HEART OF
THE NILE

Printed in the United States of America.
First printing December 2012.

ISBN: 978-0-9847738-3-1
Also available as an e-book:
ISBN: 978-0-9847738-2-4

HEART OF THE NILE

A NOVEL OF ANCIENT EGYPT

BY

LILY AARON

Wavelength Books
2012

CONTENTS

MERYT'S HOUSE

SIDE VIEW

ANTECHAMBER

MAIN ROOM

SECONDARY ROOMS

STAIRS

KITCHEN

CELLAR

TOP VIEW

SHRINE

DAIS

WORK ROOM

MERYT'S ROOM

OVEN

Chapter 1 - The Accident

12th Day of the Inundation
Year 7 of the Pharaoh Khufu

Her first hint of trouble was the sudden silence.

Meryt had grown so used to the constant babble of voices, the songs of the men hauling the huge blocks of limestone, the clink of copper chisels on stone, that it took a moment for their absence to sink in. She hefted the lunch basket on her hip.

"Might be an accident," said Kahotep to her left. The master stonemason, her brother-in-law, held a hunk of bread in his hand, one she had just handed to him as part of his lunch. He raised a hand to shade his eyes. "There's the red flag!"

Below the hill where the stonemasons' tent stood, a flash of red showed against the sand-colored landscape.

"I see it," she answered. Dropping the lunch basket, she started out on a run for the quarry.

"But your father is already there!" Kahotep called after her. She ignored him and ran on. The Pyramid of the Pharaoh Khufu (Life! Prosperity! Health!) had been under construction for five years, and now loomed over the landscape like a sheared-off mountain. The huge stones were quarried from the white rock in the quarry through which Meryt now ran.

Her long hair blew into her face as the hot desert breeze met her. As she hurried down the central lane, recruits with shaved heads pointed at her and whispered. Meryt ignored them; every year the new men had to get used to seeing a woman on the worksite. The red-flag man, recognizing her, pointed to the right. "Bench Twelve."

Meryt knew her way like she knew the streets of her village. The limestone walls rose around her, the lanes narrowing. She found herself at the back of a mob of sun-browned men in dirty white kilts gathered round a figure on the ground.

"Please let me through," she said. They gave way. She

threaded her way through the crowd, then stopped with a gasp. "Father!"

Djeti-Thutmose, physician to the "Endurance" work gang, lay on the ground like a doll flung down by a child. He was bald, middle-aged, wrinkled. His left arm and leg were bent at unnatural angles. "What happened?" she said.

A man wearing a foreman's pendant answered her in a deep voice. "He was walking along the top of the ledge and fell. That ledge is as tall as five men; he's lucky to be alive."

Meryt knelt, feeling for her father's pulse. It was fast and dangerously weak. She passed her hands quickly over her father's leg and arm, then looked up at the supervisor. "Can someone find my father's medical basket for me?"

The foreman, Sobek-Amun, barked orders, and two men dashed away. "Anything else?"

"I will need four strong staves of wood, about this long." She measured with her hands.

"Call the carpenter," the supervisor said.

"Also water," she said. She was grateful that he didn't question her abilities. She hoped he could not see her hands shaking.

The men returned with her father's basket, bearing the glyphs for "health" and "life" painted on its side. Four more approached with a makeshift litter of linen kilts lashed to poles. The linen kilts were their own, leaving all four men stark naked, their bodies muscular and tanned in the harsh sunlight. They set down the litter and stepped back respectfully.

Sobek-Amun knelt beside her. "Do you need help? Do you want me to call for Minhotep?"

Meryt shook her head. "No! He is a butcher, not a proper physician." Too late, she realized this was a mistake. Djeti would never have said such a thing in public. When would she learn to curb her tongue?

"Don't worry, Meryt. Do what you can for him." Sobek-Amun rose and clapped his hands. "You three, stay and help her. The rest of you, get back to work. If we do not make our tally of blocks today, the Renewal team will beat us, and I'll be hanged before I buy those lazy crocodiles a round of beer."

The men nodded, turning back to their work. Their talk rose around her.

"Hey, where's that water boy? ... Has anyone seen my chisel?...I think that block is marked wrong."

Meryt splinted her father's broken arm and leg with the wooden staves brought to her. The men were helping her lift him onto the litter when a shadow fell across the group.

"What is this?" boomed a voice. Everyone stopped and bowed. Meryt turned, saw the Royal Vizier, and immediately bowed from the waist, her arms held out at knee level.

Sobek-Amun said loudly, "Greeting to Hemiunu, Right Hand of Pharaoh (Life! Prosperity! Health!), Vizier of Upper and Lower Egypt, Royal Architect to His Majesty, Servant in the Place of—"

The King's Vizier waved the man to silence. A heavy-set man in his thirties, Hemiunu stood with hands on hips, gazing down at the little group. A fan bearer held a sunshade above his head. Behind him, Shushu the scribe exchanged troubled looks with Sobek-Amun.

"Your Highness, this is Djeti, the physician assigned to this work gang," Sobek-Amun explained. "He has suffered a bad fall. His daughter, Meryt, is treating him."

"Yes, he served the Osiris Sneferu when he built his Red Pyramid." Hemiunu referred to the previous Pharaoh, father to the present king. His dark gaze took in Meryt's dusty gown, her tangled hair. "Will he live?

Meryt bowed. "I believe so, Your Highness."

"How long will he take to recover?"

"My lord, I believe he will be able to walk with a cane within forty days."

He squinted at her. "Meryt, daughter of Djeti. I remember you. How is your husband?"

She bowed again. "He is dead these three years, my lord. I live with my father now, since he has no sons to be his apprentices."

"Hmm. Unusual, a woman doctor. Yet not unknown. One of my wives is the daughter of a most excellent woman physician. I hope your skills will serve your father well. Scribe!"

Shushu snapped to attention. "Highness?"

"You will issue double rations to the house of Djeti until he is fully recovered, so that his daughter may purchase whatever she needs to help him heal. You will inform the local shrines that prayers are to be said for this man's recovery, that he may continue to serve Pharaoh (Life! Prosperity! Health!). You will send a message to Perhipidje the Chief of the Royal Physicians that I require a replacement for this man. The work must not suffer because the men of this work gang have no physician."

"It shall be done, Your Highness."

Meryt's stomach tightened. A replacement? The Vizier stepped forward, moving on. Panicked, she forgot protocol and reached out a hand. "My lord!"

He stopped, looking down. "What now?"

"Shall I not take my father's place, and carry out his duties? Djeti trained me well." Her voice shook a little. To beg a favor of a royal person was a risky business.

"I have no doubt," he replied, his voice remote. "But your father will need all your care. We will consider his future when he is better."

Meryt bowed as he walked away, murmuring instructions to an aide. The three workmen stooped to lift Djeti onto the litter. As they passed out of the quarry and took the road to the village, Meryt reflected that now she had two worries: her father's health, and her father's livelihood. Because Meryt knew that the word—and the memory—of a high noble could not always be trusted.

Whoever this new "temporary" replacement would be, Meryt already hated him.

⚲

Meryt's sister Nofret opened the door of Meryt's house as the litter bearers approached. She held the door for them as they lugged it down the three steps that led from street level into the tiny antechamber.

"In here," Nofret said, and guided them into the main room. She had already spread sleeping mats on the brick bench built into one wall. Meryt and the men moved Djeti gently onto the wide bench. "Kahotep sent a runner with the news. I came over as soon as I heard. Has he wakened?" Nofret said, hovering. One hand lay on her belly, where the swell of her first child had just begun to show.

Meryt thanked the departing men with a low bow. "No, sister. His leg and arm are broken, and he has a bruise on his head. He was unconscious when I reached him, and has not spoken since." Their eyes met over their father's body, and each face mirrored the same thought. A blow to the head was always serious. "I don't even know if he can feel his toes."

Nofret knelt beside her, biting her thumb. It was an old childhood habit she had never broken. Like Meryt, her hair was black, her eyes an amber brown in a soft round face. But there the resemblance between the sisters ended. Meryt often envied her sister the slender silhouette and slim hips favored by Court fashion; her own figure tended to plumpness. Nofret swallowed. "Will he ... will he die?"

"I don't know. First I have to treat him. I'll need your help."

"Of course. But I don't know what to do. You'll have to show me."

Ignoring the hot, tight feeling in her stomach, Meryt picked up a roll of linen bandages, said a quick prayer to Isis, and set to work. With her whole strength, she grasped her father's wrist and pulled the arm bones into alignment. Meryt quickly splinted his arm, then had Nofret hold her father's shoulders while she pulled the broken leg bones straight. She ran her hand along the shin to make sure they were aligned, then splinted the leg. There was little she could do about the ugly bruise on his shaved scalp.

Finally, she sat back on her heels, wiping sweat. The main room was taller than the rest of the house, and the only windows were high on the wall just under the ceiling. They let in light, but also heat, and the air was hushed and stifling. "I don't like the look of that bruise," Meryt said.

Nofret stared at the side of Djeti's head. "Can you treat it?"

"The skin is not broken, and as far as my fingers can tell, neither is his skull. But a head injury like this..."

She didn't have to finish. Nofret may not have been the apt pupil Meryt was, but she had learned enough growing up in a physician's house to know that a head injury was a grave matter.

Meryt rose. "I'll make up some of Father's medicine for bruises and aches. Maybe when he comes around he can drink it."

"What can I do?" Nofret asked anxiously.

Meryt smiled at her sister. "It will be all right, dear Nofret. Why don't you make some of your beef broth Father enjoys so much? When he wakes, I will give it to him."

Nofret nodded and dashed for the front door, to return to her own house.

Meryt went through the door at the rear of the room. The house of Djeti had been built to the same plan as every other house in the worker's village. First came the tiny anteroom opening directly off the street, then the main room, with its high ceiling and clerestory windows, central pillar, and built-in sleeping bench. The door at the rear led to a short passage. The door on the left opened into the workroom and distillery; two doors on the right were Meryt's and Djeti's bedrooms. The hall ended in a door.

Meryt stepped through it and was in the kitchen area. This was an open, unroofed enclosure whose central feature was a mud brick oven. Stairs to the roof led off to the left. To the right, four steps led down to the cellar. Meryt ducked as she went down them. Here, sheltered from the blazing sun, she stored most of the household's food, including her special home-brewed beer. She took the lid off the next to most recent batch, sniffing it for quality.

Something soft touched her leg and she looked down. A swollen tabby cat threaded her ankles, purring loudly. "Nebet! You startled me!" She bent down to pat the cat and was rewarded with an affectionate head-butt. "Not long until your time, is it, little mother?" The pregnant cat rubbed her head against Meryt's hand, then waddled away. Gathering up her herbs and pots, Meryt trotted up the stairs.

Back in the main room, she felt her father's pulse again, and checked his forehead for signs of fever. She stirred the powdered willow bark into some beer and set it close to hand. As twilight deepened, she lit the little oil lamp. It cast shadows around the room, flickering in a dance of dark and light.

Nofret returned quietly after a while, bearing a covered bowl that smelled delicious. She looked anxiously from Djeti to Meryt, who shook her head. She knelt facing Meryt. "Will he get better?"

"I think so. I hope so. I am burning incense to Isis and every other god of healing, but oh, Nofret..." She could not say the fear in her heart, that Djeti would never wake.

"What are you going to do?"

Meryt knew what she was asking: what if Djeti died? What if this new man took over his place permanently? "I don't know," she said frankly. "Even if he lives, if he is damaged in his head, or Hemiunu replaces him, we will have no home. Of course the house belongs to Pharaoh (Life! Prosperity! Health!). It is given to us only because Djeti serves Pharaoh. We would have to leave the village."

"You could live with us," Nofret said promptly.

Meryt laughed shortly. "And your husband. And your husband's mother. And your husband's two brothers and their wives. Not to mention the child you are about to have. Yes, I can see there is plenty of room for an old man and an unmarried woman in Kahotep's small house."

Nofret looked down, but in the dim light from the lamp Meryt could see tears in her eyes. "You're right. But what else can you do? You and Father, you can't leave. Where would you go?"

Meryt shrugged. She schooled her face not to betray her inner anxiety. She took a deep breath. "I am going to take our father's place as physician tomorrow."

Nofret's eyes got big. "But...can you do that?"

"I can and I must. The vizier sent for a new man, but he may not get here for days. There must be a physician on-site, and the other work gangs' doctors have their hands full. You know how it is, this early in the building season. All the new men are clumsy and cause accidents every day. The Overseer should be glad to have someone trained by our father to take care of them."

Nofret looked unhappy, but nodded. "Then I will stay with Father while you take his place. But I do not think this is wise."

Meryt smiled, trying to look more confident than she felt. She remembered the Vizier's casual manner, his offhand orders, and how quickly he strolled away. "Men forget, Nofret. The Vizier's first concern is keeping to the building schedule. If that means it is more efficient to replace Djeti permanently, perhaps with a younger, stronger man ... well. It will mean nothing to him if we lose everything, as long as Pharaoh is served. But if I am there, in front of him, he will see me every day." Her mouth took on a determined line. "I will make sure he sees me every day, doing my duties. He will know that the house of Djeti serves Pharaoh with real devotion. He cannot refuse to reward such loyalty. But if I do not go..."

Nofret sniffed. "I know. Out of sight, out of mind. How long do you think it will take our father to recover?"

"I don't know. We should wait and see; maybe he will recover his understanding by himself. But I am running out of willow bark, and I'm going to need acacia leaves, and some *waneb* and *shemshemet*. Do you think you could go to the market for me? It would be good if we could get some antelope's horn—"

Nofret shook her head. "You know I will never remember all of that."

"I'll write it down for you," Meryt said.

"No, it would be better if you went. If I ask for a thing, and the apothecary doesn't have it, I won't know what substitute to ask for. Besides, you're always better at bargaining. I can stay with him while you go." She stood, stretching out her back. "I'll run over to Sheriti's house and ask her to go along with you."

Sheriti was their oldest and best friend, a lively girl with a ready laugh. Being around her always cheered Meryt up. "Very well, then. Is there anything you want?"

Nofret smiled lopsidedly, and her hand came to rest on her belly. "Cucumbers. Lately I am craving pickled cucumbers, for some reason." She hurried out.

Meryt sat staring at her father's profile. He looked older than he had that morning. He had always been the pillar of the family, hard working, kind, concerned for his family's well being. She remembered him teaching her the picture writing when she was just able to walk. He had made a game of it. She owed him so much. She had to do everything she could to save his life's work.

And his life.

CHAPTER 2 - IN THE PATH OF DEATH

In less than an hour, Nofret returned with Sheriti in tow. Her friend entered the anteroom, carrying two loaves of bread in a basket.

"How is he?" she asked breathlessly. The two women could not have been more different. Sheriti, called Sheri by her friends and family, was slender, vivacious, almost giddy. She plaited her hair into dozens of tiny braids, done up with flowers or bits of copper her father the smith gave her. She hugged Meryt, and gave Nofret kisses on both cheeks.

"He has not wakened. I can't be gone long."

Sheri's painted lips frowned. "I am so sorry, Meryt. Can I do anything?"

Nofret bit her finger. "I need to make more broth. Can you get a duck from the market? Or a *hin* of beef?"

"Of course." Sheri smoothed her white gown, so transparent her nipples were visible under it. "Are you ready?"

"Yes," Meryt said. She gathered an armful of her best weaving and put it carefully in a wide basket. She looked over at Nofret. "I will be back very soon with fresh aloe and acacia seeds. If he develops fever, make him drink the willow-brew. Or if he starts to—"

Nofret gave her a little push. "Go, you! I'll look after him. Come back soon!"

Meryt waved goodbye to her sister and stepped out into the narrow street. It bustled with activity, with workers headed to the quarries or the Pyramid, scribes hurrying by with arms full of papyrus scrolls, and water carriers lounging through the streets with poles over their shoulders. Over all their chatter rose the wail of a baby in the next house, friends calling to one another, two women in a corner house arguing loudly over a squawking duck. As they reached the great gate in the wall that surrounded the village, the crowd grew thicker.

A gang of workmen trudged past on their way to the quarry,

dressed only in linen kilts, their eyes rimmed with black kohl to cut the glare. Jostled to one side, the women found themselves pressed against the mud brick wall of the gatehouse. Some of the men winked at Sheri. Sheri laughed and leaned over to Meryt. "Don't you love all those muscles? And most of the men aren't married."

"Don't you ever get tired of breaking hearts?" Meryt smiled, but it felt like a lie on her face. It had been so long since she felt muscled arms around her, a man's weight on her, that sweet fire in her belly. Her shrewd friend read her thoughts easily and slid her arm through Meryt's.

"Don't worry," Sheri said. "Your good man is out there, somewhere. You know Shushu looks at you like a dog looks at fresh meat."

"Yes, that is just how I want to be looked at," Meryt said crossly.

"What's wrong with Shushu the scribe? He would be a good match for you."

"You forget," Meryt said, an edge in her voice. "Shushu's last wife divorced him. Not a recommendation. In any case, I have no time for men now."

When the workmen had passed, the women fell in behind them. As they passed through the gate, Sheri waved at a heavy-set young man carrying a staff. He waved back hesitantly.

"See Netka? He was asking my brother about me the other day."

Meryt looked him over—short, heavily muscled, running a bit to fat but otherwise healthy. "Isn't he one of the police who guard the Pyramid quarry?"

"He's been promoted to gate guard. Handsome, don't you think? A woman could hardly get her fill of that one." She blew a kiss at the young guard as they passed.

Once out of the gate, the crowd spread out. To the left, the truncated Pyramid rose above the dusty plain. To the right, the plateau sloped down to the Nile, whose swelling waters even now crept closer. A double line of donkeys burdened with water jars hurried to and from the river along the beaten road, their drivers whistling and shouting at the beasts. They looked to Meryt like overgrown ants, an endless line of plodding beasts and impatient men. Soon the rising waters would reach the edge of the plateau, and their walk would be shorter.

Meryt and Sheri swung their baskets up onto their heads to carry them. Long accustomed to this, their straight backs and graceful carriage brought them several appreciative glances from the donkey drivers they passed. The sun rising before them cast their shadows behind onto the path. The hard-packed clay was a lighter color than the surrounding sandy landscape. It wound away down the gentle slope of the plateau, dotted here and there with the distant figures of other travelers. In the distance, Meryt saw the wide shining band that was the Nile, the few fields that had escaped its rise still green with the late harvest.

Sheri sighed. "Sometimes I wish one could find a man at the market, the way one finds a fish or a good comb."

Meryt snorted. "There are thousands of men working on the Pyramid. Have you really gone through all of them?"

Sheri laughed. "No, my friend. But I have sampled a wide variety." She smiled, and a lazy, sultry look came into her eyes. "There were one or two...but no. They're too homey."

"Homey?"

Sheri managed to insert a little wiggle into her walk, without upsetting the basket on her head. "That's all they want—someone to bear their children and make their bread and beer."

"And what's wrong with that?"

"I want to go places and do things! I want to see this great ocean they speak of, or the highlands of Nubia, or maybe even the Eastern Desert where the turquoise comes from. And I want a lusty man to see it with!" Her eyes sparkled. "Or maybe just a lusty man. It's a pity a girl can't have more than one husband at a time."

Meryt smiled. "If any girl could handle them, it would be you."

In a few more minutes, they had reached the artificial harbor that had been dug for the Pyramid project. A constant stream of barges laden with huge blocks of rough-cut granite, supplies, and men came and went from the five docks. Where the road met the harbor, it widened to accommodate the streams of haulers and donkeys, and also to give way to the vendors. They squatted or stood next to their goods, along a crisscross pattern of narrow lanes. Meryt and Sheri swung the loaded baskets off their heads and entered the crowd.

Their first target was the fruit sellers. Meryt quickly filled half her basket with freshly picked lettuce, cucumbers, melons and early grapes. Sheri bought and ate a slice of melon, and the juice ran down her chin. "Mmm," she said, wiping her chin. "Where next?"

"The herb sellers," Meryt said.

Sheri shrugged. "I'll leave you to your nasty bits and roots," she said. "I'm going to see if there are any pomegranates left. Buy me some myrrh oil!"

In the herbalists' section, Meryt pored over dried roots, leaves, shredded bark. She passed over baskets full of dung, earth from tombs, dried lizard skins, and a small jar of frog's eyes. She finally bargained a two-cubit length of embroidered linen for a double measure of powdered willow bark, some aloe juice and a vial of imported olive oil. She was haggling with the seller of fir oil for her last piece of linen, when she heard shouting.

"Get out of the way! ... He's loose! ... Look out!"

Startled, she turned towards the sound. A running man careened into her, knocking her to the ground. Her basked overturned, and fruits and vegetables rolled in every direction. With a cry, Meryt knelt to try to rescue them. She heard the thunder of hoofs and looked up.

Black and huge as a mountain, with tiny red eyes set wide apart under long, sharp horns, the bull galloped straight at her. Meryt froze as the enormous animal thrust a horn through a canopy, sent a basket of dried figs flying, and crushed a watermelon to bits. The sound of his hoofs on the hard packed clay was like drums.

She had to move. She had to. But her limbs would not obey her. The bull came on, bellowing, his head down. *She was going to die—*

An arm wrapped around her waist and lifted, swinging her out of the animal's way just as it pounded past. A tangle of ripping canopies, the sound of breaking sticks, the sudden perfume of spilled aromatic oils. Vaguely she was aware of a tearing sound, a tug on her dress, shouts and running feet, the cries of sellers and herdsmen. Gasping for air, she realized that her back was crushed against a broad-muscled chest, held in place by an arm apparently made of iron. And a large warm hand cupped her naked left breast.

"Oh!" She struggled a bit, but there was no moving that arm. "Th-thank you. But let me go!"

"One moment, little dove! The beast is not yet caught," said a low voice behind her. Male, deep, with a hint of amusement. A chuckle rumbled through his chest where the back of her head met it. The hand on her breast moved slightly, fingers exploring her nipple. "Oh, yes, a very soft little dove," the voice whispered. "Lovely!" The fingers closed slightly on her nipple, and suddenly warmth bloomed in her belly, spreading outward in a long-forgotten tide of sensation. She looked down. The sun-bronzed right arm that held her bore a leather wrist cuff embossed with hieroglyphs for "health" and "life". A heavy gold ring on the third finger of the man's hand displayed a carved Eye of Horus.

She pushed at the arm. "Sir! I thank you, but let me go!" Her voice sounded a little breathless in her own ears. Distantly she heard laughing and shouting, and feet approaching. "I believe they have caught the bull."

Something nuzzled her neck. "Yes, I think so," he said. "Are you hurt?"

"No," she said breathlessly.

"Good." His breath on her nape sent goose flesh all over her skin; she felt her nipple rise. His mouth met the nape of her neck. This was outrageous, inappropriate...but delicious. Lips on her shoulder. "Very good. A shame to mar such perfection. Tell me, are you married?"

The vendors' canopies and awnings had half-fallen around them, forming a quiet, private space. She was intensely aware of their isolation, his body hard against hers, his hand caressing her breast. She trembled, slightly, and heard a tiny intake of breath from him. She knew she should squirm out of his hold; this was no behavior for a grown woman. But for a moment, she let herself remember what it was like to be held by a man, to feel his hands on her body. It was like falling into a dream.

"Who are you?" she whispered.

His breath in her ear. "Lady..."

"Meryt!" Sheri was calling for her. "Meryt! Where are you!"

Coming to herself with a jolt, Meryt pushed resolutely at the arm. "Let me go!"

His arm fell away, and she stumbled forward. She grabbed at her torn dress and held it against her as she turned.

He was a head taller than Meryt. His shoulders were broad and his arms heavy with muscle. His torso tapered to a narrow waist and hips, wrapped in a white linen kilt with a tooled leather belt. An ivory-hilted dagger hung at his waist. His broad face and high cheekbones framed a full, sensual mouth curling up in a lazy smile. Dark hair fell curling to his shoulders, and deep brown eyes rimmed with black kohl met hers as she glared up at him. There was laughter in the eyes, and also surprise.

"You..." So many equally damning reproaches rose in her that they crowded one another out in her throat. "You fondled me."

He grinned, and his teeth were as white as the sun at noon. "I did. I would like to do it again. And you did not answer my question."

"What question?" She was acutely aware of her mud-stained dress, of the broken strap of her dress, of her disheveled hair. What was wrong with him?

"Are you married?" he said.

Her face grew hot. He was teasing her, surely. What a scoundrel. "Why do you ask?"

Fumbling and tearing noises in the shredded fabric around them, and then Sheri rushed up, her dress stained with mud. "Oh, thank Isis! I was so worried about you! That terrible bull! Are you all right?" She glanced at the tall man. "And who is this?"

The tall man nodded to her. "Merely one who was glad to be of help." He winked at Meryt and strode away. When he turned, Meryt was surprised to see a mass of tangled white scars on his left shoulder, stark against the bronze of his skin. His step was jaunty, athletic; unable to help herself, she noted the strong, shapely calves and taut, rounded butt. He brushed aside one fallen awning with a careless gesture, and was gone.

Sheri's eyes were as round as figs. "Who was that!"

Meryt shook her head, bending to retrieve the tiny olive oil jar. "He pulled me out of the path of the bull, that's all," she said. "Oh, dear. Is there anything left of the aloe?"

"Don't change the subject," Sheri said. "What's his name? Oh, you broke your strap. Here." She stepped behind Meryt. Her deft fingers quickly tied a knot. "Did he do this?" she asked in a low voice. "If he hurt you or accosted you, there is a guard in the market, I can summon him."

Meryt shook her head. "He didn't hurt me."

"This was a lucky hour for you, then. then. That should hold until we get home. So?"

It seemed to Meryt as if she could still feel his hand on her breast, marked like paint on her skin. How could Sheri stand behind her and not see where he had kissed the nape of her neck, as if she'd been branded by it? "I don't know his name," she said in a low voice. "I've never seen him before, have you?"

"If I had seen him before, you would know about it," Sheri said. "Well, he's gone. Probably a sailor from one of the cargo ships. Did you see the armband on his wrist? That was a naval insignia. Here, I managed to save this fish. Your father likes fish, does he not?"

Hardly hearing her friend, Meryt set out up the street towards home. All the way back to the village, she could feel that caressing hand on her breast, the warmth of his mouth, the gentleness under that sinew and muscle.

Who, indeed, was he?

☥

By the time they returned to the village, the afternoon heat had reached its peak. The sunlight poured over Meryt's naked shoulders like molten copper. She was glad when they finally passed through the tall gate with its armed guards and entered the streets of the village. The open-weave mats strung between rooftops over the streets kept out the direct rays of the sun. Meryt waved goodbye to Sheri as the other woman turned into her own street. Meryt dodged two teenaged girls chasing a puppy and a washerman with a huge load of laundry on his head. She was glad to finally see the red door of her father's house, with his name written on it in large black hieroglyphs.

Opening the door, Meryt stopped in surprise. Shushu the scribe stood in the anteroom, looking impatient. His bald head and protruding eyes gave him a look of constant surprise. He held out a basket of figs. "For you," he mumbled. "And Djeti."

She could smell the dirt and dust on him. The kohl around his eyes was smudged with sweat, and sweat shone on his round torso. He had not even bathed before visiting her, she thought. She put down her market basket and took the figs reluctantly. "How long have you been here?" she asked.

"Not long," he said. His voice was high, even shrill. "I knew you would not expect a man of my rank to wait in the street, so I let myself in. I suggested that your sister go home for a change of clothes. She will return soon."

Meryt fought down her irritation at this presumption. Doubtless Shushu had thought he was doing her family a favor just by visiting. "How is my father?"

"He is asleep still," Shushu said.

Meryt forced herself to smile. "Thank you for the figs."

Shushu nodded shortly. He shifted uneasily from foot to foot. "I, ah, have directed the granaries and butchers to double your rations, as the Vizier ordered. However, when I spoke to the brewers, they said that you do not draw rations from them. Why is that?"

"I brew my own beer. My mother had the recipe from her mother's mother. I sell our surplus at the White Crown tavern."

Shushu's eyebrows climbed his high forehead. "Really? I had no idea. I have always liked their beer." He smiled, then the smile faltered, and he moved his feet again. Meryt felt the beginnings of unease. What did he want?

"What else may I do for you?" Meryt kept the smile on her face, though what she really wanted was a cool drink of water.

"Ah. Well." Shushu cleared his throat. "I am glad your father is getting better. I hope he will be awake soon. There is something I want to talk to him about. Or rather, I should talk to you first. Ah. I think you know what I am talking about."

Oh, she did. Meryt fought to keep a frown off her face. Here she stood, beset with worry for her father, and this was when Shushu decided to finally ask her to marry him? "This is not a good time," she said as mildly as she could. Had the man no sensitivity at all?

"I fear that if I wait, some unfortunate event may intervene," he said carefully.

Shushu expected her father to die. Meryt felt anger curl in her stomach. "You are asking me to marry you, before my father recovers?"

Shushu nodded, his face flushing a little. "I am sure we would make a very good husband and wife," he said formally.

Meryt felt her face grow hot. "I thank you," she said carefully. "For this generous offer. However, you must understand that my father's health must be my first concern right now. I cannot answer you until he is better."

"But..."

Meryt hefted the basket of figs. "Thank you for the figs. And now, I have to attend Djeti."

Shushu looked flustered. "Of course. Didn't mean to rush things. Only wanted to get matters settled before...Yes. Well." He drew himself up and executed a formal bow. "I will see you soon, I hope."

Meryt opened the door. "Tomorrow, in fact," she said. "I will be taking my father's place in the crew."

Caught halfway across the threshold, Shushu stopped and stared in surprise. "Take his place? But how? Ah. I don't think that would be wise."

"Perhaps not," she said, sliding the door until it pushed at Shushu's foot. "But I will be there nonetheless. We of Djeti's house serve Pharaoh (Life! Prosperity! Health!) in good times and bad."

The fat little scribe looked puzzled as she closed the door in his face.

☥

Inside the house, the main room held stifling heat. She opened the high windows as wide as she could, hoping for some breeze. Djeti lay on his back. His eyes at first seemed half-open, but when she waved a hand in front of them, they did not react. Frightened, she took his pulse—weak but still there. She could not think why he was not awake now.

What with all the medicine she had been brewing for Djeti, Meryt was running low on beer. Throwing on a work gown, she descended into the cellar and uncovered the earth-lined pit that held the household's barley. She measured out a half-basket and went back to the kitchen area. Kneeling over the mill, she poured the mixture into the top compartment. She picked up the cylinder of hard stone and began rolling it back and forth over the grain, crushing it and moving the flour into the bottom catch basin. To pass the time, and get her mind off the encounter in the marketplace, she sang one of her mother's grinding songs.

I planted sweet smelling flowers
I planted them near the river
Bees sang among them
And you sang there with me.
Hathor send us sweet love
Isis send us long life
Sekhmet send us good weather
Ra send us the sun.

She thought about her mother, a memory fading more and more every year. Of course, she and her father set loaves of bread before her mother's tomb in the cemetery section of the plateau, a tomb large enough to hold Djeti when his time came, and herself as well. Meryt wished her mother were here now to offer advice. She frowned as a thought came to her: if she and Djeti were evicted from the village, what would happen to their bodies when they died? Would they be buried with strangers, far from her side? Would they be buried at all? She shivered at the thought.

Her grinding done, Meryt took a few minutes to sift the flour, then put it in the kneading bowl and began to add water and oil, a little at a time. When it was a sticky mass, she shaped it and set it aside. Despite the heat of the day, she built up the fire in the oven, wiping sweat from her eyes. Out of the corner of her eye, she caught swift movement: Nebet darted out of the cellar, carrying a mouse, and disappeared under the stairs. Presently, Meryt heard delicate crunching sounds.

Leaving the bread to rise, she entered the workroom across the passage from her own bedroom. It was barely big enough for the stacked chest and work table, loaded down with tools for grinding and mixing medicines. A small worktable held pestles and mortars, chopping boards, sifters, a pierced copper strainer, and mixing bowls. Stacks of jars and baskets and chests leaned against the walls. Piles of well-worn clean linen scraps waited to be turned into bandages. She moved two baskets and a small chest, and then opened a large painted chest full of scrolls. It took her a few minutes to find the one she wanted; she knew it well, however. Djeti had often showed it to her, going over the text in detail.

The fifth case down was the one she remembered:

If you examine a man having a bruise to his skull, under the skin of his head but his skin is not broken, you should palpate his wound. Should you find that there is swelling on the outside, while his eye is askew because of it, and he shuffles when he walks, then you should say, here is one suffering from a blow, who does not move his head and who discharges blood from his nose and his ears. This is an ailment which cannot be treated.

Despite the close, hot air inside the house, Meryt felt a chill go over her. According to this ancient text, such a blow to the head spelled death. Yet Djeti did not have all the symptoms listed; he was not bleeding from the ears or nose, and she didn't know if he could walk. For the first time, Meryt wondered if perhaps she should swallow her pride and ask for help. Yet Djeti had expressly forbidden her to call on Minhotep. Perhaps it was time to look for help beyond the village.

She put away the scrolls and tidied the room, returning to the kitchen. She found that the bread had risen quickly in the heat, so she put it into the oven and popped the clay lid onto it. Nebet sat halfway up the roof stairs, washing her face with a paw. The moment she saw Meryt, she began mewing loudly.

"Oh, I know you're not hungry," Meryt said affectionately. "I don't care if you are eating for four. Or six." Nevertheless, she poured out the last of the goat's milk (which would soon sour in the heat anyway) and set the bowl down for the cat. Daintily, Nebet picked her way down the stairs and settled in to lap it up. Picking up a bowl of figs, Meryt left the kitchen.

Meryt checked on her father. His breath was loud and noisy, but regular; his pulse was unchanged. She passed through into the antechamber and opened the doors to the household shrine. Inside, a small statue of Isis stood next to one of Sekhmet, the twin sisters of healing. She dusted the images and set some of the figs before them, with a silent prayer for her father's recovery. She was not sure how much faith she had in the gods, whom she had never seen, but it didn't hurt to pray. She returned to the main room, sat down with the remaining figs, and began to eat them. She really missed her mother.

When the smell of baking bread reached her, Meryt roused herself and hurried into the kitchen. She pulled the half-baked loaf from the oven with a pad of linen, then crumbled into the vase of water standing nearby. Meryt knew that overnight, the sodden bread would magically transform itself into the beginnings of beer. Within a week, it would be ready to filter and drink. Something in the process, something even her mother and grandmother had not understood, made her beer especially good for the sick and wounded. They seemed to recover faster than when their medicines were mixed with beer made by others. Meryt hoped that some day she would understand this.

Night fell as she tidied the house, alert to any change in her father's breathing. Finally she put out all but one of the lamps, leaving one to guard his sleep as she prepared for bed.

Under the stairs, Djeti had had a bathing area built. Nofret had complained, missing the gossip and camaraderie of the public baths, but Meryt treasured the privacy and convenience. The area itself was nothing more than smooth tile laid over the usual sun-dried brick. A hole in the center drained into a pit of gravel. Meryt had hung fresh linen towels to one side. Best of all, there was a large clay pot sitting out of the sun, covered to keep out rodents and insects. She stepped out of her linen gown and tossed it in the basket of dirty laundry. She uncovered the clay pot and reached in with a gourd dipper. Standing naked in the center of the tiles, she lifted the gourd over her head and tipped out the contents.

Ah, that was good—the first shock of cool water on hot skin, the ripple of it down her back. She shivered deliciously, dipping the gourd again and again. She soaked her long black hair, running her fingers through it to untangle the knots. She could feel the tension of the day washing away with the water swirling down the drain. Her fingers slid down her skin, touching clavicle and shoulder, elbow and wrist.

Unbidden, the thought of the man in the marketplace came to mind. Her right hand drifted up to touch her left breast, the one he had fondled. It felt the same as ever. She told herself it was silly to think any man's touch could change her; still, when she remembered that hand, so large and strong, she could feel the nipple rising under her own hand. She caressed it a moment, closing her eyes.

His chest against her back had felt like a stone wall. His hand...She cupped her breasts in both hands, lifting their soft weight. His hands had been gentle. Strong, to be sure, and his wrists had been thick and solid. But his touch had been tender, not like her late husband, who had pawed and groped and fumbled. She ran a thumb over each nipple, feeling the soft, sleek skin grow taut, feeling the thread of fire slick down from her breasts to her abdomen, then lower. She thought of a wide smile and broad shoulders, of muscle and the smell of hot skin. She thought of those fine calves, the chest with its well defined muscles. Most of all, she remembered those eyes, challenging, full of laughter and a slow, sensual heat. She imagined both of those arms around her, his lips on her skin, his hands caressing, coaxing her as she now touched herself.

"Are you married?" he had asked.

Why hadn't she answered him? She was a widow, free to take any man, and his hands and voice had told her clearly he was interested in her. Why not take a little pleasure, a casual night or two with a handsome man? It didn't hurt Sheri, that was certain.

Her hands slowed, stopped. She opened her eyes. A momentary relief was all she could offer herself. A man, well, a man would perhaps offer the opportunity...

More likely he would only satisfy himself, then roll over and go to sleep, Meryt thought. Suddenly she was angry at herself, angry for letting herself feel these things again. Why? Because a handsome stranger had touched her? Smiled at her? How pathetic.

She caught the linen towel against her and dried off briskly. She reached for a small jar containing the ointment she had made up to protect her skin from the drying effects of constant desert wind. Scented with cardamom, honey, wine, myrrh, and seed of balsamum, it spread a heavy, exotic scent along her limbs. Her hands slowed, stroked more softly than usual, and for a moment she let herself think about smoothing oil on hard muscle, over bronzed male skin, along long arms.

Abruptly, she threw her towel in the basket with the other dirty linen and set the jar back on the shelf. She had better things to do than waste herself in daydreams.

Back in her room, she slipped on an old, worn gown, bound up her hair, and then carried her sleeping mat into the main room. As she stretched out on the floor beside her father's bed, she resolutely banished from her mind any thought of the man in the marketplace.

You fondled me.

Yes, I did. I would like to do it again.

Muttering, she tossed and turned late into the night.

CHAPTER 3 - THE USURPER

13th Day of the Inundation
Year 7 of the Pharaoh Khufu

In the morning, Djeti's condition was unchanged, but now his skin was pale and clammy. Meryt almost abandoned her plan to go to the worksite in his place; only her certainty that he would surely lose his position, dooming him and the whole family to disaster, held her to her decision.

Nofret arrived as she was changing Djeti's bandages; so far his leg and arm had not developed any of the tell-tale signs of putrefaction, so she could hope they were healing well. Her sister came in quietly, her face drawn with worry.

"How is he?"

"He slept well," she told Nofret. "And sleep is good, up to a point. But I am worried that he is not waking."

Nofret knelt next to the old man, taking his hand in hers. "I'll pray to Isis he wakes soon," she said.

Meryt chose her gown carefully. Obviously, she could not wear her best white linen into the dust and muck of the quarry. But neither did she want to wear a dirty rag. She settled on a beige linen gown, clean and serviceable. She had once torn the hemline, and even after her mending, it was uneven; she hoped no one would notice that. Nofret helped her to apply kohl carefully to her eyes, to guard them from disease and sun-blindness. Then she silently brought Meryt her medical basket.

"I put some breakfast in it for you," she said. "Bread and some radishes. Are you sure you want to do this?"

"I'm sure." Meryt took the basket and kissed her sister's cheek. She looked into her eyes. "It will be well. The gods will not desert our father, who has been their faithful servant."

Nofret came to hold the door as she left. "I brought some beef bones; I will make some more broth," she said.

"You'll keep checking him for fever?"

"I will send word if there is any change. Don't be late on your first day, o physician of the Endurance gang!"

Meryt hurried up the street to the central plaza. She was just in time to fall in behind the Endurance work squad and follow them up to the quarry. The men looked at her curiously but said nothing.

As they left the village and its high walls behind, her view expanded outward to the horizon. There in the east, Ra broke the seal of morning with his harsh rays burning along the sand. To the west rose the flat-topped stone mountain of the Pyramid. Since the most recent course of huge stones had been laid down, work had been diverted to the construction of the central chamber, one that would lie in the heart of the finished structure. Meryt knew that if she were a bird flying over the Pyramid, she would see a rectangular hole in its center, with men inside polishing, measuring, and surveying. Soon the great red sarcophagus would be lowered into it, and the huge granite stones laid above it to roof the chamber and support the weight of the millions of stones to come.

Someday Pharaoh would be laid to rest in the center of his man-made mountain, to rise with Ra and defeat the forces of chaos, keeping Egypt and his people safe. Meryt felt warm inside, to think that her family was part of this great work, keeping the sacred balance of Ma'at.

"Meryt! How is your father!" Meryt looked up into the kindly face of Sobek-Amun, the foreman who had helped her with her father yesterday.

"Well enough." She did not want to tell the truth about her father's failure to revive, lest rumor start burying him before he was even dead. Sobek-Amun was a veteran of five years on the project, about thirty years old and already running a little to fat. His big shoulders, calloused hands, and deep tan testified to many years of hauling stone, haranguing men, and browbeating rookies. He wore heavy kohl around his eyes, which held a permanent squint from years of working in the blazing light of Ra.

"Why are you here? Shouldn't you be home with your father?"

"My sister is with Djeti today." She hefted the basket balanced on her hip. "There has been no new man sent yet from the Vizier, has there?" She searched the older man's face anxiously.

"Not yet. Why?" He glanced ahead of them, to where a new worker was lagging behind the rest. "You! Step lively! We don't have any litters to carry lazy men like you to work!"

Meryt swallowed. "I am taking Djeti's place today."

Sobek-Amun blinked. "Taking his place?" He frowned. "I don't think I've ever heard of a woman assigned as physician to a work gang."

"You know I can do it." Meryt fought to keep a tremor out of her voice. Sobek-Amun had to accept her, if this was going to work.

"Oh, certainly," Sobek-Amun said thoughtfully. "You're the equal of your father, I know. But whether the boss will approve, well, that's something else."

"If you have no objections, why should he?"

Sobek-Amun laughed shortly. "I can see you do not know Akhti-Hotep very well. Well, let it be as you wish. It's not a thing I'd have asked for, but it's true you know your business. You know the quarry, you know how to get around in it without interfering or getting hurt." He scowled, his eyebrows like two caterpillars crawling towards one another. "Not like these new men. Some of them hardly seem to know their left feet from their right. They're forever getting hurt, dropping things, breaking tools. They're like children. I think some of them cry themselves to sleep at night."

"I met one last week who was no more than fourteen, and had never before been out of sight of the house where he was born." Meryt looked at the backs of the men marching in front of her. As soon as the Nile began to rise and farming was no longer possible, Pharaoh's scribes fanned out around the land, name-lists in hand, recruiting men into the service of the Pyramid for a season. "I thought there were more veterans this year," she said.

"Some of the men from last year have stayed on," Sobek-

Amun said grudgingly. "Tehuti and An-tetie, thank goodness, have stayed over. They're good quarry men, know how to cut stone without ruining the line or dropping a mallet on their foot. Tener-Ptah and Ameneses are here again this year. Ameneses was asking about your sister. He was unhappy to hear she was married." His eyes slid sideways, a slight smile on his face. "I made sure to tell him that you weren't."

Meryt felt her face grow warm. "I am not looking for a husband, Sobek-Amun," she said primly.

Sobek-Amun grinned at her discomfort. "Maybe you should be."

They were walking on the broad main road, paved with clay and pounded smooth by thousands of feet. It was early enough in the morning that the dust had not yet risen, so Meryt was enjoying the walk and the chat. But as they rounded a bend, they came upon a young man, almost a boy, standing by the side of way. Something about his expression caught her, and she came to a stop. "Is all well with you, friend?" she asked.

He was thin; his shaved head looked raw and white, evidence that he was only newly entered into the ranks. One of the first things that recruits underwent was a full shave, to prevent lice spreading in the close quarters of the workers' barracks. When Meryt spoke, he flinched, gaped, and then bent from the waist, hands outstretched in an obeisance. "Lady..."

"Why are you standing here? Shouldn't you be at work?" Sobek-Amun snapped.

The boy looked as scared as a rabbit, blinking and trembling.

Sobek-Amun put a hand on his hip, almost tapping one foot in impatience. "Boy, I'm speaking to you! Where are you supposed to be?"

"I...ah...great lord, I...I don't know."

"Don't call me 'great lord', or else you'll be calling the Vizier 'my good man' next. You should have learned who's who by now. What work gang are you assigned to?"

"I...I don't know. My name is Ib."

"That doesn't tell me a thing," Sobek-Amun said. "You'll have to come with me to the Overseer."

The boy looked ready to faint at mention of so high an official. Meryt took pity on him and stepped forward. "Sobek-Amun, let me talk to him. I'll catch up with you later."

Sobek-Amun grunted, glancing after his retreating workers. "Just as well. Leave these boys alone for ten heartbeats and they scatter like quail." He marched off.

Meryt put a hand on the boy's arm. "My name is Meryt. Let me see if I can help you."

The young man flushed and looked down, but he looked relieved. "Thank you. It's all so new to me."

She smiled to reassure him. "I'm sure. Tell me where you come from."

On familiar ground, the boy answered more confidently. "From Ptah-Remose. It's a little village up the river from Khetaure."

Meryt had never heard of either of those towns, and suspected they were flyspecks on any map the Vizier might have. "How long since you left it?"

He looked at her with big eyes. "Fourteen days. I...When the man from Pharaoh came, he said they needed ten men from the village. At first he didn't want to take me because I'm small, but I begged him. My wife was so proud when he said yes. It's such an honor." He swallowed, and Meryt thought he was fighting back tears. But apparently, having a sympathetic ear had unloosed his tongue. "This place is so huge. I can't remember which path to take. Everyone talks too fast. The food is all different. It's hard for me to sleep at night, with so many men around me and so much snoring. I ... I miss my wife and my children. And now, I'm all, ah, sick—" He stopped and looked away, embarrassed.

Meryt knew exactly what was wrong with him. Besides homesickness, the most frequent complaint among new men was bowel problems, brought on by eating unfamiliar food and drinking water they were not used to. Sometimes the men were too embarrassed to tell a doctor.

A caravan of donkeys laden with water jars came up behind them. Meryt stepped back to give them room. "I can help you," she said to Ib. "I'm the daughter of Djeti the physician. I can bring round a compound of honey and castor oil to your quarters. You'll be better in a few hours."

The boy looked relieved. "Thank you, Lady. I ... I can't pay you."

She resisted the urge to pat his head like a dog. "Don't worry about that. Pharaoh (Life! Prosperity! Health!) pays all the physicians on the worksite, so you don't have to. And by the way, you should learn to say that: Life! Prosperity! Health! You should say it whenever you mention His Majesty, or people will think you are disrespectful."

He nodded somberly. "Is that why some of the older men make fun of me?"

There could be a number of reasons, Meryt thought, starting with his country accent. But there was no point in adding to his discomforts in this new life. "Well, say it like I did, and they will have no cause to snicker at you on that score," she said practically. "Now, let's find out where you belong. When you came here, did you come on the river in a boat?"

"Oh, yes! It was enormous! There were forty of us in one boat, and still room to move around!"

She laughed. "Only forty men? You should see the big cargo ships from the Delta when they come in. Where did you sit when you were in the boat?"

"I sat in the back, next to the big paddle thing—"

"The rudder."

"Yes. I didn't know any of the other men, though."

Meryt shifted the basket from one hip to another. "Did they explain it to you? Why you were put in the stern?"

He shook his head.

Meryt suppressed a frown. Some of the newer Scribes of the Recruits were getting downright slovenly. They almost treated these men as cattle, rather than Pharaoh's valued workers. "Very well, listen carefully. The part of the boat you sit in decides which team you are assigned to. So you are in the 'Stern' team."

Ib blinked. "Oh. No one told me that."

"Apparently not. Now, the teams are divided into smaller

work gangs. They have names like 'Endurance'—that's my family's work squad. Some of the others are called 'Renewal' or 'Life' or 'Perfection'—"

"That's the one!" Ib almost shouted. "Yes, they kept calling us the perfect ones. Which I don't understand, because we're not perfect at all. Although we're good—"

"It has nothing to do with you," Meryt said, smiling. "Those terms refer to Pharaoh—"

"Life! Prosperity! Health!" cried Ib.

"Yes." Meryt laughed. "You have it now! You are in the Perfection squad of the Stern team. Which, if I remember correctly, is Pajasa's team—"

"That's him! Yes!" Ib clapped his hands together. "Thank you! I could not remember his name! Pajasa, Pajasa, Pajasa." He chanted the name like an incantation.

The donkeys had passed, and Meryt stepped back onto the road. Ib followed her, now looking relaxed, almost happy. "When we get to the Gate of the Crow, you can ask the guard where the Perfection squad of Stern is working today," she said. "He won't laugh at you, I promise. And if Pajasa asks why you are late, tell him you were seeing a physician. He will understand."

Ib looked as if he wanted to hug her. "Thank you! I...I do not even know your name?"

"Meryt, daughter of Djeti the Physician," she said.

"Meryt. I will name my next daughter after you!" Grinning, he took off at a run. Meryt shook her head at such enthusiasm. She walked at a more sedate pace. The day was young and soon the heat of the sun would teach even young men not to run about. Thinking like that made her feel old.

As she neared the Gate, a bottleneck to traffic, she slowed, mingling with the crowd of mostly men. Some of them leered at her, almost a reflex action, but most of them merely stared. A few knew her from last season and nodded respectfully. At last it was her turn, and the scribe standing next to the guards addressed her. When she explained her intent, he blinked, but then shrugged and wrote down her name. "Endurance is working in Bench Thirteen of the quarry today," he said, and waved her on.

In the quarry, all was dust and shouting and the constant tink-tink-tink of chisel on stone. Already a team of men were leaning into the ropes of a wooden sledge, pulling a huge limestone block up towards the paved road. Two water carriers walked backwards in front of them, slopping water into the path of the sledge to lubricate it. As they passed her, they were singing a work song.

"Where are the strong men, the bold men of Khufu?
Here they are, the men of Endurance.
Where are the weak men, the drunkards of Khufu?
There in the gutter, the men of Renewal."

The song had four verses, one for each of the work gangs, and Meryt knew it by heart. She even knew the obscene verses that were sung in the taverns. She was fairly sure that the Renewal gang had a similarly unflattering version of the song. Smiling, she hummed the tune as she picked her way down the long slope of the quarry.

Before her stretched a geometrically carved cliff of solid white, cut into a series of huge steps, or benches, that ranked back and back and back against the sky. Each bench was being measured, and huge square holes in the benches showed where the big blocks had been taken out. In one section, a crack in the natural limestone formation jagged down through several benches; no blocks were cut from this section, but steps had been chiseled out to make it into a staircase.

The administration tent was off to her left. Situated high above the main corridor to give the scribes a wide view, a large canopy shaded worktables, chests and low stools; runners came and went with messages. Inside, she knew, scribes would be planning, recording, and making lists of every detail of the work.

As she arrived, she saw Overseer Akhti-Hotep, her father's superior. He was a man in his mid thirties, with the thin shoulders and narrow chest of a scribe. He wore the simple white linen kilt of all the workers. A copper pectoral in the shape of the ibis-headed god Thoth, patron of scribes, denoted his high station, and his wrists bore hammered copper cuffs. Akhti-Hotep's narrow face and long nose had earned him the nickname "Ferret-face", though no one said it in his presence. He was leaning over a scroll laid out on the table before him; across from him, Shushu and another scribe were jotting notes, using charcoal sticks on flakes of smooth white stone left behind by the masons.

Meryt set her basket down and bowed. "Overseer," she murmured. "I am here in the place of my father, to serve Pharaoh (Life! Prosperity! Health!)." She waited for his objections, readying her response.

He looked at her a long moment, his eyes narrowing. The black kohl around his eyes emphasized their penetrating gaze. "His Highness, the Vizier, told me about your father's accident. I am sorry to hear it." He rubbed his ear. "I was told a new man is coming."

"He is not here, Overseer. But I am here, and ready to work." Out of the corner of her eye, she saw Shushu frowning and biting the end of a reed pen. "My father has trained me in his art since I was a child. I am expert in the dressing of broken bones, the treatment of bruised—"

Akhti-Hotep waved her to silence. "Very well. If Djeti has trained you, you cannot be completely without skill. I have no one else anyway. Stay out of the way." He turned back to the scroll, but Meryt cleared her throat. Without looking around, he said, "What else?"

"Sir, I can help with the tool reports."

Now he straightened and turned fully towards her.

"How can you help?"

"I read and write, sir. My father taught me."

In a corner, a young scribe bent over a papyrus snickered but did not look up.

Akhti-Hotep's eyebrows went up. "Indeed. Your father must be quite the teacher." He picked up a scroll and handed it to her. "Read it."

She unrolled the papyrus, feeling the smooth surface crackle under her fingers. Nor was the writing reassuring—she recognized the atrocious jottings of a scribe of the Perfection gang. She cleared her throat. "To the illustrious and exalted Overseer of the Endurance work gang, Scribe of the Surveyors, Assured Measure of the Workers, Akhti-Hotep, greetings from his humble servant Hebet, Royal Surveyor of the Third Grade. I pray daily to Thoth that all your endeavors may succeed. The alignment of the thirteenth course on the west side of the great work is off by one-half of a hands-breadth. I have caused the course to be re-surveyed. I humbly request permission to re-position the blocks on that side. The total of blocks to be moved—"

"Enough." Akhti-Hotep took the scroll from her. A corner of his mouth turned up. "If you can read Surveyor Hebet's scorpion tracks, you can read anything." The young scribe snickered again. "Sobek-Amun has enough on his hands today; he's behind quota. You may write up his report." He waved her to a corner of a work table, and turned his back. Over his shoulder, Meryt caught a glimpse of Shushu's face—he looked angry. But as soon as he caught her looking at him, he smiled widely, artificially. Meryt nodded abruptly to him and went to work.

The young snickering scribe moved over on the bench. Meryt sorted through the chips of stone stacked in a basket. Each one bore a jotted note, a count of tools, workers, and materials. Tools, especially copper tools, were expensive and hard to replace. They were the property of the King and thus were stored in the royal warehouses. The workers checked them out in the morning and turned them in at night. Foremen like Sobek-Amun took notes on the shards, and professional scribes wrote them up into the daily tally that went to overseers, then to the Vizier himself.

A collection of reed pens, ink jars, and palettes lay scattered across the center of the table. Meryt helped herself to them, and cut a piece of fresh papyrus off the roll next to the young scribe. He watched curiously as she sharpened the pen, mixed water with the ink, and began copying out the information on the shards. She paid no attention to him.

The sun crept towards the zenith and even in the shade of the canopy the air grew hot and dry as an oven. Meryt wiped sweat from her forehead, but did not move to a seat closer to the light breeze. Those seats were reserved for senior scribes. Instead, she bent over her work, meticulously copying in her best script. At noon, the Overseer called a lunch break. The serving boy came around with bread, beer and a dish of lentil stew with chunks of mutton, seasoned with cumin and leeks. Meryt flushed when she realized she had not brought a bowl. Well, she could make do with bread, she thought. But then the young scribe next to her nudged an empty bowl towards her.

"It's Hor-nefer's, but he's not working today."

"Thank you." She held out her bowl and the serving boy ladled stew into it.

As the men ate, they murmured among themselves. No one spoke to her, though several eyes flicked her way now and then. Shushu smiled brightly at her when he caught her eye, and patted the bench next to him. But Meryt knew that lowly copy scribes did not sit with men of his rank; to sit with him would be seen as courtship, not camaraderie. She smiled but shook her head; his smile vanished in a blank look.

A shadow fell across her as she finished; Akhti-Hotep was standing over her.

"Overseer." She started to scramble to her feet, but he waved a hand for her to stay where she was. He picked up the papyrus she had been working on, careful to handle it by the edges so as not to smear the drying ink. He scanned it closely, then nodded to her.

"Well done," he said. He laid it down and walked away. The young scribe grinned and rolled his eyes at her.

After lunch, the men of the workforce were allowed two hours rest. Most of them stretched out in whatever shade they could find to take a nap. Those who could not find shade created it by unwinding their kilts and stretching them between blocks of stone or over scaffolding. When Meryt rinsed her bowl at the common water jar, her gaze took in dozens of sleeping nude men. Her eyes lingered for a moment; when she turned around Shushu was scowling at her. She went to the other side of the canopy and sharpened reed pens for the remainder of the rest period.

When Shushu was called away, Meryt sighed with relief. What was she going to do about him? What answer should she give him? So much was uncertain, out of her control.

☥

The afternoon wore on, the men went back to work, and Meryt found herself yawning in the heat, bored with tool counts. Fifty number two copper chisels in good repair, assigned to names on a list. Fourteen number three copper saws in good repair, assigned to another list of men. Six number three copper chisels sent for sharpening. Fifty-two copper borer points sent for repair. Forty-nine copper adzes sent for re-sharpening. The lists were endless, dry, tedious. She blinked several times to keep herself alert. It would never do for the Overseer to see her nodding off on her first day.

"Help! Where is the physician?" The cry shocked her out of her half-doze.

A worker ran panting into the shadow and fell to his knees in front of the Overseer. "Sir! An accident! A chisel sharpener, one of the new men—" He looked frantically around. "Is the physician here?"

Meryt was already standing, reaching for her basket. "Here, sir!"

Akhti-Hotep gestured for her to follow the worker. "Go."

The worker looked at her askance, but at the Overseer's command he took off down the slope. Meryt hurried after him.

Once again, a crowd of men surrounded a figure on the ground. Meryt's guide shoved men to right and left. "Clear the way! Here's the doctor lady!"

The men fell back, and Meryt saw a man writhing on the ground, whimpering. Blood gushed from the man's arm. Beside him lay a scatter of copper chisels.

But he was not alone. As she dropped to her knees, Meryt saw another man leaning over him. Even as she watched, the man placed a hand on the arm wound, pressing hard. It was exactly what she would have done to slow the bleeding. A leather arm band circled his wrist, and even as recognition ignited in her, the man raised his head and saw her.

"You!" she said.

The man who had saved her from the bull in the market grinned widely at her. "It seems you are to be found wherever there is chaos," he said. He saw her basket with the physician's sign on it. His expression changed to surprise. "What's this?"

Meryt set her basket down firmly, to hide the trembling of her hands. "I am the physician on duty," she said with more confidence than she felt.

The man's eyes widened and he opened his mouth. But just then the wounded man cried out.

"Let go of him," Meryt said. She was pulling wads of linen out of her basket.

"He should have pressure applied to this wound," he said.

"I know that!" Meryt snapped. She pushed his hand aside and pressed a pad of linen against the cut. She could see that the flow was already less. Beside her, the tall man continued to kneel, watching her. She tried to ignore him as she turned the pad, then replaced it with a fresh one. She took a jar with a narrow neck and a clay stopper out of her basket. Carefully she poured it over the wound.

"What is that?" said the man across from her.

"Pure water from the temple well," she said, not looking at him. "It is cleaner than the water from the river this time of year." She washed blood off her patient's arm, sluicing it over and over until she could get a good look at the wound. The cut was long, evidently from a slip of the chisel he had been sharpening. She turned the man's arm, examining it.

"Is it bad?" The patient's voice was weak and scared. She glanced into his face—he was about twenty, with a faint mustache and soft brown eyes and high cheekbones. "I don't know how it happened. It just slipped. Will it ... will it go bad? Don't cut off my arm!"

She patted him. "I won't. Don't worry, this is a clean cut. You are going to be fine."

She looked up, meeting the eyes of the kneeling man. He said nothing, his expression serious.

"This is a long cut, but not very deep," Meryt continued. She put all the authority she had into her tone. "I will make it clean and bandage it up, and you can go home for the day."

"Where is the physician?" the workman said, gritting his teeth.

"I am your physician today," she said, reaching for her basket. It was just out of reach, and she leaned towards it. The tall man moved quickly, grabbing it and holding it out for her. She took out a small ointment jar and uncapped it. The smell of acacia leaf wafted into the air.

"Goose fat or sesame oil?" the tall man asked.

Startled, she looked up, expecting sarcasm. But his look was entirely serious, even respectful. "Goose fat," she said.

He nodded. "That is best. Mixed with honey, two parts to one part?"

"Yes, with cardamom and natron," she said. She could not meet his eyes, and glanced past him. She saw a large basket with a familiar emblem on it lying on the ground. Her stomach did a slow roll.

He reached into her basket and drew out a roll of leather. Unrolling it, he removed a short length of linen which had been smeared with pitch. He handed it to her and she took it. His movements were assured, practiced. By now, the bleeding had stopped. She applied the sticky bandage carefully to the wound; the pitch clung to the skin, allowing the bandage to draw the edges of the cut together. She looked up, and he was ready with the roll of linen bandage, which she wrapped around the man's arm.

Her suspicions confirmed, she found she could not look up at the face of the man helping her. Her entire body felt tight with anxiety, but she remained focused on her patient.

The wounded man sighed. "Thank you. That feels better."

"Can you move your fingers for me?" Meryt said.

He made a fist, then wiggled his fingers. He slowly sat up and Meryt sat back on her heels. "You should not use that arm for three days. I will change the bandage every day, and you must keep it dry. I will give you an ointment that will help keep out the fever demons. You won't be able to work. I will make sure your foreman knows this."

"Will you give me no spells for healing?" he asked anxiously. Although Meryt had little faith in spells or prayers, she knew that patients often felt better for having them. She leaned down to whisper in the man's ear. "Say the little bedtime hymn before you sleep, but say it to Isis, Sekhmet and Hathor."

He caught her hand in his good one. "Thank you, Mistress." He brought her hand to his forehead. "My name is Nerekh. My house is at your service."

She patted his shoulder. "You do me too much honor. Can you stand? You should get out of this heat. Go back to your barracks and rest."

With the tall man on one side and Meryt on the other, Nerekh struggled to his feet. "I can walk," he said. He nodded to the tall man, smiled at Meryt. "I will go home now."

"I will come look at your arm tomorrow," she said. "Which are your quarters?"

"Midship barracks, Eternity squad." Nerekh walked away, a little unsteadily.

The bystanders had drifted back to work, leaving her alone with the tall man. Meryt knelt to clean up the bloody bandages and other waste. She hoped he would leave now, and let her savor her misery in privacy before the official word came down. But he knelt across from her, his big hands moving quickly to gather up stray lint. Meryt had a sudden, vivid memory of those hands on her, and closed her eyes. She braced herself to look him in the eye. There was no point in delaying the inevitable.

"So you are the new physician," she said. Her voice sounded dry and cracked. "You are late."

"I got lost," he said frankly. "I went to the Left Hand crew and didn't discover my mistake until an hour ago. I was wandering around, looking for the Overseer's tent, when I heard this commotion."

She stood. He stood. Meryt found it impossible to meet his

gaze. There was a long, awkward silence before he cleared his throat. "My name is Nakht, son of Ra-Khuf," he said formally.

"I am Meryt-Auset, daughter of Djeti-Thutmose," she said. "He is—"

"Djeti-Thutmose? The student of Hesy-Ra, the Chief of Physicians under the Osiris Sneferu?"

This caught her entirely off guard. "Yes. How do you—"

"My father studied under Hesy-Ra as well. He said your father was a good student."

"That is, uh, generous of him." She didn't know what else to say. Her initial shock at seeing him had given way to dismay, but now he was acting as formal and polite as if he had never held her in his arms. "I suppose we should report to the Overseer now," she said. She bent down for her basket, but he was ahead of her. He caught it up and handed it to her.

"I would be grateful if you would show me the way," he said. As they set off down the path, he caught up his own physician's basket in one easy sweep of his arm. Meryt remembered that arm around her waist, snatching her out of the path of the bull. She swallowed and strode out ahead of him, resolved to start over entirely with this man.

They walked in silence back to Akhti-Hotep's canopy. Shushu stood next to his table, rolling up papyrus scrolls. He stopped and stared at Meryt's knees.

"Meryt! Gods above, have you been hurt?"

Meryt glanced down, and saw that the lower part of her gown was stained with blood. "I'm well," she said. "I was tending to a patient."

"Oh. I thought you'd gone home."

Meryt felt a slow flush of embarrassment climbing her face. What would Nakht think of her? "I would never leave my duties without the Overseer's permission."

"Oh. Of course. But still..." Shushu fluttered, his hands half-reaching out to her.

Nakht looked quizzically from her to Shushu but said nothing.

Meryt put her basket on the table. "Where is my tool report?"

"Oh, I completed it and gave it to the Overseer," Shushu said officiously.

"It was my responsibility," Meryt said. His proprietary attitude annoyed her.

The Overseer entered the tent. Meryt bowed to him. Taking his cue from her, Nakht bowed low.

"Who is this?" said Akhti-Hotep abruptly.

Nakht introduced himself. "I am sent by Perhipidje, Chief of the Royal Physicians, who was informed that you have lost your physician." He drew a small scroll from his belt and handed it to the Overseer.

Meryt drew breath to interject, to remind everyone that Djeti was only temporarily disabled.

But Nakht continued smoothly, "It appears, however, that I am not needed here. The men of your workforce are well served by the daughter of Djeti."

Akhti-Hotep squinted at him, which made him look even more ferret-like, Meryt thought. "I was not expecting you so quickly," he said. "I only sent the scroll downriver to the House of Life yesterday."

"And it was fortunate for me that I was in Perhipidje's office when he received your request," Nakht said smoothly. "I took the first ferry upriver. I knew the captain."

So he had just stepped off that ferry when he snatched her out of the path of the runaway bull, Meryt realized. Quick, indeed.

"The Royal Vizier will be pleased that his orders were so swiftly carried out." Akhti-Hotep eyed Nakht, taking in the bronze skin, the dagger at his waist, his straight bearing. "Your wrist band tells me you have been with the army," he said.

"Actually, I have been with the navy, sir. I was trained as a military physician, and served for five years on board His Majesty's royal fleet."

"We don't have many arrow or spear wounds here," Shushu said tartly.

Nakht smiled. "Already today I have seen a cut as bad as any sword could make. And it was efficiently treated."

Akhti-Hotep looked from Nakht to Meryt and back. "How fares the man who was injured?"

Meryt finally found her tongue. "I treated him and sent him back to his barracks to rest. He will soon return to work. I will of course have a report for you tomorrow morning."

Akhti-Hotep stared at Meryt's blood-stained gown. "Thank you for your service," he said to her. "I know your father will be proud of your work. But the Great House has sent this man, with proper training and the recommendation of the Chief of the Royal Physicians himself. Your services are no longer needed."

Meryt felt her cheeks flush. "But—"

"No doubt your father needs your best care," the Overseer said with a note of finality. "Report to me daily on his progress."

Nakht looked from her to Akhti-Hotep with an expression of confusion, but said nothing.

She could get down on her knees, Meryt thought feverishly. *Tell him how desperately we need to keep this position in the family. Tell him you'll copy endless reports if he wants. Or offer to be Nakht's assistant. Anything!* But pride rose in her. The daughter of Djeti-Thutmose would not beg. She straightened, performed a precise and correct formal bow, and strode from the tent.

She heard someone—Shushu?—call her name, but she only walked faster, almost stumbling when she reached the paved road. The tears in her eyes nearly blinded her. She wasn't exactly sure how she got home; her feet took the well known route of their own. She only knew that the door of her house had barely closed behind her when she burst into angry tears.

☥

Stifling her sobs, Meryt heard Nofret back in the kitchen area. Djeti lay inertly on the brick bench in the main room. Meryt slipped into her bedroom so no one would see her tears.

The room was so small she could take only three paces in each direction, but it was hers and she cherished her privacy. When the family had first come to the village, she had painted its plaster walls; although her hand had been unskilled, still the shapes of ducks in marsh reeds, fish in a blue river, and a great sun over all comforted her. This was home.

A home she might well be losing.

Her furniture was sparse: a sleeping mat rolled up in a corner, a chest for her clothes. Scrolls were piled in a basket and spilled across the floor. She cleared two scrolls off the chest and sat down on it, with her head in her hands. She was too old to cry like this, she told herself.

"Meryt?" Nofret called from the kitchen area. "Are you home? Are you hungry?"

Meryt dashed the tears from her face and stood. "I'm changing," she called out. Quickly she pulled off her stained gown and dropped it. Nebet sniffed it carefully as Meryt pulled a fresh gown from her chest. There was only one left; she had best send out the laundry soon. But then she wondered if Pharaoh's laundrymen would still consider the house of Djeti one of their responsibilities. If she could not depend on the free washing service, she would have to take her soiled laundry down to the riverbank herself. Between her work, Djeti's illness, and the usual dust of Egypt, she was running out of clean linen. She was tying her gown on when Nofret pushed aside the curtain, a steaming bowl in one hand. The smell of garlic and cumin filled the room. Meryt's mouth watered.

"There you are! I'll be frying up some fish. Do you—oh!" Nofret's eyes went wide at sight of the bloodstained gown on the floor.

"I was treating a workman who cut himself," Meryt said.

Nofret nodded. "Of course. I'll put it in to soak." She took up the gown and ducked out of the room. If her sister noticed Meryt's red, puffy eyes, she didn't say anything. Meryt was grateful; her mortification would be complete if she lost control in front of her sister, who so depended on her.

Emotions struggled in her: fear for her future, anger at this Nakht person, humiliation at her dismissal. How could she have been so foolish? Had she really thought she could take her father's place, that the powerful men of the Palace would allow this?

A soft bump broke her miserable reverie: Nebet curled around her ankles. Meryt reached down to scratch behind the cat's ears, and was rewarded with a loud purr. The cat jumped up onto her lap and began kneading.

"Ow," she said, sniffling. "Your claws are like knives!"

Nofret came back into the room. "Father is still not waking." Her troubled gaze sought Meryt's reassurance. "Meryt, if his *ka* has left his body..."

Meryt turned away to hide her reddened eyes. "If that were so, he would cease to breathe," she said. "I think when his body was broken, his *ka* fled and is afraid to return. We must help him heal, so that it will not be afraid to come back."

Nofret gulped, and tears stood in her eyes. "I ... I can do nothing, Meryt. I rely on you."

Meryt stood and hugged her sister. "Your broth will do as much for him as my bandages," she said strongly.

Nofret nodded. "Will you have some? And I baked new bread."

"Later. I have to take some medicine to a worker over in Perfection. I will be back very soon."

"At the worksite...did it go well today? You helped an injured man; was Akhti-Hotep pleased?"

Meryt wanted to tell her everything was all right, but it wasn't, and Nofret had a right to know. She turned around and sat down on her chest again. "The new physician arrived. Akhti-Hotep has dismissed me."

"Oh, Meryt! What will you do?"

"I'm not sure. It may not be permanent. I'll think of something."

Nofret tapped her finger on her lips. "Does this mean you can no longer tend to your patients? Or to Father's patients?"

Meryt cocked her head. "That's a good question. No one has told me to stop treating Ib, or the man who was injured today."

Nofret smiled. "And for every patient you treat, Pharaoh (Life! Prosperity! Health!) has to pay you, correct?"

Meryt felt her spirits lift a little. It would be good to be useful, to be doing what she was trained to do. "Anything would be better than just sitting around," she said. "I will need to make up more medicine and make my rounds."

"The latest batch of beer is ready, if you want to trade some to Wajet at the tavern for wine." Nofret pushed her hair behind her ears. "I may not be as well trained as you, but I know Father's medicines use wine."

Meryt nodded. "That's a good idea. Can you put up some jars of it?"

"Of course." Nofret disappeared, and Meryt took a moment to compose herself. She told herself that tears would do nothing. Their situation was not dire...yet. Akhti-Hotep had said that her services were not needed—he had not said her father was being replaced forever. If Djeti healed soon, if she could hold the Vizier to his half-promise, if she could keep her family's loyalty and service in front of the officials...so many ifs. So much was out of her control.

But there was no one else to fight for her family's welfare. And the more men she treated, the more of Pharaoh's people she healed, she hoped, the more favor she would earn for the House of Djeti.

There is no one I can turn to, Meryt thought. If only Father would wake, if only he could advise me. I cannot do this by myself. She thought of her mother, that strong and smiling presence she missed. Mother would do it. She would do whatever needed to be done for the family. Perhaps I can go beyond Akhti-Hotep, perhaps even to the Vizier himself.

Pondering, she crossed the passage to the tiny workroom opposite her bedroom. Meryt quickly selected her ingredients. First she made up a salve of aloe and honey for Nerekh's arm. Then she measured senna, rhubarb and castor oil into a bowl and pounded them to a sticky paste for Ib. She ducked out into the kitchen and found Nofret bringing two large jars of beer up out of the cellar.

"Here's the—drat that cat!" Nofret nearly stumbled as Nebet darted past her into the dark cellar.

Meryt caught her sister and relieved her of one of the jars. "Thank you. I'll take them to Wajet."

Nofret set them down, glaring at the direction in which the cat had disappeared. "That animal will bring you bad luck one day."

"Nebet? Of course not. She keeps the mice out of the grain."
Meryt stepped back into the workroom. In a few minutes, she
had mixed enough beer into the castor oil mixture to make it
palatable. Just for good measure, she added some honey to cut
the bitter taste. It wasn't necessary, and honey was expensive,
but she remembered the forlorn look on young Ib's face and
thought it wouldn't hurt to make the medicine easier for him.
She poured it into a small clay jar and tied a linen scrap over
the top. All the jars, and the beer, went into her medical basket
with the physician's sign on its side.

Back in the kitchen, Nofret squatted over the low fire,
stirring the ingredients in a flat pan. Meryt drew in a deep
breath. The smell of that delicious combination of garlic and
fish and onion and cumin would wake the blessed dead, she
thought. "I'll be back as soon as I can," she said.

Out in the street, the evening was advancing at the usual
stately pace of summer. Light still lingered in the west, but
already the desert air was cooling off. Meryt hurried down her
street and turned into the large central square of the village. In
the middle stood a large cistern, regularly filled by the donkey
caravans that brought water from the Nile every day.

Several women were gathered around the cistern, gossiping.
Meryt heard familiar laughter, and a woman turned, and she
saw Sheriti. "Sheri!"

"Meryt!" Her friend almost danced over to her. As usual,
she looked fresh and pretty, with a blue lotus flower tucked
behind one ear. "My dear, how are you? How is your father?"
She kissed Meryt on both cheeks.

Meryt debated whether to tell Sheri of her worries about
her father. "He's sleeping well," she said lightly. "I'm on my way
to the barracks with some medicine—"

"Wonderful! I'll go with you. It has been deadly dull here
all day. The donkey men didn't bring enough water today, so
I can't do my hair. May I come along?" Her infectious good
humor brought an echoing smile to Meryt's face.

"As long as you do not try to pass yourself off as my assistant
like you did last time," Meryt said dryly. "I don't think you fooled

that guard at all, tying a bandage on a perfectly healthy leg."

Her friend laughed. "Yes, it was a little clumsy, wasn't it? Too bad he had a temper. Did you go to the worksite today? Tell me everything!" Sheri linked arms with her, and leaned close. Meryt smelled her perfume.

"Oh, it was a mess," Meryt said. As they walked, she filled Sheri in on the events of the day.

"The man from the market is the new physician? The one who tore your dress?" Sheri frowned. "I wonder if he knew you were Djeti's daughter, and set out to embarrass you."

"Oh, I don't think so," Meryt said.

"Well, we'll have to do something about this Nakht," Sheri said forcefully. "It's a shame he can walk in here and destroy your father's position, your family's livelihood. We must encourage him to leave, or ask for another assignment. Let me see what kind of plan I can come up with."

"Don't try seducing him," Meryt said dryly. "That will hardly encourage him to leave."

Sheri laughed and dug an elbow into Meryt's rib. "Then what's your plan?"

Meryt shrugged. To Sheri, this was a game; to her, it was her whole future. It was hard to enter into the spirit of fun. "I'm still thinking about it."

They had arrived at the rows of worker's barracks, outside the village proper. Most of the people who lived in the Pyramid village were officials, artisans and craftsmen who lived year round at the site. The seasonal workmen who came to haul stones during the Inundation, when the fields were too flooded for farming, lived in the long houses that held forty men each. They were made of the usual mud brick, with many windows high in the wall to let in light. As they approached, Meryt saw a crowd of men huddled in the main square.

"Are they fighting?" Sheri said, craning to see.

The men moved to one side, and Meryt caught a glimpse. "Looks like a wrestling match," she said.

Sure enough, as they made their way through the crowd, it became apparent that the furor was just a friendly bit of sport.

The women stopped at the front of the crowd to watch.

The men were well matched: one of them was a stone hauler from the Delta whom Meryt recognized from the year before. He was built like an ox, with heavy shoulders and bulging biceps. But he was slow, relying on his bulk. Meryt had never seen his opponent before: taller, but less heavily muscled, he was quick and lithe. As was customary, they wrestled naked. The tall stranger had long hair that he had bound up out of the way, and his wiry, athletic form was heavily tanned. The Ox Man carried more fat; he almost looked like he was wearing armor.

When the Ox Man charged, the stranger dodged out of the way and tripped his opponent. Bellowing, Ox Man rose and lunged forward, grabbing his opponent in a bear hug. The new man twisted, forcing the Ox Man to move with him, and caught him in a pivoting movement with his hip. Suddenly, the Ox Man was on the ground, flat on his back, and men were cheering and clapping for the taller man. He stood, chest heaving, grinning. He caught sight of the women, and his grin slipped a bit. Meryt realized with some amusement that he was staring at Sheri, who was watching the Ox Man climb to his feet.

The two men clapped hand to shoulders to show there were no hard feelings, then slipped into the crowd on the other side. "That was a surprise," Sheri said. "I thought for certain the big man would win. Isn't he on the Perfection team?"

Meryt shook her head. "You should have taken more notice of the winner."

Sheri looked at her out of wide hazel eyes. "Winner?"

Meryt laughed. "I think you should wait for me out here. You might make a new friend." With that, she entered the worker's barracks, searching for the young man she had met on the road that morning.

Inside the mud brick building, the air smelled of sweaty men and dirty laundry. Most of the men were out at the mess hall, getting their evening meal of bread, onions, beer and meat. The interior was divided into colonnaded galleries, with built in brick platforms, wide enough for a man and his few possessions.

Some of the men were already rolled into their linen sheets, snoring. In the middle of the hall, several men were playing a game involving sticks and a square drawn in the dirt. A guard lounged just inside the door, keeping an eye out for thieves who might rummage through an absent man's belongings. Meryt approached him.

"No women allowed—oh, it's you. How is your father, Meryt?"

News traveled fast in such a small town, Meryt thought. "I'm looking for Ib," she said. She held up the small clay jar.

"Ib? Young fellow from up river? Yes, he's about fifteen rows down. I saw him come in earlier."

Meryt picked her way down the aisle, navigating around discarded heaps of linen kilts, sandals, bits of linen twisted up to hold keepsakes from home. Eyes followed her, and a few whispers, but she ignored them. Soon she saw a huddled shape on a platform and stopped. "Ib?"

He rolled over and sat up, clutching his middle. "Oh. I didn't think you would come." He looked as though he had been crying.

Meryt sat on the hard edge of the brick platform bed. Like other workers, Ib had piled several layers of straw on it and rolled out his sleeping mat. She handed the young man her clay jar. "Here is the medicine I promised."

He looked surprised. "You remembered?"

"Of course. What kind of physician forgets a patient? Drink half that off before you go to bed, and in the morning I believe you will find your trouble has cleared up. Don't drink all of it at once, or you'll spend all day in the latrine. Drink the other half tomorrow night. Say prayers to—who is your village god? Sobek? Recite three prayers each time you drink the medicine."

He took the small jar from her. "Thank you. You've been so kind—" He stopped, fighting emotions. Meryt stood, making sure she shielded him from the sight of the other men. While they were generally a good bunch, they might tease the young man if they saw him crying. Ib nodded, too overcome to speak.

Meryt felt a little sad as she walked up the aisle to the exit.

It took so little, such a small gesture of kindness, to change a young worker's day. And yet so few were willing to extend that small gesture.

Outside, she was not surprised to find Sheri in animated conversation with the wrestler who had defeated Ox Man. He was dressed now in a white kilt of fine texture, with a military harness over it. He wore a gold pendant on a leather string around his neck. He had taken the time to sluice some water over his hair and hastily finger comb it, but Meryt could still see runnels of water in the dust on his chest.

"Meryt! This is Baki," Sheri said as Meryt approached. "He's the new chief guard at the workshops."

Meryt nodded and murmured something polite. Baki's glance returned to Sheri. The evening breeze flattened Sheri's gown against her slim figure, outlining her high breasts. Baki's gaze drifted downward. Sheri was chattering gaily with him, and he was half-leaning down to listen, a smile on his face. Meryt sighed inwardly; Sheri had made yet another conquest. Her pretty face and guileless charm did it every time.

Meryt took the jugs of beer from her. "You stay here and chat. I'll drop these off on my way home."

Sheri turned to her. "Oh! But don't you want me to walk you home?"

"I'm a big girl," Meryt said. "And I've lived here as long as you. I don't think I'll get lost."

Sheri seemed to notice for the first time that it was nearly dark. "But there are night demons..." Her voice trailed off, frightened.

Baki looked from one girl to the other. "I can walk you both back to the village."

Sheri laughed and put a hand on his arm. "Oh, what a lion!"

"Yes, the village must be a hundred paces away, at least," Meryt said drily.

Baki grinned again. "Wait here." He strode off.

"You are absolutely shameless," Meryt said. "You know you don't believe in night demons."

Sheri grinned. "So? He doesn't know that. Did you see

those muscles? And those eyes? What do you think that lion pendant is for?"

"I suspect your new friend has recently served in the army," Meryt said. "Those scars on his right arm look like the kind a man might get in a sword fight, since his left arm is protected by his shield."

Sheri's eyes went wide. "Do you think he may have killed someone?"

"Here he comes. I imagine he'd be glad to tell you all about it."

Baki came back thrusting a long dagger into his waistband. "That should fend off the jackals," he said. His military posture and confident stride told Meryt that she would be safe walking into a thieves' den in his company. He bowed towards the village, extending a hand in invitation. Meryt and Sheri positioned themselves on either side of him and they walked out of the worker's area.

"It's going to be a beautiful night," he said. His voice was low and quiet, with a familiar tone to it. "Getting more beautiful all the time."

Sheri laughed a little breathlessly and put her hand on his arm. From her look, Meryt surmised that Sheri was not as careless as she appeared; the young soldier had piqued her interest. Meryt hoped that Baki would not toy with her friend's heart, although she had to admit that Sheri had toyed with a few herself.

In no time they were passing through the Gate of the Crow, which guarded the village. The evening watch, sighting Baki, saluted as he passed. Baki nodded gravely at them, and they watched him with envious eyes as he escorted the two women into the village.

♀

At the village square, Baki stopped. "A charming dilemma," he said. "Which lovely lady shall I escort home?"

"I have to leave these jars at the White Crown," Meryt said quickly, seeing Sheri's mischievous expression. "Best you walk Sheriti home before the demons get her."

Behind his back, Sheri winked at her and slipped a hand

into the crook of Baki's elbow. Meryt waved goodbye to her friend and Baki and turned off into another lane. A wry smile touched Meryt's mouth as she walked the narrow lane to the White Crown. *Another trophy for Sheri*, she thought.

The tavern was tucked into the end of a dirty street occupied mostly by the lowest rung of the social ladder. Night-soil carriers, butchers, washermen and the like lived in this warren of nooks and crannies, where houses with shared walls had been knocked together or subdivided or reconfigured until even the rats got lost in the maze. The White Crown survived its noisome neighborhood because of its reputation for excellent beer.

She hefted the jugs of said beer in her basket and pushed through the tattered door hanging. She stopped to let her eyes adjust to the gloom. Late as the evening was outside, it was even darker inside the mud-brick tavern. The room smelled of sweat and unwashed bodies and moldy bread. Loud voices off to her right told her a betting game was under way, and that the gamblers were drunk. A snore off to her left told her another patron had passed out from drink. A few smoky oil lamps contributed more to the haze than to clarity, most of them clustered near the owner himself.

Wajet sat behind a plank resting on stacks of mud brick. Behind him many jars of beer were stacked in precarious pyramids; flies buzzed around their rims. Wajet the tavern owner was obese, sweating, bald, and deceptively sleepy-looking. His half-closed eyes watched the rowdies at their game, flicking to Meryt's easy stride. He nodded as she stopped. "Meryt," he said, his voice a subterranean rumble. "May Renentet shine upon you."

Meryt nodded back. "And upon you. I've brought another batch of my beer."

Magisterially, Wajet brought up a fly whisk and flicked his shoulder. "The usual rates?"

"Two jars of beer for one of wine," she said, plunking the beer jars down in front of him. "And that means wine of Sebennytus, not that donkey swill from the upper Nile."

A half-smile spread across Wajet's fat cheeks. He picked

up a beer jar, uncapped it, and took a long swig. Then he smacked his lips and wiped foam off his upper lip delicately with a sodden rag from the bar. "Excellent," he wheezed. "Are you sure you won't tell me the secret? I would reward you well. And soon, the House of Djeti will need a friend like me." The big man's eyes slitted almost all the way closed. He looked like an overfed cat.

Meryt tried to conceal her alarm. Did everyone know of her father's grave condition? She knew that the tavern hid more secrets than any tomb, and more reliably. Gossip was the lifeblood of the village, and this was its heart.

Wajet smiled as if hearing her thoughts. "How do you brew this beer?" He picked it up for another long swig. Meryt wondered if there would be enough left for him to sell.

"If you like the beer all that much," she said briskly. "The price is now two jars of Sebennytus wine for every three of beer."

"Four beers to two wine jars," he said instantly.

"Three," she said firmly. "But I will brew another batch this week."

"Done." Wajet chuckled. "Well played, little Meryt. Alas, the wine shipment is late. May I have it delivered to you when it arrives?"

Meryt hesitated; perhaps she should take her beer back and wait for payment. Two things decided her—she would never again drink from the jar Wajet's lips had been on, and if Wajet reneged on their deal, she could and would ruin his reputation for fair dealing. For a professional gossip like Wajet, that would be fatal. "Very well," she said reluctantly. "But if it takes more than three days, you will owe me three jars of wine."

Wajet chuckled again. "I am helpless before your cunning, my dear," he said. He lifted the beer jar again. "May I offer you—"

Something slammed into Meryt. She cried out and fell to the floor. Something heavy came down on her leg, and a man fell across her, cursing. She blinked, dazed, and realized she was in the middle of a bar fight. The gamblers who had been intent on their game were now intent on killing one another.

A jar crashed next to her, splashing beer in her face along

with some of the hard packed floor-dirt. She got to her hands and knees and scampered backwards, huddling under the planks that made up Wajet's "bar". She crouched, knees under her chin, sitting in something wet that she hoped she never identified. Men fell over benches and hurled beer jars at one another's heads.

Beside her the trunk-like legs of the tavern owner stirred; Wajet was rising to his feet. Moving with calm deliberation, he stepped around the edge of his makeshift bar. But before he could intervene, another pair of well-shaped calves above leather-sandaled feet appeared in Meryt's view. Feet shifted, men grunted, pottery smashed as the tavern's entire population joined in merrily. The newcomer with the leather sandals danced out of the way of one man, there was a sound of meat hitting meat, and someone hit the floor in front of her.

Pottery smashed on the floor in front of her, spilling wine all down her dress. She thought of the hours it would take to soak the stain out, and scrambled out from under her shelter. An arm swung towards her, she ducked under it, caught a wrist. She spun, tugging the arm behind the man's back, jerking it upward until he howled. She knew exactly how much pressure to bring to keep from dislocating his shoulder, while immobilizing him. "What do you think you're—" she began.

Two men fell against her, struggling. She lost her hold on her man and scrambled backwards into Wajet. Someone came through the door, caught a glancing blow from a thrown jar, and lashed out with a fist. It connected solidly with a jaw, then Wajet stepped in front of Meryt, blocking her view. "Out the back!" he said. "Go, Meryt!"

She had no intention of fleeing.

"Wait for me!" cried a familiar voice, and Meryt peeked around Wajet to see Baki, Sheri's new friend, dash through the door. With no hesitation he launched himself at the nearest drunk. One of the fighters caromed into him; another came after his opponent, paying no attention to Baki. Baki caught each man by the back of his skull and slammed their faces together. Meryt winced at the crunch of nose cartilage and the sudden patter of red drops into the dirt floor. The two men fell in front of her, unconscious. A jar flew past her head; Meryt decided she'd be safer near the floor and knelt next to the downed men. She caught a wrist, checking the pulse.

Leather Sandals stepped over Meryt; his back, draped in a linen cloak, was to her. She saw his outstretched hand catch a beer jar in mid-flight. Holding it carefully, so as not to spill the beer, the man brought his other fist down on the shoulder of a fighter, who immediately slumped to the floor, groaning. His back to Meryt, Leather Sandals tipped the jar back, drained the beer, then brought the jar down on the shaved skull of a burly man in a leather kilt who was systematically pounding on a smaller man. Another man slipped in front of Meryt, raising a broken stool leg as a club.

Without even thinking, Meryt launched herself at the attacker's knees from behind. He crashed to the floor, yelling. His intended victim turned, leaned down, snatched the club from his hand and flung it away. The man crawled off, cursing, and Leather Sandals turned to lift Meryt to her feet.

"You!" Meryt drew her hand away.

Nakht stood before her, beer dripping down his chest and a wide grin on his face. "I am well repaid, lady, for my rescue in the marketplace yesterday."

"Duck!" someone yelled, and Nakht grabbed her, shoving her aside as a stool came sailing past his head. The man who threw it suddenly grunted as a fist plowed into his middle, and Meryt looked past him to see Baki pushing him out the door. Nakht shoved Meryt into Wajet's hands, with a fierce command. "Get her out of here!"

"No!" Meryt cried. "Men are hurt! I can't leave them!"

Wajet grunted, and pushed Meryt behind his plank bar.

"To me!" Nakht said loudly, and in two strides Baki was beside him. They turned, fighting back to back, and in the blink of an eye most of the brawlers were down or staggering out the door. Groans and heavy breathing from the fallen mingled with soft laughter from the two men who had ended the fight.

Nakht stepped over a prone victim and raised a hand in

salute to Meryt. "Thank you for taking that man down. He would have raised quite a bump with that club. Are you hurt?"

She looked down at her sodden shift. "Once again my wardrobe suffers in your vicinity." The combination of wine and water had rendered her linen nearly transparent. Nakht had seen it too; she looked up, saw the heat in his eyes and quickly looked away again.

Baki slapped Nakht on the shoulder and winked at Meryt. "Good thing I wanted a beer, or these fellows would have had him outnumbered."

Nakht laughed. "I had them on the run before you stumbled in. If there is a drink left in this place, I want it."

She heard Wajet's deep chuckle. "Your reward is on the house, my good men. Shall it be wine or beer?"

"Beer, by all means," Baki said lustily. "Now that I've worked up a thirst."

Nakht took the jar Wajet held out. "Baki, are you required to report this?"

Baki grinned. "Report what?"

Meryt knelt and checked the downed men, saw that they were still breathing, and then knelt next to a groaning man. His shoulder was bruised but not dislocated.

"Leave them," Wajet said. "They aren't worth your time."

Baki crouched down beside her. "If they're fit to travel, I can have them carried to the holding cell in the guard barracks, until they sleep it off."

Meryt stood. "They belong to Pharaoh (Life! Prosperity! Health!). He would not be pleased if they were hurt."

Wajet had sat down again, the stool creaking under his weight. He shrugged, and it was like watching mountains dance. "They will be no worse for a night in the cells. I cannot have fighting here."

Nakht met her eyes, and now it was the physician, not the man, who spoke. "Fear not, daughter of Djeti. I will tend to them myself. You need have no worry."

Unhappily, Meryt was reminded that she had no official place here as a healer. She nodded and straightened her gown, then turned to Wajet. "The wine in two days?" she asked.

Wajet nodded. "Or less. Good evening, little Meryt."

She stepped around him and ducked out of the tavern. The sun had set, the moon had not risen, and the sunshade matting over the narrow lanes blocked what little starlight there was. Nor was this a quarter whose inhabitants wasted oil on outdoor lighting. Thinking—or rather, trying not to think about the tall, dark-eyed Nakht, she took a wrong turn and wound up in the alley next to the tavern. Realizing her mistake, she turned to go back. Suddenly, a shadow slipped from a doorway and collided with her. Once again Meryt went down on hard-packed dirt, spitting. A bag landed next to her head with a metallic chime.

"Daughter of Set!" a man cursed. A large, work-calloused hand came into view, groping for the sack.

Meryt started to rise to her knees, but someone pushed her hard in the middle of her back. She grunted as she was shoved face down into the dirt again. Her breath whooshed out of her painfully.

A shout behind her, pounding feet. Feet pounded up the alley, but her rescuer did not pursue.

"Did he hurt you?" Nakht said, kneeling next to her.

Meryt felt bruised and shaken. The wind whispering along the alley felt cold on her skin; it had a lonely, empty sound.

"I ... I am unhurt," she said shakily. He helped her to her feet, silently, his hands strong on her arm. "Thank you. Again."

His hand lingered on her arm, then slid slowly down to her wrist. He raised it, turned it upward, and laid a finger on her pulse. "You should sit down," he said.

She snatched her hand away. "I do not need a physician," she said smartly.

"No, indeed. But a troop of soldiers might be in order. Is your day always so exciting? Come, I will walk you home." He held out a hand. She noticed a bruise forming along his cheekbone and found herself wanting to soothe it. She frowned inwardly. This would never do. She could not allow herself to be distracted by the man who wanted her father's place. She had to keep her distance. Meryt shook her head.

"No."

"I have no choice," he said. He turned with her and headed back to the tavern. "I was on my way to your house anyway, when I heard the fight."

She blinked. "My house?"

"Well, the house of Djeti. As the new physician, it is my duty to look in on all of the ill and wounded under the care of my office. That would include your father."

She felt anger flare in her. The new physician? Already he was encroaching on her father's work. She knew her feelings were unreasonable. But nothing about this man was reasonable.

"He doesn't need your help," she said shortly.

They had reached the mouth of the passage, and he waited politely for her to indicate which way they should turn. Reluctantly, she started for her street. He followed. "I am sure he does not," Nakht said. "But I would be shirking my duty if I did not include a visit in my report."

She could hardly argue with that. Although she wanted to. Setting her teeth, Meryt led him to her home.

Chapter 4 - Dinner on the Roof

Meryt led Nakht into the antechamber of her father's house. He stooped as he crossed the threshold, turned it into a polite bow towards the family shrine, and then straightened. She hoped he did not see the dust bunnies in the corners, or the sandals flung carelessly against a wall. She had been too busy for housekeeping. She cleared her throat. "Welcome to the house of Djeti-Thutmose," she said formally.

Nakht bowed slightly, opened his mouth to make a formal reply, but stopped at a bustle from the doorway.

"Meryt? Dinner will be ready in a—oh!" Nofret entered, carrying a bowl. She stopped dead when she saw Nakht.

Nakht bowed gracefully. "Good evening. I have the honor to address...?" He arched an eyebrow.

Flustered, Nofret bent awkwardly in a bow. "I'm Nofret, daughter of Djeti. You seem to have met my sister."

Meryt flushed as she remembered that first meeting in the market, but Nakht kept a straight face. "My name is Nakht, son of Ra-Khuf, and I had the privilege of watching your sister at work today."

Nofret's eyes narrowed. "My sister spoke of you. You have my father's duties now?"

Nakht nodded. "I do. And my duty requires that I visit your father."

"Oh." Nofret glanced desperately at Meryt. "Must you? I mean, is it really necessary to disturb him?"

"I am required to examine him and report on his condition."

Meryt felt her face go hot. "I can do that!"

"Of course. But the Overseer requires a report from me, and none other." He smiled. "Naturally I cannot refuse a direct order."

"Naturally," Nofret said quickly. She looked panicked, but stepped aside. "Meryt can show you where he is. I will be serving dinner in a moment. I hope you will join us, Nakht."

Meryt stiffened. What on earth had gotten into her sister? The place was a mess, there was a sick man in the main room, and Nakht himself threatened their father's very livelihood. But as she heard Nakht's gracious acceptance, she realized there was no way she could cancel her sister's invitation without seeming very rude.

Not looking at Nakht, she gestured for him to follow and stepped through the door. She was acutely conscious of her dirty dress, of the stuffy, unaired atmosphere of the house, of the clothes and bandages strewn about, and the pregnant cat now licking something out of a bowl. Nakht ignored it all and instead knelt next to Djeti. He reached towards him, stopped, and turned to Meryt. "May I?"

Meryt nodded, then watched as Nakht quickly examined the injured man, checking his pulse, feeling for fever, peeking under the bandages on leg and arm. He leaned close to smell the linen wrappings, then sat back on his heels. "These splints are well done. Your work?"

"Yes." Her voice sounded hoarse in her own ears.

Nakht put a hand on the old man's wrist. "And what is your diagnosis?" he asked.

Meryt was surprised. His tone was neutral, as if addressing any colleague, rather than a mere woman. She made her voice as calm as possible, and recited her diagnosis in the formal manner of a professional physician, ticking off each point on her fingers.

"As to the skull, this appears to be a bruise of the scalp with no protrusions outside the skin; there is no evidence of a breakage of the bone beneath. No treatment is called for.

"As to the arm, this appears to be a clean break of the lower bones of the arm, between the elbow and the wrist on the left side, with no protrusions outside the skin. I have set the break and splinted it.

"As to the leg, this appears to be a clean break of the lower shin, between the knee and the ankle on the left side, with no protrusions outside the skin. I have set the break and splinted it.

"As to the ribs, there is much bruising along the left side, and there may be one or two broken ribs. I have bound the ribs tightly."

Nakht nodded appreciatively. "Well said. Your father trained you well. He has wakened?"

"No."

"He has taken nourishment? Water?"

"He swallows water when we dribble it between his lips."

"Is there fever?"

"No fever," Meryt said evenly. It was strange, talking to him almost as she did to her father, discussing a case. And yet, she reminded herself, this man threatened everything she held dear.

Nakht felt her father's head again, turning it carefully, his touch gentle and sure. "I do not like this bruise," he murmured, almost to himself.

"Nor do I," Meryt said. "There is no break below the skin, however."

Nakht's fingers danced as light as a butterfly, palpating Djeti's skull expertly. "You are right," he said, sitting back on his heels. He frowned. "Perhaps all is well, it is only a bruise. Yet...you have examined the eyes?"

"No."

"With your permission, I will do so," he said courteously. At her gesture of acceptance, he leaned carefully over and lifted first one, and then the other of Djeti's eyelids.

"That is bad," he said in a low voice, almost as if speaking to himself.

"What is it?"

"See here, the black part of each eye, the eye of the eye as we call it. They are not the same size in each eye."

Meryt leaned forward, her shoulder brushing his. Nakht leaned back a little to let the afternoon light fall across Djeti's face. Meryt lifted her father's eyelids and saw that, indeed, the pupils were of different sizes. She sat back, and put her palms on her thighs to hide their trembling.

"I am not sure what this means," she said, hearing her voice crack. Meryt looked at the dark shadow spreading across her father's balding head. Her shoulder touched Nakht's; she felt his skin against hers. Was that sandalwood she smelled?

"Do not fear, yet," Nakht said, his voice low. "It could be a passing thing." He laid a hand on hers; she felt its warmth, its strength. Their faces were close enough that Meryt could see his lashes lying along his cheek, see the fleeting expression that crossed his face before an iron discipline shut it down. He sat back on his heels. "I hope your father may not develop fever," he said formally. "What treatment does he usually recommend for it?"

Meryt withdrew her hands and rubbed them on her thighs. "We use a mixture of willow bark, acacia and honey, boiled together and mixed into fresh beer."

Nakht's eyebrows rose. "Willow bark? I have not heard of this. Is this some spell which he learned from Hesy-Ra?"

Meryt hesitated. She knew nothing of this man. No doubt he was like all the other physicians, wary of any new practice. Would he report her father's unorthodoxy to the Vizier? Yet, between physicians treating a patient, there could be nothing but truth. "No," she said finally. "It ... it is a decoction of his own ... invention."

The eyebrows again, but Nakht only placed his hand briefly on hers, then rose to his feet. "I will not presume to tell you how to treat your father, who has trained you in his own methods," he said. His voice was low and quiet. "But if you need any thing, any medicine, you may call on me."

"Thank you," Meryt said, rising as well.

"And if there is any change, good or ill, send for me at any hour." He put out a hand, as if to lay it on her shoulder, but it hovered there before he let it drop. The silence grew taut between them, full of potential. She wanted him to go, he threatened everything she loved. But she also wanted him to stay, for reasons she did not want to examine just then.

⚥

"Dinner is ready!" Nofret entered carrying a cup. She smiled when she caught sight of Nakht. "I have water for my father, if I can get him to swallow. You and Meryt may eat on the roof, in the cool. It's just fish and bread and vegetables, but we hope you will honor us."

"Of course," he said politely. He took a step back. "May I wash?"

Nofret directed him to the bathing area under the stairs. As he disappeared down the passage, Meryt pulled her sister close. "What are you doing?"

"Making friends, you idiot," Nofret snapped back. "Do you want to make an enemy of the man who has Akhti-Hotep's ear? The last thing we need is for our family to get a reputation as rude or stand-offish. Now go, set places on the rooftop, while I try to get our father to drink."

Meryt bit her lip, knowing Nofret was right. Carrying two oil lamps up to the roof, Meryt could hear the sluice of water in the tiled bathing area. Just as she set down the lamps near a platter of onions, bean paste, bread and figs, Nakht climbed up into the night air, his hair now wet and sleek against his head. He inhaled deeply.

"That smells wonderful," he said. He stood, hands on hips, surveying the village. Djeti's house stood on a slight rise, but like all the other houses in the town, it shared walls with its neighbors. Two roofs over, a family with several noisy children were eating. They waved to Meryt, who waved back.

"You have a good view here," he said. "I can see the river from here. You probably get a good cool breeze after sunset."

Meryt struggled to hold onto his words. Her mind was preoccupied with the Overseer's casual dismissal, with concern for her family. "We are fortunate," she said. She sat on a mat, and he politely followed her. She passed him the plate of appetizers. He took bread and dipped it into the bean paste. In the dim light, shadows highlighted his dark eyes, his high cheekbones.

"I am new," he said simply, his expression open. "Perhaps you would be so good as to tell me something about the village. Although," he said, his white teeth tearing bread. "I would also like to hear something about you."

"There is nothing to say about me," Meryt said, feeling her cheeks grow warm. Was there no end to this man's impudence? "My father taught me all he knows about healing."

"And you live in his house, which tells me you are unmarried." His eyes danced.

"My husband died three years ago, and I returned to Djeti's house." Her voice was tight with anger, sadness, a dozen emotions.

"I am sorry, if it makes you sad," he said quietly. Seeming to realize it was a painful topic, he said, "What about the village?"

Meryt embraced the change of topic. "Of course the village is only a year older than the Pyramid," she said. "It was designed by the Royal Vizier and his architects, to house the workers."

"Oh, of course. This is the first Pyramid on the Giza plateau," he said, nodding. He turned his head, and they both looked for a moment across the village roofs, the twinkling lamps, the distant glow of lamps and bonfires to the dark bulk of the man-made mountain rising above the plain.

"We have a mayor, but he's usually at the Western House," Meryt said.

"That's the palace on this bank of the river," Nakht said. "Unusual. It is the first I have ever heard of a King living on the West bank of the Nile."

"Well, naturally he would want to be close to his Pyramid," Meryt said. "But he is not here. In fact, he is more often not here, but in Memphis. Many of the royal family come and go, and of course the Royal Vizier lives there."

"I have often wondered why His Majesty (Life! Prosperity! Health!) chose to build his tomb here, rather than at Saqqara." Saqqara, several miles to the south, was across the Nile from the capital, Memphis. It was the traditional place for kings to be buried. Already several huge pyramids rose above its riverside site.

"The ways of Pharaoh are sometimes puzzling," Meryt said politely. She dipped bread into the bean paste.

"And your family has always served the Horus Throne?"

"My great-grandfather, my grandfather, and my father have always served the King," she said, a hint of pride in her voice. "All of them physicians, all of them serving honorably."

He bowed from the waist. "I am honored to eat at Djeti's table," he said. A hint of a smile curled at the corner of his mouth. "And more honored to be served by his capable daughter. Which Pyramid did your family help to build?"

Meryt was happy to enlarge on this relatively safe topic. His compliments confused her, as did his flashing eyes and white smile. "My grandfather and my father served on the work teams that build the Osiris Senefru's Shining Pyramid at Dahshur. My grandfather was the Chief Physician for the entire workforce."

Nakht's eyes widened. "An honor!" A thoughtful look crossed his face. "I am told that the king is following his father's plan, with a burial chamber in the center of the Pyramid, rather than underground, as the old kings did. Is that the case?"

"We aren't supposed to discuss the Pyramid with outsiders," Meryt said sharply. "It is Pharaoh's law (Life! Prosperity! Health!)."

"But I am not an outsider," Nakht said reasonably. "I am here by appointment of the Royal Vizier."

Reminded of this bitter fact, Meryt's thoughts flew instantly to her father, downstairs. And to her constant worry about the future. "Even so," she said through a forced smile. "I do not presume to question the decisions of the Royal Architect. Will you have some more bean paste?"

Nofret appeared at the head of the stairs, carrying a large bowl of lentil and mutton stew. She and Meryt fussed for a moment, ladling stew into bowls, passing the first to their guest. His fingers brushed Meryt's as he received it, leaving her with an impression of warmth and strength. Murmuring compliments to the cook, Nakht dipped bread into his bowl and began to eat.

"Father was able to swallow a few sips of water," Nofret told Meryt. "I will try to get more into him later. But I am concerned that he does not wake. He must eat!"

"He will—" Nakht began.

"I think—" Meryt said. Both stopped in confusion, and then Nakht nodded at her.

"It is your place to answer," he said, and reached for a radish.

"I think he will be well, for a while," Meryt said to Nofret. "As long as he continues to sip water, his *ka* will remain."

"But if he doesn't eat!" Nofret looked distressed.

Meryt shrugged. "We will not have to worry for a few days. And I am sure he will wake before hunger threatens his life."

"What do you think?" Nofret asked Nakht.

Meryt bristled. What was Nofret doing, seeking an outsider's word against her own sister's?

Nakht said easily, "I would agree with everything your learned sister has said." He tipped up the bowl of stew, swallowing the last of it. "You have no cause to worry, as long as he is continuing to drink."

"I don't understand it," Nofret said. She pushed her bread around in her bowl, scowling. "It is as if he is asleep, yet he drinks. Yet he does not wake. This is all very strange."

Meryt opened her mouth to explain the black sleep to her sister, but before she could speak, Nakht said, "I think it is more important right now that you eat that excellent stew."

Nofret blinked at him, a hint of pink appearing along her cheek. "I, well…"

"When will the child be born?"

"Oh." Nofret fluttered a bit. "In the middle of winter, we believe. Or so the midwife and Meryt tell me."

"Your first?" Nakht smiled easily.

"Yes," Nofret said. She stood quickly. "I must fetch the fish. Excuse me." She hurried down the stairs.

"Your sister is shy," he commented when she disappeared.

"She's not used to discussing her pregnancy with strangers," Meryt said drily.

Nakht looked concerned. "I meant no offense. As a physician, you understand how quickly one falls into the habit of discussing medical matters."

As a physician. He was treating her as an equal. Meryt felt a peculiar warmth steal over her. Perhaps she had judged him too hastily…

"Your father trained you well," Nakht said. "You are almost as good as a man. Have you studied at the House of Life, or only with Djeti?"

Almost as good as a man? Bristling, Meryt snapped, "My father is a better teacher than any at the House of Life."

Clearly not believing her, Nakht smiled politely. "Of course."

Meryt finished her stew in silence. Above them, the evening had deepened to lapis lazuli blue, studded with burning stars. Sunset had brought an end to the heat of the day, and now a cool breeze wafted over the housetops, bringing with it the smell of water from the Nile, the smell of wet earth, of lotus flowers blooming in the marshes.

Nofret appeared, bearing a platter with fried fish garnished with pickled radishes and cucumbers. "Our father enjoys Nile perch, so I made him his favorite dish, should he wake. I will bring some wine."

Nakht held up a hand. "Tonight I saw men fighting over Meryt's beer. May I try some?" A corner of his mouth quirked up as he looked at Meryt.

Nofret smiled brightly. "That's up to our brewer. Meanwhile, I'll fetch more bread." She vanished down the steps, leaving them alone together again.

A quiet breath of wind ruffled Meryt's gown against her legs, tossed a strand of Nakht's hair. She could hear him breathing, close but reserved. Meryt was keenly aware of Nakht's eyes on her. She fidgeted for a few moments, and then rose to go downstairs. But as she passed, he caught her wrist in his hand.

"Lady," he said, his voice low. "I wanted to say—"

Suddenly, Meryt wanted to be anywhere but here. Panicked at the thought of what he might say, she said, "I will fetch the beer for you." She ran down the steps two at a time.

By the time she had cooled her cheeks with a splash of water and drawn a mug of beer for their visitor, Meryt was a little more composed. She reminded herself that it was important to maintain his good will.

When she returned to the roof, Nakht was chatting with Nofret. They sat cross-legged on the rooftop, with dishes arranged on an embroidered cloth between them. Nofret was telling Nakht a story about two masons, while passing him some fish. To be polite, Meryt also accepted a piece, but she could not eat for the knot in her stomach. She sat next to Nakht, and thus had a view of his profile, his animated smile, the muscles on his arms as he leaned forward.

When she handed him the mug of beer, he sampled it thoughtfully. His eyes went wide and he nodded to her. "Excellent," he said. He set the mug down with a satisfied look which made Meryt's insides warm a bit. His gaze was open and friendly, with a hint of something—sadness—behind it. "Your family is lucky," he said.

Nofret gathered empty bowls. "I don't want to leave Father alone too long," she said. "You two eat at your leisure. I will go sit with him." She slipped quietly down the steps, and silence descended on Meryt and her visitor.

She cleared her throat. "So. How do you like our village? Have you been assigned a place to stay?"

"Oh, yes. My brother is moving our family in now. There are five of us, including my son," he said cheerfully, tearing off another hunk of bread.

Meryt felt a little sick in her head. Another addition to his family? A son? He was married. His *are you married* had seemed to imply otherwise. How could she have been so naive?

Nakht continued, heedless. "We're a little crowded, I'll admit. And we've got another addition to the family arriving in five or six weeks."

Married. Why did that bother her? "Congratulations," she said. "How many children do you have?"

"Only my son," Nakht said. "Since we are new to the village, I need advice. My son is almost old enough to enter the House of Scribes to begin his education. Who is the best teacher here?"

Meryt cleared her throat and looked away, forcing herself to concentrate. Of course he had a son. Men of Nakht's age usually had several children by now. What had she been thinking? Or trying not to think? This man was a threat to her family, she must not allow herself to be charmed by him. "They tell me that Ptah-Hotep is one of the most well read scribes in the village," she said. "He tutors young children before they enter the temple school. My brother-in-law Kahotep, Nofret's husband, can tell you more about him."

She forced herself to remain calm and make her voice neutral, discussing the different scribes who lived and worked in the village. Since work on the Pyramid was the most prestigious and high-paying in the Two Lands, the scribes lucky enough to find work on it were also the finest in Egypt. Most of them also tutored young students. Meryt spent several minutes listing the most well-respected on her fingers.

Nakht shifted, and the lamp light caught the knot of scars on his shoulder. Meryt drew in her breath. "That must have been painful."

A shadow passed over Nakht's handsome features. "Yes, it was."

"How did it happen?"

"Pirates," he said. When Meryt's eyes grew big, he smiled slightly. "Off the Delta. We were coming back from Tyre with a shipload of frankincense, cedars and oil for Pharaoh's palace (Life! Prosperity! Health!). They crept up under cover of darkness, and before we knew it, they were sending spears and arrows into us like hail. I took an arrow through the shoulder; there was no other physician on board so I had to doctor myself." His mouth twisted in a wry grin. "You might now seriously doubt my skills."

"Not I. Many men would have died from such a wound," Meryt said. "Yet you have full use of the arm."

He turned towards her, his eyes bright. He bowed from the waist. "Praise indeed, from the daughter of Djeti the physician. I have had very good use of my arms lately."

Meryt blushed. It occurred to her that he was a little drunk. She said no more, but watched as he finished his dinner with slices of watermelon drizzled with date syrup. Nofret came up the steps with a water bowl to wash his hands. She handed him a linen towel, and he burped politely. Then he looked down in surprise. "Hello!"

Nebet, the cat, crawled into his lap with an air of great dignity. She sniffed carefully all around Nakht's throat and shoulder, kneaded his thigh for a moment, and then curled into a very large ball in his lap. From where she sat, Meryt could hear her purring. Nakht stroked the cat behind her ears. "Here's a little mother," he murmured. His fingers gently felt the cat's belly. "Only a few more days, I think."

Nofret reached for his empty bowl. "Please tell anyone you know that there will be free kittens available soon," she said. "We can vouch for the mother's skill at mousing."

Nebet butted Nakht's hand, demanding more petting. But Nakht was watching Meryt as she rose to clear the table. He rose with her, lifting Nebet very gently and depositing her on the floor. "Thank you for a very fine supper. I enjoyed it very much, but it is time I returned home," he said politely. "May I assist with your father in any way?"

Meryt shook her head. Nofret glared at her as she took the bowls from her hand, then nudged her towards the stairs. Remembering her manners, Meryt said, "I'll see you out."

Meryt walked her visitor down the stairs, past her sleeping father, and through to the antechamber. In the dimly lit room, she opened the door for Nakht. He ducked to go through, but as he passed, he caught her hand and pulled her with him.

She found herself in the street outside her own door. Around her she heard the murmurs of other families at their dinners, smelled the aromas of cooking and baking. The houses, after their long day in the sun, radiated warmth. The loosely woven shade mats overhead cast the street into dusk. Nakht used his other hand to pull the door shut. He stood between her and the street, her hand still caught in his, her back to the wall of her house.

"Lady, I have an apology to make."

She could not look at him, but she knew what he was going to say. She looked down at their linked hands. She remembered his hand on her. Vividly.

"I was too bold in the marketplace," he said. He tipped up her chin with one finger. His eyes were dark, troubled. He was no longer the mannerly guest, at ease on her rooftop; he seemed nervous, uncertain. "I should not have ... have handled you as I did. I didn't know ... you were ... the moment was on me before I knew it. Well, as I said. I apologize. Had I known you were promised ... I would not have done what I did. I only thought to save you from the bull."

She swallowed, or tried to. Her throat was dry. "Promised?"

He released her hand. "I spoke to Shushu the scribe this afternoon, after you left. He told me of your betrothal. I would never have done what I did had I known."

I did. I would like to do it again. His hand cupping her breast, his roguish grin, the weight of his muscled arm, his lips on her neck, oh that mouth...

"And that makes a difference?" she asked.

He straightened, as if offended. "To behave thus with another man's betrothed, that is dishonorable. I thought you were unattached. I hope you will not mention this to Shushu. We must work together, and I would not give offense to him. Or to you, lady."

So that's why he'd asked if she was married. She could smell his skin, he was so close. It was a clean, athletic smell. She closed her eyes. "What if I told you I was not promised. What would your apology be then?"

There was a long silence. "Not promised?"

She shook her head. "Shushu has asked me. I have given him no answer. Yet."

A touch on her cheek. She opened her eyes. His face was near, his thumb traced her jawline, his hand cupped it, his fingers under her ear. "*Not* promised?"

Mutely, she shook her head. And watched, mesmerized, as he leaned down.

"Little dove, I am glad to hear it."

Then his mouth touched hers, warm and quick and alive. Her eyes closed, and his mouth moved on hers, and she let herself feel, for just a moment, the bubbling excitement of her body's response. It had been so long since her last kiss, Meryt hardly knew what to do. She should pull away. She should push him away. But she didn't, and he pressed harder.

His mouth demanded, his tongue teased. He cupped her jaw in both hands, holding her head, his fingers twining through her hair. She knew one of her neighbors might come out at any moment, or Nofret come through the door on her way home. She didn't care. Then sanity returned and she put her hand lightly on his chest. He pulled away instantly, releasing her, but not before she had felt his racing heart under flat muscle.

"No more," she whispered.

"Meryt..." It was the first time he had said her name.

She turned her head, reaching for the door to her house. "No. Go home to ... to your family." She could not say *wife*, it stuck in her throat. Before he could answer, she opened the door and slipped through it into the house. She stood, arms crossed and head bowed, in front of the family shrine, until she heard his departing steps in the street.

"Isis," she prayed to her patron goddess. "What shall I do?" The little clay goddess returned no answer.

☥

Nofret came into the antechamber, wiping her hands on a towel. There were dark shadows under her eyes. "He's gone?"

Meryt nodded. She sighed. "Thank you. It was a good idea to give him dinner. I would never have thought to invite him."

Nofret patted her shoulder. "I know. You're so prickly! But I think maybe now he has good thoughts about the house of Djeti." She pulled back, looking into her sister's eyes. A corner of her mouth turned up. "About one member of it, anyway."

"You're seeing mirages," Meryt said.

"I'm seeing what's in front of me. He certainly sees you."

Meryt shrugged. "He's married, Nofret."

A small frown creased Nofret's brow, then disappeared. "Well. I won't say that's good. But it's not an obstacle unless you let it be."

Meryt closed her eyes. She was too tired for this argument, she thought. "The fish was really good."

Nofret beamed. "It was Mother's recipe." Her bright expression dimmed a little. "I only wish Father had been able to eat some."

"I'll keep watch over him tonight. You go home and get some sleep."

"I'll just finish washing up—"

Meryt took the towel from her sister. "Go home, before your husband forgets what you look like." She dropped a kiss on her sister's cheek and pushed her towards the door.

"I'll be back early in the morning," Nofret said as she left.

"If you need me during the night—"

"I'll send someone," Meryt said firmly. "Go."

Meryt closed the door of her house. Outside, the sounds of other families had died down as people prepared for bed. Workers who had spent ten hours hauling stone under a hot sun did not stay up late, nor did their wives and children. Soon the only sound floating through the night air was the croon of mothers singing lullabies.

Meryt checked on her father, whose skin still felt dry. She spent a few minutes making her willow bark mixture again, and put it beside his bed in a mug. Then she entered the bathing area, slipped out of her dress, and spent a few minutes pouring cool water over her skin. It was later than she usually bathed, and the night air bit at her. Draping a linen sheet around herself, she carried her sleeping mat into the main room and unrolled it next to her father's sleeping platform. She snuggled down under the soft linen covers, closing her eyes, hoping for the oblivion of sleep. She didn't even jump in surprise when a soft weight landed on her feet and began softly kneading them. She scooted over to make room for the cat and fell asleep.

She remembers his scent, not his hands. Maybe it's all the long hours spent with exotic herbs and oils, maybe it's the fact they first met in the apothecaries' market. But when the moment comes back to her and she remembers that arm around her, lifting her like she was a doll, she smells sandalwood and pine, a trace of musk, a whisper of mint. She hears his voice again at dinner, telling of shipments of cedar from far lands. Maybe he picked up the scent of those incense trees, so mysterious and exciting. Their scents whisper to her, enticing her. A series of images forms in her dream-mind: Nakht's hands on her breast, his fingers so gentle, the sight of his profile in the lamplight, the look in his eyes when he sees her over the body of a wounded man, over the rim of a beer mug.

Then the images change, and she is back in Butehamun's bed. She remembers her late husband's panting thrusts, the pain, the disappointment. She remembers Butehamun's growing contempt, his little slaps and punches as he expresses his disgust with a wife who cannot bear children. The tide of sadness these images brings suffuse her dream with anxiety and fear. She remembers weeping in the shrine of Min, the god of fertility whose enormous erection reflects his role in the cycle of life.

The images shift, overlap, and now Nakht embraces her, and his body is young and strong, his erection as proud and full as the god's. He smiles at her and she remembers the feel of muscled arms around her, feels heat pooling in her belly, a shiver cascading down her limbs. In the dream his mouth is ripe and slow on hers. His fingers pinch her nipple lightly, stroke the soft aureola, send waves of pleasure through her. She feels herself turning to flame, rising to meet him as Geb rises to meet Nut, earth meeting sky, kissing the heavens as her whole body shakes with delight. Just as she begins to shatter into a joyful dissolution with Nakht's strong body, peaking on a rising crest of pleasure, she wakes. And finds tears on her cheek.

Meryt slept no more that night, but sat in darkness, with the linen sheet wrapped around her. She was distracting herself with these fantasies, she thought. In her mind, she faced the possibility that soon she would be packing her household, looking for a new place to live, finding a house and a way to put food on the table, caring for an aging, crippled father—or burying him. She thought about Shushu and his proposal, and about growing old in a house without love, dependent and needy. She had no time for girlish dreams about handsome men; her future demanded more than that from her.

Nebet edged up against her, curled herself into a ball of warm fur, and purred through the night. Otherwise, Meryt was alone, in the bleakest hours of the night, facing an ugly future with an ache in her heart.

CHAPTER 5 – THE DARK SLEEP

14th Day of the Inundation
Year 7 of the Pharaoh Khufu

Dawn arrived after a fitful night. Meryt poured cold water over herself in the bathing area, shocking herself into wakefulness. It would be a long day under hot sun, on little sleep. Wrapping a worn work gown around herself, she checked on her father and found his condition unchanged. She peered at his eyes, and felt her stomach lurch as she noted his mismatched pupils. Why had he not wakened? How was she failing in her treatment?

She picked up the cup of water near the bed and dribbled a few drops onto her father's dry lips. They moved, as if in sleep, and she saw his throat move. She fed him more drops of water, until his throat stopped moving. It was too little, she thought desperately. Djeti needed more water. He needed to wake.

Nofret arrived as Meryt finished packing her basket with a newly made potion and some folded bandages. "How has he been?" she asked.

Meryt caught her sister's face and turned it to the light. There were dark circles under her eyes. "You have not been sleeping."

Nofret pushed her hand away. "The baby kicks sometimes. It's nothing. Has Father waked? Did you feed him?"

"He drank a little water, but he has not wakened." Meryt looked past her sister, seeing in her mind's eye that long night just past, when thoughts of Nakht and worry for her father stretched the hours out endlessly.

"I will make him some more broth. Maybe I can get him to swallow it," Nofret said. She looked at Meryt's basket. "You are going to the worksite?"

"Not yet. I must see to the patient who cut his arm yesterday. Then I will come home so that you may go back to Kahotep."

Nofret bit her thumb and turned away. Meryt patted her on her shoulder and then walked out of the house.

This time she bypassed the barracks where she had visited Ib, heading for Perfection. She had to walk against the tide of men heading out for work. Some whistled and sang, some grumbled, some chatted as they marched. She looked at them, each man knowing his place, knowing his universe was balanced and full and right, held together by Pharaoh and the gods and Ma'at, which was the rightness of things. Only she, and her family, were in limbo now, not sure of their place or their purpose, adrift. She put her head down, feeling obscurely ashamed.

At the Perfection barracks, she nodded to the guard, well known to her. When she stepped inside, she had to stop while her eyes adjusted to the gloom. This barrack was better run than Ib's. As her vision cleared, she saw neatly arranged bedding, stacks of sandals, a boy at the other end carefully emptying night buckets. Close by, she saw a huddled lump of blankets and stepped nearer.

"Nerekh?"

A groan, and the figure tossed. As his face came into the light from the doorway, Meryt saw that it was flushed and sweating. Oh no, she thought, her heart sinking. Fever, as she feared.

Setting down her basket, she bent over the man's bed. "Nerekh," she said clearly. "I must change your dressing. Can you hear me?"

There was no answer, and his eyes remained closed. A movement caught her eye; the cleaning boy had moved closer. The stench of the buckets he carried hit her.

"Back away," she warned, shoving at the air. "Take those outside, and wash your hands."

The boy blinked. "Wash...?"

"You heard me. Dump those buckets at the latrine, and then wash them and your hands. At the well. And dump the dirty wash water somewhere far from the well."

Plainly he did not understand, but bobbed his head and

went out, taking the smell with him. From the doorway, the lounging guard looked amused. "What do you care if a bucket boy is clean?" he said.

Meryt ignored him, lifting the bandages around Nerekh's arm, sniffing them. To her dismay, she caught the rotting-meat smell of corruption. As the bandages came free, she caught her breath. The arm was swollen almost double in size, with the long cut oozing pus. Meryt blinked against the smell.

The guard, peering curiously over her shoulder, exclaimed suddenly and stepped back. "It's gone bad!"

"I know," she said. "I must have hot water. Can it be brought?"

He nodded and stepped outside, calling for the boy again. Meryt brought out her clean linen, her ointment, her newly brewed medicine, and laid them out on the long brick bench beside her patient. The boy came back into the barracks, his hands dripping wet but clean. "Mistress?"

She looked at him. He was scrawny but strong, probably about ten. His eyes were wary but alert. "Can you boil some water for me in a clean vessel? About one hin measure. Do not let anything fall into it, and bring it as soon as it has cooled enough to carry."

He looked puzzled. "Boiled?"

"Do as she says," the guard growled at him. "Aye, if she asks for moonlight in a basket, you'll fetch it, cub!" The boy hurried away. The guard looked at Meryt respectfully. "What need you else, Mistress?"

"If he thrashes, you must hold him," she said, examining the arm. There were, as yet, none of the deadly streaks of blackish-red going up and down the arm. Perhaps there was a chance. Carefully, she finished unwrapping the arm. When the boy returned with a small copper pan full of hot water, she directed him to lay it down. She stirred into it salt, ash, natron and hemat, using a clean reed. She looked up at the boy. "Have you any rotten bread?"

He stared at her. "Rotten bread?"

The guard cuffed him on the shoulder. "Don't stand like a

donkey, boy! Run and fetch her what she asks for!" The boy ran off. The guard looked at her anxiously. "Is it to force the demons out that you ask for it?"

Meryt nodded. "As we were instructed by Imhotep the Great himself." She knew that invoking that famous physician would silence all questions. She dipped linen in the hot water and cleaned the wound. By the time the boy had returned with both hands full of moldy bread, Nerekh's whole arm was clean. Meryt drew the edges of the wound together, placed the crumbled up, gray-green fuzz along the wound, and began bandaging it again.

"Do you wish me to fetch dog's dung? Or donkey's?" the boy asked warily. "That is what the physician used on my grandfather's leg when he hurt it."

Meryt eyed him. "Did your grandfather get better?"

The boy shifted from foot to foot. "No, Mistress."

"Then we won't use it now. Here, take these bloody bandages away. Don't worry, the fever demons won't get you, but you must burn them." She loaded up the boy's hands with the bloody rags. "And wash afterwards!" she called as he hurried away.

The guard looked at Nerekh as she packed up her basket. "He's not sweating," he said.

It was true; Nerekh's face was still, in quiet and healthful sleep. She felt his forehead; it was cooler, closer to normal temperature. She handed the guard a covered jar of her willow bark brew. "When he wakes, make him drink all of this. Don't let anyone else drink it," she said. The guard held it away from him, eyeing it fearfully. She smiled. "Don't worry, it's only a mix of honey, willow bark and beer, with a little cinnamon. I only want to make sure no one else drinks it."

"Mistress," he said, bowing. "I will report this to the overseer. He will make sure your services are paid as usual."

Meryt stood, her basket on her hip. "Thank you. And now I have to go to the worksite. If he wakes and can stand, move him to the coolest place you can find, and make sure he has clean water at hand to drink."

"Yes, Mistress."

With a final glance at the sleeping man, she stepped through the door into burning sunlight.

☥

Meryt had no sooner stepped through the door of the barracks, than Nofret clutched at her. "Meryt! Meryt, come quickly!"

"What are you doing here?"

Nofret waved away Meryt's question. "Come quickly—it's Father!"

Meryt outraced her pregnant sister back to the village, through the square past the cistern, into their streets. The smell struck her as soon as she opened the door to their house. She ran to the main room; the smell was strongest there.

Djeti had fouled himself, and his kilt was a mess. But what brought Meryt up short in fear was her father's sprawled, spastic limbs. Even as she watched, his left foot—on the uninjured leg—jerked and trembled. Djeti was convulsing.

She plunged to her knees on the hard floor, reaching for a rag nearby. Quickly she rolled it and wedged it into Djeti's mouth, to prevent him from biting off his tongue. As she did so, his back arched once, then he subsided into such complete stillness that her heart nearly stopped.

Nofret burst through the door behind her, panting. "What is it? Does a demon have him? Is he dead?" she cried.

Frantically, Meryt ran through her whole catalog of knowledge, but could recall no similar incident in her father's writings. Was there time to get him to the House of Life? After midnight? And who would carry him?

Djeti suddenly subsided, as limp as a dropped string. Nofret fell to her knees. "He's dead!"

Meryt felt for her father's pulse; it was there, but it was weak. "No. No, he's still alive. But we must watch him closely." Gently, she removed the rag from between her Djeti's jaws.

"I'll get water. Towels. I, oh..." Nofret trailed off, her hands on her cheeks. "Sister, I'm afraid."

Meryt met her sister's eyes. "I am too. We'll do what we can. Let's clean up Father."

Together, the women bathed the sick man, leaving him under a clean linen sheet when they were done. Meryt did not like the hot, dry feel of his skin, or the flaccid muscle tone of his arms and legs. Her father seemed almost boneless, and his pupils were still of different sizes. She changed the dressings on his scrapes, tested the splints on his broken limbs, then sat back on her heels.

She'd been her father's right hand for many years, especially since coming back to his house after her husband died. She knew as much about healing as he did, yet now she felt completely helpless. She swallowed. It was time to put aside her pride and seek someone else's wisdom. She could go to the Chief Royal Physician himself.

"I ... I think I need to go to the House of Life."

"Yes! Yes! Or you can send for Nakht—"

Meryt scowled. The last thing she wanted was for Nakht to garner further proof that her father might not recover. "No. He ... he already saw Father. Maybe the Chief Physician can suggest something. He knows Father; they were students together."

Nofret nodded eagerly. "Yes. We must find something you can take as a gift. I can go home and get my carnelian ring. Or you have that carved amulet of ivory."

"Or ... there is the scroll," Meryt said slowly.

Nofret blinked. "The scroll of Imhotep? That is Father's most prized possession! What would he say?"

"Nothing at all," Meryt said with a wry twist of her mouth. "If it saves his life, he may consider it a fair trade. If it does not, well, it won't matter, will it." She thought of the rolled papyrus in the workroom, the record of all her great-grandfather's learning under the great physician, architect and scientist, Imhotep. Passed down from father to son, who knew what it was worth to the Chief Royal Physician?

"You're right." Nofret clutched her sister's shoulder. "You must offer it to him. Offer him anything!"

Meryt swallowed. "He will think it is a bribe."

"Who cares? Let it be a bribe, if it buys our father's life!"

"And if it does not?" Meryt swallowed tightly. "If Djeti dies, the scroll will be all we have left. We must sell it to bury him."

Nofret paused, filled with horror. Finally, she sniffled quietly. "As you wish, then. I think it is folly to go empty-handed to the most powerful physician in the Two Lands. But you will never be ruled by another's advice." Her tone was bitter. "Naturally, I must stay with Father. Will you go alone?"

Distressed at her sister's acerbic tone, Meryt answered in a subdued voice. "I'll ask Sheriti. We'll be all right."

Meryt went to her room and took the lid off her clothes chest. From the bottom, she took out the roll of linen that was her best dress. She shook it out, smoothed out a few creases. It was of fine linen, as white as Ra at noon on a summer day. She slipped it over her head. It slid over her skin like liquid, hugging her curves. The top of the skirt came to just below her breasts. Wide straps embroidered with wide and narrow bands of red and blue flowed upward, covering her breasts, looping over her shoulders and down the back. From the very bottom of the chest, she took her mother's favorite necklace of turquoise beads. She lifted it over her head as Nofret came into the room.

"Very good," Nofret said. "I'll paint your eyelids before you go. You can wear my sandals, they're better than yours, but it might be best to carry them until you get to the temple, so you don't wear them out or get them muddy. Do you want to wear your wig or do you want me to braid your hair?"

"It's too hot for a wig."

An hour later, Meryt was dressed and ready to go. She tried not to think of the imposing white Temple, which she had only visited once. Would they let her see the Chief Physician? Would they laugh at her questions? Would they turn her away? She sat patiently, knee to knee facing her sister, as the questions danced through her mind. Nofret leaned forward with her little brush, dabbed at the corner of Meryt's eye, and sat back.

"There. You look like a Court lady now." Nofret put down the brush and kohl palette and took her sister's hands. "Isis go with you, sister."

"I'll do my best," Meryt said, smiling uncertainly.

Nofret did not let go, however. She leaned forward, her

expression serious. "I know you will. But..." She bit her lip but continued. "Listen to me. You know I love you, I would never wish for you to be unhappy. But I know, everyone knows, that Shushu has asked you to marry him."

Meryt tried to pull her hands away, but Nofret hung on. "No, let me finish. Meryt, you must marry him. Even if... I mean when Father recovers, he is getting old. Soon he would be pensioned off, anyway—"

"That's not true! He can work for many more years—"

"If he recovers, Sister! If! What if he does not? What if he is ...impaired? You know your situation as well as I do! You must be reasonable. You must do what you can to secure your future. And Father's. Marriage to Shushu may be your only hope."

Not her only hope, Meryt thought. Almost against her will, the image of Nakht, his strong arms, his wide shoulders came into her heart.

Little dove, I am glad to hear it. The taste of Nakht's kiss lingered in her memory. The feel of his hands on her, the muscles under the skin of his forearms...no wonder she was dreaming about him.

Stop it, she told herself. This was foolishness. Facing a serious crisis, her heart was taking refuge in girlish daydreams. It was a waste of time to be building fantastic daydreams on a man she hardly knew, a man who already had a wife, a family. A man who wanted no more than a quick roll on a mat. She was above that. Let Sheri amuse herself with dalliances and flirtations; she wasn't like that. She was a physician, a daughter of Djeti, a woman to be respected. She was the daughter of a physician, and worthy to be her own mistress.

But only one man wanted her as a wife, a little voice inside said.

What answer should she give Shushu? Bleak prospects rose before her: Djeti might die or be disabled. Nakht would take his place. She would have no home, they would have no livelihood. Round and round her thoughts went, like a mouse in a sealed jar, seeking a way out where there was none.

Meryt took a moment to dump the ashes from the

household shrine into a nearby ash-pot, then lit incense for her morning prayers. Now of all times, she needed the help of the gods.

"Will you have time to visit the market?" Nofret asked. Her voice held a wistful note. "It's been ages since I was able to do any shopping there."

"I might," Meryt said. She smiled as her sister's face lightened. "In the workroom, top shelf," she said. "There are some packets of medicinal herbs I made up, for trade. Stuff for bellyaches, constipation, crying babies. If you bring me some, I'll trade them for whatever you need."

Nofret's eyes lit up. "Can you get some of that cassia oil? Or one of those lengths of dyed linen from Kom Ombo? Or—"

"Whatever you like," Meryt said, but she said it to her sister's back. Nofret had already disappeared into the main room.

She returned with a package wrapped in linen in one hand. She embraced Meryt. "May the soles of your feet be firm, Sister," she said anxiously, pressing it into her hand. "I'll be here with Father all day."

"Try to get him to drink, even if you have to pour it down his throat," Meryt said. Then she stepped through into the street.

CHAPTER 6 - THE HOUSE OF LIFE

Dodging dogs, children and people squatting before doorways, Meryt threaded her way through the hot, dusty streets. In a few minutes, she was pounding on the door of Sheriti's father's house.

A straight-backed teenager with a shock of black hair opened it. White teeth flashed in a grin as he looked her up and down. "Oh, what a fortunate hour! A Temple dancer come to call!" He bowed low and swept a hand towards the interior. "Enter, Lady of All Delights."

Meryt swept past him. "Good day, Amenkhau. Is your sister home?"

He placed a hand over his heart dramatically. "If she is not, I am happy to be alone with you, o mistress of grace and beauty."

Meryt rolled her eyes. "Please tell her I would like to see her."

"I am a slave to your every wish," he said, bowing his way out of the room. This poetic gesture was rendered somewhat less than elegant, however, as he bumped smack up against his elder sister. "Ow!"

"Amenkhau, what has gotten into—Meryt!" Sheri's hand flew to her mouth. "Oh, no! Not your father?"

"His condition worsens," Meryt said soberly. "I must go to the Temple of Ptah. I need to see the Chief Physician. I hoped you would come with me."

Sheri nodded. "Of course I will! Just give me a moment to change—"

"I'll come!" Amenkhau said eagerly.

"Son!" a voice bellowed from inside the house. "Amenkhau! Where are you?"

The smile faded from Amenkhau's face as he sighed. "Father. Sister, are you sure you don't need—"

Sheri shook her head. "Go back to the workshop. Tell Father where I am going." She turned to her friend. "I'll be ready before you can turn around three times." She flitted through the doorway. Amenkhau smiled ruefully, blew a kiss at Meryt, and disappeared into the passageway leading to his father's workshop.

Good as her word, Sheri reappeared almost instantly, gorgeous in white linen and yellow painted beads. Her eyelids were dark with green malachite and black kohl. She carried a linen carry-all over one arm. "Have you eaten today? No, I did not think so. It's a long walk, so I've brought melons and bread and dried figs." Linking her arm through her friend's, Sheri led Meryt back out into the street.

Meryt followed her friend as they threaded their way through the village. At the gate, they were stopped by the stocky young guard, Netka. He grinned at Sheri's finery.

"O moon of delight, breaker of hearts, where away?"

Sheriti grinned back at him, one hand on her hip provocatively. "Across the river, you donkey's cousin. Give us a pass." All villagers who left the Pyramid worksite had to have a pass, lest Pharaoh's secrets be discovered by thieves.

The young guard cleared his throat. "Yes. A pass. Wait here. Wait." He ducked back into the mud hut that served as guard headquarters.

Meryt looked at her friend. "You are shameless," she said, with admiration. "How have you remained unmarried up to now?"

Sheri shrugged. "I don't want to be married...yet. I told you. I want a man who can show me the world."

Netka came back with a scrap of limestone. The ink scratchings on it were hardly dry as he handed it to Sheri. He barely glanced at Meryt, his gaze wholly taken up with worship of Sheri. "It is only good for today. You have to be back in the walls by night. I'd be happy to wait and escort you in."

Sheri smiled, and Meryt saw the young man's knees almost visibly weaken. "Oh, I'd never want to take you away from your duties."

"It's no trouble, no trouble at all—"

"Netka!" A bellow sounded from inside the guard house.

"Why aren't you at the gate?"

Netka glanced over his shoulder, then back to Sheri. "I'll walk you out."

He strode tall and proud next to the women, as they picked their way through the bottleneck of the gate. On the other side, he bowed as they waved goodbye. Sheri leaned close as they walked away. "Look back. Is he looking after us?"

Meryt glanced over her friend's shoulder. "With every bit of his *ka* in his eyes," she said.

Sheri giggled. "He's a bit dull, but he's nice. And he kisses very well."

Meryt shook her head. "You are so spoiled." Sheri tucked their day pass between her breasts and they walked down the road towards the docks. The road thronged with donkey caravans, workers, messengers hurrying with official scrolls, laundrymen carrying piles of linen on their heads. Over it all, the glare of Ra, the smell of water; ahead of her, the green expanse of the Nile, deep and cool and quick-flowing. Boats of varying sizes were dotted over its surface, hoisting sails of buff and white and sometimes the blue stripes of a royal barge on official business. The Two Lands, prosperous under the reign of Pharaoh, blessed by the gods, lived and breathed before her.

"They say the priests predict a good Inundation this year," Sheri chattered. "A good harvest. My father has promised me that if he has any extra time he will take me down the Delta to the Festival of Bastet."

"More hearts to break," murmured Meryt. She wondered if Nakht was already at the worksite. Probably, she thought. As they drew near the market, she remembered the day before yesterday, when the bull had gotten loose. It felt like ten years had gone by since Nakht had snatched her out of the road. Her thoughts strayed to that searing kiss at her father's door last night—and she shut it out of her mind. Too dangerous, that moment.

Sheri chattered on beside her, commenting on the handsome baker's boy who winked as he passed with a basket of bread on his shoulder, or the huge barge now tying up at the largest dock, whose load of red granite for Pharaoh's burial chamber was visible even from here.

"Oh, look," Sheri said, as three white ibis rose on majestic wings out of the marsh grasses ahead of them.

Meryt felt her stomach knot. She wished she too could be as blithe and unconcerned on this beautiful day as her friend. It seemed that she had been carrying a great weight for a long time—not just the present crisis, but a burden that went all the way back to her marriage. Work, cook, work, clean, study, and work. So little time for a market excursion, or the flirtations and romances Sheri so enjoyed. Not even the comfort of children.

She cut that thought off immediately. To dwell on what she did not have, may not ever have, was a road to tears.

A sharp pinch on her arm brought her attention back to Sheri. "Meryt, are you asleep on your feet? I asked you twice, which ferry?"

Meryt blinked. They had arrived at the docks. To their right stretched the market where they had wandered two days before. To their left was the huge First Dock, with workers even now sliding ramps to unload the giant stones. Between the two were several smaller docks, crowded with lesser boats. It took Meryt several minutes to find the green-painted ferry that plied back and forth over the wide river. They hurried aboard just as a deckhand was pulling up the ramp. Sheri showed him their pass, and the crowd squeezed good-naturedly together to make room. The deckhand cast off, the rowers leaned into their oars, and slowly the boat pulled away.

"Whew!" Sheri laughed and blew at a strand of hair that had fallen across her forehead. "If we'd missed this one, we'd have had to wait until noon!" She ran her eyes over the bowed backs of the rowers. Amidships, the passengers were jammed elbow to elbow. Most of them carried something to sell: carvings, woven cloth, and one man carrying a chair. It was common for workers involved in the Pyramid to use their free time to create goods for trade. They were, after all, the finest artisans in the Two Lands.

Meryt leaned on the railing and watched the shore recede.

Below her, the green waters rushed past, carrying the occasional stick or leaf. She wondered where they had come from, how far the river had carried them. No one knew the sources of the mighty Nile; the fellahin whispered that the Inundation was the result of the Tears of Isis. She wasn't so sure; but then, there was never enough rain to explain its miraculous rise. Now it even smelled green—slow and green and fertile, carrying soil and life-giving water across the Black Lands, so called for their rich dirt. Already the reeds along the shore were halfway submerged, the eager river rising almost as she watched. She let her vision widen to take in the Pyramid. The boat moved steadily into mid-stream, and the further it moved from the shore, the more of the great structure she could see.

The edges were step-like, even from this distance. Below the great curving ramps that spiraled up from each corner, she could see course after course of gleaming limestone. On the lower rows, rough cubes of white limestone sheathed the Pyramid. She knew the plan as well as anyone in Egypt; after the top-most pyramidion had been laid, the workers would skim their way down the steep slope, chipping as they went. The rough stones would be chiseled into liquid smoothness, a slick and shining glaze on the rigid geometry of the man-made mountain.

She thought of the years that lay ahead, of how she had hoped to see the steep pyramid rise row by row, growing smaller with every course, until it towered higher than any other point of land around it. She had seen completed pyramids before, of course—most recently the great pyramid of the Osiris Sneferu Justified, father of the present Pharaoh. Her grandfather had served as physician on a work gang on that building project, the tallest structure in the world. She thought of the pride with which Djeti sometimes spoke of the great pyramid now rising before her. "People will look upon it as the work of gods," he would say. "But we made it."

It hurt her almost like a blow to think she might never see it finished, that she and her father might be sent away, forced to find a village large enough to support an aging physician and his daughter. She would have to leave Sheri, and Nofret, and all her friends.

Meryt dug her nails into her palm. No, she was not going to leave. She would find a way. Even if it meant marrying Shushu.

"Why, look at this!" Sheri said with surprise in her voice.

Meryt turned and saw Baki making his way through the crowd. His burly shoulders forced a path through the jammed passengers; even from the other side of the barge his smile was wide and white. He wore a wide collar of blue faience beads and carnelian, the lion hanging below it. His black hair was brushed back behind his ears, his hair caught in a leather fillet. A blue sash across his chest supported an official courier's dispatch case of dyed leather. Startled, Meryt read the royal cartouche on it, picked out in gold. Baki was on official business? Business having to do with Pharaoh? He stopped before them, his eyes on Sheriti. "A lucky day for me," he said. "Two ladies, and an hour or more to spend on the water with them."

Sheri laughed up at him. "Assuming we want to spend them with you."

He cocked his head to one side, hair tumbling from under his headband to fall across sun-kissed skin. "Of course you do," he said easily. "No one else can get you a seat on this tub."

Sheri's eyebrows rose. "A seat? Where?"

"It will cost you," Baki said. He glanced from Meryt to Sheri. "A kiss apiece."

"I'll stand," Meryt said dryly. "It's good for my back."

"There's also a sunshade," Baki said, nodding towards the prow of the boat. Sure enough, a tiny square of matting supported on flimsy poles shaded part of the deck.

Meryt felt sweat gathering at the nape of her neck. It would be nice, she thought, to sit in the shade a while. She saw Sheri glance at her, take in her reluctance. Then a brilliant smile spread itself across her face. Sheri touched Baki's arm, leaned in close as he bent his head. "I'll pay for her," she said, indicating Meryt. "Two kisses, if you get us a seat in the shade, and some water."

Meryt shook her head. "Oh, we'll never get through this crush," she said.

"Leave that to me," said Baki. Before she could reply, Baki bent and scooped her up in both arms.

Meryt gasped and clutched at his arm. "Put me down!"

"Certainly," he said, with no indication of exertion. "Just let me get past this fellow with the reed bundle. There." He set her smartly on her feet in the sunshade. Two low stools with woven reed seats sat under it. A man with a large belly and a short wig, probably the captain, rose and opened his mouth to protest. He caught sight of the lion pendant on Baki's chest and shut his mouth again. Nodding shortly, he stepped away, leaving the shade to Meryt.

"I will be right back," Baki promised, and stepped into the crowd again. The boat swayed in the current, and Meryt heard the water shushing against the hull. A low chant rose from the rowers as they bent, straightened, bent again. A baby in the crowd cried, and his mother nonchalantly pulled down her shift to bare a breast for it. Some men had squatted down to play a gambling game. Soon Meryt saw Baki's blocky form parting the crowd, Sheri in his arms with her hands clasped behind his neck. She was laughing, but the look in Baki's eyes was more than laughter.

Uh-oh, thought Meryt. Too bad. She liked the man, and didn't like to think of how hurt he would be when her butterfly-hearted friend flitted off to someone else's arms. Sheri never stayed with one man for very long, her restless nature pushing her to look beyond the man of the moment for the man of her ever-changing dreams.

Reaching the sunshade, Baki let the girl slide through his arms, pressed closely down his front, to land lightly on her feet. His smile spread slowly across his face. "Now that was nice." He leaned in. "My kiss?"

Meryt turned away, smiling, as Sheri leaned up to plant her hennaed mouth on the big man's. Chuckles and light applause from the crowd told her others were watching this little flirtation as well. She sank down to the stool, settling in for the rest of the trip.

The slow ferry drew nearer and nearer to the eastern shore.

Gradually Meryt began to make out the dust-colored town straggled along its banks. It did not even have a name, for it was not intended to last. Like her own village, it was built solely for the duration of the building of Pharaoh's great tomb, and would be deserted when it was finished. But that would be decades in the future, and for now, the town flourished along the muddy banks, servicing the great building and its workers across the water.

As the boat approached the shore, Meryt saw the tall white pennons of the House of Life flapping in the distance. Dedicated to life and healing, rather than to death, it was sited on the eastern shore; the western shore, as all knew, symbolized death and the afterlife. Meryt mused for a moment on her position, in the middle of the Nile, between life and death. Could she bring her father to the eastern shore of life? Or was his *ka* even now on its way to the West?

Giggling, Sheri dropped to the low stool beside her, wiping her mouth. "Well, I have paid for our shade and water," she said in a laughing voice.

"You give good value," Baki laughed above her. He held out a jug of water, his eyes bright. "Be glad the captain and crew are already paid by the king, or ..."

Sheri drank and passed the jar to Meryt. "Or?" she said merrily, her eyes on the young man.

He knelt close, one knee to the deck. "Or I'd have to fight every one of them." His smile turned lazy, cat-like; he raised Sheri's palm to his lips, lingering. Then he rose, bowed, and strode towards the stern without looking back.

"Oh, my." Even Meryt could see the slow flush that climbed Sheri's cheeks.

"He'd win, too," Meryt said softly. "I've seen him in action."

Sheri turned to her. "Oh? You mean the wrestling match? That was one on one, of course."

"He can hold his own against several at once." Meryt described the bar fight the previous night. "And I think that even if Nakht hadn't come in, Baki might have thrown every man there out of the tavern."

Sheri's mouth was a O of appreciation. "I think you are right," she said finally. She turned her head, searching the crowd behind them. "He is a warrior. I wonder...Do you think he's traveled?" Her tone was wistful.

Meryt glanced towards the prow. The shore approached rapidly. "It would depend on what you mean by 'travel'. I know that Nakht has been to the Great Green."

Sheri clasped her friend's arm. "He has? The great sea beyond the mouth of the Nile?" Her eyes narrowed. "But how do you know?"

"He...he had dinner with us last night." Meryt found herself reluctant to tell Sheri about that dinner on the rooftop.

"Tell me everything," Sheri said strongly. "Every detail."

The boat bumped against the dock, and everyone on board fought for balance. "This is not the time," Meryt said, relieved.

Sheri got to her feet with Meryt. "Later, then," she said. She linked arms. "I mean it. Every detail."

Baki appeared, threading his way through the crowd towards them. "May I escort you in the city?" he asked politely. Something about the way he turned to Sheri, the set of his shoulders, caught Meryt's eye. Why did it look familiar? Oh, of course; she was remembering the bar fight.

Baki left her little time to wonder, as he took their elbows and began to make a way for them through the crush of people fighting their way off the ferry. Without being either rough or rude, Baki somehow cleared a way, and soon the three were walking through the great western doors of the town. Guards in royal blue headdresses stood watching the crowd; one of them saluted Baki when he saw the cartouche on his dispatch case.

Meryt looked around, at the two and three story houses, the wide plazas, the fountains. The very sunlight looked different, because here it reflected off white stone rather than mud brick. The air shimmered with reflections, the shadows were lighter, less stark. As they walked, she took stock of the different houses, shops and streets. Her village had been planned by architects and built all at once, but it was clear this town had grown street by street, like a sprawling shrub.

Even more fascinating were the people. In the worker's village, the artisans and laborers were her own countrymen, but here the streets were full of foreigners. She saw black-bearded Syrians, dark-tanned Bedouin, and merchants from beyond the Great Green with oiled beards and colorful woolen robes. The babble of voices in the streets with their strange words, the sing-song cries of street vendors, the smells of bodies and herbs and perfumes and food and dust and sweat all said new to her. Sheri walked along, eyes wide, drinking it all in. Baki, however, had eyes only for her friend, and nearly walked right into a melon stall.

"Here," he said, grabbing their elbows. "It's nearly noon. We should get something to eat."

Meryt looked past him, seeking the tall pylons and flagpoles of the Temple above the streets and houses. "I want to get to the Temple as soon as I can. The line may be very long."

Baki steered them against a wall to let a string of basket-laden donkeys go past. "Temple? Which Temple?"

Meryt explained her mission quickly, noticing that while Sheri kept her eyes on the passing crowd, she did not shake off Baki's arm around her shoulders. "And so I want to make sure I see the Chief Physician soon, because we have to get back before dark," she finished. How was her father doing? Was he worse? Had he wakened?

"As to that, don't worry," he said briskly. "I can get you back into the village even if the gates are closed, on my own authority. But I have an errand of my own."

Sheri narrowed her eyes at him. "You're wearing the Royal sign."

Baki shifted, and his normally open expression closed in a little. "I will say only that the Royal Vizier has sent me on an errand."

Meryt looked at him shrewdly—something in his tone, his air of authority. Baki might look like a young soldier, but he carried an air of command. And she remembered that he was not just a guard, like Netka; he was the chief guard over the workshops, a leader. Why was a man of his rank running an errand? "Something is wrong," she said abruptly.

He caught her eye over Sheri's head. It was a warning look. "Let us eat, and then I will walk you to the Temple." He brushed a hand down the royal courier's sash. "I think I can get you in."

"Thank you," Meryt said.

"I smell roast duck," Sheri said. She rocked up on her tiptoes, peering over the crowd. "Roast duck and ... figs? Stewed in honey?"

Baki led them across a plaza, then they plunged into an area full of vendors selling everything from dates and baskets to small golden statues of the gods. Rugs, linens, jewelry, pots all spread before them, as different from their own small market across the river as the sun was from the moon. The market seemed to go on forever.

Baki bought flat bread and roast duck on skewers. Meryt bought a salad served in a loosely woven basket, dressed with thyme, fenugreek and vinegar. From another vendor Sheri bought a beaker of watermelon juice. Spying a vendor selling faience bead necklaces, she tugged on Meryt's elbow, dragging her friend over to look.

Suddenly there were men shouting, the smell of incense, and people were pushing against them. Baki planted his solid bulk in front of the women, and the crowd flowed around them like the Nile around a rock. Peeking around his torso, Meryt caught the glitter of gold, the white of waving ostrich plumes. And then everyone in the market was bowing, extending hands out at knee level.

First came a herald in white and gold, holding high his staff of office. "Make way for the Chief Wife," he cried in a booming voice. "Mother of the King of Upper and Lower Egypt, Follower of Horus, Guide of the Ruler, Favored One, She whose every word is done for her, the daughter of the God's body, Hetepheres! Make way and give honor!"

Sheri gasped and almost fell to her knees. "The Queen Mother!"

Baki caught Sheri's hand and simultaneously backed them both out of the path of the approaching men. An honor guard in royal blue sashes and white kilts marched past, with tall spears and white head cloths. Then came the litter bearers, carrying the carved chair, with gilded inlay on a platform of ivory inlaid acacia wood. The handles of the litter were carved and painted to look like lotus blossoms, and the carriers were all the same height, ten men of broad shoulder, dressed in white kilts.

Meryt looked beyond all this, daring to lift her eyes to the woman in the chair. Hetepheres, half-sister and widow of the previous Pharaoh and mother of the present, was seventy years old and looked fifty. Her strong features, lifted chin, and sharp gaze took in every detail of what passed. She wore the fine linen of royalty; she fairly glittered in the sunlight with gold and lapis lazuli and carnelian.

This was no pampered court beauty, Meryt thought. This woman is exactly what her title said: guide of the Ruler. Everyone knew that the country's scribes really reported to her, and that she held more secrets than a hand-count of pyramids already replete with Pharaohs. Kings had come and gone, and still this shrewd and wise woman guided Egypt from behind the scenes. As she passed, Meryt noted her stare, the gaze which looked over the heads of the people into the distance. Meryt wondered what she was thinking—counting gold rings? Assessing the costs of another hundred days of workers at the Pyramid? Pondering the state of the army, or the need for more naval ships? Or were her thoughts of gods and goddesses, of loftier matters?

The moment and the woman passed, to be followed by lines of servants. The higher servants wore gold-dyed sandals and fine linen with collars of faience and gold. Three donkeys bearing baskets and boxes, led by young girls and one old woman, paraded past in their timeless, unhurried manner. Finally, more guards bearing copper-tipped spears that shone in the sunlight trooped past, and the parade passed into the distance. Sheriti stood gazing after them, her eyes bright.

"Did you see that litter? Oh what a thing, to be carried so high above the dust, with a fan bearer and a gang of strong men to guard me."

Baki laughed. "Oh, if that's all you want, then all you need do is marry Pharaoh and bear him sons. Come, let us eat."

He led them out of the throng, through a narrow alley, until they suddenly emerged into cool green stillness. Meryt looked around: they were inside the boundaries of the Temple of Ptah, in the sacred park. Ahead of them the water sparkled on the artificial lake.

"You know this town well," she remarked, as he led them to grass under a tree and sat down.

"I have spent much time here," he said, handing round the meat. "Many of my duties are with the royal guard, who are housed here."

Sheri leaned over to grab some flat bread out of the basket. Meryt noticed that her breast pressed up against Baki's arm, and watched the slow flush climb his cheeks. His look roamed over Sheri, stopping at the transparent linen over her breasts. Sheri affected a nonchalance that told Meryt she was well aware of her effect on their companion. Meryt smiled to herself and kept the conversation polite.

"I hope we are not keeping you from your assignment," she said.

Baki smiled. "Not at all. I came over early, so I have plenty of time."

Sheri reached over and fingered the lion pendant. "It must be important."

He went very still. "Yes. It is. But I may not talk about it."

Sheri smiled wickedly. "I'll wager I could find it out from you."

Baki smiled, and the light in his eyes was as wicked as hers. "Please try, lady."

Switching tactics, Sheri suddenly sat back on her heels, affecting interest only in tearing her flat bread into small pieces and eating them one at a time. "Do you have family here?" She asked sweetly.

"Family?" Baki blinked, coming back to himself. "Yes. No. My parents have passed Beyond, but our house was in the capital. My brothers and I grew up there."

"And your father, he was in the army as well?"

Baki drank deeply out of the jar. Sheri leaned against him. His hand trembled a little on the jar. "No. He was a physician. But I never took after him. I liked the army more. Naki is the physician in the family, though he went off to the navy for a while. Good to finally have him back."

Meryt went very still. "Naki?"

"My brother," he said. "He—what?" Baki looked from Sheri to Meryt, both of them staring at him.

"Your brother is Nakht, the new physician on the Endurance gang?"

Sheri drew back. A worried look crossed Baki's open face. "Yes. You know him, of course."

The brawl in the tavern, Baki and Nakht standing back to back. That way Baki had of shrugging, of standing—like Nakht. Meryt frowned. "Brothers. I should have seen it."

"You should have told us," Sheri said smartly, rising to her feet. "Meryt, I believe we have business at the Temple."

Baki scrambled up. "Wait. What did I say? Have I done something wrong?"

"No," Meryt said automatically.

"Yes," Sheri said acidly. "Or rather, your stupid brother has. He got Meryt dismissed from her work."

"Sheri, it wasn't like that—" Meryt felt embarrassed for Baki.

Sheri's eyes flashed. "Of course it was. You were doing a fine job, filling in for your father, and then this Nakht fellow comes along and takes it all away. You." She squinted up at the man standing helpless before her. "Don't tell me you didn't know who she was, what she was. Or that your brother will likely get her and her father both dismissed from the village."

"What? No, Nakht would never—"

"We can find our own way to the Temple," Sheri said. She grabbed Meryt's arm. "Let's go."

Before she could protest, Meryt found herself being pulled along, stumbling on the gravel path that led around the sacred lake. She looked back once, to see Baki standing bewildered under the palm tree with the remains of their lunch at his feet. "That was ... not kind," she said to Sheri.

When they rounded a bend behind some bushes and Baki was out of sight, Sheri released her. "I was so angry! He should have told us!"

"In all fairness—"

"Oh, stop being 'fair'!" Sheri cried. "This is not the Court of Two Truths. This is your future at stake, your place in the village. Do you think I don't care if you are forced to leave! Who would be my friend? Who could I talk about men with?" To her surprise, Meryt saw tears standing in her friend's eyes.

"Sheri—"

Her friend dashed her hands against her eyes. "I am ruining my kohl. It's just that I can't bear the thought that you'll have to go away, that I might never see you again. How can they be so cruel? Can't Pharaoh's men see you're just as good as this Nakht? And now, for this thick-headed brother of his to pretend he didn't know—"

Meryt took her friend's elbow, turned her towards the Temple. They walked on. "Honestly, Sheri, I don't think he did. They only arrived here a day or two ago. They can't know everyone in the village yet."

"Don't excuse him."

"I'm not. And I'm not happy to find out Baki's the brother of the man usurping my father. But he seems to be an honest man."

Sheri sniffed. "You are so naive."

The line to get a private meeting with the Temple priests snaked through the cool, shaded interior of the outer court, through the huge pylons and onto the paved entry road. With a sigh, Meryt gave her name to a junior scribe and took her place at the end of the line. The noon sun beat down on her head, and soon her linen was wilted and her eye make-up running with sweat.

"Now I wish we had not run off from Baki," Sheri said petulantly. She fanned herself with a palm leaf. "He said he could get us in."

"I'd rather not owe Nakht—or his brother—any favors," Meryt said shortly.

A smile spread across Sheri's face, and her eyes got a sly look. "Oh, I don't know. I would not mind collecting—or paying—any debts with Baki. Did you see how wide his shoulders are?"

"I thought you were angry with him."

"His shoulders are wide, whether I'm angry or not. And did you see how big his hands are?"

Meryt snorted. "You are untamable, my friend. For all you know, he's married." Like his brother, she thought.

Sheri waved to a water seller making his way up the line. "I asked him. He said he's never been married." She tossed a carved bead to the water seller in exchange for the water jar he handed her. "But Bahu's sister says Nakht's wife is quite beautiful. As beautiful as a Great Royal Wife, even." She sipped at the water and looked sideways at her friend.

Meryt made her face blank and neutral, even as her stomach did a slow roll. "No doubt," she said. "He mentioned that she is expecting again, and they already have a son old enough to begin his schooling." Briefly she described the dinner party the night before, but did not mention Nakht's good night kiss. She felt her face grow warm with the memory of it, and told herself it was the sunshine.

As they spoke, the line moved slowly forward, until finally they were in the shade of the pylons. The smell of incense floated out of the great doors of the inner sanctuary, the enclave into which only priests and Pharaoh could be admitted. Inside, she knew the great ibis-headed statue of Ptah towered high and golden above his priests. Every morning the statue would be washed and newly draped with never-worn clothing, precious jewelry. Food and drink would be set before the god, and hymns in his honor would occupy the morning.

All would be performed in accordance with ancient ritual, as it had always been. The very size and magnificence of this temple comforted Meryt. Ma'at, the balance of things, ruled here. Surely the balance of her life could be set right by the wise men within these walls. She and Sheri sat and watched the junior priests coming and going, carrying mysterious items or scrolls.

Sheri yawned sleepily. "That young one with the side lock is pretty," she said. "I wonder how old he is."

Meryt cocked an eye at her friend. "Now I know you have no boundaries. He's serving his three-month priestly stint. You know he is forbidden to lie with women."

Sheri stretched lazily, very much aware of the appreciative glances coming her way from up and down the line. "Who wants to lie with him? I'd just like to talk to him and spend a little time in his company." She flashed a big smile and waved at a passing priest. The man stared, tripped, and nearly dropped the jar he was carrying.

Meryt pinched her friend. "Stop it! We'll never get in to see the Chief Physician if you get us thrown out for lewd behavior!"

At that moment, the young priest who had taken her name came hurrying down the line of people. He stopped, looked at his list, and bowed to Sheri. "Meryt-Auset, daughter of Djeti-Thutmose? Of the village Gerget-Khufu?"

Others in line were staring at Meryt with various expressions of annoyance.

"I am here," Meryt said, standing. The young man hesitated, then bowed again.

"Come with me, please." Without waiting for an answer, he turned and took off at a fast walk, almost a trot. Meryt and Sheri nearly had to run to keep up with him.

The deeper they walked into the temple, the darker and cooler it became. Vast walls of stone rose up on either side, columns larger around than the cistern in her village dwarfed the crowds of robed priests walking purposefully to and fro. The tops of the columns were carved and painted to resemble papyrus reed bundles; on every surface magnificently carved and painted hieroglyphics told stories of gods and kings, magic and war and triumph. The entire temple was a monument to the awesome power of the gods. Meryt felt fresh sweat break out along her back—not from the heat but from tension. What could a village girl, no matter how well trained, mean to the man who held this temple in his hand? She'd been a fool to come.

Then she thought of Djeti, lying bathed in sweat in his own

house, unable to wake. She firmed her spine, made her feet move purposefully. This was for her father, she told herself. She must be strong for him. The priest led them down a narrow corridor, through a small courtyard open to the sun, and then plunged them into a warren of roofed passages, cells. Meryt caught glimpses into the rooms they passed, mostly of shaven-headed men bent over scrolls. The priest stopped in front of a larger door, painted red. He knocked, was told to enter, and bowed them in. "The Chief Physician will see you now," he said.

Meryt stepped into a room not very much larger than the main room of her own house. She had expected something much larger than this, much grander than this tidy room with its rows of shelves, all bearing leather scroll cases. A writing desk stood near one wall, covered with scrolls, ink pots, pen cases. A small, older man sat behind it on a low chair, bent over and writing. He wore the voluminous white linen shirt of a priest over a white kilt. Gold gleamed from his wide collar, broad wristbands. His shaved head made him look like a brown egg. He did not look up as they came in, but waved to them to wait. With her hands stretched out at knee level before her, Meryt bowed deeply and then straightened. This man was the head of her own father's order of physicians.

He finished scratching on the papyrus in front of him, put the reed stylus down, and looked up. The face of the Chief Royal Physician Perhipidje was deeply etched at the corners of the mouth and between the eyes. But those eyes were brown and wise and old, and seemed to recognize her. Or something in her. Meryt searched her memory; had they met?

"You are the daughter of my old friend, Djeti-Thutmose," he said. His voice was deep and sonorous, suitable for long chants of praise and power. "I see his eyes in your face." His gaze took in Sheri. "You, I do not know."

Sheri dipped a bow nervously. She stuttered slightly when she told him her name. Meryt knew the presence of so exalted an official flustered her friend; the Chief Royal Physician's hand actually touched the body of Pharaoh. After her initial skittishness, Meryt felt herself growing calm.

Perhipidje nodded and leaned back in his chair. He waved at stools against the wall. "Please, sit and make yourself comfortable. I do not often have visits from such charming young ladies." His smile came and went. "However, pleasant as this is, I do not have much time. I understand you have a petition for me, Meryt-Auset. I should warn you, however, that I have little power in matters pertaining to His Majesty's works, even to expend in the service of an old friend."

Meryt chose to stand while her friend sat. She drew a deep breath. "You are aware, sir, that my father is injured."

Perhipidje's glance flicked to a corner of his desk; Meryt saw a small scroll in Shushu's handwriting. "I am. You have my deepest condolences. Your father was a good physician."

Was? Something clutched in Meryt's belly. "My father is not dead, sir."

"No, indeed." He picked up and unrolled a small scroll. "This morning's report from the new physician, Nakht, is very serious, however. He makes it plain that, well, it does not look good for your father. He notes that even if Djeti recovers—and of course we all wish that—he may be damaged for life."

Heat leaped into Meryt's face. "Of course," she said savagely. "Naturally, he will not give a good report of the man he intends to replace." How could he, she thought. Nakht had examined her father, said good things about her treatment, seemed hopeful. Yet it was all a lie; he had sabotaged her to the Chief Royal Physician. "My father will recover," she said fiercely. "I beg that you will keep his place open."

Sheri tugged at her hand, but Meryt shook it off, her eyes on the man behind the desk. She braced herself for argument.

Instead, the Chief Physician rubbed a hand over his face. "Tell me of his condition."

She made her report, as she had made it to Nakht, in the precise, formal terms of medical practice. "As to the skull, this appears to be a bruise of the scalp with no protrusions outside the skin…"

At her first words, Perhipidje's head snapped up, his black eyes scanning her face. When she finished, describing her father's convulsions, there was a long silence as they studied one another.

"He has trained you," the Chief Physician said. "Your father has raised you like a son, to replace him."

"Yes, sir."

"Yet he did not send you here, to the House of Life. You have not been taught by me or my scribes."

Meryt set her jaw. "I have learned as much from Djeti as any physician. I have worked at my father's side for most of my life. You only train physicians here in the scribal school for eight years."

"Yes, but they train under many physicians, not just one, so that they get the benefit of more than one man's wisdom." Perhipidje stood slowly, and stepped around the desk. He came up to Meryt, looking down into her eyes. "What is the use for the senna plant, which some call wormwood? How is it prepared?"

"It is used to expel belly-worms. One part senna is mixed with one part melilot, combined with an equal measure of fermented fruit juice. To be given over three days."

He nodded. "What is the treatment for an ache in the belly, where there is no fever?"

"Mix together one part *senejta*-fruit, one part *genegent*-plant, one part *sem*-plant and one part sweet beer equally. It should be cooked, strained and drunk all in one day."

"What spell is used for driving away a headache?"

"A headache? The potion is made up of—"

Perhipidje held up a hand to stop her. "I asked for the spell, not the drug."

Meryt hesitated. Djeti had had little faith in magical incantations, especially if not accompanied by more practical treatment. He had not taught her very many, but she was well aware that many physicians considered them even more important than bandages or drugs. "I ... I do not know. Although it is written down in my father's library, and if I needed it I could easily look it up."

He did not look impressed. "What are the signs of a demon in the leg of an injured person?"

"Swelling and redness, first at the wound or injury, then spreading up and down the leg. Heat increases, the flesh rots and then turns black. The smell is putrid."

"And the remedy?"

"If the fever demon cannot be forced out with purges, the leg will rot and die; soon afterward, the patient will die also." Meryt felt her palms sweating. She had not expected to be tested like this.

"Sometimes a man's arm or leg is crushed, perhaps so badly it will not heal." Perhipidje crossed his arms and leaned back against his desk. "And have you ever treated such a wound?"

She twisted her fingers together in front of her. "No, sir. My father would not permit me to assist."

"Nor would I expect him to," the chief physician said briskly. "Amputation would be called for. Yes, we do it rarely, but it can save a life. But your father naturally did not teach you this. A woman would be too weak to assist him, and he would not welcome the presence of a screaming, fainting female." He waved one hand as she started to protest.

"No doubt you are skilled with some simple country remedies. No doubt you are intelligent, and a good student of your father. But you do not know the spells, and I do not know if you can learn them. I know several good women doctors, but I trained them myself. With all respect to your father, you have not had the experience in actual practice that a man like Nakht has had, with five years experience in the navy. He is a better replacement for Djeti than you are."

"I am not asking to replace him, not permanently. Sir, I only ask that you keep his place open for him while he recovers." Meryt clenched her hands. "If my father had had a son, if I were a man trained by my father as he was, would you even consider any other replacement? And would you not hold it for him, waiting for Djeti to recover?"

Perhipidje hesitated. She saw the frown cross his face, the struggle on it. He was an honest man, she thought, if set in his ways. "Even if I wanted to preserve your father in his position—and I do hope he will return to it soon—I cannot leave the men your father was responsible for to fend without medical help. Who would treat their injuries, their illnesses? It would be unkind and irresponsible, not to say utterly foolish, to ignore a request for his replacement from Vizier Hemiunu." When she opened her mouth to protest, he held up a hand. "It is too early for this discussion," he said sharply. "We must first see to your father's recovery."

She drew a deep breath. "For the friendship you hold with my father, for the sake of your common calling, I beg you—"

"Please do not beg me," Perhipidje said in a soft voice that brought her to a halt. "Do not make me say no to my friend's daughter. And that is the only answer possible."

Meryt sagged as she heard the note of resignation in his voice. "You do not think he will recover."

He came around the desk, stood before her. His voice was gentle. "Daughter of Djeti, your love for him does you both credit. Your skills are good—for a woman. But his injuries would challenge my own powers. The on-site physician, Nakht, tells me in this message that Djeti's eyes do not match, that the eye of the eye is disturbed. This is an ominous sign, I know you know this."

Meryt frowned. "Nakht exaggerates—"

"Does he?" Perhipidje's tone sharpened again. "If a royally appointed physician lies, especially to me, it is a serious matter. Shall I charge him with lying to the Chief Royal Physician?"

"No, no," she said, looking down at her feet.

"Is he telling the truth? Your father's eyes are mismatched now? Look at me, Meryt."

Reluctantly, she met his eyes. "Nakht ... says truly."

"He could hardly do otherwise, and fulfill his duty. Djeti would not lie, either. No good healer would. Come, Meryt, let your good sense, which I see you have, rule your heart in this. I do not know that I myself could do for him anything you have not done. You must make up your mind, child—the gods have called your father's *ka*. He has no choice but to answer."

Tears filled her eyes, and she fought them back. "I cannot let him die."

"It is not in your hands. I speak as one healer to another. We do not always win. You know that. Patients die. Men with such serious head wounds, when the eye of the eye loses balance, who do not know themselves or their surroundings if they wake..." He shook his head. "I do not know, nor does any physician in the Two Lands know, of any remedy for this condition. It cannot be treated," he said with finality. He laid a hand on her shoulder in a fatherly gesture.

"For the sake of your father, my old classmate, I will certainly do what I can to prevent his permanent dismissal. But the Temple only trains the physicians. We do not order them, and certainly not on a royal worksite. Pharaoh (Life! Prosperity! Health!) is the living Horus, and I cannot interfere with the orders of his officials. If the Royal Vizier orders Nakht to replace your father, I cannot countermand it. Go home, girl, and tend to your father. These may be his last days."

Anger and grief and crushing disappointment blinded Meryt. She barely remembered to bow as the Chief Physician dismissed her. Sheri put an arm around her and guided her out into the corridor. There, Meryt stood with clenched fist and jaw, biting back the unseemly words, the useless words that rose to her lips. They would not listen to her. They had all dismissed her father as already dead.

"Come," Sheri said softly. "The sun is going down. We must go back across the river."

Somehow she stumbled out of the Temple precincts. She let Sheri guide her into the flow of the crowd returning to the docks. Without Baki's help, they had some difficulty finding a way onto the barge, and had to stand. The crossing seemed to take forever, with the last heat of the day beating down on the Nile. The breeze had died, and over the west bank hung a cloud of quarry dust like smoke from a big fire. By the time they had arrived, disembarked, and trod wearily up the road to the Gate of the Crow, Meryt was ready to drop. Netka waved hopefully at Sheri as they came through the gate, but Sheri ignored him and steered her friend to the village center. The two had barely spoken a word, and as they paused to part ways, her friend hugged Meryt.

"I am sorry he could not help you," Sheri said. "You know I will come to you, help you, sit with you. Whatever you need, you know I am your friend."

Meryt nodded. "I know. And I love you for it, sister of my heart. But perhaps the gods will change their minds. Perhaps it is not as dire as the Chief Physician thinks. I ... I must go home."

"Come to my house and eat first."

"No, Nofret will be waiting. I must bring her the news quickly, even if it is bad."

With a last hug, Sheri released her. "May Hathor guard your father," she said.

Meryt turned to go home, her shoulders slumped.

When she reached the street of her house, she stood for a moment outside her door. She was afraid to go in, afraid all her worst fears would be confirmed. She took a deep breath and pushed open the door.

"Meryt?" Nofret rushed out of the main room. "What did he say? Did you see him?"

Meryt entered the main room, instantly kneeling beside Djeti to feel his pulse. It was the same.

"He had two more fits," Nofret said quietly. Meryt heard an echo of her own fear in her sister's voice. "I managed to get half a cup of water in him at noon. I'll get you something to eat."

Meryt tugged off her sandals and rubbed her hands over her face. "It did not go well," she said. Nofret listened quietly as Meryt told her about Perhipidje's refusal. Meryt skipped over the incident with Baki; it didn't matter anyway.

When she finished, her sister said nothing, but her face was a mask of fear and grief.

Dusk fell as Meryt and Nofret bathed their father and changed his bandages. Meryt pulled up Djeti's eyelids to check his eyes; both pupils were still of different sizes. A cold fear clutched at her, but she said nothing to Nofret. They ate a cold meal of bread and broth, too tired to talk. When they were finished, Nofret stood, taking both bowls. "Sleep," she said. "I will watch him for awhile."

Meryt could not protest, exhausted by the emotion of the

day. As she stretched out on the sleeping mat beside the dais where Djeti lay, she whispered a silent prayer. *Don't let him die. Please don't let him die.*

☥

It felt as if she had hardly closed her eyes before someone pounded on the door. "Help! Physician! Help!"

Meryt stumbled to her feet as Nofret brushed past her, grumbling. "What is so important you must wake us in the middle of the night?" Nofret snarled as she opened the door.

A scared-looking boy in a torn kilt stared at her. "Mistress! We need the physician!"

"What's wrong?" Meryt said.

"Please," the boy said nervously. "My master sends for the physician. My mistress, his wife, is having her child."

"My sister is not a midwife," Nofret snapped. "See Khepre in the street of—"

"The midwife ran away!" the boy said, nearly in tears. "Something has gone wrong, and the midwife said she would not be responsible, and no one else will come—"

"I'll get my basket," Meryt said. She looked into her sister's eyes. "Send for me if Djeti wakes, or there is any change."

Tight-lipped with disapproval, Nofret nodded shortly.

She could hear the screams three streets away. By the time Meryt arrived at the green-painted door of the master mason's house, the air was filled with the groans of a mother in labor, with the frantic cries of servants dashing to and fro, and the bellowing of the master of the house demanding that someone, anyone, help his wife. Meryt pounded on the door with her fist. It was jerked open by a woman wearing a bloodstained gown, clutching a bloody rag in one hand.

"You're the midwife?" she said.

"I'm the assistant to Djeti the phys—"

Without waiting for her to finish, the woman hauled Meryt bodily across the threshold and shoved her toward the main room. "In there. Hurry!"

Meryt stepped through the antechamber into the large main room, and the stink of blood and feces assaulted her. A single lamp burned in the corner. A hugely pregnant naked woman crouched in the middle of the room, her feet on the traditional birthing bricks that raised her off the floor. Her hands were on her knees, but her head was thrown back, her eyes closed. Sweat covered her, her long black hair was plastered to her forehead. On either side of her, old women struggled to prop her up, wobbling as her weight shifted. Scattered all over the room were amulets in the shape of the birthing goddess, Tawaret, with her hippopotamus body, lion head and sagging breasts.

Meryt set down her basket. "How long has she been in labor?"

One of the crones glared at her. "Who are you?"

The other one said, "Since dawn. It's her first."

Meryt nodded. First babies often took longer, but this protracted labor was dangerous. She opened her basket, took out a roll of soft clean cloths, and began drying the sweat on the woman's brow. Her eyes opened, hazed with pain. She panted wordlessly. Meryt smiled into her eyes. "It will be all right. Soon you'll have a healthy baby in your arms."

The first old woman snorted. "Like you'd know, girl. You've never had a child in your life."

Meryt glared at her. "How many have you delivered?"

The other crone cackled with malicious glee. "Hah! She's right, Banafrit, you old toad. You've the one son, and that's all."

Banafrit nearly spat. "Only one, but he's master of this house. You'd better—"

Meryt interrupted. "Can I get some cold water to bathe her brow? And we need more air in here. Can someone light more lamps?"

Banafrit glared at her again. "More light? So the demons can see better? What are you thinking?"

Meryt was thinking that this old woman was as dangerous as any demon, but only said, "Water. Light. Air."

The pregnant woman suddenly stiffened all over. Meryt's gaze swept from her open mouth down to her bulging abdomen, and there saw something that made her stare in horror. The outline of the baby stood out starkly under the straining muscles of the woman's belly—and it was sideways. The other old woman saw it, glanced up at Meryt, and nodded quietly. The mother-in-law stood and waddled into the inner kitchens, calling for servants. Meryt took her place, slipping a shoulder under the mother to help support her.

"Don't be alarmed," she said in a soothing voice. "I can help you, but we have to work together. Your baby is turned sideways—"

The mother cried out, a wordless howl of terror and pain. Meryt stroked the woman's brow. "Don't worry. We can turn the baby. We have to work together. What's your name?"

The woman opened her eyes, staring past Meryt. "Sho... Shoshan."

Meryt smiled and put as much confidence into her voice as possible. "Shoshan, you are going to have a fine, healthy baby."

Across the mother's body, her eyes met the other old woman's. She read exhaustion and terror there as well. "You can't turn the baby," the woman hissed at her. "No one can! She's going to die! Better we should start reciting prayers for the dying!"

Meryt scowled. "You're wrong, but even if you were right, it does her no good to hear this." She shifted. "I cannot hold her up and turn the baby. Is there someone else here, strong enough to hold her?"

The other woman sighed, then bellowed, "Sinuhe!"

A tall, heavy-set man with the shoulders of a stone-mason ran into the room. He glanced anxiously at his wife. "Is it born yet? Is she well?"

Meryt said, "I need you to help support Shoshan."

"Me? But that is for a woman to do!"

"Is there a woman in this house as strong as you are?" Meryt said.

At that moment, Shoshan screamed and went rigid. All could see her huge abdomen convulse as a contraction rippled through it. Again Meryt saw the unmistakable outline of a head on one side of her body, a foot on the other. The child lay across the pelvis, its back blocking the exit.

Sinuhe sucked in a breath. "Gods! What's wrong with it? Is it ... cursed?"

Meryt felt like doing a little cursing herself, but she forced herself to remain calm. These people were hindering more than they were helping. "We must move quickly," she said to Sinuhe. "Your wife needs your strength. Here, support her as I am doing, and hold her fast."

Clumsily, the man knelt, a frown of distaste crossing his face as his knees plumped into a bloody patch on the floor. He held his wife gingerly, as if afraid of her. A maidservant came in with a bowl of clear water and handed it to Meryt, who began sponging the woman's face and body. Another contraction came, and a gush of blood.

Meryt looked down and saw a tiny hand poking out, where a head should be. The baby was well and truly stuck sideways in the womb, its shoulder and arm already blocking the birth canal. She plunged her hands up to the elbows in the water, shook them, then caught the tiny hand. The fingers flexed under hers; the baby was alive. Fear surged through her; not even Djeti had had to deal with an emergency like this.

Please help me, Mother Tawaret, she prayed to the patron goddess of childbirth. *Let me save this one. Let me bring this life into the world. Don't let them die.*

She felt a fierce wave of determination go through her. She would not give up on this patient. Drawing a deep breath, she gently pushed on the baby's hand. It slipped easily up into the birth canal and disappeared. Meryt let out her breath in a whoosh, but at that moment, Sinuhe jerked backwards, nearly dropping his wife. "Was that... a hand? Is it a monster?"

"Don't drop her!" Meryt said sharply. "Hold her up!"

The man just stared at her, fear in his eyes. The old woman on the other side was visibly trembling with the effort of holding up the mother.

Help me, Lady, Meryt prayed. *I can't do this alone.*

She opened her mouth to chide Sinuhe, but at that moment he mother whimpered and began thrashing about. "Hold her! Hold her!" Meryt cried.

"I can't!" Sinuhe grabbed for his wife, slipped on her sweat, lost his grip and she fell backwards onto him. He yelped and squirmed away. The old woman fell to the floor, gasping. Meryt told herself not to panic, that somehow they would get through this—

And then a large figure stepped right over her, settled behind the thrashing woman, and lifted her in strong arms. Meryt looked up and met Nakht's calm gaze.

"You!"

"I heard the screams." He settled himself, knees apart to balance the weight of the gasping woman in his arms. "I won't let her fall," he said. "Do what you must."

The old woman scuttled back against the bench, grabbing the bowl of water out of Meryt's way. Sinuhe jumped up and almost ran out of the room. Shoshan gave a low moan and thrashed again, gasping as the convulsion took her. Nakht's eyes widened as he saw the outline of the sideways baby in her belly, but he said nothing. He held the mother, his shoulders steady, a solid support for the laboring woman to push against.

"Good," Meryt told him. "I am going to turn the baby."

"Turn it?" His voice held a note of awe.

Meryt had no time for debate. "Hold her, the contraction comes!" She placed her hand on Shoshan's abdomen, feeling the muscles rippling downward, feeling the baby squirm inside.

The contraction passed, and Shoshan sagged in Nakht's arms. Quickly, Meryt placed her hands on either side of the woman's distended belly. Under her palms, she felt the baby; its head was slightly lower than its feet. She could feel the round little skull under her hand. She reached for her basket. "I need to oil her belly," she said, as much to herself as to Nakht. "Then I will try to move the baby into a head-down position." She looked at the old woman. "Can you mix two handfuls of salt into that water?"

The old woman nodded, clutched the bowl to her chest, and scampered out of the room. Nakht met her eyes over the panting woman. "Have you ever done this before?" he asked neutrally.

Meryt shook her head. "Have you?"

"I've never delivered a baby at all."

Meryt stared at him in shock. "But you're a physician!"

"I spent five years with the navy," he said, almost smiling. "I had no call to deliver babies."

The old woman came back, setting the bowl down beside Meryt and stepping back quickly. Meryt purified her hands in the salt water, then uncapped a vial of sesame oil. "Careful," she said to Nakht. "She'll be slippery." Then she began massaging Shoshan's belly, gently tugging and pushing. Shoshan took a deep breath, grunted, and then shuddered in the grip of another contraction.

"Tawaret," Shoshan gasped. "Help me." She bent forwards, almost toppling, but Nakht held her fast. His eyes met Meryt's over the woman's heaving body.

"Not yet," Meryt said to Shoshan. "Don't push yet. Let me turn the baby."

"Need to ... push ..."

Meryt caught the woman's face between her hands and forced her to look at her. "Shoshan. Listen to me. You cannot push the baby out. It is lying sideways. When the wave passes, relax and let me turn it."

She nodded, her bottom lip between her teeth. As the contraction eased, her eyelids fluttered in a half-faint. Nakht quickly wiped her forehead, supporting her in one brawny arm. He caught Meryt's eyes. "Go," he said. Something shimmered in the air between them, a connection as hot and solid as a heated bar of copper. His eyes were dark, searching. There was nothing of the rogue from the marketplace in him now, only the healer, focused on the woman struggling between them.

Shoshan panted shallowly. Meryt used her oiled hands to push gently on the distended belly, urging the small head downward. Another contraction came and went, and this time Shoshan almost passed out. She was weakening. Meryt felt her own heart speed up.

Please, help me save her, she begged all the gods.

Her knees hurt from kneeling on the hard floor. She slumped over, her hands on her thighs. The room was hot and close, stinking of unwashed bodies and blood and spilled herbs. Meryt heard whispering at the door, the sound of prayers to Tawaret, but put it out of her mind. She had to concentrate. She could not, *could not* fail.

"Meryt," Nakht said softly. She looked up and found sympathy and a tinge of grief in his eyes. His shoulders slumped a little. Meryt felt a sting of irritation. Did he think she was giving up, that she had failed already? Meryt flexed her fingers and set to work on Shoshan's belly again.

Under her hands, she felt a shift. "It's turning!" Careful not to injure the baby or the womb that held it, she steadied and massaged, encouraging the movement of the baby. She felt a tilt, a slide, as if the baby were doing a somersault in his mother's body. Nakht stared as the rounded hump of the baby's skull moved downward, rotating.

And then there was another great heaving, and Shoshan groaned, and then all in a rush there was a head and two shoulders and the baby fell into Meryt's hands. "Yes!" she cried exultantly. "A little boy! You did it!"

Shoshan, in the final extremity of exhaustion, opened her eyes and saw her child. A smile spread across her face, which did not even diminish when the next contraction brought the afterbirth out of her. The baby, a bright pink, opened his tiny mouth and cried lustily. Meryt looked up; Nakht's gaze met hers with a look of awe. He still held Shoshan, propping her up. The baby squirmed and cried in Meryt's hands.

Movement in the doorway, and then the room was full of people. As Meryt cut the cord, the first old woman secured the afterbirth and wrapped it in a linen cloth. She looked at Meryt. "Tawaret favors you." She picked up the cloth and the bowls and hurried out. The servants rushed in with mats and sheets to place on the brick bench. The baby squirmed in Meryt's arms.

Sinuhe strode in, beaming. "The babe is well? And Shoshan? She lives?"

Nakht stood, with the new mother draped over his arms, and lowered her gently to the bench. "She lives, thanks to Meryt here," he said, nodding. "You owe her the lives of your son and his mother." Banafrit sat beside Shoshan, muttering charms and tying an amulet to the woman's arm.

Sinuhe bowed deeply, his eyes on the tiny squirming bundle Meryt was wrapping in swaddling clothes. "My house will honor yours forever," he said formally. Then he straightened, his mouth trembling. "Thank you!"

Meryt nodded. She felt strangely disconnected, almost as if she were floating. The sounds of the room were distant and muffled. All except one. She looked down at the infant in her arms, at his pink mouth and bald head. He had come so close to death, so close to the afterworld before he even had a chance in this world. Suddenly she was trembling all over. Her knees buckled, but then Nakht was there, supporting her with one arm as he gently took the child from her.

His arm was firm, as strong as it had been that day in the marketplace when they met. For a moment, Meryt allowed herself to lean on him. Then she drew a deep breath and straightened. "I must see to the mother," she said, stepping away.

He let her go, turning to speak to Sinuhe in a low voice. Meryt checked her patient. Shoshan was sleeping, but her pulse and breathing were regular and her bleeding had slowed. Banafrit clutched at her. "You ... you saved my grandson's life. May the gods bless you." Tears stood in her eyes, and she trembled all over.

Meryt smiled wearily. "Make sure she rests well and drinks clean water. Beer would be better. When her milk comes in, you will help her?"

The old woman nodded. "Oh, yes. And I will fix her favorite dishes."

"I have no reason to think there is any damage," Meryt said. "But if there is fever, you must call me immediately."

She turned away, and found Nakht standing with the baby in his arms, regarding it. Something warm and strange happened in her middle, seeing his broad shoulders and sleek muscle cradling so tiny a life. His big hands could have held two babies, but held this one as gently as an egg. Catching her look, he nodded solemnly. "I counted his fingers and toes," he said. "Breath and heartbeat are normal. He looks healthy."

The baby wailed, and everyone in the room smiled. Nakht handed the boy to his proud father, who immediately turned to his wife. Nakht caught Meryt's elbow. "We should go." Her basket under one arm, he steered her towards the door. The family never even saw them leave.

♀

She needed space around her after the hot, enclosed room. He followed her from the street to the square, where the huge cistern sat deserted at this time of night. Meryt raised her face to the cool breeze, seeing the cold white stars burning overhead. She breathed deeply, smelling blood on her hands and shift, but also the smells of life around her—cooking oil, wood smoke, goats, and over it all the smell of wet earth and the dark sweet waters of the Nile, growing closer by the hour.

Saying nothing, Nakht took a large pottery jug and leaned over, dipping it into the well. She held out her hands and arms as he sluiced water over them once, then again. She shook the water off her fingers as he rinsed blood off of himself as well, then set the jar quietly on the lip of the cistern.

The numbness that had possessed her earlier was fading, being replaced with a sense of exultation.

I did it. I saved the baby and the mother.

"I have never seen anyone do that before." His voice was quiet, deep.

She looked down at her hands; they shook now like leaves in an invisible wind. "I was so afraid."

He took her hands and turned her palms up in his. "But you didn't give up. You could have given up, and no one would have blamed you."

"And let the baby die? Let her die?"

"It happens. We lose patients all the time."

"I don't care. I couldn't just ... not try." Her rising triumph and joy felt like being drunk on good wine.

"I know, little dove..." Then he was pulling her close, his mouth bending down, seizing her in a kiss and an embrace all at once. His big body pressed her up against the side of the cistern, a solid wall of masculine heat and strength closing her in, pinning her for his mouth to take hers. She opened her lips to him; he tasted of salt. His hands skimmed up to catch her waist. She felt dizzy, his kiss humming through her, her senses reeling at the closeness of him. Her hands came to rest on his broad bare chest, not to push him away but to feel his heart hammering under them.

He broke the kiss, pulled back a little. "Fighter," he whispered, brushing his lips across her forehead. "Warrior. Dove with the heart of a *lioness*..." He kissed her again. She slid her hands up his chest to rest on his shoulders. He moaned into her mouth and pulled her even closer. Now she could feel his erection pressing against her, separated from her by thin linen. Heat surged through her, a heady wildness filling her up like water in a jar. His hands cupped her breasts, and his moan sighed through their joined mouths. She pressed closer, wanting more, drunk with happy relief, joy, triumph.

His mouth broke free. "Meryt."

Her hands went around his waist, came to rest on his hips. His thumbs swept across her nipples, straining against the linen of her dress. He bent and suckled one nipple right through the thin fabric, and Meryt heard herself whimper.

She should not be doing this. She wanted to do nothing else. She wanted to celebrate her victory over death. She slid her hands down his sides, feeling the flat muscle, down to his kilt, to the bulge in his front. He laughed into the kiss, devouring her, pressing against her. His hand scrabbled, grabbing at her gown, pulling it up. It bunched around her hips and she felt his hand slide under. Then she gasped as his hand slid between her thighs and found her wet, open, soft for him. His mouth came free, to fasten on her neck. He leaned into her, panting, his fingers stroking. Meryt pressed against his hand, blindly seeking him, losing herself in the taste and feel of him. Her breath came fast and short now, gasping like the woman in labor, as her senses rioted. The entire universe spiraled down to his mouth and hands, to the hardness under her hands, to the hot quiet moment roaring between them. She had held off death with her two hands, and now life surged through her.

"Meryt, Meryt..." he whispered, and she heard the plea, the question, the demand in his voice.

Aching, her body answered his. He knew exactly where to touch her, knew where she was most sensitive, most responsive. His hands, his mouth, and the heat pooling in her belly...she felt the tension coiling in her like a cobra preparing to strike. But the strike, when it came, was wild and hot and blissful. Meryt's head fell back as she moaned through the rippling orgasm, clenching around his hand. She might have fallen had it not been for his strong arms holding her up. His fingers stroked again, slowed. He chuckled, his mouth against her hair. His hand left her to lift his own kilt, and Meryt felt a hot rush, knowing he would take her now, a little thrill of anticipation and apprehension shivering through her.

Then he groaned and stopped all movement. "No," he said. He pulled back, staring into her eyes. His long hair was tousled, his beard shadowing his jaw. "Not in the street. Not like this. You deserve better. My home is close by," he whispered. "We will drink wine and eat honey cakes, we will bathe in scented oils. I will lay you down on sheets of fine linen, and we will make love until morning. I will make you sing, my dove, my lioness!"

She opened her mouth to say yes, but then in her mind's eye she saw a bed in a crowded house, with a tall brother and a little boy and a pregnant woman.

His wife.

Awareness cascaded over her like a splash of cold water. She straightened, pushing him away. "No," she said, her voice raw with shame and anger and desire. "Not there. Not at your house..."

He stared at her, stunned. "What—?"

She grabbed up her basket. "Not with *her* there..." She turned away from him, adjusting her dress.

She could sense the bewilderment in him. "Meryt, wait!" He placed a hand on each of her shoulders.

She shook him off, not looking at him. "No." She turned and ran.

Chapter 7 - Beyond
All Boundaries

15th Day of the Inundation
Year 7 of the Pharaoh Khufu

Meryt woke with a headache and a sense of depression. She had slept poorly, unable to dismiss from her mind the feel of Nakht's hands, his hot whispered words. Had she gone mad? Yes, she ached for the man, but then, would she not ache for any reasonably handsome man who even noticed her? It had been so long...

Enough. She shook her head and struggled into a fresh gown, but did not bother to dress her hair. The burden of this day would be heavy, and she was already tired.

She peered into the main room and found Nofret sitting by Djeti, trying to dribble broth between their father's slack lips.

"How is he?" she asked.

"He drank a little water in the night," Nofret said. Her voice held cautious hope. "Also a little of the medicine you left."

"That's good." Meryt checked her sleeping father. His pulse was steady, his skin no longer flushed. Best of all, the bruise on his head had not gotten worse.

Nofret placed a hand on her swollen belly. "You should take an offering to the Temple of Sekhmet this afternoon, sister." Unlike the Temple of Ptah across the Nile, the priests of Sekhmet built their shrine to the goddess of war and healing on the Western bank of the river.

"No. I must visit a patient." Meryt rubbed her face, feeling weary. "The chisel-man, Nerekh, is still recovering from his wound."

"But the Overseer dismissed you!"

Meryt shrugged. "From the worksite, not the rest of the village. Nakht—" She stopped, her throat going dry. *His hands, his mouth on her...* She cleared her throat. "The new physician will be at the worksite, and may not have time to see him."

Even as she said the words, a sense of futility descended on her. Was there any point to this? Why continue to treat patients for Pharaoh, when Pharaoh's men were abandoning her father? The Chief Physician's words echoed in her head: even if Djeti recovers, he may be damaged for life. And Meryt knew none of them would care, would remember Djeti's long and faithful service.

"Did you hear me?" Nofret was saying. "I declare, Sister, you are so far away I'm surprised your *ka* is still in your body!"

"I'm sorry, Sister. There is so much to worry about."

"Well, don't give up hope," Nofret said. She plumped a pillow under Djeti's head. "Go get your breakfast. I will pack some bread and onions for your noon meal."

Meryt dressed, ate a desultory breakfast, and prepared for her day. She made sure her basket was well stocked with ointments and bandages. She kissed Nofret goodbye and stepped into the street.

It was going to be a day to fry eggs on exposed stones, she realized. Ra was barely above the horizon, and already the heat was oppressive. There wasn't a breath of wind to cool her as she stepped through the village gate and headed for the worker's barracks. The beaten path threw up dust to make her sneeze, and her bare feet stung on the hot ground. She passed gangs of workers headed for the Pyramid, a couple of washermen balancing loads on their heads, and a string of donkeys led by a couple of men hurrying back to the river for more water.

Perfection barracks was nearly empty, but the guard on duty did not know her. She spent several minutes establishing her authority; he was only finally convinced to let her enter when she opened her medical basket and showed him the contents.

"I'll let you in, Mistress," he said apologetically. "But I must search it when you come out. There have been several thefts, and we've been warned to search all bundles. I even searched the basket of that other physician."

"Other physician?" Meryt asked, already suspecting who he meant.

"Yes. The new fellow, the one with the scar on his shoulder."

Nakht had been there. Her stomach lurched, then fluttered. "Has he ... has he left?"

"Oh, yes. He was here and gone an hour ago."

With deep misgiving, Meryt strode into the dimly lit interior of the barracks. Nerekh was not on the same sleeping bench he had been on yesterday. She saw the water boy coming down the aisle between the sleeping benches, and gestured him over. "What happened to Nerekh?"

"Oh, the physician ordered us to move him to a place where there was more breeze," the boy replied. "We put him near the back, where the door to the roof stairs are."

Meryt thanked him and made her way to the rear of the barracks. At the far end, a wide doorway gave onto a covered patio where workers could relax; what little breeze was available would surely come through here. There, she found Nerekh asleep on his back. Setting her basket down, Meryt examined him.

She was glad to note that the man's fever had broken. Someone had sponged the sweat off him. Nerekh's skin was dry and warm. She leaned over to sniff the bandages, and found that they were fresh and clean-smelling. As she straightened, Nerekh opened his eyes.

"Mistress," he said. His voice was soft but steady. "It is good to see you."

"How do you feel?"

The man lifted his injured arm. "Much better. The physician changed my bandages and said my arm would heal well."

Despite that being her own conclusion, Meryt felt a little nettled. Nerekh was her patient, why was Nakht interfering? But the answer was obvious: as "official" physician to the work gang, he was responsible to Akhti-Hotep for Nerekh's care.

Nerekh continued. "Nakht was very good. He told me stories about when he was in the army, so that I didn't even notice when he fixed my arm. It didn't hurt at all! He is the best physician I have ever seen!"

Annoyed, Meryt busied herself repacking her basket. "Did

123

you drink the medicine I left for you?"

"Oh, yes. It was good. You make good beer, Mistress." A small smile crossed his face. "I'm a little hungry."

"That's a very good sign," Meryt said. She patted his good arm. "I will tell your water boy to bring you something. Don't eat anything more solid than bread soaked in soup until I see you tomorrow. Did the ... other physician give you any medicine?"

Nerekh made a face. "Yes, but it tasted bitter. Not like yours." He nodded at an open cup.

Meryt sniffed the mixture and wrinkled her nose. Yes, she recognized it. A standard preparation used to fight fever and infection—totally useless but hallowed by tradition. She pulled the small jug of her medicine out of her basket. "I do not wish to contradict Nakht," she said carefully. "But here is more of my medicine, if you wish to take it. It will not ... interfere with his."

"I don't know," he said doubtfully. "Two doctors. Two medicines. I ... I don't want to offend the royal physician."

Meryt bit her lip. "I understand. I will speak to Nakht and make it all right. In the meantime, you may take this medicine now and again at bedtime, if you think it will work best."

"And say the prayers," Nerekh said.

Meryt looked into the man's eyes, seeing his fear and hope and trust. "Prayers are good," she said. "Now you should rest. I will send the boy with food and water."

He lay back on the straw mat, blessing her name. Meryt gathered her things, feeling a deep misgiving. She was not used to having other physicians interfere with her or her father's work. On her way out, Meryt gave strict instructions to the water boy about Nerekh's food, and then allowed the guard to search her basket. He handled the tiny jars and pots as if they were sleeping snakes, then passed her through.

All the way to the worksite, Meryt pondered the tangle: should she make a fuss about Nakht treating her patient? Would that make her look more professional to Akhti-Hotep—or less so? Would her complaint be taken seriously, as one doctor to another, or would she be dismissed as a whining woman, unfit to intervene in the important affairs of men?

The day grew hotter as she walked, and her mood sank even lower.

♀

At the Overseer's tent, Meryt was mildly annoyed to find Nakht absent. She waited patiently as Akhti-Hotep received his daily reports from the gang leaders, architects and engineers. Then he sorted through and read dispatches from the Royal Vizier's office, and dictated two terse reports of his own to Shushu. The sun was approaching the zenith, and already the cook's helpers were trudging up the paths with big jars of stew and platters of bread for the noon meal, when he finally noticed her presence.

"What are you doing here?" Akhti-Hotep said bluntly.

Meryt drew herself up. "I am here to report on my father's condition."

"How does he get on?"

"There is no fever, and his broken bones appear to be healing normally. I am confident he will be returned to full duty within a few weeks." She emphasized the word "duty" and carefully said nothing about Djeti's continued sleep.

But Akhti-Hotep was only paying half his attention, with one eye on a gang of ten workers coming up the central aisle. "That is good to hear," he said politely. "Report to me tomorrow." He turned away, calling to the gang leader.

Well, he hadn't told her to go home, Meryt thought. And perhaps she could remain in the Overseer's eye, convince him that the House of Djeti should not be so easily dismissed.

Unobtrusively, she put her basket down by the scribe's bench, picked up a few shards of limestone, and began copying them out on papyrus. The young scribe looked at her, winked, and went back to work. By the time Akhti-Hotep noticed her continued presence, she had completed two ration lists and half a tool report. Out of the corner of her eye, she saw him frown and take a step forward. She held her breath, ready to defend her continued presence. But then he shrugged and turned back to examining the plans for the upcoming course of limestone blocks.

𓂀   125

The noon meal was served, and the workers dispersed themselves around the site for naps or gambling games. Meryt worked on through the hot hours, determined to prove her value to the Overseer. The oppressive heat bore down even through the awning; there was not a breath of wind. Sweat poured down her neck; from time to time she lifted her hair off her neck to let the air cool it. She lifted her cup and found it empty, then found the large water jar empty as well.

"They only fill it in the morning," the young scribe told her. He lifted a small water jar. "That's why I always bring my own. It usually runs dry right about now."

Meryt frowned. "But the donkey caravans bring water all day, do they not?"

The young man shrugged, picking his teeth with a bit of broken writing reed. "Not lately. They come only in the morning and mid-afternoon. Ferret-face's orders."

Meryt glanced around, glad that Akhti-Hotep had walked down to talk to three men at the bottom of the slope. "You're free with your compliments," she said.

He only grinned and continued picking his teeth. Still, what he said bothered Meryt. Shorting the men on water was a very bad idea.

She got further confirmation not two hours later, after the men returned to work and she took up her reed pen again. The familiar shout, the red flag, the hurrying feet alerted her even before she made out the figure racing towards the tent. She was on her feet, hefting her medical basket, as a young man covered in dust and sweat dropped to one knee in front of the tent. "A worker has fainted!" he cried.

Akhti-Hotep straightened from his examination of a report. "So give him water and let him recover in the shade," he said. "Why are you disturbing us with this?"

"We tried that, my lord," the young man said, his eyes cast down. "He will not wake, and he vomits up the water."

Meryt turned swiftly to the Overseer. "This is a serious problem," she said. "If he cannot be waked, if he vomits water, he may die. I must see him immediately."

Akhti-Hotep glanced around. "Where is Nakht?"

Meryt felt her stomach do a little flip when his name was mentioned, but one of the scribes, a portly man with a fuzz of hair, didn't even look up from his papyrus as he said, "Down in Bench Ten, dealing with an ankle injury."

Akhti-Hotep looked at Meryt, his squint making his narrow face look narrower. "That leaves only you. Very well then, go."

Meryt took off at a run, following the young man through the twisting alleys and aisles of the quarry.

His co-workers had dragged the fallen man into what shade there was, under the lip of a half-hewn quarry stone. Yet the sun beat down relentlessly on the man's exposed legs and torso. Meryt dropped to her knees and pulled a small water jar from her basket.

"Hold his head," she commanded, and one of the workers knelt to help her. Meryt dribbled water carefully onto the man's lips. They did not open. "Has he been drinking his water ration as he was supposed to?"

"Yes, Mistress," the man said respectfully. "But all of us finished our ration hours before the noon meal. We will not receive another for two more hours."

Meryt stared at him. "That cannot be true," she said. "The water-carriers are supposed to visit each gang six times a day."

"Here, I brought my own from home." Another man knelt beside Meryt, offering a water skin. "There are not enough drivers for all the donkey caravans," he said. "So there are fewer caravans each day. Please, Mistress, use my water for Peben."

"First we must get him into more shade. Where is your awning? Every gang is supposed to have one for emergencies."

The men looked at one another and shrugged. They looked at their fallen comrade. Two more men came forward to help carry the man, but the only shaded area large enough for him was the Overseer's tent. When the four of them shuffled up the slope and under the awning, Akhti-Hotep stood, scowling.

"Why is this malingerer in my tent?"

"He is not a malingerer, and he must be out of the sun,"

Meryt stated firmly. "We used to have an awning available to rig over men who were injured. Where is it?"

Akhti-Hotep waved a hand. "It only encouraged the men to dawdle when they should be working. I had it taken away."

"Then we have no choice but to lay him here. Clear this area," she said to the junior scribe. The boy looked from her to Akhti-Hotep, then knelt to move several baskets of pottery shards out of the way. He glanced up nervously at the Overseer, but Akhti-Hotep only watched through narrowed eyes as Meryt ordered the men to lay their burden down where the slightest breeze could cool him. The workers, with one eye on their Overseer, bowed themselves quickly out of the shelter and hurried back to work. Meryt soaked a pad of clean linen in water and used it to bathe the man's face. His skin was flushed and his breathing uneven.

"I do not appreciate having my work area commandeered in this manner," Akhti-Hotep said in a low but severe voice. "I make allowance for your inexperience, but it is not good to pamper these workers. They must be made to understand their place."

Meryt looked up at him. "My lord, this man is a valuable servant of Pharaoh (Life! Prosperity! Health!). If he is not treated immediately, he may die. Would you care to tell the Divine One's vizier that you allowed his servant to die because of a lack of shade?"

"You are impertinent!"

"I serve Pharaoh (Life! Prosperity! Health!)," she snapped. "And as long as I have breath, it is my duty to treat those who also serve him! Regardless of their station!"

The other scribes had stopped work and were staring at this confrontation. Shushu took a step forward but then stopped, wringing his hands and looking anxiously from Meryt to the Overseer.

Meryt braced herself for a lecture, for punishment, for a tongue-lashing. But at that moment, Nakht strode into the awning and unslung his medical basket. Meryt felt herself instantly go hot all over. His tall frame, those broad shoulders, the black hair like a waterfall, they all brought back last night to her, and his hands on her. Nakht did not even look at her, however, seeing only the man on the ground.

"What is this?" Before anyone could answer, he dropped to one knee across from Meryt, feeling for the unconscious man's pulse. "How is he hurt?"

"He fainted, or so his comrades said," Meryt answered, still looking at Akhti-Hotep. She could not face Nakht, not in broad daylight with the memory of his mouth on her breast. "The other workers said he also vomited."

"I see you have tried to give him water," Nakht said. "And bathed his face, of course. But we should get him somewhere cooler, and remove his clothes. We should sponge cool water over his body."

"Whatever you do, Physician, do not do it here," Akhti-Hotep said coldly. He looked angrily from one to the other of his scribes. "And what are you doing, watching an entertainment? Have you nothing better to do?"

Heads bent to papyri, fingers reached for reed pens around the tent. Nakht stood up, hands on hips. "Pardon, my lord, but I have seen this sort of thing often, in battle. This man has not drunk enough water to offset the sweating he has done in the sun. His team leader should be warned to make sure his men drink water often, or else we will have more such cases."

Akhti-Hotep said angrily, "If one fool forgets to drink, what is that to me?"

"The men don't have enough water," Meryt said sharply. "The water-carriers have been reduced to only two trips a day."

Nakht looked astonished. "Only twice a day? That is not enough."

"Do you accuse me?" Akhti-Hotep hissed.

Meryt rose, choosing her words carefully. "Not at all, my lord. I only say what the men have told me: that they no longer receive water rations as often as before. The result is as predictable as sunrise; more men will fall ill of heat stroke and exhaustion. The men must have their rations." Out of the corner of her eye, she caught Nakht's warning look but ignored it.

"You question my orders?"

Nakht ranged himself in front of Akhti-Hotep. "Pardon, my lord," he said. "Meryt speaks only out of concern for the men. Perhaps you could order more frequent visits."

Meryt scowled, flushing with embarrassment. Who was Nakht, to apologize for her where no apology was needed? "They should get water at least four times a day," Meryt said. "It used to be six—"

"I do not have the men," Akhti-Hotep snapped. "Not that it is the business of a physician, but I so short of men that I have had to press the donkey drivers into hauling stone. The ones that remain must carry water for the sledges, not for the men."

Anger caught Meryt's tongue and left her speechless.

Nakht spoke to Akhti-Hotep, his tone conciliatory. "This is a serious matter. How long has this been going on?"

Akhti-Hotep turned to Nakht, obviously relieved to find himself facing a man and not Meryt. "We are falling behind schedule because we cannot cut or haul stone as fast as the other teams. If we do not catch up, the others may be forced to halt work until we do, so as not to risk un-balancing the courses. I hardly need describe the anger of Pharaoh (Life! Prosperity! Health!) if so many men are idled by our failure."

Nakht nodded. "Is there no way to add more conscripts?"

Akhti-Hotep answered stiffly. "I am not required to explain to you, physician, but I have already petitioned for a new set of recruits. But there is sickness in some of the villages, and some nomes have not made their tally. We do not have the time to wait."

Meryt had been listening with half an ear, fuming over this silly diversion from the real problem. Something teased at her memory. She was seeing the Queen Mother's procession, when she and Sheri had been across the river. She remembered the palanquin, and the retainers, and the baggage train, and the donkeys following the royal entourage. They had been fully loaded, but were led by—

"Women!" she said abruptly.

Nakht and Akhti-Hotep stopped, turned and looked at her.

"What about women?" Nakht said.

Meryt squared her shoulders and looked the Overseer in the eye. "Why not use women to guide the donkey trains? There are many wives, mothers, and sisters among the village families. If it meant keeping their men healthy, they would probably jump at the chance to fetch them water."

"Women?" Akhti-Hotep looked at her as if a fish had suddenly spoken. "Women, working on the Pyramid site?"

Nakht's eyes showed amusement. "Meryt, you cannot seriously be asking the Overseer to make women work on the gangs. It would cause a riot."

"Why?" Meryt asked, her whole figure stiff with tension. Behind Akhti-Hotep, the scribes had stopped work and were staring at her in open disbelief. She balled her fists and stood her ground. "Are your men so undisciplined, their supervisors so lax, that they cannot control themselves when a few grandmothers walk a donkey up a hill?"

"You dare!" Akhti-Hotep spat. "Shall I have my men replaced by girls, hauling heavy stones in the sun? Or perhaps you would prefer to arm those grannies and let them replace our warehouse guards?"

Chuckles from the men behind Akhti-Hotep greeted this. "My lord jests, but I offer a serious solution," Meryt said through clenched teeth. "If it frees up more men to haul stone, why not try it?"

Nakht turned to her, a worried frown on his face. "Meryt, is this wise, to challenge the Overseer like this?" he asked in a low voice.

She looked away, her face hot with memory. She would not meet his eyes, remembering the look they held last night, seeing the distance in them now. Clearly, last night had meant little or nothing to him, or he would be defending her now, she thought.

Akhti-Hotep sputtered. "This is preposterous. Oh, I know, little Meryt, you think you're just as good as a man, with your father spoiling you and all. But really, asking women to do the work of men—"

"But it is not the work of men," Meryt said severely. "Because currently, men are not doing it at all."

Shushu rose from his place on the scribe's bench. Agitated, he hissed. "Enough, Meryt! You are making yourself a spectacle!"

Annoyed, Meryt ignored him. "My lord, at least try it for awhile."

"They will be a distraction," Akhti-Hotep said stubbornly. "The men will be stopping work to flirt with the women."

"They will be stopping work to fall down in a faint if they do not get more water," Meryt argued.

"You forget your place, woman!" White faced with anger, Akhti-Hotep turned away.

Meryt stepped forward to speak again, but Nakht interceded smoothly between her and the Overseer. "My lord, what harm will come of trying it, at least for a day or two?"

"The donkey drivers will be insulted to be replaced by women," Akhti-Hotep said.

Meryt snorted. "Then let it be known among your workers that the pride of donkey drivers counts more than the welfare of the men who are serving Pharaoh."

"Meryt!" Shushu said, outraged.

"Meryt, you go too far," Nakht said sharply. He turned to the outraged official. "My lord, she is concerned, and lets her tongue slip rein. But perhaps, for the good of the men, you might consider doing as she says. For a day or two only."

Meryt felt embarrassment and anger flare in her. How dare Nakht belittle her in this way? Had his kisses been lies? Was she nothing to him, after all?

"I have no supervisors to spare for such a task," Akhti-Hotep said.

"I will do it," Meryt said. Her cheeks burned as she took in the looks of astonishment and contempt around the tent. "If no men can be spared, I will organize the donkey caravans."

Nakht shrugged and chuckled. "Little Meryt fancies herself an overseer now." Akhti-Hotep caught his look, smiled uncertainly. Nakht pressed him. "But there is some value in what she says. You say you cannot spare the men, and we know she can read and write, so she can keep an accurate tally. Why not let her be of use?"

Meryt felt her tongue go numb with chagrin. Bad enough for Shushu to be treating her like an errant child, but for Nakht to do likewise made her feel small and foolish. "I do not—ow!" She looked down; Nakht's foot was on hers, pressing firmly.

Akhti-Hotep opened his mouth, closed it, and finally raised his hands in a gesture of surrender. "I will write to the Vizier about it. I can make no changes without his permission."

Meryt would have spoken again, but Nakht, turning away from the overseer, gave her a tiny shake of his head. Leaning close he whispered, "You have won, now leave him to save a little of his pride."

Face burning, Meryt bent to treat the fallen man again. Akhti-Hotep stalked away, his back stiff.

"That could have been done with more diplomacy," Nakht murmured. "You will get yourself into serious trouble—"

"I need no lecture from you," Meryt hissed, aflame with humiliation. "You played that well. If my idea succeeds, Akhti-Hotep will remember that you endorsed it. If it fails, you will surely remind him that it was a lowly, stupid woman who proposed it." Tears of mortification and anger threatened to spill; she turned her face from Nakht.

How could she have been so stupid as to forget that Nakht was here to replace her father? Of course he would curry favor with the overseer. Of course he would scoff at her in front of Akhti-Hotep.

Nakht touched her arm. "Meryt, I—"

His voice, that warm, silky tone, raised all kinds of conflict in her. As seductive as Min, as duplicitous as Seth, a voice in her head said. Meryt shook him off and rose. She picked up an empty water jar. "I am going for more water. Pray don't let my patient die while I am gone."

Without waiting for his reply, Meryt marched out of the tent, wishing she were invisible.

☥

In the late afternoon heat almost everyone in the village had retired for naps. The air was heavy and sultry, as still as a picture, with dust motes hanging in the air. The surrounding streets that led to the central square were covered with awnings and mats, as usual, and the cistern in the square was protected by a woven awning. Coming from intense sunlight into semi-darkness, her eyes failed to adjust and she stumbled. At the last moment she caught and steadied herself against a brick wall.

Looking down, she saw that she had tripped over a young boy of about six years. Wearing only a linen shirt, with his hair braided in the side-lock of youth, he was curled up in the fetal position, crying. Meryt dropped to one knee.

"Did I hurt you? I'm so sorry. Let me see?"

The boy sniffed and uncurled. "No, you didn't hurt me." He straightened and looked at her. "I fell."

"What are you doing here?" she asked. Surely he was too young to be a worker.

He sniffed. "I runned away. Sesekh wants me to help her with the grinding, but I'm going to join the army like my father!"

Meryt repressed a smile. "A brave warrior. But it looks as though you have already been injured in a great battle. May I see?"

Hesitantly, the boy uncurled enough to expose a skinned knee. "I fell down." He sniffed and wiped his runny nose.

A quick assessment told Meryt that his skinned knee was nothing more than that. Furthermore, the boy was healthy and well-fed, not some urchin. "I can make that feel better, if you like," Meryt said. She rose and led the boy to the edge of the cistern. "Here, sit down and let me bathe that knee."

"When my father comes home, he will make it feel better, too," the boy said proudly. "He is a physician in Pharaoh's work force!" He hesitated, then said. "Life! Prosperity! Health!"

"What is your name?"

He thrust his chest out. "I am Sefu, son of Nakht!"

Meryt felt her stomach clench. "I am Meryt-Auset, and my father is Djeti-Thutmose. I work with your father. I'm a physician, too." She felt the boy's arms and legs; no broken bones.

The boy's eyes opened. "You? But you are a girl!"

Like father, like son, Meryt thought. She pulled a bit of linen from her waist pouch. "The patron of physicians is the goddess Sekhmet, and the goddess of healing is Isis. They're both girls."

"But that—ow!" The boy flinched as she dabbed at his knee.

"Hold still," Meryt said tartly. "What kind of warrior cries out like a baby over a little scrape?"

Reluctantly, he relaxed and let her finish cleaning his knee. "You sound like Sesekh."

"Well, when we are done here, you must promise me to go home to her," Meryt said.

"But—"

"If you are going to be a warrior in Pharaoh's army (Life! Prosperity! Health!), you must learn to follow orders."

"You're not a commander!"

"No," she said, looking into that stubborn face (where she now recognized an echo of Nakht's jaw, his lively eyes). "But Pharaoh pays me, and I take orders from him. So now I am giving an order to you. You must go home."

The boy blinked, trying to work out this reasoning. Meryt took the opportunity to tie the linen scrap firmly around the boy's knee. "If you are Meryt, then you must be the lady my father talks about all the time," he said. He peered closely at Meryt. "You are not as pretty as my mother, though."

"Well, thank you for that," Meryt said, stung. Nakht talked about her? In front of his wife and son?

"But she's—"

"Ho! There you are, you jackal!" a voice boomed out.

"Uncle!" the boy cried, his face lighting in a smile.

Meryt looked up; Baki entered the square, with his long, swinging stride. He was dressed for guard duty, in a leather military kilt and headdress, carrying a spear. He paused when he saw Meryt, an uncertain smile on his face. Then his gaze returned to the boy. "Sesekh sent me to find you. Boy, don't you know I have better things to do than chase you down all day?" His jovial tone belied his words.

Meryt straightened as Baki approached. She nodded curtly at him. "Baki," she said formally. She had not seen him since they had left him at the Temple garden the previous morning.

The feeling of betrayal, of knowing that he had wormed his way into her confidence and Sheri's when he was leagued with his brother to oust her father, lingered in her heart.

Baki gave her a quizzical glance, then bent to the boy. "Sefu, I should put you on report!" He lifted the boy easily to one shoulder and glanced at his knee. "But I see you've been in a battle. Are there any enemies of Pharaoh (Life! Prosperity! Health!) left for me to fight? Or have you destroyed them all?"

The boy kicked his heels familiarly against Baki's shoulder. "I runned away, Uncle! I walked with the donkey drivers! And I saw a dead dog! And there were some boys racing but they wouldn't let me run with them, and I fell—"

"Peace, boy," Baki said. He turned to Meryt. "I see you treated his knee. Thank you."

"You're welcome. It's only a scrape. Nothing to worry about."

"Nevertheless, thank you. I hope this young pup gave you no trouble."

Meryt smiled. "Not at all."

Baki looked up at the boy on his shoulder. "And I'll stake my next jug of beer that you never even thanked the kind lady."

The boy looked stricken. "Oh." He looked at Meryt. "M-mistress Meryt, thank you for fixing me."

"You are quite welcome." She looked at Baki, and her smile faded. "Normally I would offer you advice on how to treat him, but obviously his father is well able to take care of a scraped knee."

"I want to go to the market," Sefu said loudly. "I want to see the hawks! And the donkeys! Also Imit says there is a man there with live hawks in a cage!"

Baki laughed and set the boy on his feet. "Cub, you are more of a pest than a fly in a closed room. I am taking you home—"

"Uncle!"

"And if your father forgives you for deserting your post, I may take you to see a talking bird."

The boy's eyes grew round. "A talking bird? Really?"

"Really. I have a friend who has a friend who has a little

green bird, from far to the south, which can say words like a person." Baki dropped his hand casually on the boy's head. "But of course, I can only take you if your father permits. So I think you need to get on his good side."

Meryt reached for the *shaduf* to pull water from the cistern, but Baki reached past her and took it. "Allow me," Baki said. He leaned his spear against the cistern wall and said to Sefu, "Guard that weapon, soldier!"

Sefu stepped next to the spear and regarded it fiercely. "Yes, Uncle!"

The muscles of Baki's shoulders and back flexed as he raised the weighted end of the pole, allowing the bucket at the end to dip into the water below. When he spoke, his tone was casual but the tension in his voice was not. "And how is your lovely friend?"

Meryt concealed a smile. "I believe she feels duped. You might have to do some apologizing there," she said. She held out the jar and Baki tipped water into it.

"What form of apology does she prefer?" Baki said. "Flowers? Wine? Poetry? Please don't say jewels, I can't afford them."

Merit hefted the water jug as Baki returned the shaduf to its resting position. "I think she would prefer something that seems rather rare in your family," she said tartly.

"What is that?" Baki's eyes, Meryt saw, were the same deep amber as his brother's.

"Honesty," Meryt said. "And maybe sincerity."

Baki blinked. "How have I been dishonest?"

"You should have told us you were Nakht's brother to start with," Meryt said.

"But I had no idea that—"

"Father!" Sefu squealed. A tall figure had entered the square, and the boy took one step forward, then hesitated, clearly torn between desire and duty.

"Go," Baki said, and the child ran and jumped gleefully into Nakht's arms.

Hoisting his son to his shoulder, just as Baki had done,

Nakht strode up to the pair. "Brother," he said. He faced Meryt. "You will be glad to know that your patient has awakened, and will make a full recovery. Akhti-Hotep released him from duty for two days. I have just now come from escorting him to his barracks."

Meryt looked down at the jar of water at her feet. No point in taking it back to the quarry site now, since Nakht had taken over her patient. She told herself not to resent his officiousness. "I am glad to hear that he is well," she said formally.

"Mistress Meryt here has been tending to your whelp," Baki said.

"Uncle Baki said he would take me to see a talking bird!" Sefu piped. "But you have to say he can. Please, Father? Please can I see the talking bird?"

"Why are you out here anyway?" Nakht said. He set the boy down.

"Apparently he was on a scouting mission," Baki said quickly. "I will take him home now. Ho, cub, can you walk with that war wound, or must I carry you like a baby?"

"I can walk, Uncle! Can I carry your spear?"

Arguing, the two walked off. Meryt was acutely conscious of the heat, the deserted square, and Nakht standing close beside her. As he had only hours before, tangled with her in the hot darkness.

"We parted on poor terms," Nakht said softly. He leaned casually against the cistern, his arms crossed over his chest. "And last night was so sweet. I would rather we were friends."

"Friends? When you humiliate me, insult me in front of the Overseer? What do you call enmity?"

"Meryt, you are a lioness," he said with some amusement. "And like a lioness, you charge full ahead. Sometimes it is better to be the snake who winds around and attacks from the rear."

"I don't know what you are talking about!" She shifted the heavy jug, wondering whether she should take it back to the thirsty men at the worksite. But when she stepped forward, so did he, blocking her way. He lifted it easily out of her hands and set it on the wall of the cistern.

"I mean the way you go about getting what you want," he said. He was very near; she could see the hairs on his forearm, browned by the sun. "You say immediately what you think, you care nothing for the effect of your words."

"And why should I! I am not someone to hide in shadows, to lurk, and lie! I am not a, a snake!"

He spread his hands. "Nor am I, usually. But what do you want, Meryt? If you want to persuade a puffed-up frog like Akhti-Hotep to accept a new idea, you must sweeten it for him. Otherwise, it's like trying to give castor oil to a cat."

Meryt could not help but smile at this. She could only imagine the bloody fight that would follow any attempt to dose Nebet.

"Little dove, your idea was a good one. A compassionate one. I wish I'd thought of it myself. But Akhti-Hotep is not a man who likes any ideas but his own. It is best to let him think your ideas are his ideas; he will like the flavor better." Hesitantly, his hands came to rest on her arms.

Meryt stepped back. "Oh, you're good at persuasion," she said hotly. "Smooth. Were you being a lion or a snake when you took over both my patients? You go beyond all boundaries!"

"Took over?"

"Nerekh thinks you're a minor god. Then you walked in and immediately started treating that exhausted worker, after I had had all the work of diagnosing him and having him carried..." She stopped, closed her eyes. She knew she sounded like a whiny brat, but she couldn't help it. Finally, she burst out with the truth. "You are trying to destroy my family!"

"What? What are you saying?" Nakht said in shocked tones. "I have nothing but respect—"

"Oh, do not pretend that you do not know!" Meryt said angrily. She glared up at Nakht, who stood with a bewildered expression on his face. "If Akhti-Hotep appoints you as my father's permanent replacement, we will lose everything—our house, our place, our income. My father and I will have to leave the village and wander like beggars around the countryside. He has been a respected physician these twenty years, in service to the Horus Throne. Now he will be nothing, because you have wormed your way in—" To her severe mortification, Meryt burst into tears.

"Ah, no, don't cry." Warm, strong arms came around her, pressing her to him. "I did not know. This is not what I wanted, not at all. You must believe me."

Hating herself for her tears, Meryt tried to push away, but his arms were like iron. And it was comforting, in a bizarre way, to be held by the man who threatened her entire future. "Why should I believe you?" she snuffled. "Why should I believe a word you say?"

Nakht released her a little, put a finger under her chin and tipped it up. "Because I would never lie to you, my lioness." And he kissed her.

Once again, his mouth on hers brought a dizzying, heady cloud of warmth and arousal. Her head filled up with the sweet smoke of incense, making it hard to breathe. She was pressed all up against him, warm and male and strong, lifted half off her feet. She let herself enjoy his mouth, the way his lips smiled against hers, for a heartbeat.

His hands slipped around her back, sliding up and down, his mouth trailed long slow kisses down from her mouth to her neck, his face against hers, murmuring something, something sweet—

A giggle interrupted them, then whispers. Nakht and Meryt sprang apart; Meryt felt her face go hot as fire. On the other side of the central square, two teenage girls carrying water jars were staring in wide-eyed fascination. Their eyes dropped to the front of Nakht's kilt and they giggled again.

Flushing, Nakht bowed silently to the girls, giving Meryt a long, searing look as he bowed shortly to her. Then he turned and marched quickly back towards the worksite.

Meryt turned away from the girls, who now approached the cistern hesitantly with their jars. She rubbed her hand on her cheek where Nakht's kiss still lingered.

She was confused, angry ... and thrilled.

Chapter 8 - A Challenge to Death

Meryt sat down in the shade of the an awning, next to her water jar. This plaza, with the cistern everyone visited, would be the best place to recruit her new donkey drivers. She tried to make herself concentrate on her new task, but her thoughts went back to that moment in Nakht's arms, that kiss. Should she believe him? Could she trust him? Or was he using desire as yet another way to confuse and distract her? She had to admit, candidly, that when it came to that tall physician, it would be easy to weaken her with an appeal to sex.

Women drifted into the central square with empty water jars, waiting for the afternoon delivery. Many gathered to gossip. One of them lounged against the lip of the stone of the cistern, a baby on one hip. When she saw Meryt, she waved.

"Meryt! How is your father?" she asked politely.

Meryt shoved her hair off her face and stood. "He is well, Ipi. You are kind to ask." Automatically, she assessed the baby: healthy, alert, sucking a thumb and staring. Good. "I see your nephew thrives."

Ipi laughed, her broad face creasing. "He does. Here, Henut-tawy. Take this young warrior." A younger woman took the child and walked away with him, muttering endearments. Ipi leaned back against the cistern again. "If you are waiting for water, Meryt, the caravan is late again."

Some of the other women muttered agreement with this.

"It's a disgrace," an older woman said. "It was not thus in the time of Sneferu Justified, I tell you. Men knew to step lively under that king. Now these lazy drivers think they can take all day to bring us a mug of water."

Another woman chuckled. "Yes, things were always better in the old days, Nes-Khonsu. The sun was brighter."

"Food tasted better," another woman added, with a grin.

"Water was wetter," said another.

"And the men were handsomer!" Ipi finished. Everyone laughed.

Nes-Khonsu, her gray hair neatly braided under her scarf, snorted at the amusement of her companions. "Oh, yes, it is all very well to make fun of an old woman. But I tell you, we did not have to wait by the empty reservoir for hours in the hot sun for water, not when my good man was helping the Osiris Sneferu to build the Red Pyramid at Dahshur!"

"I know why they are late," Meryt said, pitching her voice to reach the back of the knot of women. "And it is not their fault." Swiftly she explained Akhti-Hotep's changes to the water carriers' duties. Before she had finished, muttering started again.

"My husband said his team was being shorted, but I didn't know it was affecting all the men."

"Kepi took extra water today; now I know why."

"How can the Overseer expect men to work all day in hot sun without water?"

Meryt held up a hand. "I have offered an idea to the Overseer Akhti-Hotep," she said.

"You mean Ferret-face," someone sneered.

"He has agreed to let me organize volunteers to take over the water delivery," Meryt said. "Akhti-Hotep will allow women to lead the donkeys and carry water to the men. Who is willing?"

Silence greeted this announcement. The women stared at her, at one another. Finally Ipi shook her head. "What is this idea? You have been out in the sun too long."

"She thinks she's a man," someone muttered, and more giggles answered.

Meryt set her feet firmly apart. "I see women here who have raised children; how hard could it be to lead a bunch of stupid donkeys? I see women here who run their own households, oversee their own servants, manage their husbands' businesses. How then shall I tell the Overseer that they are unfit to guide an ass up a hill?"

Someone at the back of the crowd said, "Does she speak of donkeys or husbands now?" The laughter that followed was a little friendlier.

"Overseer Akhti-Hotep needs as many men as he can find, to cut and haul stone. No one is saying women should do this work forever. But in this crisis, until the king's scribes can bring more men, we women can lend a hand."

Women were looking at one another, some skeptically, some thoughtfully.

"It will not be easy work," Meryt said. "It's hot work, but basically it is just walking. Walk the donkeys to the river, fill the jars, walk back up the hill. And your men will get the water they need."

Nes-Khonsu elbowed her way through the growing crowd to the front. "I am too old to walk all day in the hot sun, poking a stick at a stubborn jackass," she said. "But I can watch the children of those who do." She turned to face the crowd, her bent figure straightening. "Are we going to let our men go thirsty? I say no. Who will step forward to show this Overseer that the women of this village are strong?"

"I will," said a voice from the rear, and Sheri pushed through to stand beside Meryt. She looked fresh and lovely, newly made up, her eyes sparkling with fun. "Think of all the grateful men we'll be bringing water to!"

A ripple of laughter greeted this, and Ipi laughed aloud. "If Sheriti is going to bring water to our men, we'd better go with her, or they will never come home again!" She stepped forward to stand beside Sheri.

Young Henut-tawy strode forward, plopped her son at Nes-Khonsu's feet, and said, "He should get a nap in the middle of the afternoon." Turning to Meryt, she put hands on hips and said, "How many women will you need?"

Other women pressed forward, either to volunteer for the donkey caravans or to offer to look after the children of women who were volunteering. Most hung back, staring and muttering, often frowning. One middle-aged matriarch said, "And who will be cooking for our men? When husband and wife both come home from a long day of work, who will make dinner?"

"We will," Nes-Khonsu said. "If I cannot tend a stew while looking after a pack of children, then lay me in my tomb now, for I am too old to live!" The other older women nodded.

"I will make sure that all of you are paid the same wages as the regular donkey drivers," Meryt said firmly. She hoped she was not making a promise she could not keep.

The women were surprised. "We will be paid for this?" They exchanged murmurs of excitement.

"But most of it will go to Nes-Khonsu and her team," Meryt said. "So that they can provide food for all the families involved."

"Hmm. We will need someone to bake bread," Nes-Khonsu said, turning to a woman her age who stood nearby. "Renit, you and your sister can do that; we will probably need at least twenty loaves. Tjetut, you have the largest kitchen, so you can make stew..." The women quickly organized a support system, while the volunteer drivers gathered around Meryt. They were full of questions.

"What should we wear?"

"Will you allow unmarried women to join?"

"How many trips will we make every day?"

Meryt drew a deep breath. She was not used to giving orders. "The first thing we must do is to make a list of everyone's names." She looked around and found a bit of charcoal that had fallen from a carrier's basket. She took it up and stepped to the wall next to the cistern.

Eagerly the women pressed forward, giving their names. Meryt wrote them on the plaster surface of the wall. When she had written the last one, she turned around. "I think we have enough for two shifts, one going and one coming."

"We shall be the Sekhmet team!" Ipi said, raising her hand. "The Lioness will make those donkeys trot!" Several women stepped forward, and others ranged themselves into a team whose mascot was Ptah, the workers' god.

Sheri sidled close to Meryt. "You have taken on a big task," she said. She laid a hand on Meryt's shoulder. "You will make enemies, doing this."

Meryt was looking at the cistern, where women were clustered, staring at her group, whispering. Her plan had not met with universal approval. "I know," she said. "Perhaps I should have let Akhti-Hotep appoint a man to be in charge."

Sheri snorted. "Do you really think the likes of Nes-Khonsu is going to take orders from a man? That woman has been bossing men around since before Pharaoh (Life! Prosperity! Health!) took the Horus Throne. But listen to me," she said, turning and placing her hands on Meryt's shoulders. "You look exhausted. What has happened to you?"

Meryt closed her eyes and sighed. She saw Akhti-Hotep's angry contempt, Nakht's easy laughter, his dismissal of her remarks. "Dealing with men," she said wearily.

Sheri patted her on the shoulder. "Go home. Rest, see to your father. And in the morning, we will show these men how it is done." Suddenly she straightened, peering past the cistern. "Who is that?"

Meryt followed her gaze, to find the entire square turning to look. On the far side, a woman emerged from the Street of Weavers, a large thoroughfare that crossed the western half of the village. She was of medium height, but her regal carriage made her seem taller. She was exquisitely dressed in faultless linen, which did not hide her advanced state of pregnancy. Despite her swollen belly, however, her stride was elegant and firm. Gold at wrist, neck and ear confirmed that she was of high status, while the short wig dressed with a lotus wreath marked her as a lady of leisure, not a housewife. She held the hand of a small boy, and with sinking heart Meryt recognized Sefu, Nakht's son.

So, she thought. *This is her.*

Conversation turned to whispers as the young woman rounded the cistern. Meryt was not sure she had ever seen a woman so lovely. High cheekbones, almond-shaped eyes, slender arms, delicate hands—oh yes, this woman embodied every feature of the desirable woman. Meryt was acutely conscious of her own dirty gown, her hair blown every which way, of smudges on her hands and arms. And she felt her face go hot with shame when she remembered that not an hour ago, she had been kissed by this woman's husband.

"Who is this?" Sheri whispered.

"I believe it is Nakht's wife," Meryt said. She was surprised at how steady her voice sounded.

"She's beautiful!" Sheri said, as if such a thing were unthinkable.

The woman had reached the knot of women, stopped, and inclined her head prettily. "Good afternoon," she said in a low musical voice.

Polite greetings murmured back, and women edged away, returning to their homes. The woman looked around, caught sight of Meryt, and smiled. "You must be Meryt-Auset, daughter of Djeti?" she said in her soft voice.

Meryt felt Sheri grip her hand. "I am," she said shortly.

"Nakht has described you well," she said. Her manner was friendly but reserved. "I am told we owe you thanks for your care of little Sefu."

Meryt's throat felt dry. "It was nothing," she said. "Only a skinned knee. I am sure his father could have done better."

"Still, we are grateful. But I mislay my manners. My name is Sesekh, daughter of Amun-en-ope," she said, and bowed slightly.

Meryt introduced Sheriti. "My friend, Sheriti, daughter of Pen-Tahut, the copper smith."

"Welcome to the village," Sheri said, nodding formally.

Sesekh eyed Sheri with curiosity. "I have heard much of you from my brother-in-law. Baki is much taken with you."

Sheri tossed her head. "Is he? I wonder that he remembers me at all, since I have not seen him since yesterday."

Sesekh turned to Meryt. "I have been meaning to seek you out, Meryt," she said, laying a hand on her abdomen. "We are only recently come to the village, of course, and I know nothing of the local midwives. Nakht said to ask you for a recommendation."

Meryt bit her lip. "He will not be attending you himself?" And she remembered how last night, Nakht had said he had never delivered a baby. Had he not even assisted at the birth of his own son?

Sesekh's lovely eyes widened, and she giggled behind a hand. Meryt wondered how it was possible for a giggle to sound elegant. "Oh, no," Sesekh said. "Birth is women's business. I would never ask him to go through that."

Meryt blinked. Why would Nakht refuse to help his own wife give birth? She shook her head. "But I am not registered with the Midwives' guild," Meryt said.

"You will not attend me yourself?"

It was a reasonable request, yet Meryt felt herself recoiling, and wondered why. She had delivered babies before—why would she balk at delivering Nakht's child? *Because it is not mine,* a voice inside her whispered. It is a child he made with someone else. Meryt was startled by this realization.

"Meryt is a very highly skilled physician," Sheri said loudly.

"I of course will attend any patient who asks," Meryt said. "But Tuy the chief midwife has delivered more babies than any five physicians combined. You would do well to consult her. She lives in the Street of Potters, in the house with a blue door."

Sesekh smiled her lovely smile again. "I shall speak with her. Thank you for your help. Come, Sefu." She held out her hand to the boy, and drifted away, leaving a whisper of perfume behind her.

Sheri drew a deep breath. "Well," she said. "Nakht can certainly pick a wife."

Meryt felt a gray weight settle on her heart. "Yes," she said, her voice a croak in her throat. She watched a moment as Sesekh swayed gracefully to the cistern, dipping one slender hand into the cool water. Then Meryt turned for home, feeling her feet drag in the dust, feeling the day turn to heat and dryness and fatigue.

♀

As she reached for the door of her house, it swung open and Meryt nearly collided with a wizened little man carrying a pair of plucked geese. "Mistress," he said, ducking his head in a bow. "Your birds are in the kitchen, on the shelf above the oven."

"Thank you," Meryt said absently.

"Double rations, as ordered," the man said smartly. "No geese next week, though, unless you order special. I'll be bringing a haunch of beef or mutton, depending on what the butchers are handing out."

"Life and health to Pharaoh, who is generous," Meryt said

automatically. She kept seeing Sesekh's manicured hands, her expertly applied makeup. Meryt doubted Sesekh did her own cooking, whether it was geese or mutton.

"Right, then," the man said. "See you next time." She watched him sling the geese, tied by their feet, over a pole leaning against the house. He put the pole over his shoulder and walked off, whistling, as Meryt entered the quiet, dark house.

The smell of simmering garlic and onions pervaded the house. She stopped to straighten the little offering bowl before the household shrine, and then stepped into the main room.

Djeti lay as if dead. Meryt knelt by him, feeling for pulse and breath. Djeti's eyes were closed, but as she counted the beats at his wrist she felt little jerks and spasms, almost too small to be felt, in the muscles of her father's arm. Worried, Meryt checked his pupils and was dismayed to find them still dilated to different sizes.

"I see you're finally home," Nofret's voice said.

Meryt turned to find her sister standing in the passageway door with hands on hips, an angry expression on her face.

"What's wrong?"

"What's wrong? You ask me that? When our Father thrashes in the dark sleep like a hooked fish, and you are not here? But no, the whole village is buzzing like a kicked beehive about your insane idea! I cannot believe you have so little sense, Sister!"

"What do you mean? You're talking about the donkey caravans? I only—"

"First you're determined to take our father's place, no matter who objects, even if he needs your care at home. Then you become a scribe of the workplace—and don't think Shushu likes it, that loud mouthed sister of his is spreading his complaints wide and far. Now I hear that you've decided to become foreman of a work team. Meryt, what has gotten into you?"

"I don't understand why you're angry with me," Meryt said sharply. "All I have done, I have done for our father, for this house."

"For your own sake, too," Nofret said. She laid a hand on her belly. "Do you have no sense of family pride? No concern with how we are made a laughingstock by your behavior? At the cistern today, some of the women were giggling behind their hands at me. I, who have done nothing strange or odd, but they know I am the sister of the woman who wants to be a man!"

"I don't want to be a—"

"Why? Why must you do these things? Why can you not stay home to nurse our father through his dying? Why must you argue with Akhti-Hotep, the other scribes, even Nakht! Do you care nothing that our family is the target of ridicule and abuse? That our father's name is made a, a joke?" Nofret swept up her hands in a melodramatic gesture.

"Sister, you exaggerate," Meryt began. "You yourself argued for me to go across the river. I told you why I went to the worksite."

"Where you have embarrassed Shushu and Akhti-Hotep! What folly! These are the men who determine who will work on the Pyramid, and you have made enemies of them! And now this absurd idea with the donkeys!" Nofret shook her head, her eyes bright with tears. "I do not know what will become of us, if you go on behaving this way."

"Maybe, I will save our father's future," Meryt snapped. "Maybe, I will be something more than a victim of bad luck. Maybe I will gain the respect of Pharaoh's overseers—"

"*Respect?*" Nofret threw up her hands and turned away. "I am talking to a wall. A wall!" She stomped off to the kitchen, complaining under her breath.

Fuming, Meryt turned back to the study of her scrolls. Her hands shook; she took a deep breath to steady them. Nofret did not understand, she told herself. She was pregnant, and breeding women got strange notions. She did not know the full story. Meryt told herself to ignore her sister's sharp tongue, but she could not shake the nagging feeling that her actions were ill-considered. Maybe she should have taken the safe path—stay home with Djeti, trust that his position would be held for him, hope that the gods would set all right.

Do you care nothing that our family is the target of ridicule and abuse?

Meryt felt a tear slide down her cheek and she wiped it away angrily. It was not fair of Nofret to accuse her thus. She cared deeply about her family. She was sacrificing much for them—her dignity, her reputation, her peace of mind. She thought of Nakht and her heart hurt so she turned from the thought of him.

She was sacrificing so much, to keep this family strong. Why could no one see that?

Nofret's sullen mood lasted through the early evening meal, after which she flounced up to the roof to sleep where it was cool. Meryt stayed with her father, feeling dull and useless. Now and again she squeezed a wet rag against her father's lips, waiting until she saw his throat move to know that he had swallowed a few precious drops. Four days he had lain in the dark sleep, as if a dead man breathed. She saw hollows at cheek and under his eyes, saw how his whole sturdy body had shrunken, thinned. He could not last much longer.

Exhausted, Meryt lit one small lamp as darkness fell. Thoughts swirled around in her head: of her father, the work site, the Chief Royal Physician. Hot shame flooded her when she remembered Nakht's caresses, his beautiful wife, his sturdy son. She stared into the darkness, empty. It was all coming to an end, and she did not know what to do.

☥

The sound of smashing pottery woke Meryt. She had fallen asleep as usual, on her mat unrolled on the floor next to her father's bench. But when his flailing hand sent the pot of willow brew to the floor, she came to her knees before she was fully awake.

Djeti lay jerking on the mud brick bench, his arms and legs out-flung, trembling. Blood and saliva ran from a corner of his mouth; he had bitten his lip. The smell of urine filled the air.

Meryt put her hand on Djeti's forehead—he felt clammy and cold. Another, stronger seizure shook her father from head to toe, like a great wave going through him. Nofret poked her head into the room from the passage, shrieked and stuck her hands in her mouth. "Meryt!"

Meryt paid no attention, holding her father's shoulders, cramming a folded rag into his mouth to keep him from biting his tongue. As suddenly as it had begun, the fit subsided. Nofret knelt beside her, gripping her shoulder. "This is worse than last time."

Unhappily, Meryt agreed. She took a deep breath. "We have no choice, Nofret. We must get help for him."

"How?"

"We must call in another physician. Some one with more training than I have." Meryt swallowed. It hurt her pride, but her father's life was at stake.

"I will fetch Minhotep," Nofret said. Her sister caught her as she turned to go.

"No! Under no circumstances! Djeti forbade it."

"A priest, then!" Nofret said. She clutched at her elbows with both hands. "We can't just stand here and do nothing!"

Meryt swallowed her pride entirely. "Nakht," she said.

Nofret met her eyes. "Do you trust him?"

"We have no choice. Go."

Nofret turned and ran. Meryt knelt next to her father, holding his hand. It clutched and loosened, clutched and loosened as the tremors shook him. Could Nofret be right? Meryt wondered. Could it be a demon in her father? Had Djeti's *ka* finally left this world for the Duat, the afterlife, leaving nothing but this dying shell behind? She didn't usually think about things like that, things no physician could heal or treat. But here in the silence and loneliness of the deep night, she shuddered with fear.

A noise at the door, and then Nakht was kneeling beside her, wearing only a white kilt wound hastily around his waist. He barely looked at her, concentrating on feeling the injured man's face, head and limbs, on counting the beats at Djeti's wrist. Only when he had finished his examination did he turn to her. "Tell me," he said tersely.

Nofret came silently into the room and knelt to Meryt's left, twisting her hands in her lap.

As Meryt quickly recited her observations, she noted his

dishevelment, his tousled hair. Nakht rubbed his hand along his cheek, staring at Djeti. Meryt saw dark stubble along his jaw. After a few moments, his eyes met hers. "So there has been no fever? At any time?"

Meryt shook her head.

"How long has he been having these fits? Do they last a long time?"

"Two days, and always for short periods." Meryt fisted her hands on her thighs.

Nofret leaned forward. "Is he possessed by a demon, do you think?"

His dark eyes flashed to hers, surprised. "A demon? No. I have seen this before."

"You have?" Meryt dared not ask: did the patient live?

"I have seen this problem in men who have been in battle. I think it is his head wound." With a glance at Meryt for her permission, he unwound the bandages on Djeti's head. Meryt gasped as she saw how black and ugly the bruise on her father's head now appeared.

"Yes," Nakht said, almost to himself. "I feared this. His head wound is worse than we thought."

Nofret blinked. "His head? But his entire body has been shaking."

"I do not understand how it is, myself," he admitted candidly. "We know the brain has little or no function, but nevertheless when it is injured, sometimes it affects the rest of the body. The *metu*, the tubes that carry fluids to the organs, reach from the head throughout the body, so there must be some connection. I have seen men with head injuries who can no longer walk, or control their muscles."

"My father taught me of this." Meryt took a deep breath. "And he told me, our scrolls tell us, that there is nothing to be done."

Nakht stared at Djeti, thinking. Finally, he turned to meet her eyes. His expression was very serious. "There may be something we can do. But it is ... unusual."

Nofret gasped and bit her finger. "An exorcism?"

Nakht shook his head. "A surgical operation."

Meryt blinked. "Surgery? But his skull is unbroken, you can feel for yourself—"

"We must open his skull." Nakht's voice was quiet.

Meryt was shocked. No physician was ever supposed to deliberately cut open a patient's skull, only to close and heal wounds. To open the skull was a desecration, save only in the House of Beautification—after death.

"What? No!" Nofret wailed. "To open the skull of a living man! You would let out our father's *ka* before its time? You would kill him!"

Meryt waved her sister to silence. "I have never heard of this. You would deliberately cut his skin, break his skull open? Why? Is there some demon you wish to release?"

In answer, Nakht caught her hand in both of his big ones. He tightened his grasp. "Free your hand," he commanded.

"I cannot. This is stupid—"

"Do it!"

Meryt strained, but his hands were tight around hers, hard as rock. "I cannot, as you know. What does this—"

"It is like the brain, inside the skull," Nakht said. "My hands are the skull bone, your hand is your father's brain. There is no space inside my hands for your hand to move."

"You want to remove our father's brain?" Nofret said, her voice full of horror. "That is something only done to the dead, when they are mummified."

Nakht ignored her, staring into Meryt's eyes. She felt a movement and looked down. Nakht had raised one finger from the hands enclosing hers. "Try it now."

She unclenched her fist, and felt his hands give way, felt his grip loosen. "You would open his skull ... to give his brain more room?" she said, puzzled.

"Yes," Nakht said. He leaned forward intently. "You know how it is when you have wrapped a broken limb, and the fever has started. The limb swells, pressing the bindings tightly so that one must loosen them. I think it may be so with your father. I think the bruise on his head is also inside his head. It

is causing his brain to swell against the binding of his skull."
He released her hands and sat back. "We need only give it a
little room. Loosen, if you will, the bindings. We must let out
some of the blood in his head."

Meryt stared down at her fist, now released by Nakht. She
shivered. What he proposed was outrageous, unheard of. For
her to agree to this would not only risk her father's life, but
possibly his soul. And hers.

Nofret sniffled. "Meryt, you cannot let him do this. It is
sacrilege. Better to let our father die in peace."

Meryt hesitated. To do something so far outside her
teachings, something even Djeti himself might not want...
She looked up and met Nakht's eyes. They were intent on her,
urging her.

"You have done this before?" she asked in a small voice.

"No. But I have heard it described, by physicians I trust."

"Where?"

"In Punt, near the Red Sea. There was a medicine man
there, who has used this procedure to cure fits and head wounds.
He told me he had done this many times."

"Did it work?"

Nakht's eyes did not leave hers. "Sometimes. And sometimes
not. But it is better than doing nothing."

Nofret squatted next to Meryt, her back to Nakht. She
grasped Meryt's upper arm. "Sister, you cannot agree to this!
It is blasphemy! You will kill our father, and the Destroyer of
Souls will eat your *ka* in the Duat!" Her eyes were wide and
dark with anger. "Do not do this!" she hissed.

Shaken, Meryt looked from her sister to Nakht. Then she
looked at her father. He lay like the dead, barely breathing, his
cheeks already sallow and sunken after nearly four days with
little food or water.

"I have done all I know, Sister," she said. Her throat was
thick with tears. "All my skill, all my medicines. I have even been
across the water to the House of Life itself. The Chief Physician
said there was nothing he could do." Beside her, Nakht made a
sudden movement of surprise, but said nothing. Meryt looked

into her sister's eyes. "Four days, Nofret! He has been dead to this world for four whole days! If we do nothing he will die. I cannot sit by and do nothing!"

Nofret shook her head angrily. "He will die anyway! At least leave him his body intact!"

"He will only lose some blood," Nakht said. "As much as if he cut a finger."

Nofret glared at him. "I wish you had never come here," she said. "You have brought us nothing but misery. Now you want to kill our father and have us all sent away. This is what you wanted—to be the permanent physician? Is it not? Is this not what you wanted?"

"I would never deliberately harm a patient," Nakht said steadily.

She whirled back to Meryt. "He lies. Send him away, Sister! We can chant the prayers for the dying together."

Meryt silently weighed her options. Nakht was a stranger, but he had the blessing of the House of Life and the respect of the men who had trained her father. He had acted swiftly and surely in the quarry, had struggled with her to save Shoshan and her baby. He had battlefield and foreign experience she did not.

She looked up, and met Nakht's dark gaze. "I think you must do this thing. To save him."

Nofret hissed and jumped to her feet. "This is madness! I will not let you do it!"

Meryt stood and met her gaze. "He is dying anyway. You said it yourself. We should do everything we can to save him." She swallowed. "He would do it for me."

Nofret's face was pale in the flickering lamplight. "I will stop this! I am going to the priests! Only the gods can save our father now!" She turned to leave.

Meryt jumped up, placing herself between her sister and the door. "No! Please, Sister! This may be his only hope!"

"You are condemning him to eternal death," Nofret said bitterly. "And we will be punished by the gods. You will do as you will, as you always have. But do not ask me to take part." She lowered her voice and jerked her head at Nakht. "Has it not occurred to you that he has every possible reason to fail at this 'treatment'? No one would be the wiser, and he would inherit our father's place. Do you trust him so much?" She pushed past her sister and went out, slamming the door.

Nakht stood. "I am sorry your sister disapproves," he said. He placed a hand on Meryt's arm. "I can only ask you to trust me."

Do I trust him? Trembling, Meryt took a deep breath and placed both her future and her father's in the hands of a stranger. "What do you need?"

"Clean water and cloths, bandages, and vinegar. We will also need a poultice with salt, vinegar, natron and honey," Nakht told her. His orders were crisp and efficient, but delivered without the condescending tone she knew Minhotep would have taken. He spoke to her, as always, as an equal, a physician. He peered closely at Djeti's eyes, carefully holding a lamp so he could see the mismatched pupils. "Prepare plenty of lint to soak up the blood," he was saying. "And after, he will need a lot of your willow brew in beer, for pain. I am glad he is not awake now."

She lit more lamps and brought them into the main room, where Nakht was cleaning her father and arranging his body to lie straight on the bench. He looked up at her. "Bring me your father's instruments. Then we must both purify our hands in salt water and vinegar," he said. "You will have to hold his head."

Her breath caught. It was one thing to watch her father splint a stranger's leg, or to sew up a cut herself. To watch someone cutting open her father's head? Could she do this?

Nakht looked up at her. "I trust no one else. Can you do this? Will you faint?"

She swallowed. "I will not." She stepped past him to the kitchen area. She poured water into a shallow pottery basin, then stirred several handfuls of salt into it. When it had dissolved, Meryt carried it into the main room.

He had lit lamps and set them all around the bench where Djeti lay, to bring heat and light into the room. The shadows were banished, and by the same token Meryt felt her spirits lifting. Nakht's quick and confident movements reassured her, as she set the basin beside him. He finished spreading a clean sheet across Djeti, and turned to dip his hands into the salt water, up to the elbow.

At which point, Meryt noticed that he was naked. She blinked, then looked away. Of course, she thought. There was sure to be lots of blood, and he only had the one kilt he had arrived in. She turned and almost ran to her basement store room, seeking the vinegar he had ordered.

She told herself to be sensible, she had seen naked men all her life, who hadn't? In the heat of summer, men and women commonly dispensed with clothing. So why did it disturb her thoughts that Nakht was being, well, practical and efficient? She herself should probably discard her gown; but she felt a hot flush go over her. Meryt gave herself a shake. *Put your mind on your work,* she told herself. *Your father needs you.* Carrying the vinegar, she returned, careful to keep her eyes on the patient.

Nakht had already unrolled the leather scroll containing her father's instruments. He sluiced the vinegar liberally over his hands and arms. She heard him muttering the prayers to Sekhmet and Isis, invoking their aid. He thrust the vinegar into her hands and turned to the instruments while she also purified herself.

Selecting a long sliver of obsidian, he picked up a shaped chunk of granite, sighted along the obsidian, and struck once. A long thin flake fell to the leather, and he picked it up carefully by one end. He held it to the nearest lamp, looking along its newly exposed edge, sharper than any copper knife. Satisfied, he nodded to Meryt.

"Turn his face to the wall, so that the bruised portion is uppermost," he said. "Then you must hold his head very steadily, while I cut. You will not faint?"

She met his eyes. There was nothing there but determination. She swallowed. "I will not faint."

He smiled, and the light threw his jaw into strong relief. "Good. I will describe this procedure as we go, so that you may remember it and tell your father. He will want to know every detail."

He was so sure of himself, of this treatment. He believed Djeti would live. Nakht's self-confidence helped un-knot some of the tension in Meryt's belly. She smiled at him, a bit wobbly.

Nakht used a pad of cloth soaked in salt water to cleanse Djeti's bald pate carefully. His touch was sure, tender. "I am preparing the skin for the first cut," he said in a steady voice. When he was satisfied, he lifted the obsidian blade. "I will now make an incision, half the length of my palm, over the center of the bruise," he said. His voice held no hint of strain.

Meryt took a deep breath. She held her father's head firmly in her hands, reciting a prayer to the healing goddess in her head. Please let this heal him, she said.

Nakht's hand was steady as he cut quickly. Immediately, blood welled from the cut, but he was already dabbing at it with a clean piece of linen. "Now I will make a cut directly across it, the same width, in an X pattern…and now we can see the bone of the skull as I peel back the flap."

Meryt swallowed, feeling a little queasy. *No, she told herself. Be strong. Be your father's daughter. Trust Nakht. He knows what he's doing. Doesn't he?*

Nakht looked up and met her eyes. "Don't worry, little dove," he said softly. "I will not kill him. Now, look away if you must, but I am going to drill down through the bone. I must be very, very careful. There is a membrane below the bone which I must not penetrate."

Meryt blinked, taken out of her anxiety. "A … a membrane?" Despite her fear, she glanced down.

"Yes," he said dispassionately. "The healer from Punt was very clear about this, and you must remember to tell your father. It is a film of skin, very tough, but it can be broken. Do not allow any rupture of the membrane over the brain, and if you find such a rupture you must sew it closed." He laid down the obsidian and dipped his bloodied hands in the basin of salt water again, washing them clean. "I must now make this obsidian edge into a drill." With two swift strokes of the granite hammer, it became a wickedly pointed awl. Nakht wiped sweat off his forehead with his arm. Meryt looked close, but saw no hint of a tremor in his hands. His dark eyes met hers. "I will make a very small hole, only enough to release some of the blood so that the brain may swell if it needs to."

She watched, fascinated, as his hands deftly twisted the long wedge, drilling a hole through the bone. Black, thick blood welled through it, which Nakht wiped away again and again. Meryt recognized it as half-congealed blood, which she knew was a dangerous thing in any part of the body. She realized, with dawning respect, that Nakht's diagnosis had been correct—blood had been pooling in her father's skull, with no way out. She watched the dark blood ooze thickly, until it was replaced by lighter, thinner blood.

"It is like the dams the *fellahin* make during the Inundation," she said, staring at the exposed white bone of her father's skull. "The bone of the skull is the dam, and the waters of the body cannot be released until a breach is made."

"Exactly. I believe his body has expelled the bad blood now," Nakht said. A note of weariness made her look up. Nakht looked tired but undaunted. She noticed that his arms and chest were splashed with blood. He met her eyes and gave her a tired smile. "I believe we may sew this wound now."

"What about the ... the hole?"

"It is small, and I believe it will heal on its own. I will sew the cuts I made very loosely, so that blood may continue to leak out but fever demons may not enter. It must be kept very, very clean and pure. We will need to cleanse it with purified water twice a day."

Meryt's arms trembled with tension as she watched as Nakht swiftly closed the crossing incisions with a copper needle and boiled linen thread. His stitches were as neat and efficient as any Djeti himself could have made. Meryt looked down at her father's face. She could not see any change in him. She swallowed. *Please heal my father,* she prayed.

"You may release his head now," Nakht said. "Be careful, as he may thrash."

But when Meryt released her father's head, he lay quietly. Her muscles were cramped. She met Nakht's look. "I have never seen this done. It was unsettling. But if you have saved his life, I owe you a debt ... my father owes you ..."

Nakht waved a hand. "There is no debt. We are all physicians. And he is not yet cured."

She laid a hand on his arm, felt the muscle under his skin move as he drew back slightly. "Nakht, thank you." She felt herself go warm all over, felt the still, hot air in the room close in on them. She could smell sweat, see his hair lying flat along his neck, saw the strong column of his neck, his wide eyes. She swallowed. "I can bandage his head."

He sat back on his heels and wiped his forehead on his arm again, rolled his head on his neck to soothe the tension of hunching over his work. "I would be grateful, yes," he said.

She reached for her poultice and the bandages. "And if you like, you may wash up under the stairs. You know where it is," she told him. She turned her eyes away as he rose, but saw enough to realize that he had been right to doff his kilt. Blood had run down his front.

As she wound bandages carefully around Djeti's head, she heard splashing sounds from the passageway. She felt her father's face, his pulse. His pulse seemed a little stronger, his breathing somewhat easier. She allowed herself to hope. It was better, she thought, than despair. She gathered up the bloodied linens and walked through the passage to the laundry basket under the stairs.

She emerged just as Nakht stepped out of the tiled bathing area. The single oil lamp flickering on the wall cast reflections in his wet skin, the highlights off his night-black hair. Naked, his skin slicked with water, her first thought was that he looked even taller than usual. Then, unable to help herself, her gaze traveled down that long, sleek sweep of muscle, the flat planes of his chest and ripple of abdomen, the narrow waist and hips. And what lay between. Or rather, what stirred between. Her gaze flew to meet his, and his was hot and open and plainly hungry. She tossed the bloody rags to the floor as he stepped towards her.

In two strides he was gripping her upper arms in his hands. "You were brave tonight," he whispered. "Brave and strong,

Meryt." His lips whispered across hers. "Many women would have wept and fainted, but not you. Not you." He pulled her against him, until they were pressed together front to front, and she could feel every inch of him, hard and male against her. His mouth teased hers, nipping one corner, drifting across to the other, his tongue trailing over her lips in invitation. Forgotten were his careless, hurtful words in front of Akhti-Hotep, his usurpation of her father's work, of her own patient. After the long, tense operation just past, the worry and fear and confusion, suddenly she felt herself releasing it all into his arms, letting herself fold against him. And he held her, solid and strong, with his mouth now trailing kisses under her ear, along her jaw.

"Nakht..." she whispered.

He chuckled, his hands roamed up and down her back, comforting and caressing. "I like it when you say my name," he murmured into her ear. "You and I, we are good for each other. I knew it the first time I held you in my arms, in the market." His hands slid down her back, cupped her against him. "You know it, too."

This was the man, she told herself, who had been ordered to replace her father. Who threatened her whole family's very livelihood. Who had supplanted even herself. Who had possibly offended the gods with his attempt to save her father. She heard these thoughts in her head distantly, as if spoken by someone else. Because all she knew right now was that he had fought for Djeti's life, and that his every touch hummed through her like a plucked harp string. She felt something warming and softening in her middle, felt little flickers of flame through her blood.

"Yes," she said. "I know it."

His mouth settled on hers, gently. His kiss was slow, sensual. She felt as though her head was filling up with incense. Under her roaming hands, she felt the bulge and release of muscle along bicep and forearm, felt hot skin, wet hair. He smelled of natron and clean water. She let her hands thread through his hair, pull him closer. It had been years since she had felt these feelings, felt her defenses weakening. So many disappointments, so many failures—could this man be different? He made her feel different.

His hands slid up her back, came around front to cup her breasts, his thumbs brushing over her aroused nipples. Without thinking, she arched against him. Nakht responded with the ghost of a moan at the back of his throat. Meryt felt a hot sweet shudder go through her, felt him tugging at the knot of her gown.

"Meryt..." he said.

"Meryt!" Sheri's voice called from the front room. Meryt heard the front door closing. "Meryt! Are you here?"

Meryt sprang back from Nakht, heart pounding. His eyes met hers first with chagrin, then amusement. "Alas. The gods send us interruptions every time, do they not?" he said. His hands slid down her arms, squeezed her fingers, and released them. "Another time, sweet." He turned away and caught up his kilt, wrapping it around his waist.

Meryt turned and stumbled, half blind with confusion and desire, back into the house. She found Sheri standing in the main room, gazing around at all the lamps. Her hair was caught up carelessly, her shift was loosely tied as if she had only just arisen, which was probably the case. She was, astonishingly, completely free of cosmetics, and her face looked small and pale. Sheri ran to Meryt and embraced her. "Meryt! Nofret came to my house, crying. I could not make out what she was saying! I thought—I feared—"

She glanced down at Djeti, and Meryt knew what she was thinking. She hugged her friend. "He is alive," she said. "Nakht was treating him. I assisted."

Nakht stepped through the doorway, his broad shoulders filling the door frame. He nodded at Sheri. "Good evening."

Sheri was taken aback, glancing from Meryt's nervous face to Nakht's relaxed one. "Oh," she said.

Nakht stepped past her, picked up one of the many lamps and blew it out. "You come at a good time," he said lightly.

Meryt thought that was a highly ironic statement, if not a flat lie, but said nothing.

"I am optimistic for Djeti's recovery," Nakht said firmly.

Sheri clasped her hands together. "Oh, yes, let us hope so! And of course, the work team physician must tend to him." Her eyes slid sideways at Meryt, taking in her disordered gown, her tangled hair. "And how is he?"

Meryt was certain that the question had two meanings, but she chose to answer only one. "My father may yet live," she said. And suddenly, she felt tears of relief starting.

Nakht paused in the doorway to the anteroom. "I will take my leave now. I fear my son will wake in the night and call for me; he will cry if I am not there to tell him his nightmares are not real. Sheriti, I am glad you are here. Your friend has been up all night tending her father. Can you stay and watch the patient while she rests?"

"Me? Oh. Well, yes, of course..." Sheri was a little taken aback. "If you really think I—"

"Thank you," he said smoothly. "I will return in the morning to check on him. Daughter of Djeti, you need no advice from me in his care." He nodded to Meryt, smiled a brilliant smile at Sheri, and ducked through the door. They heard the front door shut softly behind him.

Silence settled across the room. Meryt felt shy, reluctant to meet her friend's curious gaze. She turned away, kneeling beside her father. He lay still and quiet beneath the white sheet, but the rise and fall of his chest was regular. Were his cheeks showing a little color now? Meryt hoped.

"What has happened here?" Sheri's voice was quiet.

Meryt laid a hand on her father's head, very lightly. Was it her imagination, or was he breathing a little easier? "Nakht may have saved my father's life. But what he did was...unusual. Some might call it ... wrong."

"And what do you call it?"

Meryt met her friend's searching gaze. "I call it heroic. He has gone well beyond the common effort, well beyond what even Djeti might do."

"And has he done this for Djeti? Or for you?"

"He ... he has been most kind to my father—"

Sheri grasped her shoulders, and turned her gently. "I am not a fool, and I have eyes. Open yours, my friend. I saw the way he looked at you. And the way you looked at him."

Meryt dropped her gaze to her lap, where her fingers were trying to tie themselves together in a knot. "I ... I don't know what to think."

"Think? What is there to think, when a man is involved? You know what he wants. I warrant he's already shown you what he wants. The question is, do you want him?"

Meryt stared at the floor, unseeing. Did she? She had hated and feared him before she even saw him. But just now... "I don't know. It's been so long since....and probably any man would have the same effect..."

"This is not just any man," Sheri said firmly. "Consider, my girl. He is young, he is well-placed, he has a profession. He is probably going to permanently replace your father, come what may. No, look at me. Look at me, Meryt." Sheri's eyes, no longer rimmed with malachite and kohl, looked older and wiser than usual. "Meryt, you should marry this man. If he does not want you now, we can make him want you. Even if, no, when your father recovers, you know he is getting on in years. You cannot live in his house forever. You must marry. Why not Nakht?"

Meryt closed her eyes. Felt his mouth on hers again, felt his hands on hers. "He is already married."

Sheri shook her. "Again, so what? To have a man who looks like a young god, any sensible girl would be glad to be a concubine. Why let your pride stand between you and a future? Especially a future with shoulders like that!"

Meryt rubbed her temples, feeling tension in the muscles of her neck and shoulders. "I cannot think. I cannot decide this now. I have to watch over my father. The next few hours—"

Sheri stood, pulling her friend to her feet. "No. You will go sleep and I will—"

"I must watch—"

"Nonsense. You're swaying on your feet. I will bring a fresh mat in here, and you will lie down next to the bench. But you will sleep, and I will wake you if your father moves."

Meryt wanted to protest, but knew her friend was right. An exhausted physician was useless. While Sheri fetched the mat, rolled it out, and went around the room snuffing all but one of the lamps, Meryt stared into the darkness, thinking.

You and I, we are good for each other, he had said. *You know it, too.*

Yes, she thought. *I know it too. But there are things between us. We need time...*

Chapter 9 - Minhotep Steps In

16th Day of the Inundation
Year 7 of the Pharaoh Khufu

Pounding on the door of her house shocked Meryt out of restless sleep. Disoriented, she sat up on the mat as Sheri hurried to the door.

"Tell them to stop that racket!" Meryt called irritably. "My father must not be disturbed!"

"Come quickly!" Sheri cried.

Meryt stumbled sleepily into the anteroom, then stood swaying. Sheri held the outside door open; framed in it was a man in full military garb: leather kilt, crossed pectoral straps, shield and spear. His red headdress and dyed leather armlets proclaimed him as a high-ranking member of the guards of the Temple of Sekhmet. "Are you Meryt-Auset, daughter of Djeti?" he boomed.

"Yes. What—what is this about?" Acutely aware of her untidy hair, her disheveled appearance, Meryt shifted from foot to foot. Surely the Temple had not sought her out for her medical expertise.

A small, wiry man with shaved head and white tunic shoved past him. He held a papyrus scroll in one hand. "You have brought down the wrath of the gods on this village!" he said in a high, nervous voice. "You have endangered us all!"

Sheri turned to stare at Meryt, her eyes big in her face. "Who is this? What's he talking about?"

Behind the guard, a growing crowd of her neighbors shifted and muttered.

"I have done nothing to offend the gods," Meryt said.

"You have allowed the physician Nakht to commit an unholy act upon the person of your father, a servant of Pharaoh (Life! Prosperity! Health!)! This is a sacrilege!"

"What? Nakht was treating my father—"

"He has cut a hole in Djeti's head, that demons may enter! The High Priest of Sekhmet orders you to cease this blasphemy at once!"

"I have done no wrong!" Meryt said, panic knotting in her core. "Nakht has done no wrong!"

"That is for me to say, not you," said an oily voice, and a large fat man pushed the Temple priest aside with a pudgy hand. Minhotep, physician to the Resolve work gang, entered the room. His fine gauze tunic was stained with grease. His heavy wig only accented his beetling eyebrows and heavy features. "Step aside, little one. I have orders to examine your father, if he still lives."

"Of course he lives! Don't touch him!"

The temple guard crossed the threshold in one step, gripping Meryt's arm painfully. "Orders from the Royal Vizier," the guard said coldly. "You may not interfere."

He pulled her against the wall as Minhotep, brushing breadcrumbs from his hands, stepped into the main room. Meryt twisted free and followed him inside, trembling.

Minhotep wheezed as he bent over the bench, feeling along Djeti's limbs. He did not touch the bandages on his head, but pulled first one and then another eyelid down to examine the pupils. He counted the beats at the patient's wrist, then straightened, shaking his head. "Very bad," he said.

"What?" Meryt flew to her father's side, relieved when she saw he was breathing normally. "He is better," she said. "Look, see how his eyes are the same now? And there is no fever. He is—"

"He is lucky to be alive," said Minhotep. "It is as I feared, a false look of health."

"False? That is ridiculous!"

Minhotep sneered down at her. "And who are you to tell a physician trained in the House of Life what is and is not false? I am a priest of Sekhmet, a scribe of the God's house! Your father has indulged you beyond reason, child, but now it is time for the real physicians to handle his case, before your ignorance kills him!"

"And threatens us all!" said the little priest, behind him. He shook the papyrus scroll in her face. "Here! Right here it says, if you can read, 'a wound of the head, where he does not wake up, it is untreatable'! The wisdom of our ancestors, and yet you and your accomplice flout it!"

While Meryt fumbled for an answer, several white-clad, shaven-headed priests crowded into the room. One of them sniffed and wrinkled his nose in distaste. "Is this a house or a pigsty?" he sneered.

Meryt's face flamed. Sheri grabbed her arm. "What are they doing?"

Meryt put her head close to Sheri's. "Run! Fetch Nakht, if you can find him!"

Sheri's eyes met hers. "As I live, I will bring him." Then she was gone, sliding through the crowd of men.

The priests crowded around her father, poking and testing. Meryt tried to push her way through. "Let him alone! Don't touch him!" But the guard took her arm and pushed her to the back of the room. She watched fearfully.

Ignoring her, Minhotep continued pressing on the wound, moving Djeti's arms and legs, and even laying his head on Djeti's chest to listen to his heart. Finally, he turned to the other priests, muttering together. He turned to speak to the guard and to Meryt.

"As I said, some demon has entered him and has seized his *ka*, which is why he cannot waken. We will enact the required ritual and say the usual prayers, but this rash act may have damaged your father beyond repair." He shook his head ponderously, its beaded artificial braids clashing together. "This is a serious breach, young lady. You should have called me right away."

"It was my father's wish that you not touch him!" Meryt said hotly. "He called you a butcher!"

Shock rippled through the crowd now pressing into the room. Immediately Meryt regretted her angry outburst. Insulting Minhotep in front of his people would earn her no favors.

"As I said," Minhotep said icily. "A demon. Come, we must clear this room of everyone except physicians and priests!"

Meryt struggled, trying to stay with her father, but the guard dragged her into the anteroom, herding everyone else ahead as well. He placed himself in the doorway, spear in one hand, feet planted. "No one may enter," he said.

Meryt stamped her foot. "He's my father!" The guard ignored her.

From inside the main room of her house, the drone of chanted prayers began, and shortly the air began to fill with the smoke of incense. Meryt opened the door to the street for more air, and found herself the object of attention of a crowd. Men and women she had known for years gazed at her with suspicion and fear.

"It's all right," she said, trying to smile.

But the crowd took a step back, continuing to stare and whisper.

Then there was a disturbance, and Meryt saw Sheri, and then a tall figure pushing its way to the front. Meryt ran to Nakht.

"Oh! They are with my father! They say he has a demon!"

Someone in the crowd shrieked, and Nakht pulled her against him protectively. "Come, we must go inside." He stepped over the threshold of the door, taking her with him. Inside, he strode to the guard and demanded, "What is going on here?"

The guard, reacting automatically to a commanding tone, saluted but held his place. "Orders, sir. No one but physicians and priests allowed."

"I am the physician of the Endurance work gang," Nakht said forcefully. "I demand to be admitted at once! This patient is my responsibility."

A small hand slipped into Meryt's; Sheri stepped up beside her.

The guard hesitated, and nearly moved aside. But an oily voice contradicted him. "Your patient no longer." Minhotep shoved past the guard, bringing with him the smell of frankincense and myrrh. "Djeti-Thutmose is now under the protection of the priests of Sekhmet."

"By whose authority?" Nakht said, his eyes flashing with anger.

"By mine," said the high-pitched little scribe. He squeezed past Minhotep's bulk.

"And you are?"

"Henet-kha, of the Temple of Sekhmet," he said. Wizened, stooped and skinny, the little man nevertheless conveyed a sense of quiet menace. "I am in charge of this investigation."

"Investigation?"

Meryt stepped forward. "They believe my father has been possessed by a demon."

"Not necessarily a demon," Henet-kha said fussily. "Perhaps merely an evil spirit, or it may be a visitation from an angry god. Either way," he said, fixing a baleful eye on Nakht. "The vital balance has been upset. You have disturbed Ma'at, the way of things. Anyone or anything that unbalances the Ma'at of Pharaoh's workforce (Life! Prosperity! Health!) touches his well-being. What you have done is a threat to Pharaoh and to his people!"

"It is nothing of the kind!" Nakht snapped. "It is merely a new procedure, one you don't know. Therefore you think it is evil."

Minhotep snorted. "Young dogs like you always think they know better than the ancestors. But who can surpass the mighty wisdom of physicians like Imhotep?"

The priests crowding the doorway behind Minhotep murmured their agreement.

Henet-kha drew himself up, which made him almost as tall as Meryt. "Nakht is a stranger to this village and this workforce," he said. "And we do not yet know the ultimate outcome of this outrage perpetrated on the helpless, defenseless physician Djeti."

More muttering from the priests. Meryt stepped forward to speak, but Sheri pulled her back. "No," she whispered into Meryt's ear.

"Therefore," the little priest continued. "Nakht will not be arrested at this time—"

"Arrested!" Meryt cried.

"—Nor will he be fined or punished. He is free to continue

his duties as physician of Pharaoh's work team. However, he is forbidden to touch a head wound. If any worker suffers a head injury, Minhotep or some other qualified physician shall be called to treat him. Is this clear?"

Meryt felt hot rage bubble up in her like a boiling pot, but she took a deep breath and forced it away. It was all she could do to avoid screaming her anger, fear and frustration to the walls. She drew a deep breath.

"Nofret," she muttered to herself. "This is your doing. You went to the priests. Oh, Sister, you fool!"

Minhotep turned to the priests and said loudly, "Prepare the patient for transport!"

"What? No! You cannot take him away!" Meryt cried.

At the same time, Nakht said forcefully, "Stop! He should not be moved!"

"Be silent," Minhotep said. "From this moment onward, all care of this man is in the hands of the priests of Sekhmet, who know their business. They will be overseen by myself and by Henet-kha here, as representative of the Temple and of the Royal Overseer. Djeti will be treated at the Temple of Sekhmet." He stepped forward, his bulk forcing Nakht to step aside. Minhotep took advantage to press up against the younger man, and his sweating face thrust close. "And mark you, pup. If this man dies, you will be charged with murder as well as sacrilege."

Helpless, Meryt was forced to stand aside as the shaven-headed priests assembled a rude stretcher out of poles and linens taken from her chests.

Sheri put her mouth close to Meryt's ear. "I am going to find your sister," she said with determination. "No matter what has happened, she should be here."

Numbly, Meryt nodded and Sheri slipped out. Soon the priests were shuffling past, carrying Djeti between them. She cried out and pressed a fist against her mouth at the sight of his pale face, the fresh blood seeping through his bandages. Nakht held her against his side, his body tense with anger and frustration. As the priests passed through the doorway and Minhotep made to follow, Nakht stepped into his path.

"At least let the girl attend to her father," he said. His voice was low and menacing. "Would you offend Ma'at so far as to deny a daughter the right to do her duty?"

Minhotep's beady little eyes darted from Nakht to the guard at the door, to Meryt. "Count yourselves lucky that you are not both prisoners."

He turned, and Meryt collapsed on the steps of the household shrine, sobbing.

☥

Nakht stood uncertainly as she wept, then silently closed the door. The heat and light of the street were cut off, along with her neighbors' prying eyes. He disappeared into the inner room, as Meryt fought to control her tears.

They will kill him, she thought. She would be alone in the world. She did not even have her sister any more. Tears welled and slid down her cheeks as she stared at the little household goddess, silent and useless in her niche.

A nudge against her arm, and she looked down. Nakht held a cup of water. She drank thirstily until it was all gone. Silently, he took the cup from her and tilted her face up with one hand.

"You may want to rest," he said quietly. He smoothed a cool, wet cloth over her forehead and cheeks. "Have you eaten today?"

She looked into his eyes. "They wanted to arrest you," she said. "And all you did was try to help." Tears threatened again, and she took a deep breath. "I ... in any case, thank you for all you have done for my—"

His mouth on hers silenced her, as he cupped her face in his hands. His mouth was warm, generous, comforting, with none of the sexual heat of the night before. He broke from her gently, laid his forehead against hers. His breath mingled with hers as he said, "We will not abandon him. Come, refresh yourself, change your clothes—"

"Oh, what does any of that matter! My father—"

"Is in the hands of stupid fools, who will drown out anything you have to say with their sneers if you appear before them looking like an orphan. They are foolish men, who will weigh your words against what you look like, rather than against the feather of Ma'at." He pulled her to her feet. Nakht tilted her chin up again, gazing into her eyes. In the dim interior light, his eyes were as brown as the earth, warm with compassion and some other emotion.

"Meryt, find that lioness heart you showed last night. Find that courage you showed to save your father's life, to save the life of Shoshan and her baby. I know it is in you." He kissed the corner of her mouth softly. "Little dove, little lioness. I will take you to the Temple, and you can be with your father. Even if I have to fight the guards at the gate."

Seeking comfort, she slid her arms around him and laid her head against his chest. Weariness seemed to settle on her like a blanket, and she closed her eyes. Under her cheek, she heard his heart, felt his warm skin against hers. Part of her wanted to stay here, to let go of the burden of her responsibilities, if only for a moment.

Meryt released him and stepped back out of his arms. "No," she said decisively. "I will not go to my father. I will ask Nofret to take him some broth, but there is only one person who can override the Temple priests." She stiffened her spine, readying for the task ahead of her. "I must appeal to the Royal Vizier himself."

Nakht stepped back, his expression amused. "Yes, there is my lioness. You would take on the Divine One himself, would you not? But for our humble purposes, perhaps his Right Hand will suffice. Do you want me to come with you?"

"Of course," Meryt said, rubbing her cheeks briskly. "My father is still your patient, whatever that crocodile Minhotep may claim." She ran over her mental list of clothing, cosmetics.

She darted into the main room. It was strewn now with discarded incense cones, bloody bandages, a knocked-over pot of water seeping into the packed clay floor. She continued on to her room, where she rummaged in her chest. Down at the very bottom, carefully wrapped in linen, was her most prized possession, her mother's heavy necklace. As she drew it out into the light, a ray of sun struck it and the room was filled with gold reflections.

Red carnelian, turquoise, and the deep, gold-flecked blue of lapis lazuli stones set in gold filled her hand. Tiny ankh symbols—the knot of Isis, her name-goddess—were spaced around the wide collar with simple gold beads. The necklace hung heavily in her two hands as she gently untangled the counterpoise at the back. Designed to hang down the middle of the wearer's back, it distributed the weight of the necklace across the chest and shoulders. It had been made for Meryt's grandmother, and she had never worn it.

A hiss of indrawn breath; Nakht stood in the doorway. "Magnificent!" he breathed. He stepped into the room, blocking some of the light, and nodded at the necklace. "Fit for a princess, to be sure."

She looked down at the glittering thing in her hand. "I would gladly trade it for my father's life," she said, her voice choked.

He took it from her hands and draped it across her shoulders. "Let us pray that is not necessary," he said. "Wearing this, Hemiunu will not mistake you for a servant or a peasant. He must see you as a woman of dignity. As I do, my lioness." He leaned down and kissed her again.

With all her being, Meryt wanted to melt into that kiss, to drown herself in the feelings sweeping through her, making her knees weak and her heart race. But she pulled away, putting a hand on Nakht's chest. "This is not the time."

"I know." He caught her hands, pulling the necklace from them and dropping it onto Meryt's sleeping mat. The heat in his eyes warmed her all through. "I hope there will come a time, though, my dove. I hope there will come a time when we are not hurried, or interrupted, or—"

"Meryt!" Nofret's voice, shrill with panic, rang through the house. "Meryt, where are you?"

Nakht's eyebrow rose in frustrated amusement. "As I said..." he whispered.

Meryt stepped through the door into the passageway, just as her sister caromed through the door. "I am here."

"Oh, Sheri came to my house! I saw Father! Priests were

taking him through the streets! What has happened? Where are they taking him? Oh, gods, do not say that he is dead, that you and that fool Nakht have killed him!" Her hair was tangled, flying around her head, her dress was muddied, her eyes red with weeping. "Where are they taking him?"

Meryt steadied her sister with hands on her upper arms. "You told the priests about Nakht opening Father's skull."

Nofret pushed hair off her forehead distractedly. "Well, of course I did! How could I not? But now—" Nakht stepped out of Meryt's room behind her. Nofret drew back with alarm. "Why is he still here?" Her eyes went from Nakht to Meryt's room. She gasped. "Meryt! To lie with him, while father is dying, how can you—"

It was all Meryt could do to refrain from slapping her sister. As it was, she shook her roughly. "Be silent, if you cannot be wise!"

Nofret jerked herself away. "You cannot talk to me like that! You have put our father in danger! And you—" she nearly spat at Nakht. "If he dies, it is on your head! I will see you executed for murder—"

"Stop!" Meryt cried. "You fool, if Djeti dies, it will be because you foolishly told the priests about the procedure! He should not have been moved, he should be lying here, recovering, but now thanks to you he is in some cold, dark temple, stinking of blood and incense! How could you have betrayed us so!"

Nofret burst into tears. "I only wanted to do what was right!" she wailed. "I was afraid!"

Meryt released her sister. "The damage is done," she said coolly. "Now I have to go to Hemiunu and beg—beg, mind you—for permission to tend our father, in accordance with his own teachings. I am going to the Royal Vizier now, so get out of my way."

Nofret dashed tears from her eyes. "Oh, let me help! You cannot go looking like that! You could never do your eye makeup right."

Meryt shook her head. Behind her, Nakht stepped back

into her room and reappeared with Meryt's necklace. "You have done enough, Nofret," Meryt said. "Go home to your husband. I am going to Sheri for help, and then to the Western Palace."

"Meryt, please—" Nofret wept. "I didn't know. I'm so confused. Please, don't hate me!"

"I don't hate you," Meryt said. "But I have so much to do. I can't be your comforter now."

"What can I do?"

Nakht's voice was deep and soft. "Your father likes your broth, does he not?"

Nofret blinked tears away. "Yes."

"When he wakes, he will be hungry and thirsty. Perhaps you could take some of your broth to the Temple—"

"Oh! Oh, yes!" Nofret said, energized. "Yes, I can do that! And I have bread new-baked this morning! And beer, made with Mother's recipe!"

"Then fetch it to him," Nakht said kindly. "The priests have no grudge against you, who reported to them. When he wakes, it will be to a friendly face."

Nofret nodded eagerly, then faced her sister. "Meryt, will you come with me? Together, we can—"

Meryt shook her head. "I am for the Western House." Seeing Nofret's hopeful expression fall, she reached out and touched her sister's cheek. "But Nakht is right. It would be good if you could take our father something. Who knows what they will feed him in that place?"

Impulsively, Nofret hugged her sister, nodded half-suspiciously at Nakht, and darted out again.

"You are kinder to her than I would be," Meryt said, staring after her departed sister.

Nakht took Meryt's elbow and steered her towards the door. "Come," he said. "I will take you to Sheriti's, and then go home to change. I will come for you and we will see the Royal Vizier together." Snatching up a discarded rag, he wrapped the heavy necklace in it and handed it to her. "And perhaps I will get my brother to bring his spear. The last thing we need today is a robbery."

Meryt followed him out of the door, then turned and pulled it to. She stood in the street uncertainly, looking at it. That red door was the only one she remembered, the door to the house she had always called home, the familiar goal at the end of every day. If Djeti died, would she ever cross its threshold again?

Nakht touched her shoulder. "Come," he said quietly. "We will want to catch the Right Hand of Pharaoh (Life! Prosperity! Health!) before his afternoon nap." He held out a hand.

Slowly, aware of her neighbors' eyes on her, Meryt took his hand. His hand was large, warm and firm. He gave her fingers a squeeze and then led her along the street. Her bundled necklace under one arm, Meryt followed.

She wondered if she would ever see her father alive again.

Chapter 10 - The Western House

The sun was high and the heat of the day rising fast when Meryt and Sheri finally stepped out of Sheri's house. Meryt's borrowed wig was perfectly braided and coiled, her face made up with Sheri's most expensive malachite-green eye shadow. Sheri had rubbed oils and unguents into her friend's skin, powdered her face with fine-ground flour, and polished her friend's nails until they shone. The jeweled necklace lay heavily on her shoulders, clashing faintly with every step. Meryt could feel its heavy counterpoise in the middle of her back.

"Mind you don't trip over the threshold," Sheri said as they exited. "If you trip and tear that gown, I will weep for a week."

"I am almost afraid to move." Meryt looked up and halted.

Nakht had been pacing back and forth in the street before the house, but now stopped. "You..." he breathed.

That seemed to be their usual greeting for one another, Meryt thought, even as she sized him up. He was shaven, kilted in flawless white linen, his black hair wet and curling on his head. He wore a wide pectoral of carnelian and gold and turquoise, showing a warrior in battle. The bracelets now on his wrists were hammered copper instead of leather. Fine sandals adorned his feet and an ivory-hilted dagger hung at his waist.

"Well, aren't you two a fine pair?" Sheri purred. "One might think you were getting married."

Meryt felt her face go hot. "Shush, insect," she said. "This is no time for joking."

A small smile wobbled across Nakht's face. "Indeed," he said, his voice soft. "You are a vision, daughter of Djeti. Like cool water in a desert." He offered a hand.

Sheri giggled. "Oo, a flirt! Who knew he had it in him?"

Meryt hesitated, then put her hand in his. His grip was warm and firm. He drew her close, and his eyes burned amber and gold at her.

"Ho, brother! Wait for me!" a voice said. Baki hurried into

the street, carrying a spear and wearing his military kilt.

Sheri drew herself up like a little cat confronted by a dog. "Why is he here?"

Baki blinked at her. "Why, to help Nakht, of course. It will lend presence to my brother to have a soldier escort." He cocked his head on one side. "Come, Sheriti. Can we not be friends, when our friends are friends?"

Sheri sniffed. "Friends do not conceal things from one another."

Nakht snorted impatiently. "Play this game another time, brother. The sun does not stand still for your dalliance."

"Dalliance!" Sheri blazed at Nakht. "Why, of all the—"

"We should go," Meryt said hastily, pulling on Nakht's hand. Reluctantly, he turned, and led the way down the street. Behind them, Sheri and Baki fell in silently, an arm's length apart.

As they marched through the central square, down more streets, and out through the Gate of the Crow, Meryt was acutely conscious of Nakht's hand in hers. She could not help but wonder if his wife had helped him shave, had adjusted his kilt and smoothed its creases, done all those little wifely things for him. She liked his solid presence next to her, liked walking beside him, enjoyed the warmth and strength of his hand holding hers. She tried not to think of his hands on her, as they had been that night after she delivered the baby. As they had been that night when he may have saved Djeti's life. As his kiss had lingered on her mouth only this day.

I hope there will come a time when we are not hurried, or interrupted.

She thought about the beautiful Sesekh, swollen with pregnancy. Many men, she knew, turned to other women while their wives were breeding, and then went back to them afterwards. She had always despised men like that, yet here she was daydreaming about just such a man.

"It's a long walk," Nakht said to her. "I wish I had thought to borrow a sedan chair for you."

Meryt clucked her tongue. "Don't be absurd. I'm a physician's daughter, not a nomarch's wife."

They came to the crossroads, where the road from the village met the road to the river. They halted to allow a donkey caravan laden with empty water jars cross their path, headed for the river. With a jolt of pride, Meryt saw that they were led by women, with their heads veiled in scarves to keep the sun off their skin. Boys walked with them, too young to work at men's jobs but too old for nurses and tutors. Several of the women hailed Meryt and waved as they walked by, then went back to prodding the plodding beasts. The last in line was Ipi, driving a braying donkey before her. She glanced at Meryt, at Nakht, at their linked hands; smiling, she nodded as they passed.

"You've done well there," Nakht murmured to her. "The men will not die of thirst today."

From this crossroads, Meryt usually turned west, to enter the road to the quarry. But now they faced north, along the Palace road. Meryt felt her heart speed up. The Western House! Not, of course, the Great House in Memphis, where Pharaoh himself held court, but the smaller Residence on the west bank of the Nile.

"I've never been to the Western House!" Sheri said in an awed voice. "Perhaps they will not let us in."

Meryt turned to her friend. "You don't have to come, of course. I am grateful you have come this far, so—"

Sheri drew herself up. "Don't be insulting, Meryt!" she declared. "I will not leave your side."

Baki smiled at her, then turned to his brother. "It's only an hour's walk."

Nakht glanced at the sun overhead. "With luck, they'll be ready to break for their noon meal by the time we get there. The less formal this meeting is, the better."

Meryt was a little stunned at how casually Nakht treated a visit to the Western House. She felt small as she trudged along beside Nakht, regretting her heavy wig in this heat.

"We must stop and fix your eye makeup as soon as we reach the palace," Sheri said to her. She held up a small wooden case. "I brought my supplies."

Suddenly Meryt wanted to laugh and cry at once. The

strain of this crisis, her lack of sleep, the emotional tension were beginning to wear on her. So many new feelings, new problems, new solutions. Part of her longed to go back to the days when all she had to worry about was fixing Djeti's lunch. And Sheri's biggest worry was her smudged cosmetics.

They topped a small rise and paused for a moment to take in the sweep of plain below. To their left, the truncated Pyramid rose to its abrupt, flat top; even from here Meryt could see the line of workers that snaked up the earthen ramps, bent into their pulling ropes, with the great cubes of white limestone behind them. Distantly came the *tink-tink-tink* of copper chisels in the quarry. To their right, the Nile teemed with white-sailed boats and a few huge cargo rafts. Before them, between the river and the quarry, lay the brick-walled "working palace" of the Lord of the Two Lands.

Built, as was every non-temple in Egypt, from sun-dried brick, it sprawled like a small town, almost as large as the worker's village itself. The walls were twice the height of a tall man, plastered in white and painted with huge murals depicting the exploits of the Divine One. Looking down from their slight height, Meryt could see artificial lakes, trees, gardens, flat-roofed houses for palace officials. Towering above everything was a massive hall. A steady stream of lords, scribes, overseers and their retinue streamed in and out of the wide gates. In the distance, a cloud of moving dust indicated the drill field where young soldiers were training.

Sheri gripped Meryt's hand. "Do you want to turn back?" she whispered.

Mouth dry, Meryt shook her head. Baki and Nakht swung into the path, marching nonchalantly down its beaten surface. Sheri squeezed her hand and then released it. With a deep breath, Meryt followed.

Travelers before them had kicked up a cloud of dust, and Meryt blinked several times to clear her vision. The burning sun, her hot wig and the long walk combined to leave her thirsty and tired. She could hardly spare a glance for the streams of odd folk converging on the gates: outlander merchants in heavy wool, with curled and oiled beards, warriors from Nubia in their elegant braids and gold hoops in their ears.

A herald shouted leeway for his mistress, a dark woman in a formal vulture-winged headdress, being carried in a palanquin by sweating retainers. As they watched her pass, Sheri whispered, awe-struck, "Princess Nefert-Nesu, the Divine One's sister!" She bowed from the waist as the woman passed, extending her arms out parallel to the ground in the royal salute. The others followed her lead.

When the palanquin had entered the gates, Nakht grabbed Meryt's hand and they walked on. Guards on either side of the gate, outfitted in magnificent helmets of copper-studded leather, nodded as Baki held up his official courier's dispatch case with the royal cartouche, and passed them without challenge. Inside, Meryt halted in wide-eyed wonder.

The smell of water hit her first—deep and green and wet. Everywhere there was water—pools, fountains, little rivulets running in artificial channels beside brick paths. Tall palms of every description, leafy groves of sycamore, lacy overhanging willows dotted the gardens and open spaces, creating cool shade. Birds sang in every tree, the scent of flowers perfumed the air. From a distant pavilion came laughter and the sound of a harp. The bustle and dirt of the Pyramid construction site seemed miles away. They walked past a small shrine; from within the sound of chanting and the scent of burning myrrh reminded Meryt of their errand.

"Where do we find the Royal Vizier?" she asked.

Baki sighed and nodded towards a long line of people waiting patiently near the entrance to a huge hall. "We'd best get in line," he said.

Meryt sagged. "We'll never get in today."

Nakht shook his head. "Not through the front door, at least. Follow me."

Baki shrugged and followed his brother as Nakht struck off along a footpath that wound among trees and beside ponds. Soon they came to a small brick building, plain and undecorated, with several soldiers lounging about in the shade and eating a watermelon. One of them snapped to his feet as Nakht appeared. "Sir!"

The others got to their feet as well. Nakht put his hands up. "No need for that, I'm not in the army any more."

The first man grinned, showing a couple of missing teeth. "Never mind that," he said. "I remember how you patched Mintauf together after that Sinai raiding party put a fistful of arrows through him." He picked up a leather wineskin and held it out. "Care to wet your throat, sir?"

"No, thanks," Nakht said. "It's good to see you again, Nesut. How is your son?"

"Serving the Great House in Nubia," the grizzled soldier said proudly. "Earned his honors with the bow and spear."

"Congratulations. I'm sure he'll do your house proud," Nakht said. He half-turned to his brother. "You'll remember my brother, Baki."

The older man's eye widened. "This is the fledgling? A young hawk, to be sure!" The two men exchanged salutes. Then the veteran turned his gaze on the women. "And this would be your lovely wife? Wives?"

"No," Nakht said hastily. "In fact, we're trying to get in to see the Vizier. The life of this lady's father is at stake." He indicated Meryt. "We must get in, and we can't wait all day in line."

The veteran squinted, thinking. "Ah, well. Let's see. First gong went a half-hour ago, so they'll be serving the noon meal. If you promise not to get me put on report, I think we can find a way in the back door, sir. You, Khafy! Get your lazy ass up and look sharp! Your kilt is a mess, are you some peasant? I want you and Wehem dressed, armed and ready for escort by the time I count to twenty! Go!"

The two younger men scrambled inside the building. Nesut turned back to Nakht. "The Divine One (Life! Prosperity! Health!) is not in residence today, so things are less formal. Otherwise, this would never work. But if you hold your head up and look like you've got a stick up your arse—beg pardon, ladies—you can march right on by those soft-bellied children

184

they call guards in the Horus Hall. You know the look, sir. Rather like Captain Ia-sen, back on the *Horizon of Ra?*" He chuckled.

Nakht smiled. "I know the look. Can my brother's badge get us into the private apartments?"

Nesut looked Baki over carefully, noting the courier bag, and nodded. "Most like. 'Course, you'll have to leave your weapons here."

Baki nodded and handed over his spear, as Nakht took the knife out of his belt. Nesut smiled when he saw it. "Aye, I saw that knife do good work against those—" On Nakht's look, he shut up, but his eyes danced.

The two soldiers came out, dressed in full military rig. The royal cartouche was embossed on their leather chest protectors; their helmets were fastened on their heads. Nesut scowled as he walked around them. "Pigs. I tell you, this outfit has gone to the pigs. But you'll do, I suppose, if no one important looks close. Escort Captain—er, physician Nakht and his party to the royal apartments, and look smart about it. If you embarrass me, you'll be standing guard over the latrines for a month."

"Thank you," Nakht said. "I won't forget this."

"Only balancing things out, sir," the veteran said. "After that time when you—"

"We'll be back soon," Nakht said hurriedly.

Nesut waved them on, and the guards strode quickly ahead down an obscure path. Rather than winding through the trees and garden, this one cut quickly behind sheds and outbuildings, obviously a shortcut intended for palace servants. In no time they were entering a small door at the rear of the massive Hall. Meryt barely noticed the paintings of rare animals, trees and animals surrounding the door as they entered, passing bakers with new-baked bread on trays.

Inside, they entered a crowded but cool passage. People hurried past carrying trays, baskets, musical instruments, scrolls. A dozen voices talked at once, and somewhere a calf lowed mournfully. The tiles were cool under Meryt's feet, the walls plain plaster with a red checkered border along the floor.

"Where are we?" whispered Meryt.

"Looks like we're heading for the kitchens," Sheri replied. "We're lucky Nakht has friends in a place like this!"

Indeed, Meryt felt hope rising in her for the first time since her father had been taken. Anger and fear had kept her going through the long, hot walk, but now she began to feel encouraged.

At a juncture, the guards turned left, then right, then left again. They passed a granary, two kitchens (where the smell of roasting duck made Meryt almost dizzy with hunger), a sewing room full of bolts of linen, and a room full of water jars.

"I'm lost," Sheri said. "Don't fall behind, or we'll never get out of here!"

The guards opened a narrow door, and the party stepped through into a different world. As the door closed behind them a hush fell, and the guards stopped a moment to confer. Meryt gazed around her at the blue tiled floor, the exquisite wall paintings showing a hunting scene, a harvest, even a fishing boat on the Nile. Chests and boxes sat around the room, and a large, ornate chair sat against one wall. "Is this the Throne Room?" she asked.

One of the young guards snorted, and the other nudged him to silence. "No, Mistress," he said politely. "This is the changing room for the servants of the Queen Mother. The Vizier is dining with her today. This way."

Nakht turned to her and held out his hand. "Come. We will see an end to this trouble."

Meryt, intimidated by her surroundings, put her hand in his. "May it be as you say," she said.

The guards opened a blue-painted door on the opposite wall, and stepped through. A man with a shaved head, immaculate linen tunic and solid gold pectorals immediately blocked their way. "Who are you?"

Nakht stepped forward. "Nakht, son of Ra-Khuf, with my brother Baki. I am the physician to the work team Endurance, on the Pyramid of Khufu (Life! Prosperity! Health!). We are here on a matter of life and death."

As he introduced the party, Meryt looked past him into the opulent room before them. It was as large as the entire worker's barracks, but the overall impression was light and airy rather than dark and crowded. The walls were plastered white, decorated with scenes of women dancing or playing musical instruments. The floor was painted to look like a lake, with fish swimming among lotus. In a corner, a girl in a white gown played a flute softly, while servants silently hurried to and fro.

The focus of all attention, however, was the group at the center. Seated in ebony chairs, Hemiunu the Royal Vizier and several women were having lunch. Small tables in front of them held roasted duck, small dishes with fruit, bowls of stew. Fine bread baked in the shapes of fish or animals sat before each diner, and cups of wine were being filled by young women wearing little more than paint. Behind each chair stood a fan-bearer waving ostrich-plume fans with great dignity.

"Oh!" whispered Sheri. "Isn't that the Queen Mother?"

Meryt recognized the woman who had passed them in the streets of Memphis only days ago. Regal in her bearing, she was dressed in a court gown of spotless linen, wearing heavy make-up and a necklace of lapis lazuli. Upon her head sat the Vulture Crown, its golden wings falling behind her ears and covering half of her heavy braided wig, denoting her status as the mother of the Divine One. Beside her sat two other women in court dress, eyeing Baki and Nakht curiously.

Almost as an afterthought, Meryt noted the Royal Vizier seated beside the Queen Mother, holding a papyrus scroll in his hand.

"What is this?" came an imperious voice. The man arguing with Nakht immediately turned and bowed to the Queen Mother.

"Noble lady, these intruders are mere commoners, workers in the Pyramid site. I will have them sent—"

"Ah!" the Queen Mother said, with a note of triumph in her voice. "Exactly the kind of people I want to speak to."

"Grandmother," said Hemiunu irritably. "We are in the middle of the reports. This is hardly the time—"

"There is no better time," the older lady said imperiously. She waved at the doorman. "Come."

Nakht turned and gestured for Meryt to come with him. Together they walked up to within a few feet of the group, then bowed from the waist, arms held parallel to the floor.

"Greetings to the Mother of the King of Upper and Lower Egypt, Follower of Horus, Guide of the Ruler, Favored One, She whose every word is done for her, the daughter of the God's body, Hetepheres, may she live forever," Nakht said; he turned towards Hemiunu. "Greetings to the Guardian of Nekhen, Mouth of Pe, Priest of Bastet, Staff of Apis, who loves his lord—"

"Enough," said the old lady. "We will be here until tomorrow if you insist on all this formality. Besides, you left out half my titles anyway. What service do you perform on the Horizon of Khufu?" she said, using the official name of the Pyramid.

Nakht introduced himself and Meryt. The Queen eyed her closely. "You are a physician, as well?"

"I was trained by my father, Djeti, the physician to the Endurance work gang."

"This Nakht just now called himself the physician to the Endurance work gang. I can see at least one problem with that." The old lady shifted in her chair, beckoning to a servant. "Take this away and bring me a cup of cool buttermilk. And beer for our guests."

"Grandmother, surely you would prefer a nap—" Hemiunu began. His grandmother's sharp eyes silenced him.

"While I sleep, the Two Lands decay," she said. "Who has kept this kingdom in balance these forty years? Who has worked tirelessly behind two Pharaohs, to ensure the continuation of Ma'at in this land? I was managing building projects before you were weaned, Grandson. You, girl!"

"M-majesty?" Meryt said.

"Your name, I heard it in the reports." She snapped her fingers, and a fat scribe behind her stepped forward, head bowed, to lay a rolled papyrus in her hand. "Are you not the one who devised this scheme whereby women drive the donkey caravans?"

Hemiunu snorted with laughter. "This is a jest, Grandmother."

She looked at her grandson through slitted eyes. "Is it?" she said dryly. "I find nothing amusing in the threat of a work slowdown. Nor will His Majesty (Life! Prosperity! Health!)."

Hemiunu shifted in his seat and picked up a wine bowl. "Well, if you must..." he muttered.

The Queen Mother turned her attention back to Meryt. "I would have this story directly from you, child," she said. Her tone softened a little. "Do not fear. I like smart women. Tell me what happened."

Haltingly, Meryt stammered out the story of the water bearers, the labor shortage, of her suggestion to Akhti-Hotep. Meryt felt as though sand coated her throat. This was not what she had come for, yet she didn't know how to broach her father's case. How could she digress from the Queen Mother's conversational track?

The women on either side of Hemiunu leaned forward, and she knew they were cataloging every detail of her appearance. She suddenly felt shabby and ugly and under-dressed, a poor display against these princesses.

Meryt came to the end of her tale and fell silent.

The Royal Vizier snorted with laughter. "How absurd! Women driving donkeys! What, will they dress them in flower wreaths, and put cones of perfume on their heads? Or will they braid painted beads into their tails?"

Coolly, the Queen Mother peered at Meryt through half-closed eyes, considering. "How many women?"

Hemiunu looked at her in amazement. "You cannot seriously—"

The old queen met his look with a level look of her own. "Cannot seriously consider that mere women are capable of running a simple donkey train? When I have run the estates of this family for more years than you have lived? You jest poorly, Grandson."

Meryt was surprised to see the powerful Royal Vizier taken aback. "I mean no disrespect to you, Majesty—" he began.

"And yet, I feel the lack of respect nonetheless," she retorted.

189

Turning to Meryt, she gestured her forward with a ring-covered hand. "Child, come closer."

Meryt felt nearly dizzy as she advanced to the foot of the Queen Mother's chair. Close up, she could see the heavy makeup caked on her face, smell the heavy perfumes and ointments. Her nose also detected a medicinal smell. *She is being treated for pain in her joints,* Meryt thought.

"And when does this new workforce begin?" the Queen Mother inquired.

"We passed a train on our way here."

Suddenly the old woman cackled. "Excellent! Grandson, she has done what the great men of Egypt cannot! She has actually solved a problem rather than just barked about it!" She smiled at Meryt, her face crinkling up at the corners of her kohl-lined eyes. "I like women who get things done," she said. Her glance took in the simpering females next to Hemiunu. "Alas, there are too few in the Black Lands," she said, referring to the fertile soil of Egypt. She waved her fingers in dismissal.

"Since my grandson chooses not to honor your efforts to serve Pharaoh—" Her glare almost visibly withered the Royal Vizier. "I appoint you to walk in the rear of my procession during the Hathor Festival." She turned to Hemiunu, dismissing Meryt with a wave. "Which reminds me, Hemiunu. Your plans for the Festival are incomplete. How can you have possibly overlooked the Singers of Isis? They have not been assigned a place in the procession, and no one has ordered—"

"But that is not why we have come!" Meryt burst out.

Everyone in the room stared at her, frozen in shock.

"Meryt!" Sheri whispered behind her, panic in her voice.

Meryt wanted to sink into the floor and become one with the painted fish. "I ... I am sorry," she stammered. She bowed from the waist. "All respect to the Royal Wife, the—"

"Don't start that again," the Queen Mother said. "Why did you come here, then?"

Meryt bowed her head. This was not going to work. "Because my father's life is in danger. And we are being unjustly accused of sacrilege."

Silence fell like a blow. Hemiunu rose to his feet. "Sacrilege?" he said in an ominous voice. "What do you mean?"

Meryt fought for words, fear silencing her. *Oh why, why had she not held her tongue?* Before she could speak, however, she heard Nakht beside her, his voice even and smooth as he explained.

Meryt's thoughts flew to her father. Was he waking in a room full of incense and strangers? Was Minhotep even now committing some serious mistake that would kill Djeti?

"And you believed this procedure would work?" Hemiunu was saying incredulously. He turned to his aunt. "This is sacrilege. The gods will surely destroy anyone who violates the body of a living man in this manner. I will have them arrested—"

"Don't be a fool, Hemiunu," his aunt said calmly. "First we must see how this ends. For all we know, the man may recover."

"But they have let demons into his head!" Hemiunu cried. Meryt saw the women beside him shudder delicately; one placed her hands over her eyes.

"No," Nakht said earnestly. "I swear, on my own *ka* and the *ka* of my son, that this procedure has worked before. It has a good chance to work here—"

"I will hear no more," Hemiunu said angrily. "In this matter, I will not overrule the priests of Sekhmet." He cast a baleful glance at the elder woman. "Nor will Pharaoh (Life! Prosperity! Health!) allow me to, even if I wished. In matters touching the gods, the Divine One is very careful, as you know. Ma'at demands that justice be done."

"If justice is to be done, then it should wait to see if it is needed," said the Queen Mother evenly. "Let this matter play out, and see what results."

Hemiunu opened his mouth to protest, but the Queen Mother silenced him with a look. "Be reasonable," she said mildly. "Will you allow the priests of Sekhmet to stampede the wisdom of the Royal Vizier like a yearling calf? Wait but a day or two."

Hemiunu's eyes narrowed, then he flung himself down in his chair. "You mock me. Oh, I know you. It is useless to argue.

Very well, let it be as you wish, but Pharaoh will know who to blame when famine and plague strike the Two Lands." He picked up a honeyed fig and popped it in his mouth.

"Will you do nothing?" Meryt cried in anguish.

The women beside the Royal Vizier reacted with little cries of dismay. The Queen Mother regarded them with distaste. Hemiunu scowled at Meryt. "Impudent! Djeti has spoiled you beyond reason! I thought better of him—"

"This girl has cleverly solved a problem in the service of my son," Queen Hetepheres said resolutely. "Is this how a Great House shows favor?" She tapped a long, polished fingernail impatiently on the arm of her chair. "Send for the Chief Royal Physician, at least," she said.

"But—"

"I will do it myself, to spare you the wrath of the King, my lord Vizier." Her voice held irony.

Sheri grabbed Meryt's hand and tugged. Now was their chance to leave, before becoming further embroiled in the royal family's infighting.

The Queen Mother spoke. "Go, all of you. Pray that the girl's father recovers. And obey the orders of the Royal Overseer, who is commanded by the Living Horus." She glanced at Meryt. "The Chief Royal Physician will be sent for. I will expect you in eight days' time, at the Festival. By then, I expect to hear favorable news of your father."

Nakht, Meryt and the rest of their party bowed their way out of the dining room. As the blue-painted doors closed behind them, all sighed with relief.

"I thought I was going to be ordered to arrest you," one of their young escorts said.

Meryt scowled at the floor. "We wasted our time." She thought of her trip across the Nile earlier, when she had appealed, fruitlessly, to the Chief Royal Physician. "They will do nothing for us. They do not care about us. We mean nothing to these great ones."

"Shush!" Sheri tugged her arm. "Don't say such things! Pharaoh pays us well to work on his great Pyramid, he pays your father for his services, he is the source of all health and Ma'at!"

Does she really believe all that? Meryt wondered. But seeing the troubled glances exchanged by the young guards, for once she kept her mouth shut. All the way back through the palace maze, through the lush gardens, and across the plain seared by late afternoon sun, she was sunk in gloomy thoughts. She could not even take pleasure in the Queen Mother's mark of honor for her, knowing it had been offered more as a taunt to her grandson rather than as a measure of Meryt's own accomplishment. Ahead of her, Nakht and Baki walked together, heads down, talking in worried tones.

Meryt looked up at the horizon, seeing the great, rising slopes of the unfinished Pyramid, the taste of dust and failure in her mouth.

♀

By the time the little group had walked all the way back to the village, evening was falling. In the west, the setting sun painted the unfinished Pyramid in shades of red and gold, and sent long purple shadows across the road. When they stopped to let a work team trudge wearily past, Sheri leaned in to Meryt.

"Baki wants to walk me home, but I said I would stay with you as long as you need me."

Meryt sighed, feeling the weight of failure lying heavy on her shoulders. "No, you should go home. I am going to the Temple to see my father."

"Then I should come with you," her friend said staunchly.

Meryt shook her head. "There's no reason. They probably won't even let me see him."

"I'll go with you," Nakht said.

Meryt swallowed a bitter laugh. "They will certainly not let you in to see him."

Nakht's hands made slow fists at his side. "I will insist."

Meryt put a hand on his arm. "I thank you for your dedication to my father," she said. "But there's nothing you can do."

Baki scuffed at the ground and cleared his throat. "I don't know about that."

The work team had passed, and the foursome started up the slight rise that led to the village gate. "What do you mean?" Meryt asked.

Baki exchanged glances with Nakht over the women's heads. "I have an idea. Let me think on it."

Sheri elbowed him. "We'll be waiting on your slow thoughts until the Pyramid is finished."

Baki grinned down on her. "Some of my thoughts move very fast."

Meryt was surprised to see a slow flush climbing her friend's cheek, but all Sheri said was, "I'll go with Meryt."

They had reached the village gate, and the guards saluted Baki as they passed through. "No," said Meryt. "Go home. Rest. We will talk tomorrow." She halted by the cistern, embracing her friend. "And thank you. I would have looked a mess today without your help. You are a good friend."

Sheri sniffed and blinked back tears. "Yes, I am," she said tartly. "Don't forget it, next time I need someone to braid my hair."

Meryt smiled as her friend turned away, Baki following. As the pair turned into the street where Sheri's house lay, Baki leaned down to whisper. Meryt could not hear Sheri's soft reply.

"I think they're friends again," Nakht said. He touched her arm. "No matter what you say, Meryt, I am going to visit your father in the Temple, if I have to climb down from the roof."

Too tired to argue, Meryt nodded wearily and turned west, towards the Temple precincts. This meant they had to walk against the flow of workers coming home from the quarries, stonemasons hurrying towards dinner, woodworkers and scribes and painters all trudging home after a long day.

A knot of women at the village gate called greetings to sons and brothers and husbands, and one or two called flirtatiously to lovers. Through it all, the dust and heat of the day died down under the fast retreat of day. Soon a cool breeze stirred the hem of Meryt's gown and teased the braids of her wig. She considered taking it off, but then remembered she would be confronting the priests of Sekhmet. A sigh left her lips as they left the crowded avenue and entered the nearly deserted approach to the Temple of Sekhmet.

"Thoughts, oh my dove?" Nakht said softly.

"I wish my sister was here," she confessed. "I wish we had not quarreled."

Nakht took her hand in his; she did not resist. "When Djeti wakes, your quarrel will be forgotten," he said firmly.

Meryt laughed shortly. "It seems that only you and I have any faith in your skills."

"And your faith is weakening," Nakht said.

She glanced up. The fading light gave an amber tint to his brown eyes, but even in shadow his expression was kind. "A little," she confessed.

He squeezed her fingers, undaunted. "I will not lie to you," he said seriously. "He is at risk. The more so with those jackals like Minhotep attending him. But he is strong—I could feel his strength under my hands. And he has your prayers." He stopped, pulling her hand to draw her out of the busy lane.

"Meryt, listen to me. If they let me in to see him, that will be well. But if they do not, know this. I have known men to wake from just such a dark sleep as Djeti is in now, to tell me that they remember the voices and sounds around them. I believe your father may hear you, even if his body seems like so much clay right now. His *ka* can hear you, I am sure of it. Talk to him. Tell him to come back to you."

Meryt's hand trembled in his. "Most of the Two Lands seems to think my father is already as good as dead."

Nakht drew her closer, and put two strong arms around her. "'As good as dead'? You and I, my lioness, know that that means nothing. There is life, and there is death, and the two are day and night, white and black. Until he is well and truly dead, beloved, he is alive and there is hope."

Beloved. Meryt caught her breath. Did he mean that? Words whirled in her head, a thousand questions—or one question. Before she could voice them, Nakht was turning, leading her towards the white gleaming temple at the end of the causeway.

It was a smaller temple than the one across the Nile, but it still towered over the reflecting pool before it. The whitewashed mud-brick walls rose to the height of four men, and the tops of the pylons before the great door were still bathed in the last rosy glow of sunset. Junior priests carrying torches emerged as they approached, and began lighting oil lamps at the bases of the towering twin statues of the lion-headed goddess Sekhmet that stood on either side of the entrance. Just before the door, two guards in red leather harnesses stood forth, barring the way.

"Nakht," one of them said. He seemed embarrassed but determined. "I have orders that you may not enter the temple."

"I must see my patient, Mertash," Nakht said evenly. "It is a violation of Ma'at to keep the physician from his patient."

The guard shifted from foot to foot; he looked young and embarrassed. "I ... I have my orders."

Meryt stood forth. "Do your orders bar me from seeing my father?"

Mertash's eyes widened a bit. "M-mistress Meryt, I did not recognize you. Your hair—" He straightened and stood aside. "I have no orders to keep you out," he said. He eyed Nakht. "But he must stay here."

She turned to Nakht, but he shook his head. "We cannot win this fight, little dove," he said softly.

"Tell me what signs to look for," she said urgently. "Will he be feverish? Should I check his eyes?"

"Do all for him that you were doing before," Nakht whispered. "And remember what I said—speak to him."

Wordlessly, she nodded and then walked past the guard, head held high.

☥

Inside, the temple was dark save for a wall sconce here and there holding an oil lamp. Her sandals made rasping sounds on the tile floor, raising faint echoes that whispered off into the darkness. The lights danced over the painted walls, making the images of gods and men and animals dance and slither as if they were alive. Meryt felt a shiver go over her that had nothing to do with the coolness of the evening. The smell of frankincense drew her onward, and in a few steps she heard the distant sound of chanting. Skirting around a tall pillar carved with formal hieroglyphs, she turned towards a dark side passage, whose doorway yawned like an open mouth. She stopped to lift an oil lamp from its bracket, and advanced into the gloom.

"Come! You who drives out evil things.
We bow down to Sekhmet's name.
Powerful lioness, you whose face is beautiful
Strong of heart appearing in your temple
Lady of one million years, make strong the weak one,
Protect and heal him, make all fever far from him ..."

Feeling her way along the wall, the light wavering before her, Meryt felt her fingertips pass over carved faces, hieroglyphs, raised images of things she could not name. The chanting grew louder as she approached, and now the fetor of burning dung wreathed along the close corridor.

"Preserve him from all evil and sickness.
Goddess, arise in the horizon! Give ear, Lioness!
You who issue forth, you who summon Ra, give ear!
Flame-bearer, you of eternal light, deliver him!..."

The light ahead grew stronger, and finally Meryt came to a stop in the door of a small room. Inside, bald men in white linen lifted censers to the ceiling, filling the room with dense gray-white smoke. Frankincense, she catalogued automatically. Dung of some kind. Willow bark and cassia, oil of fir, charcoal—her trained nose identified the ingredients. Through the haze, she could just make out the figure of her father, wrapped tightly in a linen shroud. *Oh gods,* she thought. *Is he dead already?* But then she saw his chest rise and fall slightly. She raised a hand to cover a polite cough.

Instantly, a young priest wearing only a white kilt stepped into her path, raising a hand. "None may enter," he said officiously.

Meryt felt her last reserves of patience ebbing fast. "He is my father. You may not keep me from his side."

He shook his head. "The physician Minhotep has forbidden—"

And at the sound of that name, her last restraint drained away. Meryt stepped forward, forcing the young man (who was forbidden contact with females during his priestly service) to step backwards in alarm. "I will see him," she snapped. "Though all the armies of Pharaoh stand between us. Be gone from my path!"

The chanting cut off, and every eye in the room turned to her. An older man stepped forward, but Meryt pointed to the door. "All of you! Out! Now!"

"You cannot—" the older man started.

Meryt stamped her feet and drew herself up as tall as she could. Sekhmet, give me strength to deal with these your priests, she thought. And then, as if in echo, she remembered Nakht's words: find that lioness heart.

Yes, she thought fiercely. *Give me the heart of a lioness now!*

And perhaps the goddess heard her, because the men backed out of the room. "Get Minhotep!" one of them hissed, and a young priest took off running.

Meryt turned her back on them and knelt beside her father, who lay on a bier. "Father," she said. His chest rose and fell regularly, to her relief. But the bandages on his head were dark with sweat—did he have a fever? Impossible to tell, smothered as he was. Quickly, she began un-tucking and unwrapping the heavy linen sheets. They were not just ordinary sheets, she noticed: each one was painted with signs and symbols and prayers of protection.

As she worked, she forced herself to observe, to see with the eyes of a physician and not a daughter. No trembling, she noted. No convulsions. She sniffed—no putrefaction from the broken limbs, no smell of urine or feces. His leg and arm were well splinted and straight. Laying aside all but the lightest sheet, she passed her hands quickly over her father's head and neck. All seemed well, and there was no sign of bleeding. Finally, holding her breath, she brought the little lamp near and pried open first one, and then the other of her father's eyes.

The pupils matched. Even more, as she moved the light, they shrank in response, as they should.

Meryt let Djeti's eyes fall closed, and set the lamp down

with trembling hand. He was alive, and not feverish. His eyes, oh thank the gods, his eyes were normal. Maybe his *ka* was returning to his body. "Father," she whispered. "I don't know if you can hear me. I hope you can. Let your *ka* return to us, Father. Let your body heal. I have done all that I can. The priests here, they think dung and prayers will bring you back to me." A tear dropped hot onto her hand, and she wiped her cheeks. "All you have taught me, all I have learned, I have used to fight the darkness you are in. But now, you must fight it, too."

Noises in the corridor outside—Meryt knew she had little time. "Father, wake, I beg you! Come back to us! I don't know how to live without you!"

"You!" Minhotep stood in the doorway. "Do not touch him! Guards! Take her away!"

"It is my right—" Meryt began, but two large guards with fierce expressions shouldered past Minhotep and jerked her to her feet.

"Right?" Minhotep thrust his face close to hers. "Be grateful I do not have you confined in the guardhouse like some thief," he snarled. His gaze caught the linen sheets on the floor. "You fool! You have stripped him of his protections! The demons will enter him now, unless we begin again—"

"No!"

Minhotep sneered at her. "Take her out. We have work to do."

The guards hauled her towards the door, with Meryt struggling in their hands. She wrenched herself free and whirled to face Minhotep. "If you kill my father with this barbarous nonsense, I will have your life!"

"Threats? To the priests of Sekhmet in her own Temple?" Minhotep sneered. "Throw her out!"

One guard grabbed at her, but the other stepped back, making the sign against the evil eye. Meryt evaded the other's reach, turned on her heel and strode through the door. Her dignity carried her only a few feet, however, before a sob rose in her throat. Half-blind with tears, blundering in the semi-darkness, she stumbled out of the temple into the night.

☥

Nakht caught her as Meryt stumbled down the steps of the temple. "Meryt? Don't tell me he's—"

"He lives yet," she said, turning instinctively to the shelter of his arms. "And his eyes, oh, Nakht, his eyes match! They look normal!"

Nakht gave a shout of joy, which had the guards turning to them with scowls. He slipped an arm around Meryt and led her down the causeway towards the reflecting pool. "Normal, you say? This is good news, indeed! Any fever?"

"No, but they have wrapped him almost as close as a mummy, or a swaddling child," she said. "You really think he can live?"

"If he yet has no fever, and no shaking, and you say his eyes are balanced again—as you know, that is the most important sign. I have seen men recover from wounds at this stage. There is no sign of corruption in the limbs?"

Meryt drew a deep breath and straightened. Remembering her training, she looked up and met Nakht's anxious eyes. Wordlessly, he pulled her to him and wrapped both arms around her. For a long moment, they stood there in the cool night, with the pond making ripple sounds behind them and the first frogs cheeping tentatively at the edges. In the village at the end of the causeway, Meryt heard a dog bark, a baby's cry. The smells of cooking—frying fish, new bread—reached her. But here, for now, it was only him and her and their two hearts turning wearily to one another.

And for the first time in a long time, Meryt felt hope again. *I have seen men recover,* Nakht had said. She thought of his strong hands holding Shoshan, of his quick and skilled handling of injured workers, of his dedication and skill as he cut into her father's skull, and for the first time she began to look ahead, to the day when her father would wake, and walk, and talk again. Dared she hope that on that day, she and Nakht would have a future? That he would turn to her and—

Like water dashed over her head on a hot day, the thought shot through her. *He is married.*

As though stung by a wasp, Meryt backed out of Nakht's arms. How could she have forgotten? Shame rose in her face. This meant nothing. He had a wife, a son. Soon he would have another child—

"Meryt? Have I said something?" His voice was puzzled.

"No, nothing," she said hastily. She refused to compound her mistake by confessing her feelings, her hopes. "It's late. I must get home."

"I will walk you," he said, and turned her towards the village.

"Not necessary," she said, stepping out ahead of him. "You should go home, as well."

"Home?" Now he sounded amused. "Not until I've walked you home. I will accept no denial," he said firmly.

Stubborn man, she thought, secretly pleased. And then she felt shame again, allowing herself to feel ... warm ... towards a married man. Suddenly, she could take this yanking back and forth on her emotions no longer. She whirled to face Nakht. "No," she said, forcing her voice to sound calmer than she felt. "You have been away too long from your wife. She is close to her time, you should be with her."

Nakht stopped dead. Behind them, in the East, the full moon had tipped over the horizon and now spilled milky light across his handsome features. Features which now registered shock and puzzlement. "Wife?"

"Yes," she said, determined to do the right thing. "You keep saying you hope for a time when we will not be interrupted, when we will be alone. But we cannot be alone," she said. He stepped closer, and Meryt backed up a step. "We can never be together," she said. "I know some women would accept some arrangement, but I am not such. I will not dally with a married man, especially one whose wife—"

"Who told you I was married?" he said abruptly.

Meryt blinked. "The women of the village. And I met Sesekh. And your son, you said he—"

Nakht took hold of her upper arms. "Listen to me, daughter of Djeti. I have no wife."

"B-but, I met—"

"—My very lovely sister-in-law. Baki and I have a brother, Harkhuf. He is a surveyor, but he is fulfilling his duty to Ptah this month."

Meryt gaped. A brother? Her mind raced. Most priests were volunteers who only served a few weeks of the year. During their service, they shaved all the hair from their bodies and refrained from their wives until their time was up. Nakht's brother would have been required to stay away from Sesekh. "He ... he is across the river? At the Temple?"

Amused, Nakht said, "Naturally. And Sesekh would be across the river, as well, except that none of us wanted to leave her alone in their house when she is close to the birth."

"Of course," Meryt said, stunned. "And Sefu?"

"Is my son," Nakht said, brushing a hand across her cheek. "His mother died of fever when he was a year old. I was away with the army. By the time I came home, she was four months in her tomb." Meryt heard pain in his voice.

"You loved her," she said numbly.

"Yes," he said. A cool breath of air lifted the hair on his forehead. "But she is with Osiris now."

Realization began to dawn on Meryt. Not married. *Not married.* And he had called her beloved.

Which might mean anything, she realized. No matter that his hands on her arms felt warm and firm, that his kisses drugged her like lotus-infused wine. It could mean nothing, only the way of a seducer and a rogue.

Except her heart told her different. "Nakht," she whispered.

He answered her with a kiss, gentle and slow. He tasted of sunlight and laughter, and she wanted it to go on forever. She pressed up against him, his broad chest sheltering her from the cooling air, his fingers ranging up to cup her chin.

He broke the kiss, panting. "Meryt," he breathed. "Dove, oh my dove..." He turned her face to him. "I am walking you home," he said firmly, with laughter under it, laughter and something else, something warm and exciting. "And do not say nay. You have not eaten all day, and I daresay you hardly slept. You must rest and eat."

"Yes..." she replied, breathless. But she didn't feel hungry. Or sleepy.

She saw a small, trembling smile spread across his face. Was this charming man of the world feeling shy?

Meryt felt her whole body hum as he pulled her into his embrace again. "Oh, yes," he breathed against her cheek. "I am definitely walking you home." He took her hand in his and pulled her into the roadway. Walking fast, he almost towed her along the walkway.

"Nakht," she said breathlessly. "I don't know—" But then there were men walking towards them, dressed for temple service, and two dogs chased themselves across the path. A woman walking with a child stared at Meryt curiously, her gaze going from her to Nakht and back.

"Not now," Nakht hissed in her ear. "Say what you need to say, but say it indoors."

She agreed. The last thing she wanted to do was add wind to the gossip storm raging through the village. Half-dazed, she stumbled at his side as he wove through the knots of conversing villagers, past a group of young girls playing a singing game, around the cistern, where the village gossips clustered and clucked.

Then they were in her street, at her father's red door, and then they were inside and he closed the door behind them. The room smelled musty, as though it had been centuries, not hours, since she was inside it. Nakht released her and reached into the corner behind the door. He picked up the wooden bar and dropped it into the slots on either side of the door.

"I refuse to be interrupted again," he said fiercely.

Suddenly Meryt laughed. It was all happening too fast, and too slow, and there was so much uncertainty, and yet with him she felt a deep kind of surety.

My father will live, she thought, and hope went through her. *Because of this man, he will live.*

She reached out in the semi-darkness, and he took her hand unhesitatingly. She led him through the darkened antechamber, through the main room. It smelled of medicine and spilled incense and stale, closed-in sickness. Her foot connected with something that rolled into a corner, and then she was through the main room and into the corridor. Anticipating her, wordless, Nakht stepped past her and grabbed a small oil lamp set above the oven, blowing on the smoldering wick to fan it into life.

"Bread?" he said.

"And wine," she answered in a half-whisper, though there was none to hear them. He snatched the loaf of bread and a jar of wine sealed with wax from the top shelf. Meryt caught up the basket of figs and led the way up the stairs to the roof. He climbed so close behind her, his breath warmed her neck. And then they were on the roof, with the stars above, and a cooling breeze from the western desert making the lamp dance.

They were not entirely alone—two houses away, a family ate on their roof, laughing and singing. On the roof of the house across the street, behind a screen of potted vines, someone was practicing on a harp. Unlike the house below, Meryt's roof was tidy and clean, smelling of fresh air and the container garden of cooking herbs that lined the edge in clay pots. In one corner, the sleeping linens from two nights ago lay neatly folded.

"Sit," Nakht breathed into her ear, taking the figs from her. He tugged at her elbow as he seated himself on the warm roof, now giving back some of the heat it had absorbed through the long day. He pried off the top of the wine jar and held it out to her. "Sit, before you fall down."

Slowly, she folded her legs and came to rest next to him, their thighs and shoulders touching. She accepted the jar and drank deep of the sweet, dark wine. Worth four jars of beer, she thought absently.

Nakht reached over and lifted the heavy wig from her head. He stroked a hand down her hair, let it linger on the nape of her neck. His fingers worked at the clasp of the broad collar, loosened it, lifted it away and set it aside. He rubbed her tight shoulders and neck.

"You are knotted like a rope here," he said, moving around to sit behind her. His fingers gently massaged her neck and shoulder. Meryt shivered as his fingers worked. She set down the wine jar and broke the loaf. The smell of fresh baked bread rose to her nostrils. She tore off a hand-sized piece and passed it over her shoulder, felt him take it from her.

This moment was both intimate and familiar, as if in another life they had done this a hundred times, shared an evening meal and this contented quiet between them. But as his hands worked their way from her neck to her shoulders and then her upper back, as she relaxed and breathed more deeply, she felt something deep and warm rising to the surface. She lifted her hands, placed them over his.

For a long, quiet moment, they sat that way, her back to him, his hands on the bare skin of her upper arms. She felt both at peace and thrumming with tension like a plucked bowstring. Under her hands, his fingers spread, trapped hers, wound their hands together. She heard him catch his breath, felt him lean forward, and then felt his mouth at the back of her neck, the way he had kissed her that first day.

She shivered, and held her breath, and then, as inevitably as sunlight, his hands slipped down to circle her waist, to pull her back against his chest, until he had buried his face in her shoulder. He said nothing but she could feel him trembling. He seemed to be waiting for something.

He's waiting for me, she finally realized. She did not know what to say, caught between desire and fear, between her overwhelming concern for her father and the dizzy feeling in her heart. *What to say? When I can't even say it to myself?*

He already knows, her heart told her.

Slowly she turned, shifting her weight until she lay half in his arms (strong arms, as she had known from the first day he held her, in the market). She looked up and found him looking down on her, his gaze open, questioning. Meryt lifted her hand to cup his jaw (feeling light stubble there), to run her finger across his cheekbone, up around his ear, and finally to pull him down to her mouth.

Soft, hungry, feather-light. This was not the devouring, ravenous kiss he had shared after the birthing, or the delicate comfort of the shared kiss after working on Djeti's skull. This was something more intimate, new and scary and exciting. She leaned up into him, felt his breath catch, felt his arms tighten. She caught his face between her hands, opened her mouth for him, felt him taste her. Felt his delight and his need and his wonder.

Twisting further, she pressed up against him, heard the half-moan at the back of his throat. His hands held her firmly at her waist, his thumbs rubbing against her linen dress. She reached up to the knot of her dress, tugged. Shrugging, she let it fall, baring herself to his touch. The heavy pectoral on his chest pressed into her breast and she shifted. Without breaking the kiss, he reached up, curled fingers around the jewel, and jerked it so hard the chain broke. He tossed it over his shoulder and it fell with a clink. Against his mouth, Meryt smiled and felt him smile back.

He broke the kiss, looking down at her breasts pressed against his chest. "Soft, so soft," he whispered. One hand released her, came up to cup one soft weight. "A feast, a treasure, beloved." His thumb stroked across one nipple, sending delightful ripples throughout her torso.

Beloved. He'd said it again. Meryt felt her cheek grow hot, tipped her forehead against his chest. "Beloved," she whispered.

"Yes," he said, and lifted her chin. "Can you doubt it, Meryt? Do you not feel it, between us? Can you not feel that we are meant to be together? That we are so right together?"

Yes, she could feel it. But she could not say it, could not trust her feelings. "It's … confusing," she whispered.

"Then let me make it clear," he said, amusement in his voice. And then he was kissing her deep and hot and wet, bending her backward until she lay on the warm surface of the roof. His hands skimmed down her, shoving at her dress until it slipped down to her ankles. She kicked it off and was naked under him, under the stars, hidden from distant eyes by night and his big, broad body above her. His shoulders blocked the moon, his hair fell forward against her face. Then he was kissing his way down her neck, to the valley between her breasts. He measured the distance from nipple to peaked nipple in kisses, moaning as his lips grazed her delicate skin. "Meryt, so beautiful..."

Meryt felt like she had when, as a child, she had ridden on a neighbor's rope swing, soaring up towards the sky before swooping down again. Breathless, she giggled when Nakht kissed his way down to her navel with hot, open-mouthed kisses, his tongue trailing a wet line. Her fingers roamed over muscle and skin, feeling now the tickle of chest hair against her fingers, then the smooth curve of bicep, the flex of muscle and sinew in shoulder, forearm, chiseled abs. Meryt found his leather belt, pushed at it in frustration. Her breath came short; heat washed over her skin where his mouth touched her, where his fingers touched her.

Then he drew away, unwound his kilt, cast it aside, and the moonlight showed him to her: hard and smooth and muscled, skin of copper and gold and amber, shoulders carved in marble like the god-statues in the temples. Her gaze traveled slowly down his body, widening when it dropped below his waist and saw what waited for her there, proud and demanding.

She caught his look: open, vulnerable, a little shy. "Say the word, lady," he murmured, his voice like warm honey in the darkness. "Say the word, and I am yours."

What word? She felt her face go hot, then cool. Then a great certitude settled on her, and something in her said yes, and she answered him with one word: "Beloved."

His hands slid to her hips, lifted her, opened her, and found her ready for him, as she had been from the day they met. And when he joined them in one long thrust, when they both gasped, when they moved as one in a slow, sensual rhythm, he matched her every move, every breath. Until finally there was nothing but the stars above and the two bodies below, tangled and moving, seeking closer and closer union.

Meryt, feeling half-drunk, eyes closed, gave herself over to the heat of him, the weight of him, the feel of their joining, and the rising spiral of tension in her center. She felt herself opening to him in every way, felt his breath on her neck and heard her name in his mouth. Then she was quivering under him, in a soft explosion that sang outward from her center. She gasped, trembled, and then felt him shuddering his own release into her. Gradually he slumped onto her, warm and heavy. His fingers caught hers, intertwining them.

"Where has all the air gone?" he murmured after a moment. "I cannot catch my breath!"

She laughed softly and stroked his hair, feeling their bodies cooling. He shifted, easing from her, rolling to one side. He let his gaze wander over her body, taking in every curve, every detail, until Meryt felt a hot blush flooding her body. "You have seen women before," she said.

"Not one so beautiful," he said.

"Flatterer," she said. To cover her confusion, she reached for the basket of figs.

He caught her hand, drew her hand to his mouth, and plucked the fig from her fingers with his teeth, eating it in one gulp. He slowly licked her fingers. "I have not seen another woman so sweet, so brave," he said. There was no laughter in his look now, no overt sensuality. He threaded his fingers through hers and squeezed. "Meryt, we must be together. You know it. If your heart does not know it, if your *ka* does not know it, your body knows it. It has just told me how much you love me."

Meryt felt her breath leave her in an astonished rush. "L-love?"

"Can you not feel it? Please tell me I am not alone in feeling this," he said. He pressed her fingers against his lips. "Meryt, be my lover. Be my wife. Say we will live together all our days, and enter the afterlife together. Say you will bear our children and laugh with me and argue with me and stamp your foot when you get angry, and always, always be my lion, my dove, my beloved—"

This time her mouth stopped his, and she felt him laugh against her lips before he returned her kiss, first sweetly, then with growing passion. Then he pulled away, took her face in his hands, and said, "Is that yes? You will be my wife?"

Wife. She'd never thought to carry that title again, never thought she would want it. *You will never have to leave the village, never have to go wandering with Father,* a little voice inside her said. But mostly she heard *love love love* in her head, so she nodded and put her head against Nakht's chest. "Yes," she said, so quietly she didn't think he could hear her.

But he had. He wound long arms around her, and she heard his heart beating wildly against her ear, and she closed her eyes. "Wife," he said, turning the word over in his mouth. "Wife. Lover." He kissed her hair. "I will make you glad, little dove. You will never be sorry."

Memory dredged up something she had read, a long time ago, when she was a young girl with dreams of romance, dreams she thought long dead until one day in the market when a dark-haired soldier had plucked her from the path of a bull:

"I seek your love by day and night,
In the hours when I sleep
And when I wake at dawn;
When the sun rises and when it sinks.
No one else is in balance with your heart
Except me alone."

He smiled, and brushed a kiss into her hair, and took up the poem:

"Would that I had a morning of seeing her,
Like one who spends her lifetime doing this.
I would make festival to the god
Who stops her from straying away."

A festival to the god, Meryt thought. She rubbed her head against Nakht's shoulder, felt his arm tighten, and then felt a shiver go over him. "You're cold," she said. The night air had grown cool. "We can go downstairs. Or perhaps you ... you must go home?"

He shook his head. "No. I never want to leave you again. And it is clean and cool here on the roof. Have you any sleeping mats?"

Meryt scrambled up, heedless of her naked state. Two steps, and her arms were filled with the folded linens kept stored for sleeping on the roof. She turned and found Nakht, equally naked and equally heedless, stretched out on his back, arms behind his head, looking at the stars. Giggling, she dumped an armful of linens on him and laughed as he fought his way out of them.

One long arm shot out to catch her, drag her down to his chest, and then he was drugging her senseless with long, slow kisses. As he rolled, bringing her on top of him, she found the fire lighting inside her again, found it kindling in his eyes as his hands slid possessively down her body. As the last of her words left her, her only thought was the memory of their words, from what seemed like ages ago, but was only a few days:

You fondled me.

I did. I would like to do it again.

So she let him.

Chapter 11 – Sorcery and Murder

17th Day of the Inundation
Year 7 of the Pharaoh Khufu

Sometime before dawn, Meryt woke, shivering. A long, sinewy arm snaked around her waist, drawing her backwards against a wide chest, long legs. A deep voice growled in her ear. "Good morning."

Memory returned—wild, passionate sex, the two of them coiled around one another, hot and panting. Meryt felt her cheek warm—had she really…and while he was… and had he really—

"Um. Good morning," she said shyly.

Nakht nuzzled the back of her neck, his breath warm on her skin. A large hand slid up to cup her breast. "My sweet dove," he murmured.

She shivered. "Your cold dove," she said. "You've stolen all the covers."

He chuckled, unwrapping the cocoon of sheets and blankets that had wound themselves around him in the night. He flung them over her, pulling her against him at the same time. He was naked, and his skin was hot.

"You feel good," he said. "I want to touch you. Here." His fingers traced a circle around the aureole of her breast, squeezed her nipple gently, then flowed downward, slowly. "And here." Further down, past her belly which fluttered under his touch. "And here." His fingers slipped lower, lower yet, and then Meryt gasped as they slid between her thighs.

"Nakht!"

"Hush," he whispered. His fingers teased, tickled, as his other hand pressed her back, hard against his erection.

Meryt quivered, awash in sensation. He had been powerful, passionate in the night; now he was tender, teasing, gentle. There were so many sides to this man. His fingers slipped lower, and she tensed with surprise.

He chuckled again. "Don't worry, I am a physician."

She snorted. He kissed her neck, and his tongue danced over her shoulder and his fingers danced in her and Meryt arched, gasping. His hips rocked against her, in a rhythm she was beginning to know.

"Open for me," he whispered. Nakht's hand slipped under her thigh, raising it, and then he was sliding home hard and strong. Meryt moaned blissfully as he filled her, and his fingers stroked harder. "My dove," he whispered. "My lioness."

"Yes," she gasped, and "Oh!" and then he shifted and his angle changed and all her words left her in a delirious rippling spiral. Moments later he convulsed against her, driving hard and deep, until his breath burst from him against her neck and she felt him shudder through his own climax. He held her close, breathing hard against her back, before releasing her slowly.

"Beloved," he murmured. "You are almost the perfect woman."

Meryt turned in his embrace. "Almost?"

His smile was lazy, teasing. She smoothed a hand along his stubbled cheek. "If you were to get up and make me breakfast, now..." he said.

She laughed, and kissed him. Her heart felt as light as the feather of Ma'at, goddess of truth. Would she ever get used to feeling like this: loved and treasured, desired and cherished? She didn't know, but she hoped she never did. She wound her arms around his neck, pressing close—

Someone pounded on the door of her house so loudly she heard it even on the roof. "Open up!" a harsh male voice called.

"What in the name of Set?" Nakht struggled to his feet, running a hand over his tousled hair. "Is there no peace in all of the Two Lands for us?"

But Meryt jumped to her feet, heart pounding. "My father—"

Nakht met her eyes, and she read his own fear there. His mouth moved, but he said nothing.

And really, she thought, what could he say? If Djeti had died in the night, when she was not with him, would she ever

212 ☥

forgive herself? No words of Nakht's would make it right. Her good mood vanished in a welter of self-recrimination as she clutched her discarded gown to herself and dashed downstairs.

She tied the gown onto one shoulder and left the other bare as she yanked on the bar, then swung the door wide. She gasped as her worst fear was made manifest: several armed men stood scowling at her.

"Is Nakht, son of Ra-Khuf, here?" said the leader.

"I am here," Nakht said behind her. She turned, to find him standing with his feet apart and his head held high. His kilt was askew and his hair needed a comb, but there was strength and dignity in his stance. "Who are you?"

The leader, dressed in the blue and white livery of the royal house, stepped forward. "Where is the body of the physician, Djeti?"

"Body?" Meryt cried out and clapped her hands to her mouth. Her father, dead? "When?" she choked out.

The guard looked down at her out of obsidian eyes. "You are his daughter?"

"I am. Did he … when did he …"

"Your father's body was stolen from the Temple in the early hours of this morning," the guard said. "Three masked, armed men entered the Temple and stole it."

Nakht stepped up beside Meryt; his hand brushed against hers. "He was recovering when we last saw him in the Temple. How did he come to die?"

A familiar figure pushed through the guards. Henet-kha looked as if he had not slept in a week, and his once-white tunic was sweat stained and dirty. He glared at Nakht. "He must be dead; why else would you steal his body away, unless it was to conceal your sorcery? You will come with us, by order of the Royal Vizier."

Meryt swayed. "N-not dead? But how…why…I don't understand." Nakht's hand on her shoulder steadied her.

"You fool!" Nakht snarled at Henet-kha. He put an arm around Meryt, supporting her. "You torment her deliberately!"

Henet-kha squeaked and stepped back behind the guards.

The captain glared down at him. "You said the physician was dead! Is he not?" The captain's voice held a menacing note, and Henet-kha shrank back.

"He might as well be dead," the little priest hissed. "Without the attendance of the great physician, Minhotep, he is sure to die!" He raised a narrow hand and pointed at Nakht. "And it will be all his fault! And now he has blasphemed against the gods! He has used sorcery to steal the physician's body away!"

Meryt felt the room reel around her. She would have fallen had not Nakht steadied her with an arm around her shoulders. "This is madness," he snapped. "My lady here is faint with shock, and you prattle nonsense. Captain, do your orders encompass both of us, or only myself?"

The captain, casting a withering glance at the priest, said, "Only yourself. I am commanded to arrest you and bring you before the Royal Vizier tomorrow. He has already sent for the Chief Royal Physician, as well as your overseer and the others involved."

"I am involved," Meryt said. She forced herself to stand erect. "He is not only my father, he is my patient. If Nakht is sent for, I must come as well."

Nakht turned to her. "No, Meryt, you must not—"

The captain shrugged. "I will not take you, but you may follow if you wish. Nakht, you will come with us now."

"May we not send for her sister? Meryt has had a shock, and has not eaten today," Nakht said.

"No need for that," cried a familiar voice, and Sheri pushed her way past the soldiers. "Leave her to me." She put an arm around Meryt's shoulders. Looking up at Nakht with a serious expression. "Your brother sends his regards."

Nakht cocked his head, puzzled, but said nothing. Henet-kha, emboldened, nudged the captain of the guards.

"Are you not going to bind him?"

The captain, annoyed, snapped, "I do not need you to tell me my business, priest." He jerked his head at Nakht.

Nakht whirled to face Meryt. "Do *not* follow. I will talk to Hemiunu, and then we will find your father."

Sheri, leaning in, said in a low voice, "She will not have far to look." With this cryptic comment, she stood back and said loudly. "I am taking my friend to my house to rest."

Nakht took Meryt's face between his hands and kissed her fiercely. "My lioness," he whispered, and then he turned to press through the crowd of guards at the door. In passing, his foot somehow came down on Henet-kha's instep, and the little priest squawked.

The captain bellowed a command, accompanied it with a blast from his whistle, and the company fell into place around Nakht. Head held high, he marched away in the center of the formation, not looking back.

"It is my duty to search this house," Henet-kha said primly. Without waiting for an answer, he swept past them into the main room, where Meryt heard a lamp break.

Meryt sagged against her friend. The world was surely collapsing around her. "Father...." she whispered. "Nakht."

Sheri hugged her and drew her back into the antechamber, away from prying eyes. "Fear not," she whispered in Meryt's ear. "Your father is safe, and nearby."

Meryt straightened, blinking. "What? I don't understand."

Sheri closed the door of the house, to the disappointment of Meryt's very interested neighbors. "You must pack a medical basket quickly, and change your clothes. We do not have much time. I don't know if I am being watched, but we have to move quickly." She gave Meryt a little push. "And while you are packing, you can tell me just exactly how it comes to be that Nakht is at your house this early in the morning."

⚲

Henet-kha threw a clay cup against the painted wall of the main chamber of Meryt's house.

"Stop that!" she cried hotly. "Does the Royal Vizier say you may destroy my things?"

"They are doubtless all cursed," he sneered. He pushed his face close to hers. "What have you done with your father's body?"

Her anger turned from hot to cold in an eyeblink. "Get out of my house."

Henet-kha turned away and lifted the mat on which Djeti had laid. "Did you hide spells under here, to bewitch his *ka*?"

"No, and you have no right—"

Cold water splashed over Henet-kha, and Meryt jumped back. The stench of urine filled the house.

"What—"

Sheri tossed the piss-bucket into the corner. "Get out," she said, and Meryt had never heard such anger in her gentle friend's voice. "Get out or I will take a knife to what little manhood you have."

Henet-kha sputtered. "I will have you cursed for this! Minhotep—"

Meryt and Sheri both stepped towards him, and the little priest slunk back. Cursing under his breath, Henet-kha slunk past Meryt and Sheri, then left the house. Sheri barred the door behind him.

"Come," she said. "There is no time to lose. We must let everyone think you are going to my house."

Dazed, Meryt allowed Sheri to push her down the corridor into the kitchen area, to the bathing area under the stairs. She stood shivering while her friend untied her dress.

"Here," Sheri said, prodding her into the tiled bathing area. "Rinse off and I'll find you something clean to wear. Then you must pack your basket and we must leave. Only don't use your medical basket." She turned to the kitchen, scanning the shelves. "Here, let's use this bread basket. I'll put this half-loaf on top, so no one will know what you're carrying."

Meryt dashed cold water over herself, wrung out her hair swiftly. "What has happened to my father? What's going on?"

"We rescued him," Sheri said with a distinct note of self-satisfaction.

"'We'? And what do you mean, 'rescued'?"

Sheri picked up some grapes and added them to the basket. "I won't tell you another thing until you are dressed and we are out of this house. Move now!" She ducked into the corridor.

By the time Meryt had toweled off and stepped into her own room, Sheri was ankle-deep in the contents of Meryt's clothes chest and baskets. "This is pitiful," Sheri said. She shook her head. "When this is over, we are going to have a serious conversation about your wardrobe. Really, Meryt, this yellow gown—"

Meryt grabbed her friend's arm. "Tell me what has happened to my father!"

"Ow! You'll leave a bruise! Oh, very well. Put this gown on and I'll tell you." Sheri bent close and lowered her voice. "It was Baki's idea, of all things. Walking back from the Western House, he said that if Hemiunu would not help, we should help ourselves. You told us, you told everyone, that Djeti was in danger as long as he was in the hands of the Temple priests—"

"Yes, yes," Meryt said, slipping the dress over her head. "I know all that. What did Baki do?"

Sheri let a little smile of admiration play over her lips. "He is cleverer than I thought. He found two of your patients to help him, and they sneaked in last night and stole your father out of the temple. They have hidden him in the house of another one of your patients."

Meryt stared. "What? Which patient?"

"Baki went to Sinuhe, the husband of Shoshan, and reminded him that if it weren't for you, his wife and son would be dead. Sinuhe was not happy with the plan, but he agreed. So Baki and his friends carried your father to Sinuhe's house."

"And my father? Did he wake? Does he have fever?"

"He appears to be as he was in the temple, but there is no one to tend to him. You must come quickly with your medical supplies."

Overjoyed, Meryt dashed across the corridor to the workroom and plowed through her supplies at top speed. She threw bandages, ointments, and her father's surgical instrument roll into the basket Sheri held out. Sheri threw on a linen cloth, slapped the half-loaf and the grapes on top, and nodded at her friend. "I hope you are not angry with us?" she said anxiously.

Meryt shook her head. "I don't know whether to laugh, cry, scream or knock you on the head. It will depend on how Djeti is when I find him. Let's go."

Together, the two women hurried down the street. The smells of cooking, the cries of washermen, the song of a woman grinding grain in a nearby house, all whirled around Meryt as she followed Sheri through the town to the street where Sinuhe's house stood. As they approached, Sheri leaned close. "The mother-in-law has given out that Shoshan needs your care, some complication from the birth. In case anyone asks."

Meryt glanced around nervously. Was that old woman in the corner watching her a little too closely? Who was peering out of that half-screened doorway? But even as she took note of her surroundings, she felt something inside her turn hot and strong. She had felt helpless ever since the guard had taken Nakht away, as if she were stuck in Nile mud. Now things were moving again, maybe in her direction. She followed Sheri into the house.

It was dark and hot in the antechamber, and Meryt stopped to let her eyes adjust. "Come!" Sheri hissed, and pulled at her hand. Meryt stepped blindly across the threshold of the main room, sited exactly as her own; on the brick dais a still form lay under a linen sheet.

"Father!"

Meryt dropped to her knees, grateful to see the linen sheet rise and fall over his chest. She laid her fingers on his wrist and counted the beats—the number was normal. Her father's chin showed a light stubble, and his skin looked healthy. She pulled the sheet aside and carefully examined him. The splints on his leg and arm had been replaced, but whoever had done them had done a serviceable job. Finally, she pressed gently on the bandages on Djeti's head, holding her breath. No red stain seeped through. Tears gathered at the corners of Meryt's eyes and she bent her head, fighting a sob of relief.

"Meryt?" Sheri touched her arm anxiously. "He is worse?"

Meryt clutched her friend's hand. "He is well, as well as can be expected," she said, and put her forehead against Sheri's hand. "Thank you!"

"Oh, you should be thanking Baki! He did all the work."

A noise behind her, and then Baki was kneeling on Meryt's

other side, an anxious look on his face. "Did we hurt him? We carried him in a linen sheet, as carefully as a basket of eggs."

Some corner of Meryt's mind noted how Baki had his brother's chin and shoulders, and remembered the night just past. Then she put those thoughts aside and smiled. "You did well," she said. "Thank you. You took a great risk, you and your friends."

"We were glad to do it," a familiar voice said, and Meryt turned. Ib, the young worker, knelt on the other side of the room, next to the chisel-sharpener, Nerekh, whose white linen bandage showed stark against his sun-bronzed skin.

"We both owed you, Mistress," Nerekh said.

Meryt felt warmth gather in her center. "Ib, Nerekh! I can never thank you enough!" She bowed from her sitting position. "The house of Djeti is in your debt. You have risked the wrath of the priests to save my father."

Ib blushed, and Nerekh cleared his throat. "Nothing to it, really," the older man said. "Ib and I just put a couple of sacks on our heads, with holes cut for the eyes, and followed Baki where he led us."

"Nakht and I once sneaked our company cook out of a, well, a place he shouldn't have been, using the same tactic," Baki said. "Only Cook was drunk, not injured. I hope you're not angry."

Meryt thought of the incense·choking the air of the Temple, of the unspeakable concoctions Minhotep may have forced on her helpless father. She leaned over and hugged Baki, who grunted in surprise. "Thank you! Oh, thank you!"

Baki coughed when she released him, and the twinkle in his eye definitely reminded her of his brother's. "Ah, if only Nakht could have seen that," he murmured.

Sheri snorted. "Baki! Meryt isn't going to hug you again. You might as well fetch her something to eat."

As she rose, Ib and Nerekh rose with her, shuffling and murmuring. Ib nodded to Meryt. "If you need anything for him…"

Meryt rose, took his hands in hers. "Thank you. I can care for him. You two should get to work before you are fined for being late."

"Not that we'd mind," Nerekh said stoutly. "We still owe you for your kindness." Nodding at Baki, he led Ib out of the house.

Meryt turned to unpack her medical basket. "Meryt?" a low voice called.

"Father!"

Meryt sprang to her father's side. Djeti's eyes were open, blinking. He coughed, raising a hand to his face. He felt the bandages on his head and looked puzzled. "What is this? Where am I?"

"Father! Do you know me? How do you feel?" Meryt took his wrist, feeling for the heartbeat. It was strong.

Djeti blinked again, but when he focused on Meryt his gaze was clear, sober. "Know you? Of course I know my daughter Meryt. What has happened? Why am I here?" He started to rise, winced, fell back.

"My arm? My leg? They hurt."

"Does your head hurt? Do you feel hot?"

A small smile crossed her father's worn face. "Now, is that any way to question a patient? I taught you better than that."

Almost weeping with relief, Meryt knelt beside her father and put her forehead on the dais. "Father, I cannot tell you how worried we have all been. It has been five days since you fell."

"Days? What happened to me?"

"One moment, Father," Meryt answered. She fought back tears and giddy laughter. Father is alive, and awake! All will be well now! "Sheri!" she called.

Her friend popped into the room from the antechamber, where she had been barring the door. "Meryt? You—oh!" Her hands flew up to cover her mouth as she met Djeti's gaze. "Sir! You're awake! How—"

"Can you fetch some water for my father?"

"Yes! Oh, yes, at once!" Sheri fairly flew from the room.

Djeti turned his head, sniffing. "Is that hippopotamus dung I smell? Meryt, you know better."

"It was not my idea, Father," she said. She settled comfortably beside him, reassured at the sound of his voice. Quietly, she explained his fall, his injuries and his long sleep. When she came to his convulsions, his eyes narrowed.

"Unequal pupils, you say? The eye of the eye distorted?" Djeti closed his eyes. "That is very bad. I see that you had reason to worry. I recall none of this. I do not even remember falling." His hand again felt his head bandages. "I can hardly believe that a mere bruise warrants all these bandages."

Meryt cleared her throat. Slowly, she described the procedure where Nakht had drilled a hole in her father's skull. He listened closely, eyes on her face. Afterwards, there was a long silence, and he lay back with closed eyes.

"Remarkable," he said quietly. "I have never heard of such a thing."

"Oh, Father, do not think I gave consent lightly," Meryt said anxiously. "I was so afraid, and I did not know what to do."

"You made a hard decision, daughter," Djeti said. "It is a risk, a terrible, terrible risk, to open the skull. I have never heard of it being done. What we know about the skull and the brain inside it, we only know from wounds that have already opened it, or from the methods of the embalmers in the House of Beautification." He opened his eyes. "I would like to meet this Nakht."

Meryt felt her cheeks warm. "He is accused of sacrilege, for doing this thing."

A sardonic smile flitted across the old man's face. "No doubt. And it will be even worse for him, when I live. Did I hear you correctly, that Minhotep is mixed up in this?"

"Yes, but not by my will."

He sighed deeply, and Meryt noticed the lines etched deeply in her father's face.

"Bar the door against him. His mother was a jackal. No, that is an insult to jackals."

Meryt smiled. "Don't worry about him now. Rest, while I bring you some food. Do you think you could eat some bread soaked in broth?"

"I could eat raw crocodile, my dear." Djeti closed his eyes.

Meryt went out to the kitchen area, grateful that Pharaoh's builders had made all the village houses to the same floor plan.

Sheri was stoking the fire in the clay stove.

"Sinuhe's family has rigged up the canopy on the roof and are spending the day up there, to give us the house," Sheri said. As she spoke, Meryt heard a baby squall and heard the hum of quiet conversation. "Shoshan left us some soup and bread." She handed Meryt a clay bowl.

As Meryt broke bread into small pieces and put them in the broth, she said, "Someone should tell Nofret what has happened. She will be in a panic, thinking our father is dead or missing."

Sheri's expression hardened. "She reported you and Nakht to the priests."

Meryt sprinkled a little salt into the broth. "I know. But she was frightened. When she sees our father awake, perhaps she will change her mind about Nakht."

Sheri met her eyes. "I will go. But if she is still angry with you, I will not tell her your father is here."

Meryt nodded unhappily. The last thing she needed was for Nofret to betray her again.

Back by her father's side, she offered the bowl of cooling soup. Djeti opened his eyes. She held the bowl to his lips. "This is good soup. Did Nofret make it?"

"The mistress of this house made it," Meryt said. She explained how he came to be in a stranger's house.

"Where is Nofret now? How is the baby?"

Not wanting to bother him with the true state of affairs, Meryt shrugged. "She's at home. Don't forget to eat the bread."

Slowly, Djeti finished the bowl and laid his head down again. "Promise me you will write down the order of that procedure this Nakht did on me," he said drowsily.

When he slept, Meryt took the bowl back to the kitchen and rinsed it. Suddenly her knees buckled and she slid to the ground bonelessly, weeping with relief. Her father was alive, and speaking. Nakht's procedure had worked.

Surely everything would be all right now. Surely it would.

☥

Djeti slept soundly, and Meryt dozed by his side, holding

his hand in hers. She heard hushed voices in the kitchen, the clack of clay bowls being stacked, smelled onions and rabbit being stewed. Then the sounds retreated to the roof again and left her to her peaceful drowse. A fly buzzed languidly in the rising heat, and the sunbeams slanting through the high, narrow windows climbed the wall.

Sinuhe had had his main room painted with a scene of duck hunting, and Meryt lost herself in a daydream about poling through the papyrus reeds with Nakht, perhaps with a basket of fruit and bread for lunch, maybe a jug wine tied to a rope in the water to cool it…

The front door flew open, and as Meryt came to her feet Nofret burst into the room, eyes streaming with tears. "Father!"

Meryt caught her sister before she could throw herself onto their father's body. "Careful! He is still very weak!"

Nofret hovered over her father, tears streaking her face. "Father?" she said in a trembling voice.

Djeti's eyes fluttered open. "Nofret?"

"Oh, Father!" Nofret bowed her head, letting tears flow freely. "It's so good to hear your voice!" She laid one hand gingerly on her father's splinted arm.

Djeti patted her hand. "Dry your tears, child. I am feeling much better." He darted a glance at Meryt. "Your sister and her friend, this new physician, have worked a wonder for me."

Sheri entered the room, with Baki close behind her.

Nofret raised tear-filled eyes to Meryt. "Oh, Sister, how can you ever forgive me? I should have trusted you. I am so sorry. Now Nakht is arrested, and it is all my fault!"

Djeti blinked. "Arrested?"

Meryt put her arms around Nofret's shoulders. "We don't need to go into that now. Dry your eyes, Sister, and let us see what we can do to make our father comfortable."

Nofret flung her arms around Meryt, squeezing tightly. "Yes! Oh, we must move him back home, and let him rest in his own place!"

Baki knelt beside the sisters. "That would not be wise," he warned. "The priests are watching your house."

"That Minhotep had better not lay a hand on me!" Djeti snapped. "Put a knife in my hand, or even a stone to cast, and I will make him regret 'treating' me with his foul concoctions!" Belying his fierce words, his head fell back on the pillow. "I need to sleep now. Nofret, if you would, could you make me some of that beef stew your mother used to make? The kind with garlic and leeks?"

Dashing tears from her smeared face, Nofret nodded. "Oh, yes! I will go home and make some right now! Oh, it is so good to hear you, to see you—" She looked ready to burst into another storm of weeping, so Meryt helped her to her feet.

"Walk, don't run, on your way home," she cautioned her sister, as she led Nofret to the door. "Don't let anyone suspect Djeti is here. No one will question if you are crying, under the circumstances, but if you look joyful, people might begin to wonder."

Nofret nodded, rubbing her hands on her swollen belly. "Yes," she said. She glanced back into the main room and leaned close to Meryt. "Soldiers came to the house this morning, looking for Father. They searched *my* house!" she hissed. "They suspected me of hiding Father, and that awful Henet-kha hinted that he was dead! I didn't know what to do, until Sheri came to us." She scowled. "I would not give those priests my own name, now!"

Sheri came in, carrying an empty basket. "I will go with Nofret, and then come back alone with the stew. It might look suspicious if she were seen coming and going frequently from this house."

"Oh, I must go home immediately!" Nofret said. She darted out, followed by Sheri, who paused on the threshold to exchange speaking looks with both Baki and Meryt.

Meryt returned to the main room, to find her father asleep, breathing normally. Baki stood uncertainly, looking down. "He looks the same," he said.

Meryt collected some stray bits of gauze, an overturned water cup. "Believe me, he is much better," she said in a low voice. "How … how is your brother? Have you seen him?"

His voice low and angry, Baki said, "They have tied him

up in a room in the guardhouse at the Gate of the Crow. They would not let me in to see him, but one of my men is on the guard detail. I sent word to Nakht that I and five of my men were prepared to rush the guards and free him, but the fool refused!" He kicked at a stray bandage.

Meryt's heart ached to think of Nakht tied up, alone, perhaps afraid. She swallowed. "He is right, though," she said. "If you freed him, where would he go? No one would believe in his innocence if he ran away."

"But they have set the trial for tomorrow morning!" Baki snarled. Meryt could see sweat on the young man's brow. "If they find him guilty, it is a death sentence!"

Meryt's heart turned over. A death sentence! She pressed her hand to her stomach, which fluttered. "No," she whispered.

"We must free him," Baki said. "We cannot risk Minhotep winning his case."

Meryt clutched at his arm. "There may be another way. If my father were to meet with the Vizier, so that Hemiunu could see that he is alive, that he is well—"

Baki shook his head. "I thought of that, but how to get him there? Henet-kha's spies are everywhere. And Minhotep has been making threats against your family; he has friends among the guards. It was one thing to sneak your father through the night, with three men to carry him. It's something else to carry him in broad daylight, when the priests may seize him as soon as they see him. And if there were a fight? What if Minhotep's men slew him, to prevent him from speaking?"

Meryt's jaw dropped in shock. "Would they do that?"

Baki's expression was grim. "Minhotep is a proud man. It was one thing for Nakht to dare some new treatment. I don't know anything about that. But when we took your father out from under his nose, he became a laughingstock. Or he thinks he did. Either way, if I know men, he is angry enough to kill your father and make it look like Nakht's work, or hired work."

"It was just a simple rivalry," Meryt said, stunned. "Now Minhotep wants his life? You are right, Baki. We dare not reveal where he is."

Meryt stared down at her father. It was almost like a story from a Temple wall, she thought. Risk her father's life? Or see her lover executed on false charges? She closed her hands into fists at her sides.

Don't make me choose, she prayed. *Because there are no good choices here.*

☥

The long summer evening gave way to dusk before Djeti woke again. Meryt heard him stir, and was beside him instantly. "Father!"

His eyes opened, and her father smiled. "Daughter." He patted her hand; Meryt noticed that it shook slightly. "Water?"

She held the cup for her father to drink, then fetched bread and broth. As she sopped the bread in the warm broth, Djeti scowled. "I am not a child," he said peevishly. "And there is nothing wrong with my teeth. Bring me meat."

"You told me once that physicians make the worst patients," she said, smiling. "I find that, as usual, you are entirely correct."

"Hah. Such impertinence!" he said, but there was a smile in his eyes. "Well, if I cannot have meat, can I have some of your willow beer, at least? My leg hurts."

In the kitchen, Sinuhe's housekeeper loaded a platter with figs, fish cakes fried in oil, sliced cucumbers and leeks. "My mistress says you are to have whatever you need," she said. "For the honor of the house, and the life of her child."

"I only did my duty," Meryt said, touched by the gratitude of her patient. From a room built on to the back of the house, she heard a baby cry, and then a crooning lullaby.

Djeti's eyes lit up at sight of the food, but he was still too weak to sit up on his own. Meryt helped him to a sitting position and propped cushions behind him. Djeti's hand tremor increased when he tried to lift the soup bowl to his lips, so she held it for him, then handed him food bit by bit from the platter.

"I feel like a child again, being fed by your grandmother," he groused. Seeing her face, however, his look changed to concern. "Oh, do not fear, daughter. As I have taught you, when the heart receives bread again, the patient will recover. Dying men have no appetite."

Meryt blinked tears from her eyes, and turned her head to hide them. But her father put a hand over hers. "Meryt, this will take a long time, you know that."

"I know," she said, blinking away tears. "Your leg and arm are healing well. It's the head injury that worries me."

"Well, now, I think we're past the worst of that," he said comfortingly. "I have treated several head injuries in my time, and I can safely predict my own recovery." A shadow passed over his face. "However, it will take a long time. I do not know how long this hole in my head will take to heal, but I know that when a patient has been in the black sleep, sometimes they wake up with less than they started with."

Cold seeped around Meryt's heart. "What do you mean?" Her whole future depended, had always depended, on her father's ability to function as a physician. "What … what have you lost?"

He shrugged wearily. "Many things can be lost. Thanks to this leg, I have not even tried to stand; perhaps I will no longer be able to walk." He lifted a hand, examined its tremor dispassionately. His eyes, in their nests of wrinkles, squinted with professional acumen. "It may be that I will be unable to write, or measure a potion accurately. It may be that my memory is damaged. I do know this, daughter." He sighed deeply. "Men recover from head injuries, but they almost never come all the way back." He closed his eyes. "I must sleep soon."

She moved the platter aside and helped him to stretch out on the padded dais. As she did so, she rested a hand on his wrist, counting. She looked up to see her father watching her with approval.

"Well done," he said softly. He laid a had on her hair. "You have carried a heavy burden, my dear. And you have done it well. I am proud of you."

"Father…" Then her tears came in earnest, and Meryt hid her hands, as her father stroked her hair affectionately. "Tell me," he said.

She knew he was still gravely ill, that she should wait for a better time. But after days of carrying the weight of grief, fear, anger, and even love, Meryt broke down and sobbed. And as her father listened with his usual quiet patience, she told him all of it: of her fears that she would not be able to save him, of her trips to the House of Life and the Western House, of Minhotep's enmity, of Nakht and their growing love. She told him of her fear even as Nakht worked to save his life, to open his skull. She even told him of the donkey driver crisis, and heard his soft chuckle. He stopped chuckling when she told him of Nakht's arrest and impending trial.

"Oh, *why?*" she said angrily, when she could weep no more tears. "Why has this happened, Father? All this bad luck, all these crises—have we offended some powerful god? Has someone cursed the House of Djeti?"

"Hush," he said, his voice fading with age and fatigue. "Meryt, you are not a child, you are a woman. And you should know that the things that come to us, whether through luck or the will of the gods or our own choices, do not matter as much as how we meet them." His thin, trembling hand patted hers and slid away.

As she watched her father sleep, Meryt wondered how she would meet the news of Nakht's execution.

☥

Late that night, Baki returned to Sinuhe's house with news. Sheri and Meryt, who had been tending Djeti all day, met him in Sinuhe's anteroom.

"How is your father?" Baki asked. Sheri silently handed him a cup of beer and a half loaf of bread, which he tore into hungrily.

"Sleeping. He is extremely fragile, though he won't admit it," Meryt said wearily. "Have you seen Nakht?"

Folding himself into a sitting position on the floor, he leaned against the wall and sighed. "No, but I've found out where the trial is being held tomorrow. Minhotep wanted him tried across the river."

"That would be a long trip," Sheri said.

"Worse, it would mean Djeti could not make it to the trial to testify for Nakht."

"He cannot travel anyway," Meryt said anxiously. "He is

228 ☥

improving, but it will be a long time before he can travel farther than to our house, when the time comes."

Baki nodded. "I thought as much. I talked to Sobek-Amun and a couple of the other work team leaders. They also talked to Perera, the Overseer of the Left Hand Side." The workforce building the Pyramid was divided into two great forces, the Left and Right Hand Sides. The Overseers of those sides were second only to Hemiunu, the Royal Vizier. "Perera remembers your father, Meryt. He persuaded the Royal Vizier to hold the trial on this side of the Nile, on the grounds that anything else would eat up time and interfere with the work schedule."

"And Akhti-Hotep?"

Baki shook his head. "He could not be bothered to meet with me. He is deep in Minhotep's counsels, anyway. Did you know that Akhti-Hotep is married to Minhotep's cousin?"

Sheri snorted. "If she is anything like Minhotep, I almost feel sorry for Ferret-face."

Baki smiled wearily. "Nevertheless, they are a powerful family. I don't think Akhti-Hotep has anything against Nakht personally, but he won't counter his cousin-in-law." He sighed again and drained the cup of beer. Silently, Sheri took it and refilled it. Their fingers lingered on the cup when she handed it to him.

Meryt knelt beside Baki, her hands in her lap. Darkness had seeped into the corners, and the little lamp in front of Sinuhe's household shrine had gone out, leaving the three of them in shadow. "So where is the trial?"

"Minhotep claimed that if the trial could not be held over the river, it should be held in the Temple of Sekhmet," Baki growled.

"That's not usual," Sheri said, frowning. "Most trials are held in the Temple of Ptah. He's the worker's god."

"Minhotep reminded him that the kidnapping took place in the Temple, and said the trial should take place where the crime took place, and Perera agreed. 'In the interests of justice', he told me." Baki made a disgusted face.

A knock at the door: everyone tensed. Sheri opened the

door cautiously, then wider. Nes-Khonsu stepped into the room, holding a flickering oil lamp. Nebu and Ipi crowded in behind her. "We're here to help," Nes-Khonsu said.

Baki scrambled to his feet, frowning. "Who told you we were here?"

"My nephew, Nerekh, owes his arm to the daughter of Djeti and this Nakht," she said quietly. "He said you are tending your father alone?" She gestured, and the other women stepped forward holding baskets of linen bandages. "We know enough about sick men to help take care of him."

Meryt felt tears gathering at the corners of her eyes, but fought them back. She stood up straight and bowed to the other women. "My house is in your debt," she said formally.

Nes-Khonsu snorted. "Don't be absurd, girl. None of us can repay the House of Djeti for all he and you have done for us, whether Pharaoh (Life! Prosperity! Health!) paid you to do it or not. Now show us where he is."

Sheri gestured for the women to follow, but Baki laid a hand on the old woman's arm. "No one can know he is here," he said.

Nes-Khonsu patted his hand. "Don't worry, son. We can keep a secret. Come, ladies." They followed Meryt and Sheri into the main room.

Djeti came out of his doze long enough to recognize Nes-Khonsu as she bent over him with a damp cloth. "Nes? How is your daughter?"

The old woman gestured Ipi forward. "You mean the baby you delivered more than twenty years ago? Here she is, with a child of her own. Now hush and let us wash your face, and then you'll have some gruel and a good sleep." Her tone was exactly the same tone Meryt had heard grandmothers take with fussy infants all her life.

Djeti muttered something and drifted off again. Anxiously, Meryt checked his temperature and pulse. He tossed a little in his sleep, which Meryt told herself was a sign of recovery.

As the other women cleaned and cared for him, Nes-Khonsu came to Meryt and took her hands in her older ones.

"Girl, when did you last sleep?"

"Last night," Meryt said vaguely. "I caught a nap—"

"Napping is not sleeping. Here is what you're going to do," Nes-Khonsu said in her no-nonsense tone. "You are going to go to Sheri's house. You are going to eat and sleep—"

"I can't leave—"

"Yes, you can. It is important that people see you at your friend's house, not at the house of a stranger, or people will start wondering why the daughter of Djeti is spending all her time in the house of Sinuhe?"

Sheri put her arm around her friend's shoulders. "Minhotep's slimy little scribe, Henet-kha, searched our house today. My mother enjoyed it very much."

Meryt blinked. "She enjoyed it?"

"Yes," Sheri grinned. "She got to try out a few words even my little brother didn't know."

Meryt worked up a smile, but inside felt tired and discouraged. Most of all, she felt guilty about leaving her father in someone else's care. But as she watched the older women expertly arrange the sickroom, prepare food for an invalid, and adjust the window shades for a cooling breeze, she realized that what Djeti needed now was not doctoring, but nursing. And at that, these women were experts.

And Nakht needs me now, she thought to herself. She allowed herself, for the first time in hours, to think of him. Tied, helpless, maybe afraid. Did he know she was thinking of him? Did he know she loved him? She had not told him that. She had said she would be his wife, but she had spoken no words of love. Was she afraid to lay her heart at his feet, as he had laid his at hers? Had she held some part of herself back, afraid this love would not last?

But it was all different now, and her inner vision cleared. Nakht could die tomorrow, a horrible death, torn apart by crocodiles on the orders of the Royal Vizier, and would never know how she felt.

"Time to go," Sheri said, a hand on her arm. "Come. My mother has been puttering around all day, preparing for you.

She ordered up a roast duck specially from the bakery, so let's not disappoint her." She glanced over her shoulder at Baki. "You, too, if you want to come," she said, with studied carelessness.

Baki smiled, one that reminded Meryt achingly of his brother's carefree grin. "I can't wait," he said, opening the door for the women. "I want to hear these new words your mother is so proud of."

☥

The journey through the village was swift but memorable. Wherever they went, people stopped talking to stare and whisper as Meryt passed. One or two spat in the dust behind her, but Baki's glare put an end to that. Meryt could not help but notice the soldiers and scribes on every corner, or the priests who followed them from the central square to Sheri's abode.

At Sheri's house, her brother Amenkhau opened the door, staring in awe at Baki's military trappings as he entered. Out of the corner of her eye Meryt saw a priest in a torn robe slip up the street.

Sheri's home was a little larger than most, as befitted the home of a master coppersmith. From the forge in the built-on addition at the back of the house, Sheri heard the tink of a hammer on copper, but the rest of Sheri's home was cool and quiet. Her mother, Ikhtay, the mistress of the house, met them at the door.

"It's a shame, what that Minhotep is doing," Ikhtay said, her broad, pleasant face creased in an uncharacteristic frown. "You know, that man gave me an ointment for a rash when Amenkhau was a baby, and it made the rash worse! I had to wonder if the man knew what he was doing. You sit right here in the main room. You too, Baki. Sheri, fetch a washing bowl and towels for our guests!" She bustled her daughter out of the room, leaving Baki and Meryt alone in the brightly decorated main room. At the back of the house, bowls clacked and voices were raised, but here it was homely and peaceful.

Baki sighed and sat down on the edge of the brick dais against the wall. "You're worried about him," Baki said.

Meryt looked at the younger man. He looked tired and worn, despite his customary carefree air. "We both are," she said.

"You know he's in love with you."

232

"Is there anyone who does not know that?" Meryt said, half-laughing. She sat next to him, facing a wall painted with bright geometric patterns. "He was found at my house."

But Baki did not laugh. "You never knew his wife, of course. The Osiris Hemet-re. She was an extraordinary woman." He dropped his eyes, making circles on his knee with a finger. "He loved her like ... well. I didn't think he would ever love another woman. Then he came home from the market one day raving about a girl with a basket. It was you. His eyes...I hadn't seen that look in his eyes since she died. Nakht had ... hope, I think." He cleared his throat. "I'm not good at this."

"I'm not either," she said ruefully.

Baki shrugged. "All I'm trying to say is, even if, or rather when my brother is free again, if you're not with him, it won't matter to him if he's alive or dead."

Meryt glanced at the passageway, hoping Sheri was not listening in. She leaned close and lowered her voice. "Are you asking if I love your brother?"

"I suppose I am," Baki said. His eyes met hers, full of trouble, yet so like his brother's it brought a pang to Meryt's heart.

Meryt swallowed. "He asked me to be his wife," she whispered. "I said yes."

Baki's eyes lit up, and he beamed. But before he could speak, Meryt shook her head. "Not a word to Sheri. Not yet."

At that moment Ikhtay entered, carrying a wide tray of sliced cucumbers, leeks, and radishes, surrounding a dipping sauce of vinegar, honey and herbs in a blue-glazed bowl. "Here's a little something to get started," she said, setting it down between her guests. Behind her, Sheri entered with a bowl of fresh water and a towel over one arm. Summoning her good manners, Meryt made sure to wash her hands before dipping into the vegetable platter.

Ikhtay smiled broadly at Baki and Meryt. "Sheri, stay and make sure our guests have whatever they need, and I'll see to dinner." She disappeared into the passageway, whence wafted the delicious scents of baking bread, roast duck and beans cooked with cumin and onion. Meryt's mouth watered.

Sheri sat next to Baki, shoulders touching, careful not to look at him as she offered him a mug of beer. "So," she said. "How are we going to get Djeti to the Temple in the morning for the trial?"

"The priests and scribes are watching everywhere for a sick man carried through the streets."

And the idea came to Meryt then, an echo of that morning and the guard standing on her doorstep saying—

"My father is dead."

The others stared at her. Meryt leaned forward, a smile spreading across her face, and began to explain.

CHAPTER 12 - THE TRIAL

18th Day of the Inundation
Year 7 of the Pharaoh Khufu

Sheri woke Meryt well before daybreak. Meryt, curled on the spare sleeping mat, felt as though she had been running a long race over hard ground. She remembered a morning, one that seemed years in the past, when she had waked in Nakht's arms. Would she ever feel them around her again? She yawned hugely; she, Baki and Sheri had sat up very late, discussing and refining their plan for the trial today.

"Come," Sheri said. They had slept in a small bedroom off the main corridor of Sinuhe's house. Now the smell of morning beans was drifting past the dyed curtain. "We must bathe and dress quickly." She smiled, a fleeting, self-satisfied look. "Baki has finished already."

Catching her friend's look, Meryt raised an eyebrow. "You spied on him," she said. It was not a question.

"What kind of hostess would I be, not to make sure a guest had all the towels he needed?" Sheri's response was wide eyed. Then a look of mischief crossed her face. "It was well worth a look, believe me."

Despite her many worries, Meryt felt her heart lifted by her carefree friend. "You have already seen him naked," she pointed out. "At the wrestling match."

"Assuredly," Sheri said, as smug as any cat. "But now I have seen him wet, as well."

Meryt shook her head, as a maidservant came through the curtain bearing fresh linens. "We must hurry," Sheri said. "I will barely have time to get my own cosmetics on, let alone do yours."

"I do not need—"

Sheri lifted eyes and hands skyward. "Isis bless us, but we cannot go to a criminal trial looking like the accused! If we dressed up for the Western House, we must be twice as dressed up for this!"

So by the time they left for the Temple, both Meryt and Sheri had been bathed, perfumed, made up, dressed in oiled wigs and adorned in the finest linen they could lay hands on. Broad collars borrowed from Ikhaty's considerable collection lay on their shoulders, embroidered belts with tassels cinched their waists, and every finger winked with rings. Baki fairly glowed from the scrubbing he'd undergone, and his military kilt was white enough to blind the unwary.

Leaning close, he whispered, "I have already heard from Ib; everything is ready and he is with the others at Sinuhe's house. You sent a message to your father?"

Meryt nodded. "Amenkhau went last night. My father will do anything he can to help Nakht."

Baki nodded, then straightened as Sheri gestured for them to start out. The street in front of her house was narrow, and now crowded with curious on-lookers. Meryt slipped one finger between the edge of her broad collar and her neck, easing its weight a bit.

"Everyone is staring at us," she whispered to Sheri.

"So don't slouch," Sheri said. The younger woman was careful to maintain a calm expression, looking neither right nor left as they advanced up the main street of the village. Villagers, mostly women left behind when the workmen left for the day, whispered behind their hands to one another; children held on to their mothers' skirts and stared, sucking on fingers.

The day was only an hour old, but already the heat seared naked skin. Bald priests with sharp eyes noted their approach, and one ran ahead. Baki's hand tightened on his spear, but he said nothing. The crowd grew thicker as they approached the Temple; regardless of what they thought of Djeti, Nakht or Minhotep, no one was going to miss the sensation of the day if they could help it. Meryt wondered how many men had taken a "sick day" to be here.

The whitewashed mud-brick walls rose ahead of them, and the red pennons of Sekhmet snapped in the breeze from the tops of the pylons. The twin statues of the goddess seemed to glare down at the trio as they approached. The crowd parted to let them pass up the avenue that bordered the reflecting pool; in daylight, the frogs were silent. As they reached the door, two guards in red leather harnesses stood forth, spears crossed.

"Let me pass," Meryt said. "I speak for my father today." The taller man opened his mouth to speak, took in her finery, shrugged and stepped aside. She heard Baki and Sheri following her. This time the great hall was crowded with priests, officials, curious onlookers. A rectangular skylight let in a shaft of light that burned down into the shadows like the eye of Ra himself. Even before they reached the center, Meryt could see the tall peacock feather fans, the ceremonial staffs borne by bearers, and the spears of a royal honor guard. Her eye took in the robes of white linen, the bright jewels, the flash of gold. But she saw only one thing: Nakht.

He stood straight at the edge of the shaft of sunlight, wearing only a clean white kilt. His hands were bound before him; his black hair fell in a midnight waterfall to his shoulders. He turned as the party approached, and his eyes lit when he saw Meryt and then Baki. But he said nothing, only watched them draw near with hope and anxiety in his eyes. Meryt's heart leaped to see him, and then sank in fear. He looked so alone.

Beyond Nakht stood Hemiunu, the Royal Vizier. He wore a full length linen tunic cinched with a golden belt and decorated with panels of embroidery. His heavy formal wig fell to his shoulders, and black kohl highlighted his eyes. Around his neck hung a pendant of hammered gold, the image of Ma'at, the goddess of truth, her arms and wings outstretched. Made of gold inlaid with faience and precious stones, she flashed and winked in the sun, symbol of the justice of the gods. A carved stool indicating his high status sat behind the King's vizier, a reminder to all that he stood in the place of the Living Horus, the King of the Two Lands. For a moment, Meryt forgot to breathe, so overcome was she with the time and the place.

Then a disturbance off to the right drew her attention, and the Queen Mother's sedan chair was carried in.

"Don't set me down in the middle of that light! Are you trying to blind me? Back on the other side, idiots!" Queen Hetepheres grumbled at her attendants as they carefully lowered the chair. A woman in a heavy wig scrambled to place an inlaid ivory stool next to Hemiunu, signifying her equal status with her son's lieutenant. Slowly, with the help of two of her strong young bearers, the aging mother of Pharaoh climbed out of her chair and sat. Instantly another attendant took his place to the side, holding a sunshade over the royal head. A small girl brought a cup and handed it to the queen mother, then knelt quietly at her feet. Meryt saw Akhti-Hotep, an unhappy frown on his face, shift position in the shadows behind the Queen Mother.

Hemiunu turned to Queen Hetepheres with a slight frown on his face, then seemed to remember where he was and made his face a mask again. But Meryt had caught that fleeting moment of annoyance, of humanity, and she breathed again. She returned her attention to Nakht, who now looked rigidly ahead at the Vizier. He stood straight, but she saw how his shoulder slumped to one side—the side where he bore spear scars, and his fingers worked restlessly behind his back. *He is tired,* she thought. *And perhaps afraid. But he will not show it.*

Finally, after an eon, a chamberlain banged his staff on the granite pavement. Instantly, the entire assembly apart from the Vizier and the Queen Mother bowed from the waist, holding out their arms parallel to the ground. The chamberlain called out, "The Place of Two Truths, under the Living God Khnum-Khufu (Life! Prosperity! Health!) and conducted under the aspects of Amun, may he live, and Ma'at the Goddess of Truth, is established! Presiding is Prince Hemiunu, Chief Justice and Royal Vizier, Right Hand of the Living God, King's nephew of His Body, Seal-bearer of the King of Lower Egypt, Guardian of Nekhen, Mouth of Pe, Priest of Bastet, Priest of Shesemtet, Priest of the Ram of Mendes, Staff of Apis, Staff of the White Bull, Eldest of the Palace, Greatest of the Five in the House of Thoth, who loves his lord, the Sole Friend, Overseer of the Royal Scribes, Director of the Singers of Upper and Lower Egypt, Overseer of all Royal Works."

"Oh, get on with it, or we will be here all day," Queen Hetepheres muttered irritably. She drained her cup and handed it down to the child at her feet, who disappeared silently into the shadows.

The chamberlain, a short, fat man sweating under a heavy wig, flushed slightly but continued. "Greatly is the Place of Two Truths honored by the presence of the Chief Royal Wife of the Osiris Sneferu, King's Daughter of His Body, Mother of the King of Upper and Lower Egypt, Follower of Horus, Guide of the Ruler, Favored One, She Whose Every Word is Done for Her, Hetepheres."

The pain of holding the exaggerated bow was making Meryt tremble slightly. She took a deep breath and forced herself to maintain it, and so missed the introduction of the other members of the Court who would rule on Nakht's case. Since there was no fixed judiciary, a trial could be conducted by the highest ranking member of the royal family available, with a few other judges called as he saw fit. With half an ear, she caught the introduction of Akhti-Hotep, Nakht's immediate superior, and Perhipidje, the Chief Royal Physician.

She caught the swirl of white robes out of the corner of one eye, and was dismayed to see Henet-kha swishing his way up to the pavement before Hemiunu. He bowed low, intoning a truly majestic line of titles, until the Vizier waved him to silence. Others were introduced, most of whom Meryt had never seen. How were these strangers supposed to judge Nakht's case?

Finally, when it seemed she must collapse from fatigue and embarrass not only herself but Nakht as well, the chamberlain rapped his staff again, and the people around Meryt straightened. The relief was so great she nearly forgot herself with an audible sigh. A whisper of release threaded through the crowd, and now Hemiunu seated himself on the stool beside the Queen Mother.

"Who brings this case before Pharaoh (Life! Prosperity! Health!)?" he said in his deep voice.

Ponderously, Minhotep bowed before the Royal Vizier. Even from several feet away, Meryt's nose wrinkled at his heavy, overpowering scent. The Queen Mother recoiled, flapping her hand before her face, as Minhotep sonorously intoned a list of prayers, good wishes, and praise directed at the King's deputy. Hemiunu heard him out patiently, but Meryt could see the restless movement of one foot that betrayed impatience. She promised herself that if and when she was called on to speak, she would be quick and to the point.

"...And so the physician Nakht has endangered Pharaoh (Life! Prosperity! Health!), his workers, and his Pyramid. He has risked the wrath of the gods by bringing strange magic into the Two Lands, foreign ways practiced by—" Here he paused for a sneer. "Practiced by witch doctors from Punt and other barbarous lands. He has abjured the wisdom of our forefathers, who fashioned our medicines and practices in ancient times, handed down from the time of the first Osiris—"

"Are you claiming that this physician has killed his patient?" Hemiunu interrupted. "I thought Djeti-Thutmose was only unconscious. What charge are you bringing?"

Of course Hemiunu knew as well as anyone in the crowd what charges Minhotep was bringing, but the words had to be said, so that the scribes busily scratching off to one side could get it all down.

Minhotep brought himself to his full height. "Great Vizier, I charge this man with kidnapping, sorcery and murder!" Dramatically, he thrust a finger toward Nakht. Members of the Court murmured in the background, and Meryt heard Nakht's name spoken in undertones of scorn and fear. Her stomach tensed.

"I deny all of these lies, my lord," Nakht said quietly, his voice raspy. "I did not kidnap Djeti-Thutmose, nor did I kill him, nor did I bewitch him. I am a physician, not a priest, a scribe or a sorcerer."

"Blasphemer!" sneered Henet-kha, but a guard elbowed him to silence.

"These are serious charges," the Royal Vizier said. His dark gaze lit on Meryt for a moment, and she felt weighed. Would he believe the powerful and influential Minhotep, or her? "What evidence do you have?"

Minhotep struck a dramatic pose, throwing up one hand.

"Great Prince! Blessed Queen Mother of Pharaoh! On the night before last, masked men stole into the holy Temple of Sekhmet, the Golden One of Healing! Shameless in their sacrilege, they restrained the holy priest on guard and made away with the body of Djeti, which we had taken into our care after the infamous assault on him by—"

"And you have witnesses?"

Minhotep turned to Henet-Kha, but before he could speak, Baki stepped forward. "My lord!"

Hemiunu gestured for him to speak. Baki drew himself up, saluted, and spoke loudly. "I am Baki, the brother of the accused. And I was the leader of those men."

"No!" Nakht took a step forward, alarm on his face. His guards pulled him back.

Baki ignored his brother's protest. "I freely admit to rescuing Djeti-Thutmose from the evil ministrations of this crocodile." He spat the last word at Minhotep.

"Crocodile!" Minhotep gasped. Giggles rippled through the watchers, and Queen Hetepheres cackled aloud.

Meryt darted a glance at Nakht, who stood pale and solemn.

Baki detailed his kidnapping of her father, to murmurs from the crowd, gasps of outrage from Minhotep, and snorts of suppressed laughter from the Queen Mother. When he finished, he bowed low to the Vizier and spoke the formal oath of a witness. "As Ra endures, as the Great House (Life! Prosperity! Health!) lives in truth, if I am found to be lying, let my body be fed to the crocodiles and my *ka* wander the desert of the Afterlife forever."

"And who else committed this act with you?" Hemiunu demanded. "Name them."

Baki shook his head. "With respect, my lord, they but followed me. I am responsible, not them."

"That is for me to decide," Hemiunu said coldly.

Meryt was close enough to see the sweat rolling off Baki's brow, but his hands and stance were steady.

"My lord, they only wanted to rescue an injured man from a pack of fools."

"He lies!" hissed Minhotep, stamping a foot. He turned to the Vizier and nearly spat. "My lord, he lies! The body of the physician Djeti was stolen by demons, to hide the work of this man's blasphemous hands!"

"What, exactly, did this man do that was so impious?" Hemiunu asked patiently.

"A sacrilege I shudder to recount!" Minhotep said. "He committed an unholy act—he opened the skull of a living man!"

Horrified whispers lanced through the watching crowd.

Gratified by this reaction, the fat physician swept a hand out dramatically. "My lord, you know that it is forbidden to cut into the flesh of the living. You know that only the embalmers in the House of Beautification may do so, in order to preserve the body of the dead for the Afterlife."

"This is not quite true," said a steady voice. The Chief Royal Physician, Perhipidje, stood with quiet authority beside the Prince. "It is allowed, sometimes, to make an incision."

"But not into a man's head!" Minhotep said.

More murmurs in the crowd, and someone gasped. The Chief Royal Physician pursed his lips. "Sometimes circumstances permit … change."

"*Change?*" Minhotep cried, outraged. "Change the wisdom of our fathers, our ancestors?" He turned to the Royal Vizier. "Your Highness, are the teachings of our revered elders to be set aside on a whim?"

The Royal Vizier hesitated. Watching him, Meryt thought *he does not know how to decide this, but cannot say so in public.* A cold tendril wound around her heart. What will Hemiunu do, if he thinks this trial will embarrass him?

"It was not sorcery," Nakht called out forcefully. "My lord, what I did can be done by any physician, taught to any man. Or woman." His glance flicked to Meryt, then back to the Royal Vizier. "It is not a secret, and it is not magic. It is only a new way to heal." He turned to Perhipidje. "I could, with permission, teach it to yourself, sir. Or to any of your students, as I was taught by a medicine man in Punt."

"Foreign medicine," snarled Minhotep contemptuously.

"There must be a way to decide this." The Queen Mother tapped a foot impatiently. "Make him swear the oath, like Baki did. Will you swear to your truth, priest?"

Minhotep blinked, taken aback, and began to stammer excuses.

"Where are they?" Sheri whispered impatiently. She craned her neck, looking back into the crowd. "They should have been here by now!"

Hemiunu raised a hand to silence the muttering that swept through the Court. "Baki, son of Ra-Khuf, if you took Djeti-Thutmose from this Temple, tell us now where he is."

Baki bowed low, then straightened, his head held high. "I do not know, Your Highness."

Angry comments rippled through the crowd, and the Royal Vizier scowled. "I will not tolerate lies and impudence," he said.

Baki bowed again. "Highness, I neither lie nor am I impudent. I speak only the truth. On the night when we rescued Djeti, we took him to the house of one of his patients, a man who has innocently sheltered his benefactor and who is guilty of no offense against Pharaoh (Life! Prosperity! Health!). But this morning, when I went to visit him, he was no longer there."

Meryt knew this was true, and knew why. Her hands clenched one another as Hemiunu's scowl darkened.

"What game is this?"

Minhotep shrilled triumphantly, "Your Highness! This man claims to have kidnapped the body of the unfortunate Djeti-Thutmose, to conceal his brother's sorcery! Now he lies even to you, to conceal—"

Cries at the entrance to the chamber interrupted him, and then the crowd behind Meryt was parting, shoved aside by guards carrying spears.

"Finally!" Sheri said, clutching Meryt's arm. Nakht, on the other side of the room, stared at the procession entering the chamber.

First came Nes-Khonsu, nearly unrecognizable in her finest linen, wearing a formal black wig, with her hand raised to her brow in the traditional gesture of mourning. Behind her, carrying a simple rectangular coffin, came Ib and Nerekh, Kahotep and Sobek-Amun.

"Make way for the Osiris Djeti-Thutmose!" Nes-Khonsu cried. "May way for him who is dead!"

The crowd quieted, and many raised their hands to their brows as well, out of respect for the departed.

Nakht cried out and stepped forward; his guards yanked him back.

"You bring a corpse into the sacred precincts of Sekhmet!" Minhotep recoiled, and Henet-kha slid silently out of the sunlight into the shadows. Baki, after a brief bow to the Vizier and the Queen Mother, stepped up beside the coffin, which came to rest just inside the shaft of sunlight.

Meryt felt Sheri's hand at her back, urging her forward. She stepped into the light.

"My lord Vizier! My father, Djeti-Thutmose, begs leave to speak!"

Cries of astonishment went round the chamber. Hemiunu rose from the stool and strode forward.

"Sacrilege! You mock this court, and this trial!" Hemiunu cried.

The coffin-bearers set down their burden with a thump.

"Take that out of—"

The lid of the coffin rose. Cries from the crowd, with everyone stumbling backwards. "The dead man rises!"

Ib and Nerekh quickly set the lid aside, and reaching in, Baki gently lifted Djeti in his arms. Nes-Khonsu bent to retrieve a mat and the sick man was laid on it. Gasps and whispers rustled around the room.

With an exclamation, Perhipidje the Chief Royal Physician hurried past Meryt.

Djeti pushed himself up on his good arm and bowed his head. "Your Highness, forgive me for not rising."

Meryt, ignoring all protocol, was at his side in a flash, supporting him as he tried to sit straight. "Your Highness, he is still very weak—"

Hemiunu's face was tight with fury, but the Queen Mother

laughed. "No apologies are necessary, from one who has risen from the dead. Djeti-Thutmose, we rejoice to see you alive and speaking."

"Demon!" hissed Minhotep.

Hemiunu looked around, finally striding toward Baki. "Explain this!"

Baki bowed low. "Highness, this ruse was necessary to get Djeti to this trial in safety. Minhotep and his accomplices would have stopped at nothing to prevent his appearance, which gives the lie to their accusations."

"Never!" Minhotep blustered. "This is infamous!"

Hemiunu stood with his hands on his hips. "You could have asked for my protection," he said.

"Would you have believed them, Grandson?" The Queen Mother bent forward in her chair for a better look.

The Chief Royal Physician stepped forward, bowing. "Highness, if I may? We must be sure of his condition."

Hemiunu gestured his permission, and Perhipidje knelt beside the mat. "Old friend, it is good to see you," he said, taking Djeti's hand.

"And you," said Meryt's father. He smiled, but there were tired lines around his mouth. "Although I hear you had given me up for dead."

Perhipidje glanced at the bandages around Djeti's head. "As would you, had you heard the extent of your injuries. But now, at Pharaoh's command, I must examine your injuries."

"If it is required, to clear this young man of the charges against him, I am willing. Perhipidje, my friend, proceed."

The Chief Royal Physician turned, and a shaven-headed assistant was instantly beside him. The assistant helped the Chief Royal Physician remove his bracelets and rings, and brought him salt water to purify his hands. Intoning a blessing from Sekhmet, he began by gently examining Djeti's head.

Silence reigned in the hall as the physician carefully unwound bandages, sniffed at the healing incision on Djeti's scalp, and noted the precision of the stitching. He dictated his findings in a low voice to a hovering scribe. Behind him,

Minhotep leaned forward, listening with a frown on his face.

Every eye in the place was on the scene, except for Meryt's. She already knew what Perhipidje would find; instead, she stared at Nakht, willing him to see in her eyes the love and support she held for him. Nakht's attention was all for Djeti, however, as he craned his neck, trying to see past the people blocking his view.

"...arising from a disturbance in the *metu* of the hands, which disturbs the heart," Perhipidje was saying.

"Nonsense!" Djeti snapped. "The *metu* were not disturbed in the least. The trembling is merely weakness, caused by being in bed so long and by being pestered by idiots with crocodile dung!" This last was delivered with a glare at Minhotep.

"You live only because the gods heard my prayers," Minhotep snapped back. "And as for crocodile dung, the great Imhotep himself declared that—"

"Stop!" cried Hemiunu, hands on his hips. "If this has become a quarrel among physicians over a treatment, I see no reason to continue. Obviously no murder has been done, as Djeti is alive and well. There remains only the charge of kidnapping—"

"And sorcery!" Minhotep cried.

"I am grateful that this young man rescued me from the ministrations of this fool," Djeti said, indicating Baki. "My house owes him a debt of honor. Without his help, and his brother's extraordinary skill, I would probably be dead now."

"Your Highness, the charge of sorcery must be considered," Minhotep insisted. "We cannot allow—"

"Let me through!" A cry arose from the crowd near to the door. People muttered, cried out, someone laughed. The disturbance spread, like someone pushing through a field of wheat. Then the edge of the crowd parted, and a small figure dashed into the sunlight. Behind him, a guard snatched at him but missed.

"Father! I want to see my father!" Sefu cried. Blinded by the sudden glare pouring down from the skylight, he blundered into a guard, darted past Hemiunu, and stumbled towards the center. Dodging another guard, he tripped over the corner of the fake coffin and collided with Hemiunu's carved wooden stool. Even as Meryt cried out and took a step towards him, the boy went down in a heap of arms and legs. Everyone in the room heard the crack as his head hit the stone floor.

"Sefu!" Nakht cried out, his voice ragged with alarm. He tore free of his guards and flung himself to his knees beside the crumpled heap of his son. "Sefu!"

Everyone in the room was frozen, except Meryt. She dashed to kneel beside the boy, already seeing the blood pooling under his small skull.

In the shocked silence, Minhotep intoned solemnly, "Thus do the gods mete out justice."

Baki did not hesitate. His right arm shot out, his fist connected with Minhotep's nose in a satisfying crunch. The fat physician fell backwards into the arms of his henchman, Henet-kha, blood pouring down his face.

"Shut up," Baki snarled, and turned his back on him. A guard stepped forward, but Baki didn't even look at him as he strode to Nakht's side and knelt. "Sefu?"

Meryt slipped her hand under the boy's head, careful not to move him. She felt carefully along his small neck, her fingers probing. She heard shouts around her, heard feet moving. She paid no attention, all her focus on the boy sprawled in a pitiful heap on the pavement. Finally, she sat back on her knees. Her hand came away bloody.

"How is he?" a voice said beside her. She looked to see Perhipidje kneeling beside her, his assistant already opening the Chief Royal Physician's box of instruments. "Has he broken his neck?"

"No," Meryt said. "I felt no break, no looseness in the neck. There is no wound. All the blood is coming from his ears." She spoke briefly, caring nothing for rank or status now. Across from her, she was aware of Nakht, rigid with fear, his eyes fixed on his son's face. She could see his shoulders strain as he fought to free his hands.

"My son..." Nakht lifted his gaze to her, his eyes blind and staring. He bowed in the direction of the Royal Vizier. "Lord, I beg you. Let me help him."

"We will do all we can," Perhipidje said. "We must not move him until we are sure it will not hurt him further."

Meryt glanced around. The crowd milled about, uncertain about this dramatic turn of events. Djeti urged his bearers forward until he was almost on top of Meryt. Minhotep scowled in a corner, holding a bloody pad of linen to his nose, while Henet-kha whispered in his ear. In the center of the sunlight, Hemiunu stood with his arms crossed, anger in every line of his body.

"Who let this child in here? Who is he?" the Royal Vizier snarled. "Where are the guards?"

A sweating, middle aged man wearing an officer's medallion said, "My lord, he was very quick. He slipped past us because he was so short, we weren't expecting—"

"The boy is not to blame," the Queen Mother said strongly. She sat straight on her stool, no longer looking frail and harassed. When she spoke, the snap of authority sizzled in every word. "What son would not want to be with his father at such a time? You, young man!" She gestured for Nakht to rise.

Nakht stumbled clumsily to his feet, blinking. "Your Majesty?"

"Where is your wife? She must see to your son."

"She is with Osiris," Nakht said. He looked down at his son. "He is all I have."

"Hemiunu, dismiss the Court," said Queen Hetepheres briskly, all trace of fatigue gone. "Clear these people out of here. This is not an entertainment. You!" she crooked a finger at the guard captain. "Release the prisoner from his bonds. Guard him if you must, but if I know men he will not stir from his son's side, bound or not." Nakht's guards looked uncertainly from her to the Royal Vizier.

"Majesty, this trial is not conclu—" Hemiunu's tone held steel.

"The trial can resume another time. For now, clear this chamber!"

The guard captain rushed to do her bidding. A servant hurried up with a cup for the Queen Mother, and white-robed priests huddled around Minhotep and Henet-kha.

Meryt paid scant attention, but came around to stand next to Nakht as his bonds were cut. He rubbed his wrists and then knelt beside his son again. He stared at Perhipidje as that worthy finished examining the boy.

The Chief Royal Physician shook his head. "It's bad," he said quietly. "He bleeds from the ears."

"Check his eyes," a voice echoed through the emptying chamber. Djeti was leaning forward. "Are they the same?"

"We must turn him over to see that," Meryt said before Perhipidje could answer. "I think we can do that safely."

"Agreed. Meryt and Nakht, brace him on that side. I will support his head. On three…"

They gently rolled the boy onto his back. Immediately, the great black bruise on the side of his head came into view. Nakht groaned and leaned over the boy.

"Sefu! Can you hear me!" There was no response. With the lightest of touches, he opened first one and then the other of Sefu's eyelids. Meryt's heart sank as she noted the differing sizes of his pupils. Across Sefu's body, Perhipidje pursed his lips, shaking his head sadly.

Sefu's body suddenly jerked, his arms and legs flailing as if fighting some nightmare. The guard captain stepped back, awed. "He is possessed!"

"It is a demon!" Minhotep snarled from across the room. "Nakht's black magic has redounded on his son."

Ignoring him, the Queen Mother turned to Perhipidje. "You are the senior physician here. What is your diagnosis?"

Perhipidje rose, bowed. "He has injured his head, Majesty. There is no treatment that can heal him but time."

"That's what you said about me," Djeti snapped. "You were wrong then and you are wrong now."

Perhipidje stood, bristling a little. "Are you saying you should allow Nakht to perform the same procedure on his own son?"

"I think that is a very good idea," the Queen Mother said with authority.

"You would have him practice sorcery here, in the very precincts—" Hemiunu said.

"If it is sorcery, what better guardian could we have than Sekhmet Herself?" Queen Hetepheres said. "And if it is not…" She eyed the small knot of healers, apprentices and scribes before her. Her gaze drifted to Meryt. "Nakht said that his procedure is not sorcery, but medicine. He said it could be taught to anyone. Do you still hold with that?"

Nakht came shakily to his feet. He swallowed. "I did not lie, Majesty. The procedure is merely a matter of knowledge and skill, not prayers or incantations."

"Then you can teach it to Perhipidje here?"

"Majesty!" The Chief Royal Physician was aghast. "I am the body physician to Pharaoh himself! I cannot make myself impure by such a practice!"

Meryt swallowed. "Majesty, the boy is in grave condition. It is urgent that we act now. Nakht has the wisdom and the exper—"

"He is on trial," the Royal Vizier said. "I will not allow him to possibly escape justice by working some kind of spell."

Nakht sank to his knees, arms parallel to the floor. "Highness," he implored. "Let me save my son. Do with me whatever you will, but let me save my son."

"I will perform the procedure," Djeti said firmly. "I am still a physician."

"With respect," Perhipidje said gently. "You are in no condition to be treating a patient."

"Me. Let me do it. Please, Majesty, my lord, I beg you…" Nakht's voice broke. Neither Hemiunu nor the Queen Mother paid him any attention.

The Queen Mother swung her gaze to Meryt. "That leaves you."

Sefu thrashed silently again; a shudder ran through his small body and then subsided. Meryt heard gasps from the litter-bearers, a servant or two. "M-me?"

"She is not a physician," Perhipidje said strongly. "She has some knowledge, yes—"

"I trained her myself," Djeti said, black eyes snapping. "Nor has she any knowledge of magic. Furthermore, she has already performed this procedure on me."

The Queen Mother raised one eyebrow. "Is this true, girl? You helped open your own father's skull?"

"She is ignorant of the great matters of medicine," Perhipidje said urgently. "She has some knowledge, yes, but she is not learned in the ways of—"

"Let her do it!" From the floor at Hemiunu's feet, Nakht's voice rose in an anguished plea. "For the love of all that is holy, let someone act now!"

Meryt looked down at the little boy, saw the blood pooling in his ears. Nakht looked at her out of desperate, pleading eyes. "I will do it," she said, her voice small. "I will try."

Hemiunu, looking harassed and angry, said, "Grandmother, this is outrageous!"

Perhipidje shook his head. "I cannot allow it," he said in a loud voice. "It is not permitted—"

The Queen Mother struck her hand smartly on her thigh. "I will hear no more argument. A life hangs in the balance. If you men are too squeamish, withdraw." She glared at Meryt. "Be sure, girl."

Meryt swallowed, desperately running over in her memory the steps she had gone through with Nakht. What if she forgot one? What if she killed his son? She knew that if Sefu died, she would never forgive herself. And Nakht would not, either.

"Daughter," her father said softly beside her. "Trust yourself."

The final decision lay not with her, she realized, but with the man she loved. She met Nakht's eyes, imploring her. His lips moved soundlessly, but she read them: *Please*.

She drew a deep breath, turned to the Chief Royal Physician, and bowed. "If I may borrow your instruments."

"You may," the Queen Mother answered for him. She clapped her hands. "Bring this girl whatever she wants. Send some priests into the inner sanctuary to say prayers to Sekhmet. We will see this done, and quickly."

251

Hemiunu stepped forward. "I will let you do this," he said in a low voice. "I will let you usurp my authority, though I answer only to Pharaoh, but on one condition. This man—" he gestured at Nakht. "This man cannot be in the room. If this is sorcery, there will be none of it done against the boy."

Meryt gasped. "But my lord! I need his guidance! I have only done this once!"

Hemiunu's face was stone. "I have spoken. Guard, remove the prisoner. And bind him again."

"No! Let me stay!" Nakht fought like a madman, and Baki, too. But they were quickly subdued and dragged, still struggling, from the chamber. Meryt's protests were ignored.

When they were gone, with their shouts still echoing in the chamber, Hemiunu signed to his chamberlain. "Since you have dissolved the Court," he said acidly to the Queen Mother. "There is no longer any need for my presence here. Amuse yourself as you will. I have work to do." He turned on his heel and stalked out, his retinue scrambling to catch up. Soon all that remained in the center of the great Temple hall were the Queen Mother, her servants, Meryt, her father, the litter bearers and Perhipidje. And one other: a soft touch on her shoulder told Meryt that Sheri stood with her.

"What do you need?" Sheri asked in a low voice.

Desperately searching her memory, she said. "I will need clean water and salt. I will need many linen bandages."

The Queen Mother growled an order, and servants went running.

"Bring me closer," Djeti told his bearers. "Daughter, I will assist."

"I shall observe, as Pharaoh's representative. He will require a report of this," Queen Hetepheres told the Chief Royal Physician.

In short order, Sefu had been lifted onto a low table brought by priests, and bowls of vinegar and salted water prepared. From the inner chamber of the temple came the sound of chanting. A hand on her shoulder; her father leaned close. "Daughter, remember your training."

"He must not interfere!" Henet-kha shouted. "Djeti must be removed, or he will teach his daughter the spells of the demon inside him!"

Perhipidje stood up angrily. "This is beyond outrageous! Your Majesty, may we have that man gagged?"

Before she could answer, Minhotep sidled up, wearing his most ingratiating expression. "Majesty, it is not an unreasonable request. For a fair test, the girl must be allowed to work unaided."

"This is not a test!" Meryt snapped. She picked up a ewer of water and poured water over her left hand, then her right. "This is not some game! This is life and death!"

The Queen Mother looked at Minhotep, then at Perhipidje. "You will both observe, but you will not speak or aid her. Djeti, that goes for you as well. Guards, remove all three of these physicians out of hearing. They may watch, but not speak."

Djeti struggled to rise. "But Majesty—"

"I have spoken. We will see if this new procedure is sorcery or not. Bring me a cup of wine and tell my fan bearer to come back." She sat straight on her ivory stool. "Proceed, daughter of Djeti."

Meryt finished washing her hands. Sheri silently took the bowls and washing materials away. She clasped her hands to keep the shaking at bay, then took a deep breath. *Remember your training.*

First, cleanse the wound. She gently blotted blood and dirt off the boy's head. She could see swelling in the flesh over the bruise, but what really worried her was the faint trickle of blood from nose and ear. She checked the boy's pupil; sure enough, they were unequal in size. "I ... I must have the instruments," she said.

Sheri brought the soft roll of leather containing Perhipidje's surgical implements. Meryt's hands shook so much that it took her several tries to strike off a flake of obsidian sharp enough to cut. As she lifted it, the boy suddenly thrashed, his limbs convulsing. Meryt waited, her heart in her throat, until the fit passed. She did not have much time, she knew. It was one thing for a grown man to sustain such a head injury, but a young child would be in far more danger if she did not act quickly.

With a whispered prayer, Meryt bent to her work. She laid the blade against the boy's close-cropped scalp and made the first cut.

And as she did, her hands stopped shaking and a great sense of calm settled over Meryt. She had trained for this. She could do this. With swift, sure strokes, she opened a flap of skin, dabbing away seeping blood. Remembering Nakht's strong hands, she flaked off a drill point. It took only a couple of turns to open a tiny hole in the boy's thin skull; blood welled red in the shaft of sunlight.

Meryt heard the guards muttering, but ignored them. She waited until the blood flowed a healthy, thin red, then slowed. Swiftly she sutured the wound, and bound the boy's head with clean linen. Finally, she sat back on her knees, her back aching.

"It is done," she said.

"Majesty—" Perhipidje said, in an imploring tone.

Meryt looked up. All eyes were on her and the boy. The shaft of sunlight had crept across the floor while she worked—for an hour? Two hours? At the edge of it, the Chief Royal Physician, Minhotep, and her father all strained like dogs on a leash.

The Queen Mother, her expression an enigma, waved a hand and Perhipidje strode swiftly across the space. Djeti tried to climb off of his mat, but Kahotep held him with a firm hand as he and the others carried him over. Minhotep advanced slowly, suspicion in every line of his face.

"Well?" the Queen Mother said. "Will the boy live?"

"It is too early to tell, Your Majesty," Meryt said wearily. "We must wait."

"Prayers must be offered. I have incense waiting, and the dung of lions," said Minhotep.

"If you have lion dung handy, you should eat it," snarled Djeti.

"Enough of this!" the Queen Mother snapped. "We will wait here to see if the boy lives or dies."

Meryt swayed with fatigue; suddenly, Sheri was there, propping her up quietly on one side. "Majesty," Meryt said in a faint voice. "May Nakht be allowed to visit his son now?"

"No!" Henet-kha said, striding forward. "It is part of his plan!"

"Remove that man," the Queen Mother said wearily. "I do not wish to see or hear him again."

A fat guard led the little priest from the chamber, protesting volubly.

Meryt paid no attention to the quarrel, slumping against her friend. She heard the snap of command from the old Queen, heard hurrying feet. Perhipidje and Djeti argued in subdued voices. Someone offered her a soft cushion on which to sit. A fine faience cup of beer was put into her hand; a plate of food was set before her. All her attention was on the boy; every few minutes she laid fingers on his wrist or neck, checked his breathing and his eyes. The square of sunlight from the skylight inched across the floor, placing the boy and herself deeper into shadow with every passing moment.

"He is sweating," someone said. Perhipidje? Her father? Meryt hardly knew.

"Bring cool water," she said, her voice a croak. "It is not fever," she said, no longer aware of who might be listening. "It is only the heat."

More orders, more hurrying feet. Sheri knelt beside her with a basin of water, and Meryt bathed the boy's cheeks and body. The sunlight retreated further across the floor, as if oozing away from the scene of injury, perhaps fleeing from death.

Her eyes rimmed red from exhaustion and worry, Meryt knelt through the long afternoon, keeping vigil for a boy who lay like one dead.

☥

Meryt woke with a snap from a doze, and immediately leaned forward to touch Sefu's head, wrist and chest.

"All is well," came a soft voice. Across from her, Djeti lay on the floor on his litter. "I have been watching him closely, daughter. There is no change, either for better or for worse."

"I do not know if that is good or bad," she said dully.

Djeti smiled, his face lined with fatigue. "It is not bad." He sighed. "I have sent your sister and her husband home. With the child coming, it is important that she sleep."

"You need sleep also, Father. You should have gone with her."

Djeti chuckled. "And leave this highly entertaining moment?"

"He should have shown some recovery by now, should he not?"

"It is enough, for now, that he is alive," came Perhipidje's voice. He knelt on a soft cushion near Sefu's head. "I did not expect him to live so long."

"Has anyone told Nakht that his son yet lives?" Meryt asked.

Djeti nodded. "Your friend Sheri has made it her personal mission to visit him with news every hour."

"And how ... how is he?" Meryt asked.

"Anxious," Perhipidje said, with a wan smile. "As any father would be." His expression sobered. "I have had to bandage his wrists; he has rubbed them raw, struggling against his bonds."

Anger flamed in Meryt. "He should not be bound at all!"

"If he is not bound, he must be removed from the Temple," came another voice. The Queen Mother still sat on her carved ivory stool, her back as straight as a plumb line. "I cannot overset my grandson entirely," she said. She motioned Meryt to approach. "How is the boy?"

Meryt knelt wearily in front of the royal lady. Again she caught a whiff of a medicinal scent. She bowed her head. "Majesty, the boy breathes, he has no fever or convulsions. The bleeding from the ears has stopped."

"Will he live?"

"I do not know."

Queen Hetepheres peered closely at her. "Have you eaten? Slept?"

"Yes, I thank you, Majesty."

Silence fell, as the Queen studied her and Meryt waited for dismissal. The Queen Mother suddenly leaned forward. "You are the donkey girl."

256

Startled, Meryt blinked. "Donkey girl?"

Queen Hetepheres waved a hand. "The one who organized the women to drive donkeys."

"Oh. Yes, Majesty." It felt like a lifetime ago. Meryt wondered if this woman would ever let her go; she needed to get back to her patient.

"That was well done. Akhti-Hotep tells me that there have been fewer men suffering from water sickness," the Queen Mother said. "He wants me to believe it is his doing; I know better." She tapped one hennaed fingernail on her thigh. "You are a clever girl. I like clever women." She leaned close. "We run the world, you know," she whispered.

Meryt glanced up in surprise, and caught a twinkle of mischief in the older woman's eye. She mustered a tiny smile in reply.

"So," the Queen Mother said. "Are you going to marry that young man of yours?"

Meryt felt her face grow hot, then cold. "Not if I let his son die, Majesty," she said somberly. "May I return to my patient now?"

The Queen Mother waved a hand in dismissal, and Meryt hurried to Sefu's side.

Night crept onward. Lamps burned low, then were re-filled by bald Temple servants on bare feet. Silence drifted like sand over the company, punctuated only by the soft snores of the Queen Mother, leaning against the stolid captain of her guard.

Let the boy live, Meryt prayed silently. She did not care what gods were listening, only that the words spiraling out of her heart were heard by someone. *Let him live. Do not scar Nakht forever by taking his son. We cannot start a life together in the shadow of death.*

Gingerly she bathed the boy's forehead, though his flesh had cooled when the heat of the day retreated. She lifted a small clay lamp and leaned forward to raise one of Sefu's eyelids to check on his pupils. But when she touched the boy, his eyelids fluttered open.

"F-father?" the boy said, his voice no more than a breath of air.

Her heart leaping, Meryt smiled down at him. "Hello, Sefu. Do you remember me?"

The boy blinked, then stared around as Perhipidje approached. Behind him, Djeti was furiously commanding Ib and Nerekh to haul his mat closer to the boy. Queen Hetepheres woke in mid-snore.

"What is it?" she said, blinking.

Meryt paid no attention to the commotion, instead bathing the boy's face carefully. "Sefu, do you know where you are?"

The boy looked around, confused. His hand came up to touch his head, felt the bandages. "You are Mistress Meryt." His expression grew fearful. "Father! I want my father!"

The Queen Mother snorted. "He sounds healthy to me." She turned to her guard. "Bring the prisoner."

Sefu looked up at Meryt fearfully. "My head hurts. Where is my father?"

"He is coming soon," Meryt said. "Can you follow my finger?" She moved her finger back and forth across the boy's face; his eyes tracked it perfectly.

Perhipidje, who had been feeling the bandages on the boy's head, grunted with approval. "Excellent," he said. "And still no fever." He looked up at Meryt. "Well done, daughter of Djeti."

Sheri silently handed a cup of water to Meryt, then helped her raise the boy to a sitting position. Meryt held the cup to the boy's lips while he drank thirstily.

A noise of running footsteps at the door, then Nakht and Baki burst into the lamplight.

"Sefu!" Nakht landed on his knees with an impact that made Meryt wince in sympathy. "My son!"

"Father!"

The two embraced, Nakht cradling his son's head as carefully as an egg. "Do you hurt? Are you well?" Nakht sat back, running his hands over his son. "Do you feel hot? Can you move your arms and legs?"

Perhipidje tugged on Nakht's arm. "He is in good health, Nakht," he said with all the authority of a Chief Royal Physician. "Meryt and I have conducted the proper examination. There is no impairment that we can see." As Nakht turned to him, gratitude on his face, the older man nodded towards Meryt. "She has performed a remarkable feat. I would not have said this thing was possible, to open a person's skull and let sickness or injury out."

The Queen Mother leaned forward. "Well, Chief Physician? You are satisfied that this is no sorcery?"

Perhipidje stood and bowed formally. "Majesty, I have watched and listened, and I find no evidence of sorcery here." He stood, his face lined with fatigue but his eyes sharp. "This man, this physician, has brought a great gift to the House of Life. With this new knowledge, we may save lives that might have been lost."

"And this new knowledge, it can be taught to others?"

Perhipidje bowed once more. "Clearly it can, as the girl has shown us. With the permission of Pharaoh (Life! Prosperity! Health!), I will have Nakht teach it to every physician trained in the House of Life."

Meryt paid no attention to the conversation of the Court; rather, she was holding Sefu's wrist, counting heartbeats. On the boy's other side, Nakht was doing the same. His gaze met hers across the boy's body, and the look in them sent warmth from her head to her toes.

"Meryt," he said, and his voice held a hundred tones of different meaning. "I owe you my son's life," he whispered.

"Then we are even," she whispered back. "For you saved my father's." She placed a hand on the boy's head and smiled. "Let there be no talk of debts between us, beloved."

Nakht left one hand on his son's wrist, and reached for hers with the other. Across the boy, they joined hands.

"Meryt!" her father hissed from his litter. "The Queen Mother is speaking to you!"

Meryt blinked, then rose quickly to her feet. "M-majesty?"

Queen Hetepheres regarded her with some amusement. "As I said, I like clever women. I like strong women. You are both. It is not enough that you walk in my retinue in the Feast of Hathor. You! Nakht! Is it your intention to marry this girl?"

Nakht did not rise, but bowed from his kneeling position. "Immediately, Your Majesty."

"Good. You would be a fool not to. But will you permit her to continue practicing the art of medicine?"

"What?" Perhipidje said, startled into rudeness.

Nakht offered up a wan smile. "Majesty, I am not a fool. I would never attempt to stop the daughter of Djeti from doing whatever she wishes."

The Queen Mother laughed shortly. "A wise answer. Then as you are continuing as the physician to the work team, you will continue to live in this village. Good. And your wife will live with you. Good."

Meryt blinked, reeling. Had all her work, all her prayers been for naught? "But Majesty, my father is healing! Should he not return to his duties?"

"Majesty, I must counsel against it," Perhipidje said slowly. He looked sadly at Djeti. "Djeti, you know why."

Meryt turned to her father. "Father? What is he saying?"

Djeti sighed deeply and held up his hands. All could see the tremors that shook them. "Child, I feared this from the time I woke up. I told you that those who come back from the dark sleep often do not come all the way back. I fear I will never be able to hold my instruments again, or take the heartbeat of a patient." He dropped his hands, a sad look on his face. "I fear I may no longer be fit to serve the Great House."

"Nonsense," quipped the Queen Mother. "You have already told me of two new remedies for my joints, as we waited through this night. You are in possession of medical knowledge unknown to the House of Life." At Perhipidje's exclamation, the Queen Mother cocked her head. "Perhipidje, you really should listen more." To Djeti she said, "You can still dictate to a scribe, no? Then do so. I would have you compile a book of medicine, to be used by the work gangs on the Pyramid."

Awed, Djeti bowed from where he sat. "Majesty, you honor me—"

"No, I don't," she said. "I expect you to work on it quickly, because my own pyramid, humble as it is in the shadow of the

Horizon of Khufu, is behind schedule. And I am not a young woman." She signaled to her guard, who stepped forward with a supporting arm. "Scribes!"

Two bald scribes who had been dozing in a corner leaped to their feet and padded over with their palettes. As they seated themselves cross-legged in the traditional posture, ready to write, the Queen Mother hauled herself painfully to her feet, putting off the offered arm of the Chief Royal Physician.

"Hear my word," she said in a clear, thin voice. "I speak as the representative of the Living Horus, Khnum-Khufu, King of Upper and Lower Egypt, who is given life."

Everyone in the room fell flat on their faces.

"This is my ruling: all accusations against the physician Nakht, son of Ra-Khuf, are erased. Let them never be spoken of again. The physician Nakht is to be restored to his position with the Endurance work gang. The physician Djeti-Thutmose is assigned to the House of Life, his service to the Horus Throne to continue as a teacher and adviser. Let it be inscribed that his ration shall be as before." She smiled, her face lined under the fading cosmetics, her sharp features softening. "Djeti, you have earned an honorable retirement."

Nakht prostrated himself beside his son. "Majesty, I thank—"

"I am not finished." The Queen Mother's tone turned cold and hard as stone. "The Physician Minhotep has sworn falsely before the representative of Pharaoh. He has offended Ma'at, the balance of truth. As he was appointed to his post as physician by the Horus Throne, I cannot overset it." Her tone made it clear that she would like to. "However, he is hereby stripped of his privileges in the Temple of Sekhmet; he shall function as scribe-priest no more. His house is taken away, and his rations shall be reduced by one-third."

The scribes scribbled busily in the utter silence. There was a smothered whimper from where Minhotep knelt with his nose on the floor.

The Queen Mother's eye gleamed fiercely. "Let the house of Minhotep be given over to Djeti-Thutmose, that he may recover in peace and serve Pharaoh (Life! Prosperity! Health!).

Let the house of Djeti be given over to Minhotep, that he may learn wisdom and humility."

Meryt stifled a gasp. The house of Minhotep was one of the largest and finest in the village.

"Daughter of Djeti, stand forth."

Dazed, Meryt struggled to her feet, then bowed from the waist before the authority of Pharaoh. "M-majesty."

"Look at me, girl," the Queen Mother said, and her tone was kindly.

Meryt met those wise old eyes.

"I speak now as the mother of the King, as an old woman soon to go to the West," the Queen Mother said, and Meryt caught the weariness behind the regal tone. "My pyramid is rising even now in the shadow of the Horizon of Khufu," she continued. "I have all authority over my own tomb. I need a trustworthy physician. I appoint you to the position of Chief Physician to my work force."

Gasps from Perhipidje, a suppressed chuckle from Djeti. "M-majesty?" Meryt repeated, stunned. "Chief Physician? But I am not enrolled as a physician in the House of Life."

"I suspect," the Queen Mother said dryly. "That you will be, before noon of this day. Am I correct, Chief Royal Physician?"

From the floor, Perhipidje's muffled voice assented. "As the Mother of Pharaoh wishes."

"Good. Meryt-Auset, daughter of Djeti-Thutmose, you have ten days to get married, set up your house, and enjoy your husband. On the eleventh day from today, you will report to the worksite of my pyramid. Your wages shall be the same as that of your husband, lest there be strife in the household." Her mouth turned up. "I know you will earn it, daughter of Djeti."

Overwhelmed, Meryt fell to her knees and put her forehead on the floor. "Majesty, I cannot thank you enough. This is too much kindness."

"Nonsense," the Queen Mother said. "I am never kind, I have no time for it. All this will ensure that my son's Pyramid is completed in a timely manner, and mine as well. Scribes! Write it down, with copies to the King and my grandson. Where is my

262 𓂀

litter? I will return home now. My bones are old and need rest."

Everyone remained on their faces as the old woman was helped into her sedan chair, then carried out of the Temple. In the great skylight overhead, the stars were fading toward dawn. The lamps had guttered out by the time the Queen had departed and everyone rose to their feet, stretching with fatigue.

Meryt turned to Sefu, who lay asleep on the floor. "How is—"

Nakht caught her up in a crushing hug. "Goddess. Lioness. My heart..." He kissed her, long and deep and thoroughly.

Behind them, a discreet cough. "We must get this boy to his home," Djeti said, a chuckle in his voice. "And I, too, am weary. Come, Perhipidje. You can refresh yourself at my humble home. I have a scroll you might be interested to see."

Ib and Nerekh, still awed by an evening spent in the presence of royalty, picked up Djeti's mat. Meryt leaned down to touch her forehead to his. "Father? I have your blessing?"

He patted her cheek. "To marry the man who saved my life and earned the favor of the Mother of Pharaoh? Need you ask? Be happy, child."

"I am," she whispered. She kissed his hand and he was carried away, already deep in a discussion with Perhipidje, who trotted alongside the litter.

Perhipidje's silent assistant came forward with two more litter bearers, but Nakht shook his head at them. Stooping, he gently gathered his sleeping son into his arms. Hugging him close, he turned and met Meryt's gaze.

"Let us go home," he said.

CHAPTER 13 - BELOVED

19th Day of the Inundation
Year 7 of the Pharaoh Khufu

The chill air of dawn felt like walking through cold water. Meryt half-stumbled after Nakht, who strode through the streets with his son in his arms. Meryt didn't even think twice about turning to follow him; when Djeti's litter bearers turned off towards her home, she followed Nakht unthinkingly. Sefu was her patient; she would not leave him now. Baki murmured something and stepped away with Sheri, steering her friend towards her house.

Then it was just the three of them walking down the dusty street as the rays of the sun finally climbed above the horizon. Already men were stepping out of houses, lunches wrapped in linen slung over one shoulder, saying goodbye to wives and children. Nakht swerved to avoid a woman with a jar on her head, and then stopped before a large house with a blue-painted door. He turned to Meryt.

"I cannot open it," he said, indicating the sleeping boy in his arms.

Without ceremony, Meryt pushed on the door and it swung open. The interior was laid out exactly like her own house, although the scale was larger: the little house shrine on the left as they entered, the neat row of sandals on the right. Before them, the door to the main room was hidden by a curtain, even now swept aside by Nakht's beautiful sister-in-law.

"Oh! Nakht! How is he? We've been so worried!" Sesekh barely glanced at Meryt, all her attention on the boy. "We heard rumors from people who had been at the trial, but they were made to leave. We didn't know what had happened to you or Sefu." Fluttering, she held the curtain aside as Nakht strode through it. Meryt, left alone in the antechamber, paused.

This was not her house. Nor did Sefu need her, not when

his own father was so well qualified. Perhaps she had better return home…

"Meryt!" Nakht called.

She pushed aside the curtain and entered. Sesekh and a young maid were straightening a sheet over Sefu, who had been laid on the raised brick platform on the left wall. Nakht knelt over his son, feeling his wrist. Meryt noted the larger size of the room, the bright paintings of birds on the wall, the light seeping down from the high windows, before kneeling at his side.

"He is well," Nakht assured her. "Sleeping normally."

"Sleep is the best thing for him now," she agreed. Suddenly she swayed, and he caught her.

"Softly, my dove," he chuckled. "How long since you slept?"

"How long since you slept?" she said. She caught his wrists, noted the bandages. "I should dress and re-bandage these."

Sesekh entered with the young maid, carrying a water jug. She knelt awkwardly next to Nakht. "Brother, you must rest. We will watch him."

Nakht blinked. "I should stay with him."

Sesekh pushed at him, her gesture that of a sister teasing a brother. "You will fall asleep where you sit, and your snores will wake him. Go. I have laid a sleeping mat under the canopy on the roof, with food. Go rest and eat; no one will disturb you."

Meryt laid a hand on Nakht's arm. "She's right."

Nakht smiled ruefully. "All you women order me about like a donkey."

"No," Sesekh said briskly, settling her feet under her. "A donkey would have more sense. I will call you if he wakes."

Meryt rose with him, and turned to go. It was time to go back to Djeti, she thought. But Nakht caught her hand and pulled her through the rear door, down the corridor to the kitchen area of his house. "No," he said. "I'm not letting you go now. Or ever."

"But my father—"

"Is currently arguing medical theory with the best physician in the Two Lands," Nakht said firmly. "You need not worry about him. But I do worry about you."

He tugged on her wrist as he turned to the stairs, and she stumbled up after him. The morning sun broke across her face as she emerged onto the large, flat roof. Pots full of medicinal and cooking herbs lined the edges, and a tall trellis covered with cucumber vines shielded them from neighboring rooftops. Over the southern half of the roof, a brightly striped awning cast cool shade across a sleeping mat, a tray of sliced melon, and a jug of wine beaded with moisture. Releasing her, Nakht stepped to the street side edge of the roof and stretched mightily, his hands rising over his head. Meryt watched the muscles of his shoulders and back move with oiled precision under his skin. She smiled appreciatively.

He turned and caught her look, and grinned. "Meryt." In one long stride he held her hands in his, then her face in his hands. He kissed her long and slow, then wrapped long arms around her. "Wife," he murmured into her hair. "Wife."

The sound of it settled into Meryt, like a missing piece of a broken pot settling back into place. She laid her head against his chest and heard his heart beating strongly under her ear.

"When my son wakes," Nakht said. "I will tell him he has a new mother now. We will throw the biggest wedding feast this town has ever seen. We will invite everyone."

"Not Minhotep," she said immediately.

He chuckled. "No, not Minhotep. Or Shushu." He pulled back and looked down at her. "When my brother Harkuf's service is up, he will take Sesekh back across the Nile to their home. Baki can go sleep in the barracks. That will leave just us. You, me, and our son."

Meryt blinked. "Our…"

"He is your son too, now." His brow creased slightly with worry. "Unless you don't want to be his new mother. But if that's so—"

She silenced him with a kiss. His mouth on hers was hungry but hesitant. They had a lot to learn about one another, Meryt thought as she nuzzled his neck. And a lifetime in which to do it.

He pulled her, and she followed, and they sank onto the

sleeping mat, curling up together. His skin against hers felt warm, comforting. His arm gathered her against him as he reached for the wine jug. She shared a slice of melon with him. He licked the juice off her fingers. Meryt sighed with contentment. He smiled sleepily, his eyes drooping. Meryt felt herself falling into a happy doze, surrounded by love and looking into a happy future.

"Look," Nakht murmured, lifting an arm. He pointed towards the Pyramid. "Look how it shines in the light."

Meryt gazed out across the rooftops at the Horizon of Khufu, the great Pyramid rising layer by layer, each stone placed with care and precision to the glory of Pharaoh, to shelter the protector of Ma'at and the defender of the Two Lands even after his death. The rays of the sun caught the fresh-cut surfaces of limestone, and they gleamed white as new linen.

"Will we ever see it finished?" she asked.

"We will," he said drowsily. "And the one after it."

A pyramid was a monument to death, she thought. Yet in the shadow of immortality, she and Nakht served the living, not the dead.

"Life..." she said.

"Prosperity!" Nakht smiled and raised her fingers to his lips.

"Health!" she finished, and smiled down at him. "And love."

"Forever, oh my heart," he murmured.

They watched the sun rise over the great stone mountain of Pharaoh, and listened to the village stir to life around them.

THE END

Author's Note

Hollywood and Herodotus have combined to persuade generations that the Great Pyramid of Giza was built by slaves or aliens from outer space. In fact, recent excavations on the Giza plateau have revealed not only the graves and tombs of the actual men and women who built this great monument, but the remnants of the town they lived in, the quarry they dug from, and the harbor built to service it. While the workers who built Stonehenge and Chartres Cathedral are still unknown to us, we now know the names of many of the real people who built the Great Pyramid.

The making of the pyramids (the Great Pyramid was neither the first nor the last to be built along the Nile) required organization on a hitherto unknown scale in human history. While some work went on year round, the bulk of the hauling and laying of stone would have taken place during the Inundation, the yearly flooding of the Nile. While the fields lay under water, farmers were available to act as unskilled labor. For this work, they were paid high rations in bread and beer, given lodgings, and provided top notch medical care, all made available by Pharaoh. To keep track of men, materials and progress, literacy was essential. We might consider the Egyptians as having invented bureaucracy, the foundation of civilization.

The physicians of Egypt were famous throughout the ancient world, and justly so. Surviving medical papyrii show that, while magic and faith played a huge part in the practice, the Egyptians also had an extensive practical knowledge of surgery, medicine, pharmacology, and dentistry. The knowledge of trepanning, or opening of the skull, was in fact known in the Stone Age, but I am here "introducing" it to Egypt via the physician Nakht. And recent research has shown that some Egyptian beer, brewed as Meryt does in this story, actually contained a form of tetracycline, a powerful antibiotic. No wonder Meryt's patients did well!

As for women physicians, there is an inscription dating to the age of the Great Pyramid, a title that can be translated as "chief woman physician of the women physicians". There is strong evidence that, while rare, it was possible for women to become physicians in ancient Egypt, a career not open to women again for another 4500 years.

Finally, some readers may be surprised by the freedom enjoyed by the women in this novel. In ancient Egypt (less so in later ages), women had a higher legal and social status than they did during Europe's own Age of Enlightenment. Women could marry as they pleased; divorce was possible for both sexes. Women could buy, sell, inherit and pass on property. Literacy was possible if private tutors or family members taught them; probably more women of ancient Egypt could read and write than could do so in the Middle Ages.

Ancient Egypt is a fascinating country; if you are intrigued by any of the cultural background you have read here, please consult the Sources for more information.

SOURCES

A bibliography, in a romance novel? Why not? If you enjoy reading about ancient Egypt and the men and women who lived there, here are some excellent guidebooks to get started. Most of the research for this book came from them.

Books

Allen, James P., Ed. *The Art Of Medicine in Ancient Egypt.* Metropolitan Museum of Art, October 20, 2005. Contains photographs of all pages of the Edwin Smith Papyrus, one of the oldest medical textbooks in the world.

Baker, Rosalie F. and Charles F, III. *Ancient Egyptians: People of the Pyramids.* Oxford University Press, New York, NY. 2001. General overview of ancient Egyptians. Good maps.

Bierbrier, Morris. *The Tomb-Builders of the Pharoahs.* American University in Cairo Press, 1993. Slightly dated, but lively overview of the excavations at Dier el-Medina, the worker's village for the Valley of the Kings. Much detail on the lives of ordinary workers, craftsmen and supervisors, including names, pay rates, and work assignments.

Capel, Anne K. and Glenn E. Markoe, eds. *Mistress of the House, Mistress of Heaven: women in ancient Egypt.* Essays by Catharine H. Roehrig, Betsy M. Bryan, and Janet H. Johnson. New York:Hudson Hills Press in association with Cincinnati Art Museum ; [Lanham, MD]:Distributed in the USA, its territories and possessions, Canada, Mexico, and Central and South America by National Book Network, c1996. Essays and photographs from an exhibition at the Cincinnati Art Museum, with particular reference to ancient Egyptian textiles and domestic furniture.

Casson, Lionel. *Everyday Life in Ancient Egypt.* Baltimore, MD:Johns Hopkins University Press, 2001, 1975. The lives of everyday Egyptians in pharaonic times.

Clayton, Peter A. *Chronicle of the Pharaohs: The Reign-by-Reign Record of the Rulers and Dynasties of Ancient Egypt.* Thames & Hudson, New York, NY. 1994. Excellent overview of the dynasties, titles and reigns of all known kings of Egypt. Short biographical sketches. Illustrations of cartouches, statues and mummies.

Dodson, Aidan and Dyan Hilton. *The Complete Royal Families of Ancient Egypt: A Genealogical Sourcebook of the Pharaohs.* Thames & Hudson, New York, NY. 2004. Invaluable sourcebook for the complicated family histories of the Pharaohs. Includes most known titles and offices for royal family members.

Graves-Brown, Carolyn. *Dancing for Hathor: Women in Ancient Egypt.* Continuum Press. London, 2010. Scholarly analysis of both recent and early finds relating to the status and lives of women in Egypt. Ms. Graves-Brown is careful to distinguish between periods of Egypt's 3000-year history, giving us not only a valuable perspective on how women's status changed over time but a reconsideration of some previous conclusions from the point of view of a modern feminist. Most valuable are the specific details regarding the "jobs" available to and held by women throughout Egyptian history.

Halioua, Bruno and Bernard Siskind. *Medicine in the Days of the Pharaohs.* Cambridge, MA:Belknap Press of Harvard University Press, 2005. Comprehenisive overview and summary of what is known about early Egyptian medicine.

Hawass, Zahi A. *Mountains of the pharaohs:the untold story of the pyramid builders.* New York:Doubleday, c2006. Bantam Dell Pub Group, Westminster, MD, USA, 21157 SAN 201-3975. A good introduction to the workers on the pyramids, written by one of the archaeologists who uncovered their graves. Includes Hawass' own fictional recreations of ordinary workers at the Giza Plateau. Good account of pyramid layout and construction.

Lehner, Mark. *The Complete Pyramids.* Thames & Hudson, 2008. Introduction by Zahi Hawass. The definitive work on the pyramids of Egypt, from the director of the Giza Mapping Project himself. An exhaustive resource on pyramid building.

Lichtheim, Miriam. *Ancient Egyptian Literature: Volume I: The Old and Middle Kingdom.* University of California Press; 2 edition, 2006. Poetry and literature from ancient Egypt.

Manniche, Lise. *An Ancient Egyptian Herbal.* University of Texas Press, Austin, Texas. 1989. Excellent collection of recipes for perfumes, ointments, and medicine. Especially valuable for the list of identified Egyptian plants.

McDowell, A. G. *Village life in ancient Egypt:laundry lists and love songs.* Oxford:Clarendon, 2001. A series of scholarly translations of texts discovered at the Deir el-Medina worker's village in Thebes. Especially valuable for translations of letters and court cases.

Mertz, Barbara. *Red Land, Black Land: Daily Life in Ancient Egypt.* New York:Dodd, Mead, c1978. Lively and engaging recounting of ancient Egyptian life.

Nunn, John F. *Ancient Egyptian Medicine.* Red River Books, November 2002. The most exhaustive work on ancient Egyptian medicine, with lists and tables of remedies, diagnoses, and pharmacology. Overviews of diet and general health, discussions of all the major medical papyri, and even includes an index with the names of all known physicians from ancient times. Invaluable resource for research in this field.

Siliotti, Alberto. *Guide to the pyramids of Egypt.* New York:Barnes & Noble Books, 1997. Preface by Zahi Hawass. Notable for maps and discusions of workers' villages in and around the Giza plateau.

Silverman, David P. General Editor. *Ancient Egypt.* New York:Oxford University Press, 1997. Overview of daily life; especially good on the subject of internal domestic arrangements.

Smith, Craig B. *How the Great Pyramid Was Built.* Washington:Smithsonian Books, c2004. Foreword by Zahi Hawass. Photography by Andy Ryan. This unique and outstanding book covers the building of the pyramid of Khufu from the point of view of a modern-day project manager, complete with analyses, GANTT charts, and timelines. Priceless.

Strudwick, Nigel C. edited by Ronald J. Leprohon. *Texts from the Pyramid Age*. Leiden, the Netherlands ; Boston:Brill, 2005

Tyldesley, Joyce A. *Daughters of Isis: Women of Ancient Egypt*. Penguin Books. London; New York. 1995. Comprehensive and well written discussion of the lives of ancient Egyptian women, including detailed descriptons of their houses, dress, furnishings and what few written texts from them remain. Very detailed without being dry, extremely informative.

Websites

Arab, Samuel M., MD. Medicine in ancient Egypt. http://www.arabworldbooks.com/articles8.htm Visited June 2010. An overview and discussion of ancient Egyptian medical practice and its efficacy, by an associate professor of cardiology at Alexandria University in Egypt.

Armelagos, George M. Take Two Beers and Call Me in 1600 Years. Natural History. http://findarticles.com/p/articles/mi_m1134/is_4_109/ai_62324477/ A discussion of the discovery of tetracycline in the bones of Egyptian mummies, and the archaeological investigation that led to the discovery of beer laden with antibiotics in ancient Egypt.

KNH Centre for Biomedical Egyptology. University of Manchester, UK. http://www.knhcentre.manchester.ac.uk/ Includes links to seminars, postgraduate theses, and exhibitions related to the practice of medicine in ancient Egypt.

Menon Menon. King Tut's Tipple. http://discovermagazine.com/1997/jan/kingtutstipple979. Visited June 2010. Discussion of brewing techniques of the ancient Egyptians, and how a modern taste-test fared.

Roach, John. "Antibiotic" Beer Gave Ancient Africans

Health Buzz. National Geographic News. http://news.nationalgeographic.com/news/2005/05/0516_050516_ancientbeer.html A discussion of research showing that some forms of beer brewed in ancient Egypt contained tetracycline.